R.J. KAISER

Squeeze Play

MIRA

ISBN 1-55166-713-4

SQUEEZE PLAY

Copyright © 2002 by Belles-Lettres, Inc.

Visit us at www.mirabooks.com

Printed in U.S.A.

For Helen Breitwieser

After they'd both come—she for the fourth time and he for the second—she'd lain moaning in ecstasy and, right out of the wild blue yonder, out popped, "Nick, would it upset you if I invited my parents to the first-anniversary party next week?"

Her hand had been resting on his cock when she dropped that little bombshell. Okay, so maybe every muscle in his body tensing was an overreaction. Maybe the question wasn't as portentous as he thought. In any case, Bree noticed his privates go limp and she did a fast one-eighty.

"Not that it's important or anything. It's just that Daddy's going to be in town on business and since Mom's been wondering what's so special about Dominick's, I thought maybe I could suggest she come along...but, if that makes you uncomfortable..."

"No, no, that's fine," he assured her, though to make his position clear, he added, "As long as they don't get the wrong idea."

"Oh, no, it'd be nothing like that."

Nick wasn't so sure. He'd had more than a little experience interpreting the female mind—and getting blindsided seemed fairly routine. Bree, who was supposedly a free spirit, had been showing signs of possessiveness, and that wasn't good. Since his divorce, Nick had considered women the dessert of life—not the entrée. His ideal woman was in the game to have a good time.

"If your folks are going to be here anyway, then invite them, if you want," he said, hoping she saw the nominal courtesy for what it was.

Bree Davis—a child of the Philadelphia suburbs, a graduate of Curtis Institute of Music and an aspiring Broadway actress—was no dumb bunny, even if she fucked like one. "No," she said, "it's our night, yours and mine and the rest of the crew's. Parents would only put a damper on things. Bad idea."

Nick had rested easier after that, choosing to take her at her word. Besides, this day could be a turning point in his life, and he wasn't going to let his divorced-guy-jitters get in the way of maximum enjoyment. No, Nick Sasso chose to see sunshine in the dark clouds. Besides, those big fat raindrops looked mighty fine on Bree's bare shoulders and milky thighs. Damn it, he had two tickets to a Yankees game at forty bucks a pop. He wasn't going to be denied. Period.

Taking Bree's hand, he hurried them toward the entrance under the approving eye of a few cops, a handful of die-hard scalpers, a platoon of street kids and a couple of bums. Yes, this was definitely his day.

Once inside the stadium, they made their way to their seats, skirting the long lines at the refreshment stands, giving wide berth to a pregnant woman barfing into a trash can, two kids engaged in a shoving match and, of course, the pigeons, one of which he accidentally kicked. "Sorry, birdie."

Bree laughed, a sound almost as gratifying as a coital moan. Ah, the House that Ruth Built. Nick was a transplantee to these environs, but at some superficial, though significant, level, he loved New York.

As they took their seats, Bree caused quite a stir. The wolf whistles coming from up in the stands behind them weren't aimed at Derek Jeter. When she gave Nick a smile and snuggled against him, he felt great. Maybe it was wishful thinking on his part, but that business about her parents seemed to have been nothing more than a blip on the screen. All was well in Mudville, he decided. Patting her knee, he checked the scoreboard and brought himself up to date on the game.

It was the top of the fourth, two outs. Garciaparra had singled and was on first. On the second pitch, Ramirez grounded to second and Soriano flipped the ball to Jeter for the force. Nick applauded along with the rest of the crowd. Bree did as well.

"This is great," she enthused. "I'm really glad we came."

Nick decided he really liked the girl, though they hadn't been together all that long. Bree had been on staff at Dominick's for three months, starting as the weeknight hostess and working her way up to a sort of assistant manager. They'd been dating for seven weeks and screwing for seven weeks. Mostly their dates consisted of a rented movie at her place or his, a concert in Central Park or take-out Chinese food and sex. Two weeks earlier they'd gone to see the revival of *The Music Man* because she had played Marian the Librarian in a hometown production and simply "*had* to" see it on Broadway.

"So, explain again," she said. "Your father named you after who?"

"Dom DiMaggio. Joe DiMaggio's brother."

"Well, how come he didn't name you after Joe, if he was the famous one?"

"Because he named my older brother after the famous one."

"Bummer. But they called you Nick instead of Dom."

"My mother preferred it."

"Nice she got a say. Your father must have loved his Yankees, if he named his kids after them."

"It was the DiMaggios he loved. Grew up with them, knew the family."

"In San Francisco."

"Yeah, North Beach. When my old man opened his restaurant back in the fifties he called it the Yankee Clipper. The DiMaggios gave him tons of memorabilia over the years. The Clipper is full of the stuff. It's a San Francisco institution."

That was the environment Nick grew up in. To his father, Joltin' Joe was a god, right up there with the Catholic saints, if not higher. When he was young, Tony Sasso had had aspirations of being a Major League ballplayer, but when that hadn't materialized he'd looked to his sons to put the Sasso name in Cooperstown. Ironically, Nick's brother, Joe, was not an athlete and had zero interest in sports. While Nick enjoyed the game and was talented with the glove, playing a pretty mean short by sandlot standards, he couldn't hit a fastball— not a good one.

And so, Tony Sasso's aspirations for him had died on the ball fields of places like the Moscone Rec Center. But was that Nick's responsibility? Was he the keeper of his old man's dreams? Nick loved the game, but not the sacrifice. Sensing that, Tony would say, "Nothing important ever comes easy, least of all hitting a Major League fastball. What it comes down to, son, is how bad you want it." Evidently Nick hadn't wanted it enough.

Like most kids, he had to figure out what he *did* want. Finally, he settled on a career in law enforcement, though even that he'd embraced only halfheartedly, which may have been why that had ended in failure, as well. To his credit, though, he had put in the time and effort necessary to get his badge. About the same time he got a wife and thought his life in San Francisco was set. Then disaster struck. The wheels came off his personal and professional life in quick succession, costing him both his marriage and his career. It was at that point that the Big Apple beckoned.

Having grown up in the restaurant business, that's what he went back to. In fairness, he'd always loved cooking. He could whip up a mean pasta dish from the time he was a kid. Not a genius in the kitchen, but he had flair and imagination. Over the last few years he'd worked in some of the best restaurants in Manhattan, but he decided he needed his own place and made that his dream. No bank had been willing to front the money, so he'd called his brother in San Francisco. Though it had been years since they'd talked, let alone seen each other, in the course of twenty-four hours they'd worked out a deal. Nick sold half his interest in the Yankee Clipper to Joe for a hundred and fifty thousand, under the condition Joe not tell the old man, who now lived in a nursing home.

"What does it matter?" his brother had asked. "You haven't spoken to each other in what, three years?"

"I'd rather it be confidential, that's all."

Whether Joe understood, Nick didn't know. But the fact was, Nick had always been the favored child. And, deep down, he knew that disappointing the old man hadn't changed that. He might be the prodigal son and he might be in exile, but all he had to do was pick up the phone to be welcomed home with open arms. Somehow, he just hadn't been able to do it. Nor had his father reached out to him. The way Nick figured, they were both too damn stubborn.

Maybe, at some level, Tony knew that Nick had to be his own man, that he had to look forward and not back. And San Francisco, much as he'd loved it his whole life, had become Nick's personal chamber of horrors. That was why he'd chosen a fresh start in New York. It had been a battle, but Dominick's California Cafe was finally coming into its own and Nick with it. If he wasn't on the top of the world, he sure as hell could see the summit ahead.

Just then the skies opened and God dumped Niagara Falls on Yankee Stadium. Maybe on the whole eastern seaboard, for all Nick knew. Bree let out a yelp. As one, the crowd rose and headed for the aisles. Beer, popcorn and peanuts went flying, along with scorecards, newspapers and stadium seats. Umbrellas popped up, too, as well as rain slickers and plastic sheets. The umpires and players jogged toward the dugouts as the ground crew ran onto the field.

By the time Nick and Bree reached the shelter of the upper deck, they were both soaked. Her strawberry-blond hair, darker now, trailed limply down her back and she was shivering. Nick put his arm around her and they went to look for coffee.

"Bummer," she said.

"It's all part of the game." He grinned at her.

"You're feeling it, aren't you, Nick?"

"What?"

"The review."

"It's a nice turn of events."

"Nice? Nick, you'd have given your firstborn child for that review. The taxis will be lined up to the corner with customers. This is going to make you. I know it is." She squeezed his waist. "And you deserve it."

Nick wanted to think so. He *did* think so, but he was also afraid to admit it. Maybe he'd been lucky, which was a worry, because luck had a way of changing. After the life he'd had, he could knock on every piece of wood in Yankee Stadium and still not feel secure. Yet, for the first time ever, something he'd done was turning out right. Still, it was dangerous to think you'd get what you deserved. "Let's see what happens," he said.

"Why don't you call and see how the lunch service is going?"

"Naw, I'll wait until I get there this evening."

"Nick, how can you?"

He shrugged. "I've waited thirty-seven years."

"Where's your cell phone?"

"Why?"

"If you won't call, I will."

"Bree..."

"I'm serious," she said, feeling his pockets.

Nick pulled his cell from his jeans. She reached for it, he moved his hand away.

"Give it to me!" she demanded.

"Give it to her, man," a teenager in baggy pants and a Yankees jersey said as he and a buddy walked by.

"See!" Bree said. "The world agrees with me." She wrenched the phone from his hand, then dialed the restaurant. "Hi, Eddy, it's Bree. How's the lunch service going?" She listened, her eyes getting round. "Oh, my God! No kidding?" She let out a little yelp of joy. "Nick, they're lined up down the block!"

"Really?" he said, hardly able to contain himself.

Bree hopped like a high-school cheerleader. Nick wanted to kiss her. But she was listening to Eddy. "Yeah, he's right here." She extended the phone. "He wants to talk to you."

Nick took the phone, his heart going crazy, as if he'd just stretched a triple into an in-the-park home run. "Yeah," he said, "it's me. Things are going well, huh?"

"Not just well, man. Fabulous."

"How many?"

"Double last Sunday and we're a long way from finished."

"Hey, great." He gave Bree a wink. "Maybe I ought to get my ass over there," he said to Eddy.

"We're hustling, and things are a little slow coming out of the kitchen, but so far nobody's come unglued."

"Maybe we need to increase the waitstaff."

"Yeah, maybe. But that's not what I need to talk to you about. You got a telephone call a little while ago. An urgent call."

"Who from?"

"A guy in San Francisco. Somebody named Mort Seidel."

God, talk about a name out of the past. "Mort called me? On a Sunday?"

"Yeah, he said it was really important, man."

Nick's brain locked momentarily. Mort was his old man's accountant. Nick knew him, of course, but hell, he and the old duffer didn't exchange Christmas cards, much less talk on the phone. He wasn't sure they'd ever discussed business. It had to be something personal. "Did he leave a number?"

"Yeah."

"Give it to me, Eddy."

He read off the telephone number to Nick. Nick didn't bother repeating it aloud. He knew it well. It was the Yankee Clipper's.

As he hung up, Bree saw his dark expression and said, "What's happened?"

A loud clap of thunder exploded, quieting the buzz of the crowd.

He looked at Bree, not seeing her. "My father's accountant and longtime friend called from San Francisco."

"What about?"

Nick shook his head. "Eddy only said that it's urgent."

"What do you suppose it is?"

"I hate to say it, but I think the old man is dead."

Nick decided to call and get it over with. He took a ten-dollar bill from his wallet and asked Bree if she'd mind getting them some coffees. "I'm going to find a quiet spot and phone San Francisco. Meet you back here in a few minutes."

Only moments ago he'd been on a high. Fate, pissed apparently, decided to fire a shot across his bow. Nick walked along, looking for a corner he could duck into. The first likely place was already occupied by a boy and girl on a guided tour of each other's anatomy. Finally he stepped into an alcove accessing some kind of maintenance room. He dialed the number of the Yankee Clipper back in his old hometown.

A woman answered, probably a hostess. He didn't recognize her voice. There'd undoubtedly been ten since he'd left.

"Hi, is Mort Seidel there?"

"Mort Seidel?"

"Yeah, the accountant."

"Oh, oh," the woman said. "Yes, I believe he's in the office. Hang on."

Mort came on the line a few seconds later. "This is Seidel." His gravelly voice was familiar, time and alienation notwithstanding. Nick's heart raced to keep ahead of his fear. It had to be about his father.

"Mort, it's Nick Sasso in New York. I had a message you called. Is something wrong?"

"Nick, your father, Tony...well, he asked me to call you to discuss a situation."

Nick, not hearing what he thought for sure was coming, sagged against the wall with relief. A second later he was angry at being given such a start. But then, maybe Mort had no idea he'd scared the piss out of him. "What kind of situation?"

"It's the books. There's anomalies. Even though Joe runs the business now, this was something I felt I needed to discuss with Tony. So I went to the nursing home and told him what I'd found. I asked what he wanted me to do about it and he said, 'Call Nick,' and that's what I did."

"If there's a problem with the books, why don't you talk to Joe?"

Mort cleared his throat again. "You want that I say it over the phone? God knows who could be listening."

Nick couldn't help but smile. Mort was a dignified little man who seemed to have walked into the twenty-first century directly from the 1950s. Always in a bow tie, regardless of the time of day, the season or the occasion, he was a throwback. He believed in order, frugality, accountability and directness. He saw himself as the servant of sound business practices.

"Short of you hopping on a plane, I don't see an alternative," Nick said.

"Okay," Mort said, relenting. "There's sixty-eight thousand, four hundred and thirty-two dollars and seventy-seven cents unaccounted for. Now, I'm not accusing him of anything, but it appears Joe has taken funds without accounting for where they're going. Eleven times in the last six months. Five, six, seven thousand dollars at a time."

"You're saying he's putting it in his pocket?"

"I don't know that, Nick. All I know is there have been withdrawals without corresponding ledger entries, so there's no way to know what it was used for. Sixty-eight thousand, four hundred and thirty-two dollars and seventy-seven cents."

"You're sure about this, Mort?"

"I tabulated it three times."

"No, I mean you're sure the entries weren't made in the wrong ledger, that the receipts weren't misplaced, or that the bank screwed up."

"Nick, I've been an auditor for forty-six years. I've done your father's books from the time he first went into business. I know all the tricks."

"I don't doubt that for a minute. I thought there could be an easy explanation that we're missing. Like that Joe is in some kind of trouble."

Mort Seidel was silent for several moments, his uneasiness detectable clear across the country. "Naturally, a man in my position hears a lot. I'm in offices all over town and, well, since you asked... There's talk that Joe's got financial diffi-culties. I heard, for example, he was in foreclosure on some of his real estate holdings. And his investment firm could be in bankruptcy."

"Bankruptcy?"

Nick was caught totally by surprise. This did not sound like Joe. But even if everything Mort said was true—which Nick was inclined to believe—it still didn't mean his brother was pulling a fast one. He couldn't imagine Joe stealing from his own family.

"When you talked to my father, did he give any indication what he expected me to do about this?"

Mort hemmed and hawed a bit, then said, "Well, I think he'd like for you to come and straighten things out. He's stuck in that place, you know. In fact, to be honest, Tony's pretty far removed from things, mentally as well as physically. I thought long and hard even before I took this to him. He was pretty upset."

Nick could imagine that. What he didn't know was whether his father saw this as an excuse to lure him back to San Francisco. He hated being cynical about a family crisis, but he wouldn't put that past his old man.

"This is coming at a very bad time, Mort," he said. "It would be difficult for me to get away right now."

"Do you want me to tell Tony that?"

Nick wondered if he shouldn't just take the bull by the horns and call his old man. In a sense, Tony had reached out. He was old and sick, and Nick had no excuse for being hard-nosed or selfish. "No, I'll tell him."

"All right, fine. But Nick, before you go, there's something else I think I need to share. As I said, an important part of my job is minding my own business, but sometimes you have to think of the human beings behind the numbers."

"What are you trying to say, Mort?"

"Yesterday, while I was here, doing my audit, a phone call came in on Joe's private line. I didn't answer it, of course. The machine got it, but I heard what was said."

"Yeah...and?"

"Let me put it this way. If I was Joe's brother, especially one who was an ex-cop, I'd want to hear it."

"Go on. What was the message and who was it from?"

"I don't know. The guy didn't say. But instead of me trying to explain, why not listen to it yourself? It's right here. Joe's out of town, so it hasn't been erased."

"Okay, put it on."

While Mort fooled with the machine, Nick could hear a siren in the background. On the other side of the country, some emergency vehicle was going through the streets of North Beach, probably on Columbus Avenue. It soon faded away. He couldn't hear any other sounds, but if he were there in the office that had once been his father's, the clank of dishes and the muted voices of the kitchen staff would be coming through the ventilation system from below. As a kid, he'd spent more than one afternoon in Tony Sasso's office doing his homework but wishing he was downstairs in the kitchen, watching Carlo Cordoni doing his magic.

"Okay, sorry," Mort said, "here it is."

The first message was from a woman who spoke with an accent. She sounded Chinese. "Joe," she said, "I need to talk to you about tomorrow." That was all. No name, no number. Obviously, she'd counted on being recognized by Joe, but Nick had no idea who she was. The second message was from the same woman. "Please, Joe, it's about the meeting. Do you want to go with us, or meet us there? Call me." Still no name or number.

The third message had to be the one Mort was referring to. It was a man's voice. "Joe, sorry I missed you this morning. We've got problems, buddy, and we need to talk, I mean seriously. Like I told you, this has ramifications that go beyond your deal. Hell, it's bigger than both you and me, Joe. I'm sure I'm being followed. Everywhere I go, it seems. The hell of it is, I don't know who I can trust, if anybody, including the police. Maybe it's paranoia on my part, but I'm concerned for my safety. And maybe you should watch your backside, too. I mean it, Joe, this is bad. Give me a call, huh?"

There were no other messages.

"Did you hear that all right?" Mort asked.

Nick was stunned. It was so unreal. These things didn't happen at Yankee Stadium in the middle of a rain delay. He looked out of his cubbyhole at the milling crowd and saw Bree coming toward him in her sexy little shorts, bare midriff, belly button. She'd homed in on him like an infrared beam, two steaming coffees in her hands. He reminded himself that a couple of hours ago he'd been fucking her, but that didn't seem real, either. Nothing did.

Another clap of thunder. Bree, standing in front of him now, shivering. On the other end of the line, San Francisco in chaos.

"Nick, did you catch that?"

"Yeah, I did."

"You know better than me what to do about it."

He wished that was true. He wasn't even sure what he'd just heard. "Play that for me again, will you?"

"All right."

While he listened to the messages on his brother's answering machine, he put his arm around Bree, smoothing her goose bumps with his palm. She sipped her coffee and huddled against him while a stranger's fear-tinged voice came to him from the far Pacific shore. "I'm sure I'm being followed. Everywhere I go, it seems. The hell of it is, I don't know who I can trust, if anybody, including the police...."

When Mort came back on, Nick asked him where Joe was.

"They said out of town. I think maybe I heard Reno, but I'm not sure."

"Okay, thanks, Mort." He hung up.

Bree looked into his eyes with deep concern as she handed him his coffee. "Is it your father?"

"Yes and no. He's okay. I mean, it's not a health problem. But the family business is in trouble, more particularly my brother." He took a quick sip of coffee.

"What kind of trouble?"

"It's a long story," he muttered, checking his watch. Then, looking into her trusting blue eyes, he said, "I don't think they're going to finish this game. Do you mind if we flick it in?"

"No, of course not."

Nick bussed her on the cheek. "I'm going to have to spend

some time on the phone to see if I can straighten out the mess at home. What say we go to the restaurant? I'll call from there."

"Looking like this?" she said, glancing down at herself.

"Could help business, babe." He gave her a wink. "Come on, we'll take a taxi."

As they walked arm-in-arm, the smell of ozone, which Nick loved, hardly touched his consciousness. He was thinking about Joey, five years his senior, family man and father, existing, it seemed, on the margins of Nick's life, in the penumbra of the family circle.

Joey, his body soft, his heart hard and filled with a yearning Nick never understood. The two couldn't have been more unalike. Nick had coasted through life, getting by on his natural talent and his charm, riding whatever pony was available. Joe, on the other hand, was always striving for something, if only their father's approval. Nick never worried about that, taking what he got for granted, not caring about the rest. Joey tried so hard, but the money he made never was enough, his achievements always falling short of his aspirations. Tragic, sad Joey—his body failing him on top of everything else.

When last Nick had seen his brother, Joe was in the early stages of MS. It had to be worse by now—but how much worse Nick had no idea. Poor Joe. What had he gotten himself into? How desperate had his desperate life become?

It was still pouring as they left the stadium and ran across the pavement to the street. Bree waited on the curb while he battled for a taxi. It took a couple of minutes. She was dripping as she slid across the cracked vinyl of the rear seat. Nick glanced up at the sky before ducking inside. There was no sign of the sun and powerful little indication it would ever be seen again. Wonderful days weren't meant to last, apparently. This one hadn't even made it to nightfall.

CHINA BASIN, SAN FRANCISCO

Wilhelmina Fox, known to the world as "Billie," did what bleacher bums did at Pacific Bell Park—she gazed through her binoculars at the luxury suites, scoping out the rich and famous. An inveterate Giants fan, Billie came to the ballpark early to take in batting practice and watch Barry Bonds launch ball after ball over the right-field wall and into the bay. What the hey, she was into cheap thrills.

But this game and this occasion were different. Activity on the field took a back seat to goings-on in the stands or, more particularly, in the luxury suites. Because Billie was looking for Wilson Dahl.

Sure, it was an exercise in morbidity, but she had a morbid streak to rival Mary Shelley. Besides, what woman alive wouldn't be at least a little curious about the shenanigans of a former lover?

It had been months since Wilson Dahl had so much as entered her thoughts, so inconsequential was he in the greater scheme of things. But as she and Emily, her six-year-old daughter, had entered the stadium, who should she see walking ahead of them but Wilson himself, cuddling a Latina chicky—most likely the camp follower of the hour. Billie observed the saccharine display with disgust, not because of any residual feelings for Wilson, but rather because seeing him with his current floozie gave Billie a perspective on herself that she didn't particularly like.

Moving the glasses from suite to suite, she finally spotted him in the Bachman, Carlisle, Cummings & Glick luxury suite, laughing and snuggling the bimbo. But the pair weren't alone. Checking out the box more thoroughly, Billie realized it was practically an annex to the Hall of Justice. The D.A., Henry Chin—Harry to his detractors—Bart Carlisle and Jessica Horton, both hotshot lawyers at B.C.C.&G., were in the party. The bimbo didn't look familiar, but then Wilson was known to prefer outsiders, Billie being a case in point, though she, at least, had been a member of the bar. Chiquita, on the other hand, looked like a refugee from an escort service—boobs, lipstick and hair worthy of an exotic dancer.

"Mommy, can I see?" Emily said, tugging on her arm.

"Honey, there's nothing to see."

"Then why are you looking?"

Six-year-olds came up with questions like that from time to time, questions requiring answers comprehensible only to the duplicitous mind of an adult. "I'm watching some people I know, pumpkin."

"Who?"

"Harry Chin."

Emily began to laugh. "Mommy, that's not a name."

"Oh, yes, it is."

"Let me see a hairy chin."

Billie handed over the binoculars. The little girl began peering around the stands. Billie pondered the happy five-some in the B.C.C.&G. suite, wondering where Harry's girl was. Surely he knew that no self-respecting big shot would venture out without his PalmPilot, his beeper and his bimbo. In truth, there seemed to be an epidemic of mistresses in the San Francisco legal community at the moment, not that there wasn't a time when the courthouse boys didn't have a girl on the side. Apparently, today, Harry was without, poor baby. Her compassion wasn't genuine, though. The D.A. was Montgomery Street's man in City Hall, and Billie, a self-proclaimed proletarian, couldn't have had less respect for the man.

She felt pretty much the same about all the boys in the legal establishment, including Wilson Dahl, though he didn't practice law. A graduate of Stanford Law School, he'd gone into banking, instead, later becoming a bankruptcy trustee. "Having seen so many properties run into the ground by inept managers," he'd told her, "I decided there was room for somebody with a modicum of competence." The false modesty could be forgiven. Wilson had a lovely home in Pacific Heights and was a millionaire many times over. He knew Bart Carlisle from law school—they'd been buddies down on "The Farm"—and it was actually Bart who'd introduced Billie to him.

Their fling had been part of her divorce-recovery program, a course of action made necessary by the trauma of her husband's infidelity. It was hard to say which had embarrassed her more, Sonny's duplicity or the desperation sex that followed. But then, that had been the point—crafting a second wrong to make things right.

Fortunately that phase of her life was very much in the past now, but it didn't mean she wasn't still curious about what was going on in the upper strata of the legal community. Nor was she alone. Gossip was the communal pastime—more so in San Francisco, it seemed, than most places. Billie wasn't immune. Not by a long shot.

Seeing Bart Carlisle and Jessica Horton together, for example, was no surprise. Everybody in town knew they were screwing. Most of the heavy hitters relished the opportunity to play kissy-face with some dewy young thing sporting perky boobs and pouty lips. These guys all lived for billable hours and a fresh piece of ass.

Some of the girls set their sights on a greater reward than a few months of high living. Jessica was a good example. Her strategy was obvious to even a casual observer. She was counting on Bart making sure she became a partner in the firm so that the fortune he lost when his wife divorced him would soon be replaced by the earnings of a young and industrious second wife.

Billie sighed. Why the shenanigans of the high and the

mighty was so fascinating, she didn't know. She was neither unhappy with her modest, though spiritually rewarding, law practice nor was she envious of the big boppers. Maybe it had something to do with an innate sense of self-preservation— when you swam in shark-infested waters, you needed to keep your eyes open and your wits about you.

In this day and age, survival was a complex matter. There was the struggle to earn a living, to keep your personal life on an even keel, all the while maintaining your sanity for your child's sake, if not your own. But for Billie, the biggest stress-inducer of all was her health. She'd had to face that demon, too. A few months before the demise of her marriage, they found a spot in her breast during a routine mammogram. It proved to be a cancerous tumor, a tiny one, but cancer, nonetheless. Early detection had saved her, but it had caused a scare. And because of the possibility of a relapse, she still contended with her mortality on a daily basis, a particularly ominous prospect for a single mother.

Billie put her arm around her child.

"Mommy," Emily said, "I see lots of hairy chins."

"On the gentlemen, I hope."

"Huh?"

Billie gave her daughter a hug. "Emily, how'd you like to let me have the binoculars for a while?"

"Then can I go on the slide again?"

The creators of Pac Bell Park had added a few features for the kids to give the place a carnival-like feel. Emily's favorite was the slide inside the giant Coke bottle above the left-field bleachers. Billie herself liked the thirty-foot-high, ten-ton base-ball glove next to the Coke bottle, maybe because it reminded her of her own career as a jock—first base, high-school softball, Fresno County and South Central Valley Regional champs.

"You went on the slide three times already, pumpkin. Now the game is about to start."

"Grandpa would take me."

"But Grandpa's not here, honey. He's at home." Billie was sorry now she hadn't gotten three tickets and brought along her dad to baby-sit. Mel Fox lived with them and adored entertaining his grandchild, but he wasn't a fan and had little interest in baseball.

"Can I go by myself?"

"Definitely not."

"How come?"

Billie was not going to bring up the incident in the supermarket three years earlier when she'd turned her back for a few seconds to find Emily had disappeared. Luckily a clerk had seen some creep carrying a crying child out the door and Billie caught up with the SOB a block from the store, wrenching her daughter away from the flabby pervert and pasting him a good one before he finally made his escape.

"Tell you what," Billie said. "I'll trade the binoculars for some popcorn."

"Oh, goodie!" the little girl said.

She handed her mother the binoculars. Billie hailed the popcorn vendor.

Once the transaction had been completed and Emily was munching happily, Billie turned her attention to the field where the Braves' lead-off batter had just stepped into the batter's box. The really important stuff was about to begin.

Where the hell was Joe Sasso? The game was under way and he still hadn't arrived. Elaine Chang, in a French-blue St. John skirt and white-and-gold St. John tank top, did her best to hide her anxiety from the man who sat in stoic silence beside her.

Ken Lu was not one for small talk. She knew that, despite his outward calm, his gut had to be churning. They waited for Joe, waited to learn their fate. Elaine had more on the line than just a fee. She'd devoted the better part of a year to this deal. She'd expended money, time and risked her reputation. Hell, she'd gone to bed with a cripple to make it go. But she couldn't allow herself to get upset. Not now.

Though her heart refused to slow down, Elaine distracted herself by watching the sailboats plying the waters beyond McCovey Cove. The majestic Bay Bridge, the sweeping panorama, the play of the gulls and boats were much more interesting than baseball, a pastime for which she had little taste and almost as little knowledge.

Elaine had purchased a luxury suite at the new ballpark to see and be seen, to entertain and conduct business. And, since baseball was secondary, Elaine had commissioned her *fung shui* master to examine the plans to determine which orientation would be the most propitious for her purposes. All she'd asked was a clear view of the bay. Exclusivity was a given.

There was much about her adoptive city of San Francisco that reminded Elaine of Hong Kong, where, in relative poverty, she'd spent her youth. The boats always brought to mind the times she would accompany Auntie to the fish market. Sometimes they would go to the docks to have their bowl of rice and watch the freighters, ferries, motor yachts and sampans zig and zag between Kowloon and Hong Kong Island. Elaine especially liked the cabin cruisers because the rich men and pretty women on them seemed to be so happy. Even as a child she'd dreamed of such a life.

There was a sudden roar from the crowd. Ken Lu leaned forward for a better view of the field.

"What happened?"

Elaine glanced down at the field and saw a player in the home uniform rounding second base. He was trotting at a measured pace. "A home run," she replied in a matter-of-fact tone. She said the words in English, though virtually all of their conversation had been in Cantonese.

"This is obviously good," he said, pushing his large sunglasses back up on his nose, partially covering the scar over his right eyebrow. He was a portly man with a deceptively quiet manner and a penchant for white suits. "It's like a goal, isn't it?"

"Yes, Ken. The object, I think, is to hit the ball over the wall. Beyond that it's a mystery to me. Joe knows all about baseball. He can explain the game when he arrives."

"I hope he can explain why there is a holdup on the money. *That* is of immediate concern, Elaine. I have a virtual army under pay and they can be very fickle. I'm sure I don't need to tell you that."

"No, I understand fully. And surely you understand that two million dollars is not easily raised."

"What about the fifty thousand I was supposed to have last week?"

"You'll get it, Ken. I promise."

She hated using the word *promise* unless she knew she could make good, because credibility was important in her line of work. Joe had used the term with her when they'd spoken that morning, but Joe was desperate to do the deal. Of course, so was she. Her cut could be in the mid to upper six-figure range, maybe even seven. That was pressure.

Elaine had promised herself that by the age of forty she'd be in a position to retire into a life of luxury. She only had a little over four years to make it. This deal was a major step toward her goal. Everything was riding on Joe Sasso.

Growing more antsy by the moment, Elaine decided to try and reach him. "Ken," she said, placing her hand on her companion's arm, "will you please excuse me for a few minutes?"

He nodded his compliance.

Elaine slipped out of her seat and left the suite through the door at the rear. A waitress passed by and Elaine stopped her, asking her to take a beer to the gentleman inside. She took a twenty-dollar bill from her purse. "If he wants food, bring whatever he wants."

"Yes, ma'am."

"Keep the change."

Elaine went to a quiet corner, took her cell phone from her purse and dialed Joe Sasso's cell number. To her relief, he answered.

"Joe, where the hell are you?"

"On my way, sweetheart. I should be there in fifteen minutes or so."

"Do you have the check for Ken?"

She held her breath, afraid of what he'd say. The deal meant everything to her. She'd prepared herself for the worst, though. If the bastard didn't have the money yet, but might still come through, she'd have to keep her cool, figure out a way to buy them a few more days. She simply couldn't afford to fail.

"Got it!" he said.

Elaine closed her eyes, saying a silent prayer, thanking the gods. "Good," she said evenly, refusing to show any trepidation. "Now if we can just come up with the rest, everything will be fine..."

"We will. We will."

"We've come this far, it would be a shame not to put this one to bed."

"Speaking of which, how about we celebrate after the game? Just the two of us." He hesitated. "I could spend the night."

"What about your wife?"

"I told Gina I was going to Reno on business. Supposedly I left this morning."

"And she believed you?"

"Not the part about it being for business. She figured it was to gamble. But she didn't say anything because I haven't been to Nevada in a long, long time. So, what do you think about having a party, you and me?"

Elaine wasn't in the mood, but if he was bringing fifty thousand for the pot, she could do that much. "Of course," she said.

Ending the call, she decided to go to the ladies' room before giving Ken the good news. She felt better about things. At least now, the evening would be easier to endure.

Minutes later, as she came out of the stall, she noticed an attractive blonde at the mirror, checking her makeup. She looked familiar but Elaine couldn't place her. The woman wore no rings on her left hand, so she wasn't a wife. She was thirty, give or take a year, about five years Elaine's junior, and was wearing a very expensive gold watch. A mistress, perhaps?

It was rare that Elaine didn't recognize an acquaintance and place a name with a face. It was a special knack. That was why it bothered her not to be able to place the blonde. When the mystery woman left, Elaine followed her out the door. On an impulse, she trailed along behind her as she made her way along the concourse.

The blonde was tall, with a very good figure, shapely legs and a sense of style. She was dressed casually, of course, but her shorts were nicely tailored and her tank top was designer. She carried herself with confidence and grace. Elaine knew class when she saw it, something unusual in a woman so young.

The blonde entered a luxury suite on the first-base side, a less desirable perspective according to Elaine's *fung shui* master. As she passed by, Elaine caught a glimpse of the occupants—three men and another woman. Ever curious, Elaine pondered how she might find out who they were.

In the end, she decided to walk right in, feigning a mistake. Her chutzpah had gotten her from the bottom rung of the socioeconomic ladder in Hong Kong to the loftiest heights on the Golden Mountain, so why be shy now? Opening the door with a flourish, she charged right in, stopping when all five occupants turned.

Before her was a snapshot of some of the more important movers and shakers in San Francisco's legal establishment. The Asian was Henry Chin, the district attorney, the man next to him was Bart Carlisle—Bartholomew Carlisle II, to be precise—managing partner of one of the three largest firms in the city. The identity of the third man she wasn't sure about, but he looked vaguely familiar. Perhaps a judge or something. The other woman, a brunette with olive skin, maybe Hispanic, seemed to be with the judge. Elaine didn't have the vaguest idea who she was.

"Oops!" Elaine said, not showing immediate recognition. "Sorry, wrong suite." She pretended only then to recognize him. "Henry!"

"Hi, Elaine," he said, grinning. "What a nice surprise."

"Nice" was hyperbole. "Unexpected" would be more accurate. She and Henry Chin had been lovers years ago—the better part of a decade, to be exact—before he'd moved from the world of corporate law into politics. It was also before she'd climbed the heights of the business community. They'd both been single at the time, Henry one of the few men she'd considered marrying. Unfortunately she'd had a past a bit too rich in lore for his requirements, and he'd opted for a safer bride, a woman endowed with pedigree rather than brains and sex appeal.

Not that their paths hadn't crossed in the years since their liaison. They'd had a drink together on half a dozen occasions, schmoozed at social events, and had lunch two or three times. There'd always been a good reason to get together but it hadn't gone beyond talk, though she had seen desire in Henry's eye.

"Forgive the intrusion," she said to the group. "I feel so

stupid. I was looking for Max Harrison. Somebody said he was in a suite along here somewhere."

"Wrong law firm," Carlisle said, chuckling.

He was the quintessential establishment lawyer, early fifties, blue-eyed, all-American boy, now middle-aged, with thinning blond hair. Carlisle had a sharp nose and high sculpted cheekbones, but to her his most attractive feature was his lean, athletic frame.

"So it *is* the wrong firm," Elaine said. "Hi, Bart."

"Nice seeing you, Elaine." He seemed amused—Bart Carlisle always seemed amused. "Hey, why don't you join us...unless finding Max is critical."

"I just wanted to confirm an appointment. It's not urgent."

"Sit down then."

Bart was being cordial and Elaine figured what the hell. When you hung around power, bits of information that could prove useful sometimes filtered down. "Perhaps for a minute or two," she said. "I've got clients in my suite."

Elaine glanced at the blonde, who'd taken a seat next to Bart Carlisle, realizing then who she was—one of the rising stars in Carlisle's firm. Elaine remembered now. They'd met at a reception six months or so ago.

Bart made introductions and Elaine acknowledged everyone. Dahl was a courtly-looking gentleman, WASP undoubtedly, roughly the age of the other two men. His lady friend—busy, painted, cheap—scarcely earned a nod. Elaine slipped into the seat next to Henry. She gave his hand an affectionate pat, one former lovers might use to say, "Hi, how've you been?" As regards to skill, Henry Chin was not at the top of her list of former lovers, but he was large for a Chinese and showed more consideration in bed than most. Mainly, she'd been attracted to his instinct for power.

Henry was rumored to be positioning himself for a run against the mayor. That would explain why he didn't have a cutie on his arm, like the others. Considering Mayor Bobby Green had a well-established reputation as a womanizer, making sport fucking the game of choice at City Hall during his two terms in office, any opponent shooting for the moral-outrage vote simply had to keep his or her transgressions within reasonable bounds to outstrip him.

"So, how's the game?" Elaine asked, just to make small talk. "Have I missed much, running around looking for Max?"

"Braves have two men on," Bart said, indicating the field, "but there are two outs."

She only vaguely understood, but she nodded, assuming cause for grave concern. When the next batter grounded out to short, eliciting a cheer from the crowd, Elaine knew the danger to the homeboys had passed. She leaned forward and glanced over toward her own suite. Joe had arrived. She had to get back.

"Tell me, Elaine," Henry said, apparently having sensed that she was about to take her leave and not wanting her to go, "what's in your bag of tricks these days that's worthy of note?"

Elaine wasn't sure if it was an innocent question or if murmurings about her big project had made their way to City Hall. There was nothing illicit about the deal, but she preferred to keep a low profile.

"The usual, Henry," she said casually, looking for signs he might have heard something. Chin was a sly operator and rarely tipped his hand.

"Nothing is usual when you're involved, Elaine."

"I hope that was a compliment," she said, sensing he was just bantering.

He put his hand on hers. "What else?"

She realized then that her old flame had a sudden hankering to get laid. Well, too bad for good old Henry. She wasn't about to accommodate him. She had a reputation and a lot of history, but she wasn't a slut. Everything she did, whether in bed or elsewhere, was for a purpose. There probably weren't more than half a dozen times in her life that she'd had sex purely for pleasure. She'd learned long ago, the highest and best use of her body was as a tool of the trade.

"Much as I'd like to stay and chat, I'd better get back to my guests," she said. She gave Henry's cheek a pinch. After saying goodbye to the others, Elaine left the suite. She started up the concourse, having taken only a few steps, when Henry came running after her.

"Elaine!"

She stopped.

"I know this is out of the blue," he said, "but do you have plans for dinner?"

"Why, Henry, you surprise me."

"Yes, I know. But it's not *just* for the pleasure of your company, though that in itself is a very good reason. I have business I'd like to discuss with you."

"What sort of business?"

"I'd like to talk to you about a role in my campaign."

"Me? Politics? Henry, surely you jest."

"It would be a discreet role, of course. I know how you abjure the public spotlight."

Elaine couldn't help but be amused by his earnestness when he tried to be seductive. Henry's problem as a politician was that he was too formal and stiff. And intellectual. As a grad of Princeton and Yale Law, it was to be expected, perhaps. Bobby Green, by contrast, was a man of the people—San Jose State and Hastings College of Law. Scandals or not, Elaine's money, though not her sympathies, were with the mayor.

"I work for myself, Henry, as you well know."

"At least hear what I have to say. You may be surprised by how interesting it could be."

Her inclination was to demur, but Henry had always been adept at piquing her curiosity. And since it was possible he could end up being mayor, maybe it was in her interest to play along for a while.

"We're all going to Jessica's place for dinner after the game," he said. "Would you care to join us?"

"Henry, I'd love to, but I've got plans for the evening."

"That's too bad."

"Yes, isn't it?"

"How about lunch next week, then?"

"You're determined, aren't you, you naughty boy?"

"Monday, Tuesday. You say when."

"Call me Monday and we'll find a time."

With victory in hand and the crowd heading for home, Inspector Dickson Hong, a homicide detective with the SFPD, and his wife, Suze, made their way down the ramp and out the gate into Willie Mays Plaza. Hong was largely indifferent to baseball, but Suze loved it, adored it. She had earned the "Croix de Candlestick"—a pin awarded to fans who stuck through to the bitter end of extra-inning night games out at the refrigerated wind tunnel on Candlestick Point where the Giants once played. Suze's Giants cap was a veritable helmet of commemorative pins she'd collected over the years.

Suze Hong's favorite player was the Giants' shortstop, Rich Aurelia. She had a picture of herself and Aurelia taken during spring training in Arizona the year before. The picture was on the mantel of their house in Daly City, right next to their wedding picture. Hong sometimes wondered—not entirely facetiously—if his wife would leave him for Aurelia, given the chance.

"Now that wasn't so bad, was it, Dickson?" she asked him, taking his arm. "At least they won."

"No, it was a good game."

Hong indulged his wife by attending a game or two with her each month, though Suze went to several other games with a friend, or even alone. The woman was addicted to baseball and, given ticket prices, it put quite a dent in their budget, making him wonder if he wouldn't be better off having to contend with a wife with a mah-jong habit like most Chinese husbands. But Dickson's toleration had its compensations. It earned him the liberty of one or two evenings out each week to play chess at his club, chess being *his* passion.

"I don't know what's wrong with Richie," she said with concern. "This is the second game this week he's gone without a hit. Until the Cardinal series he was on fire."

"These things happen," Dickson said, trying to be supportive.

The crowd was dispersing in all directions from the plaza. The Hongs would take the Muni along the Embarcadero to the BART station, where they would catch a train to Daly City. Parking was expensive and it was a nightmare.

"Dickson, look!" his wife said, jerking on his sleeve.

"What?"

"Look who's getting into the limo."

He peered through the milling crowd, spotting a black limo at the curb some distance away, but couldn't pick out who she was talking about. "Who?"

"Henry Chin! See him next to that white woman, the blonde. You don't suppose... No, there's two other men with them. The woman's probably with one of them. Yes, one's taking her arm. For a second there I thought..."

Dickson's wife, like many women her age, was a ready gossip, but this was more than idle chatter, because there was a personal element at work. Every time the subject of Henry Chin came up, Suze found a way to bring up the fact that years ago, when she was twenty, she and Henry had dated. To hear her tell it, they were all but engaged and their families had talked marriage.

Dickson knew little about Henry Chin except that his father had once been the mayor of Shanghai, back when it was in the hands of the Nationalists. Though Chin's accomplishments had been significant, they fell short of the standards set by his now-aged father, who at one time had been a young protégé of Chiang Kai-shek. Chin, according to the gossip in Chinatown, wanted desperately to be the mayor of San Francisco, if only to show his father he was as worthy and as accomplished as he.

True or not, the Chins were a formidable family, and Dickson had doubts about the accuracy of his wife's characterization of her relationship with them. He never expressed them, of course. Suze was best controlled by indulging her, which he did with a deftness that brought him pride. Though friends considered him henpecked, to Inspector Dick Hong, the name of the game was domestic tranquillity. The same principle applied at work, as well.

"And to think that could be me going to Giants games in a limousine," Suze said.

"Don't be too sure," he rejoined, unable to resist. "More likely he'd take a mistress."

Suze didn't like the rebuff and gave him a harsh glance, as though it had been a put-down. It didn't matter that they were discussing a hypothetical situation. The implication was that she would lose out to some younger, more attractive woman.

"Joyce might not be able to keep him in line, but I wouldn't have had that problem."

Dickson rolled his eyes, sorry now he'd brought the matter up.

"Who do you suppose those people are, anyway?" his wife asked as they made their way toward the Muni stop.

"Movers and shakers," he said glumly.

Dickson had never had any direct contact with Henry Chin, either in his personal or professional life, though the district attorney seemed always to nibble at the edges of his existence. Chin was the highest law enforcement official in the city and the most prominent member of the Chinese community, whereas Dickson was a simple police inspector, if a senior one because of longevity. And then there was his wife's well-timed reminders of what might have been. He never complained, though. Jealousy was nothing more than outward-directed feelings of inadequacy. Dickson Hong had the satisfaction of being an honest man.

UPPER WEST SIDE, MANHATTAN

Dominick's California Cafe was in pandemonium—the good kind. Upon arriving, Nick and Bree had pitched in with the rest of the crew, working right through the dinner service. He'd taken over in the kitchen and she'd waited tables, donning a chef's jacket with rolled-up sleeves so as not to scandalize the clientele with her skimpy outfit. Her legs had drawn considerable attention nonetheless, prompting one guy to ask if she was going to be in the floor show later. Nick had found that more amusing than Bree.

At ten o'clock they staggered into the extra room at the back of the restaurant, which Nick had converted into a studio apartment—windowless and illegal, yet convenient and economical. They were both sweating like battery mates in the ninth inning of an afternoon game in August, humidity at ninety-eight percent. Nick pumped his fist in the air and fell backward onto the single bed, roaring, "*Yes!*" as Bree went off to take a shower.

He would have joined her, except that the shower stall was the size of a phone booth. Anyway, he wanted to savor the moment a bit longer. He knew his problems would be intruding soon enough.

"Hot damn!" he shouted.

"Hot damn!" Bree shouted back.

He glanced at the bathroom doorway and saw her stark naked, her arm behind the shower curtain, groping the water, her chin tucked into her shoulder, turned his way, a smile on her pretty mouth. It was an arresting sight, making him want her. No surprise there. They would likely have sex, but probably not until he'd decided what to do about his family. Even while working furiously in the kitchen, Nick had felt their presence—Joe and the old man at his elbow like a pair of ghosts from Christmas past.

Watching a cockroach skitter across the wall opposite him, he pondered how he should approach the situation. Where did he start? With Joe?

Nick had no desire to go to San Francisco. It was make-or-break time for his restaurant and even two or three days away could be crippling. He'd taken a hell of a risk running up to the Bronx to see the Yankees. Of course, he had no idea the effect of the *Post* review would be so dramatic and immediate. Now that things were happening, there was no way he was going to let this opportunity slip through his fingers.

Then he got an idea. He'd call Benny. Benito Vocino was an old friend of his father's, a guy who'd practically been an uncle to him and Joe. Benny, considered by many to be the honorary mayor of North Beach, had for years proclaimed himself "the richest wop in San Francisco." He could say that because he was generous and used his money wisely—God knew, he'd helped Nick's old man out of more than one jam. The restaurant business was not easy, Benny would say, and when a good eating joint was in danger of going under, "A man had to do what a man had to do."

Benito Vocino meant so much to the family that Tony Sasso reserved the corner booth—the most sanctified spot in the dining room—just for him. Above it, Tony had placed his most prized possession, a photo of Joltin' Joe with Marilyn Monroe holding Sasso's firstborn, baby Vince, in her arms. The boy had died a year later of scarlet fever, which made the photograph even more precious to the family. The original was bolted to the wall above the old man's bed at the nursing home.

Nick could picture Benny practically as well as he could picture his old man. Vocino was a short, stocky man, usually wearing an open-neck shirt with the collar spread neatly over the lapels of his tweed sports coat, a look that had been out of style for twenty-five years. Benny had made it his signature fashion statement, and that was that.

About the time Nick had left San Francisco, smoking in restaurants was banned entirely. Benny, an inveterate cigar smoker, had nearly gone ballistic, but he'd had little choice but to comply. It didn't stop him from keeping an unlit cigar in his hand, though. More than once he'd vowed to light up the second the people of California had the sense to elect public officials who valued personal freedom.

Even if Benny didn't know what was going on with Joe, he'd be ready with advice. Nick was sure he'd have some harsh words for him, too, given Nick's estrangement from his family. But it would be worth a lecture if he could get Joe straightened out and spare himself a trip to California. The trouble was, he didn't know Benny's number. Maybe somebody at the Yankee Clipper would have it.

As Bree splashed happily in the shower, Nick got on the phone. Because of the time difference, things would be just getting under way at the Yankee Clipper.

He was surprised when a hostess didn't answer. Since his father had opened the place, the Clipper was known for the pretty women who greeted customers. "Tall, beautiful and preferably with tits," was the way Tony Sasso liked them. Instead, Nick got a gruff male voice.

"Yankee Clipper. Can I help?"

"Hello, this is Nick Sasso in New York."

"Jesus Christ, I thought you were dead."

The bluntness of the remark told him it was Gennaro Ravara, the crusty waiter who'd been hustling pasta at the Yankee Clipper since the old man was Joe's age. Gennaro was nothing if not outspoken.

"How's it going, old buddy?"

"If there was a chair here," Gennaro said, "I'd sit down."

"What are you doing answering the phone, anyway? They don't have you in a skirt, do they?"

"Jesus Christ, they might as well. No, the girl is off taking a leak and she asked me to guard the door."

Nick had forgotten how fond he was of Gennaro. The guy was an institution in North Beach, as famous as Carol Doda, the onetime topless dancer at the Condor who'd been as equally well-known in her day as then governor Ronald Reagan.

At the party they'd thrown for Gennaro's seventieth birthday, Nick had introduced him as "The Yankee Clipper's own Carol Doda." Gennaro had risen to his feet, hushed the applause, ran his hand back over the pencil-line strips of hair glued to his nearly bald pate and said, "Yeah, but think of the tips I'd have gotten with her knockers."

"I've got a favor to ask," Nick said. "I'm trying to reach Benny Vocino. Does anybody there have his number?"

"Probably. But Benny's here, sitting in his booth, waiting for me to bring him his coffee. Why don't you talk to him so I can earn my gratuity? This phone don't got a cord. I'll take it to him."

Gennaro didn't wait for a response. Nick could picture him shuffle-stepping his way over to the booth of honor. After a brief moment of garbled conversation amid the crowd noise, Nick heard another familiar voice.

"Well, if it ain't the family's culinary genius. Last person on earth I'd be expecting to hear from. How are you, Nick?"

"Doing well, Benny, doing well."

"I suppose I'm glad to hear that. Don't have to tell you that your stock ain't what it once was in this town."

"No, you don't."

"But you're family, Nick, and you haven't killed nobody that I know of, so I'm happy to talk to you. What's on your mind?"

"I'm concerned about Joe and the old man and I thought maybe you could give me a feel for what's going on back there."

Benny gave a snort. Nick could picture the cigar rolling between his fingers. "Let me tell you about Tony Sasso. Here's a proud man, practically confined to a bed, dying a little each day. That's not your fault, I know, but put yourself in his shoes. The son he loves runs off, never sees him, never calls him. It's a goddamn shame, that's what it is."

Nick had known this was coming, but he hadn't expected such passion. "I know," he said. "I'll be talking to him soon. I thought maybe you could make it a little easier by giving me the lay of the land, Benny."

"Tony Sasso is a loving father," Benny continued, really pouring it on. "I'll never forget the time when you were in high school, playing ball for the city championship. Me and Tony went to the game. I don't know if you were aware of that. He was so goddamn proud, Tony was. The two of us and a couple of the other boys come back here afterward and Tony breaks out the Chianti. It was between lunch and dinner and there was nobody much around. So, we start drinking and talking about the game. I'll never forget this. Tony looks at me with wet eyes and he says, 'Maybe I'm going to have a DiMaggio of my own, Benny.' Never forget that as long as I live. That was a proud father if I ever seen one."

Nick, sinking into a morass of guilt, realized this had been a bad idea. If he'd wanted to be chastised, he could have gone to confession. "Too bad I couldn't hit worth a damn," he said, hoping to deflect the reproval.

Benny snorted. "Hell, there aren't many who can. A Joe DiMaggio only comes along once in a lifetime. He was truly special. Now, Vince and Dom were damn good ballplayers, mind you, but Joe...well, put it this way, how many Napoleons have there been? Huh?"

"You're right about that."

"We could use another Joltin' Joe."

"Right again."

"Speaking of guys named Joe, what's with that damn brother of yours?"

Nick was glad the conversation had finally moved on. "Actually, that was what I wanted to ask you. What's with him? I hear he's having problems."

"He sure as hell hasn't discussed them with me," Benny said.

Across the way, Bree stepped out of the shower. Nick checked out her ass and her tits because there was no way he couldn't. But if he was going to have a halfway coherent conversation, he had to avert his eyes. It was like being fourteen and knowing that looking at the *Playboy* centerfold was a sin yet having only enough willpower to stick the magazine under the mattress, not in the trash.

"What's the word on the street, Benny?" Nick asked, bringing his mind back to the matter at hand.

"There's always talk," Benny said. "Joey's into a lot of things, which you already know. But if you're asking about specifics, I haven't heard nothing special."

Nick was surprised. If Mort Seidel had heard talk about Joe's financial woes, then Benito Vocino would surely have. Benny knew everything about anybody in town who counted. Then it occurred to him whatever he'd heard may have been related to him in confidence.

"I can tell you this," Benny went on, "he hasn't been himself lately. They tell me, for example, it's been a few days since he's been around. You're in the restaurant business. You know how important it is to keep an eye on things."

Nick wanted to say, "Yeah, that's exactly why I can't be running off to San Francisco." There was no point, though. His issues were not with Benito Vocino.

"Speaking of which," Benny said, "how's your restaurant doing?"

"Great. We got a good review in the *Post*. Things are looking up."

"New York's a tough town for restaurateurs. The fact you've lasted this long is a tribute. I wish you luck."

"Thanks, Benny. I'll let you go so you can enjoy your coffee."

As he hung up Bree came striding across the room, a towel wrapped around her, her pale flesh as inviting as clotted cream. She sat down on his lap. Nick put the cell phone next to him on the bed. He ran the back of his finger along her jaw, just for the sheer pleasure of her silky skin.

"You are an eyeful," he said.

She raked her fingers through his damp hair. "And you need a shower."

"I know."

"So, did you get things straightened out with your family?" she asked.

"Not yet."

"You going to make more calls?"

"Yes, but not now. I've got to talk to my brother, but I'm going to sleep on it first."

She stroked his cheek. "Maybe I can find a way to get your mind off your troubles."

Nick kissed her lip. "Babe, I can guarantee you will."

GOLDEN GATEWAY CENTER

The limo pulled up outside the complex where Jessica Horton's condominium was located. "Henry," she said, "are you sure you don't want to join us? I bought five steaks."

"Five, as in fifth wheel."

"But that was the plan," she insisted.

"You can have more fun without me. Besides, I have to return that call that came in a while ago. It's very important." Looking at Bart, he gave a half nod and his friend seemed to understand.

"You could come in, make your call and join us for a drink," Bart said.

"Yes," Wilson Dahl chimed in. "Do join us, Henry."

Henry realized Bart and Wilson were as eager to know what was up as he. "Okay. Perhaps a short one."

They made their way up the stairs and into the town-house complex, which was like a village accessible only by foot. The fog had flowed in through the Golden Gate, already obscuring Coit Tower.

Once they were inside Jessica's peachy-beige town house—the sort of place a bright, ambitious professional woman with taste would be expected to occupy—Rosa Ostos, Wilson's squeeze of the moment, began gushing. "This is so pretty. Like a flower. I love your house, Jessica. It's wonderful."

Henry took advantage of the effusing to step into the study. Bart closed the door behind him to give him privacy. Henry took out his cell phone and dialed the number.

"Yes?"

"It's me," Henry said. "What happened?"

"I talked to her."

"And?"

"Your friend has decided to go after you, Mr. Chin. With guns blazing."

"You mean he's going to the feds?"

"No, the courts. She's seen a draft pleading, naming names."

"Good Lord."

"I didn't think you'd be pleased."

"Why, for God's sake?" Henry said.

"He thinks he's macho man, I guess."

"A very dangerous one."

"You'd know better than me."

Henry thought for a moment or two. "I'm with my associates now. We'll discuss this."

"What are you going to do?"

"Leave it in our hands," he said. "You've done your part. Now keep your head down and your mouth shut."

"No problem, Mr. Chin."

"Where did you find her, by the way?" Henry asked.

"In Oakland."

"East Oakland?"

"No, she hasn't sunk quite that low. But she's hurting and therefore vulnerable. I convinced her it was in her interest to talk."

"Well done."

"Thanks."

"Okay," Henry said with a weary sigh. "I'll be in touch."

He hung up, took several moments to gather himself. What had once been a ripple on calm waters had turned into a tidal wave, threatening the end of everything he'd worked for. This was a disaster, an absolute disaster.

The image that flashed through Henry's mind was of his father, now little more than a loose bundle of flesh and bone, passing the hours in contemplation, gazing backward at lost glory and ahead at dreams for his son, dreams still unfulfilled. Chin

Wan took the small fortune Henry had accumulated in stride, respectful of the accomplishment, but not overly impressed. After all, anybody who works hard can make it in America. And old Chin saw the legal profession simply as a stepping-stone to power. When Henry was elected district attorney, his father nodded his approval. "It is a good start, my son."

Chin Wan was an old warrior who'd outlived his times. Henry knew that, but he couldn't ignore the fervor of the old man's desire, a desire that was like a dominant family gene. "A man's son is his destiny," his father had said. Over the years Henry had learned what a terrible burden that could be.

Taking a deep breath like a pitcher facing a three and two count with the bases loaded in the bottom of the ninth, Henry Chin now knew it was do or die. He took a second or two to reflect, then returned to the company of his friends.

Bart and Wilson, drinks in hand, were on their feet, anxious expressions on their faces. They were alone. Henry joined them. Bart handed him a scotch.

"Where's Jessica and Rosa?" Henry asked, peering back toward the kitchen.

"Freshening up. They can't hear." Bart took a gulp of his drink. "What happened?"

"The bastard has declared war. Total war." Henry let the words settle on his friends, taking a sip of scotch before going on. "He's decided to go the civil route, apparently. He's working on pleadings."

"Oh, shit."

"Yeah."

Wilson Dahl's shoulders slumped. Bartholomew Carlisle II stared off, his jaw working. He shifted his weight nervously. "We can't let this happen, Henry."

"I know."

Bart glanced at Wilson, then at Henry. "Maybe the time has come to talk to my Russian contact."

Henry Chin spun the ice and scotch in his glass, staring down at it. "Yes, Bart, I think maybe it has."

MONDAY SEPTEMBER 2ND

VAN NUYS

Igor Andreyevich Sakharov loved America. He especially loved L.A. He loved the palm trees and the smog, the beaches and the girls, the cars and the supermarkets and the pizza parlors and the Lakers and the movie stars and the freeways and especially the money. And, yes, he even loved his wife, though Eve could be a pain in the ass at times.

Stretched out on his lawn chair next to the kidney-shaped pool in his backyard, Igor listened to the hiss and gurgle of the pool sweep, which was cheeky enough to bump up against the tiles and piss on him from time to time. But he didn't mind. It was all part of the great symphony of American life. How many places were there where you could make a fortune killing people?

Igor Sakharov was an assassin, now semiretired, who'd decided to become a capitalist. Why not? he'd said to himself when Eve first proposed the idea. After all, he was fifty-eight; he had bad joints and digestive problems. A man had to settle down and make an honest living sometime before he died. It was the American way.

Eve, who sat under the umbrella table on the other side of the pool working on the laptop computer, was the genius behind their enterprise. She was the classic entrepreneur—always thinking, always calculating, always finding the angles. But she liked to spend money as much as she liked to make it. That was a problem.

They had a nice house, but Eve wanted to live in Holmby Hills in the worst way.

"What's so important about living there?" Igor demanded when last they fought over moving. "Don't you have everything you could want right here?"

"I want better, Iggy. I want the best."

Just then the cordless phone at Eve's elbow rang. She picked it up. Igor heard her say, "Happy Labor Day to you, too, Viktor."

He cringed. It was Viktor Chorny. He did not want to talk to Viktor. Not on a holiday. Actually, not on any day. At one time, perhaps, but not any longer.

"No, we're just having a quiet day at home," Eve said into the phone. Then, after a moment, "Sure, come on over. We're barbecuing later. Stay and eat with us, if you like."

Igor groaned. Why did the woman do these things? Why couldn't she think of him, just once?

Eve hung up the phone. "It was Viktor," she announced across the pool. "He wanted to talk to you. He's on his way over."

"Eve, why didn't you ask me first before inviting him? Did it occur to you that maybe I don't want to talk to Viktor?"

"Will it hurt to find out what he's got?"

"You know how I feel. I'm tired and I'm old...old for the work, I mean."

"Iggy, how can you say no to a job without finding out

what it is? You know how tight things are at the moment. You should come and look at these figures, the expenses. My God, if you knew..."

"I don't want to hear about it," he muttered.

"Then all the more reason to talk to Viktor."

This was the one thing about America he did *not* like—the pressure. Freedom meant the freedom to fail. In communist Russia there was no opportunity, so there was no failure. Instead there was bitterness and frustration. Igor knew which was worse, but that didn't make the struggle to survive pleasant. His wife was not going to let him take the easy road.

Any way you cut it, Eve Adams was a hard woman to say no to. She'd had him in the palm of her hand from the day they'd met, nine years ago at Venice Beach. She'd gotten out of the slammer a couple days before, and he'd just arrived in L.A. Fate put them on adjoining bar stools.

Igor was immediately attracted to her pretty face and her breasts—the best set he'd ever seen, and they were still great—but it was her sassy, no-nonsense personality that he loved best. Eve wasn't afraid to tell it like it was.

"What is your profession?" he'd asked, trying to strike up a conversation.

"My *profession?*"

Eve used to tease him mercilessly about his English. Not that he didn't speak it well, because he did—virtually accent free—but it wasn't idiomatic. Since they'd been together, she'd taught him to talk more like an American, or more specifically, a Southern Californian.

"Yes," he'd said, "what is it you do to make your living?"

"Until a few days ago I was a guest of the state," Eve replied. "Before that I ran a string of girls out of a massage parlor in the valley, and before that I was a topless dancer—Eve Adams, maybe you've heard the name."

"I'm not sure I understand. You are a performer?"

"Honey, either you're on the slow side, or you just got off the boat."

He chuckled. "To be precise, it was an airplane, but it's not important."

Amused, Eve had unabashedly explained exactly what she'd done in her life.

"This is very interesting," he'd said, impressed.

"What about you, lover boy? You have a profession?"

"Yes," Igor had said. "I am an assassin."

"A *what?*"

"I kill people for money."

"Yeah, sure."

"I know, because of my kind face, it is difficult to believe. But it is true. First, I do this for the Soviets and now that the Soviets are no more, I do it for myself. In America, like in Russia, there is much need."

"You're shitting me."

"If you are so honest with me, why should I not be honest with you?"

That had been the beginning of their affair. Eve had gone with him to dinner, then to his hotel where they fucked their brains out for two days. When he'd noted she had a remarkable appetite for sex, she'd pointed out the obvious: "You caught me at a good time, Iggy."

From day one she'd refused to call him Igor, a name she'd said was half a step better than Dracula or Frankenstein.

Considering the early success of the relationship, they'd proceeded to find an apartment to share. Six weeks and one hit later, they married in Vegas, and they'd been together ever since. About the only time they were apart was when he was away on business.

It was a successful marriage by most standards. And, though things had slowed down some in recent years, the sex was still great. There was never a boring day with Eve. She'd managed the money, steadily moving them up the economic ladder. His wife had worked hard, doing her damnedest to become a success in her own right. Using Igor's earnings, she'd started a couple of small businesses, which, for no lack of effort on her part, had failed.

First, she peddled beauty products from a shop in a strip mall in Northridge and had just started making money when not one, but two big chain drugstores opened up within three blocks of her place. Selling out to a Vietnamese, she'd managed to break even, contributing nothing to the family income but a tax loss. She'd bought a yogurt-shop franchise next, but her timing was bad. Yogurt was on its way out.

Then, a couple of years ago, she'd hit on her brilliant idea: Lovers International. "There's tons of lonely, horny jerks in this country," she'd explained, "and a million Russian girls who'd marry any of them just to come to America. With your connections over there, and my ability to sell pussy, we can make a fortune supplying the demand. And it's all perfectly legal!"

And so Lovers International was born.

For a while they'd felt their way along, but once the kinks were out, their business had taken off. Eve, having an instinct for the jugular, pressed ahead, rapidly expanding the operation. They went from advertising in men's magazines to the Internet. There had been several trips to Russia to find a partner and set things up on that end, all of which took money, but Eve was right about the demand. "Sex and companionship never go out of style," she explained. "And, since somebody's going to make a killing bringing those girls over here, why shouldn't it be us?"

The endeavor had kept them both busy, and Igor found less time for his vocation, a fact which pleased him. But a new business was subject to cash flow problems. They had only one way to raise money fast and that was for Igor to do a hit.

Killing was like anything else—do it often enough and you get used to it. But not only was murder for hire risky, it was demanding. Igor had never put it so bluntly as this, but he was not sure he was still up to the physical and psychological demands. The last two jobs had made him sick—not because of the gore, but rather because of the tension. Maybe his days as an assassin were over.

Igor closed his eyes and tried to put it from his mind. He let the hazy warm sun bake him. Having spent his childhood and youth in Siberia, he could never get too much sun. Southern California was paradise on earth. What a shame a guy had to kill people to heat his pool and keep the blow jobs coming. When you thought about it, life in America was *very* complicated.

Igor had tried to explain that to his kid brother, Alexei, who'd followed him to America five years ago, but all Alexei could see was the glitter of gold, the fast cars and the women. Since his arrival in this country, he'd sustained his lifestyle doing little jobs for Viktor Chorny, giving no thought to the future.

Recently, though, Alexei had turned forty and it resulted in an awakening of sorts—he knew that, if he was going to make something of himself, he'd have to make a run at the big time now, before it was too late. Unfortunately, the big time he had in mind was to become a celebrated hit man, like his big brother. Igor knew in his gut it was wrong for Alexei, but he was hard-pressed to explain why.

The doorbell rang and Eve jumped up from the umbrella table. "I'll get it," she said as she pranced off in her platform sandals, shorts and tank top to get the door. Her blond hair piled high on her head, the walk, the tits—his wife was still a sexy, attractive woman. How many guys could say that about someone they'd been with for nearly a decade?

It had been several days since they'd gotten it on and, between the sun and the relaxing morning, sex had entered his mind. While Eve buttered the toast at breakfast, Igor had come up behind her, taken her luscious breasts in his hands and pulled her body firmly against his. "Got any plans for the afternoon?"

"I've got to work on the books."

"Anything else?"

"Alexei's coming over for dinner."

"Anything else?"

"I was kind of hoping you'd fuck my brains out." She turned around and kissed him then, making his heart stutter to the point of pain. When he rubbed his chest, she'd said, "Iggy, what's wrong?"

"Damn indigestion. I guess I'm going to have to stop drinking coffee."

"I think you should see a doctor."

"No, I'm fine." Igor hated doctors because in Russia they were mostly butchers. His father had died under the knife and his mother's cancer had gone undiagnosed until it was too late. Maybe the doctors were better in America, but once you had a phobia, it wasn't easy to change your attitude.

But he didn't need to think about that. It was Labor Day in America and he was on easy street. Other than their cash flow problem—and Alexei's mania—he didn't have a problem in the world. A little sex tonight, and life would be perfect.

"Привéт *Hi,* Igor Andreyevich!"

It was Viktor Chorny, waddling toward him from the house. Viktor was in a short-sleeve white shirt the size of a small tent. Chorny seemed to have added another twenty pounds every time Igor saw him.

Back in the days when Viktor Chorny was a key figure in the Third Chief Directorate of the Komitet, Internal Security, he was among the most feared and hated men in the USSR, a man whose middle name was synonymous with the slogan of the directorate he served—*smert shpionam,* "death to spies." Now his slogan was simply death to whoever had a price on their head. In his American incarnation, Viktor's greatest concern was not state security. It was cholesterol. "Морóженое *Ice cream,*" he would say, "this American ice cream is going to kill me." It wasn't a vacuous comment. Viktor had the scars of two bypass surgeries to prove it.

Igor got to his feet and, when Viktor reached him, the two exchanged bear hugs. "And how are you on the heroic day of the American working people, Comrade Colonel?" Igor said in Russian. His greetings invariably made Viktor flush.

Igor pulled over a chair and Chorny settled his corpulent frame into it, causing it to creak and groan. "You look good, Igor Andreyevich," Viktor said in Russian as he glanced across the pool at Eve, who'd retaken her place at the computer, "but not so good as your wife. You are a very fortunate man, but I'm sure I don't need to tell you that." Taking out a handkerchief, he mopped his brow.

"Every day I thank God that I am no longer in the lines of the state stores back home, waiting for a loaf of bread." Igor hesitated. "Though I must say there are days when I could use a nice bowl of борщ *borscht* like my mother used to make."

"Chilled," Chorny said. "With сметána *sour cream.*" He sighed. "Democratic Russia is different, you know. There is plenty of bread and often the quality is good. The only problem is nobody can afford to buy it."

They both laughed. Chorny blotted his forehead again. They silently admired Eve's enticing profile. Igor knew that Viktor, who in the old days had a reputation as something of a pervert, lusted after his wife. But Victor's health had deteriorated so badly during his sojourn in America that, should he attempt a sexual encounter now, the danger would be to the paramedics with the unenviable task of carrying him to the ambulance.

Igor cleared his throat, wanting to get right down to business. "Forgive my directness, Comrade Colonel, but there is only one issue of consequence—how much does the job pay?"

Viktor regarded him with the beady, colorless eyes of the man who'd once terrified a nation. "Two hundred thousand, Igor Andreyevich."

Igor's eyebrows rose. It was considerably more than he expected. Considerably more than he'd been paid in the past. Such service could be had much more cheaply. He was suspicious.

"For that kind of money you must be asking for the life of the president."

"No, my clients want the *termination*—" the word was spoken in English, a favorite of Chorny's because he was a big fan of Arnold Schwarzenegger "—of two very ordinary persons, though one is a professional."

"А дóктор *doctor?*" Igor said, brightening.

"Better. А адвокт *lawyer.*"

"And the other?"

"His client."

"That's strange."

"Yes," Chorny said. "It is, isn't it?"

Igor knew he wasn't going to get any details until he'd accepted the job. He wondered if Chorny might have already whispered the figure in Eve's ear, knowing the effect it would have. He contemplated his wife, who continued to work on her computer, giving no sign she knew what was up.

"There is a caveat," Viktor said.

"And that is?"

"You must take Alexei with you."

"Why?"

"Two reasons, Igor. First, he wants to go, and second I want him to. I need to replace you, my friend, because we both know your heart is no longer in the work. If this were the old days, you already would have been transferred to Siberia. But you have skill and knowledge and I am a desperate man. Do this job, teach your brother the fine points, and you will be paid handsomely. It's a once-in-a-lifetime opportunity, Igor Andreyevich. If not for me and not for yourself, then do it for your wife."

Igor knew then his goose was cooked. Viktor and Eve

were conspiring against him. Which meant that if he didn't do the job, there'd be hell to pay. And no sex for a very long time.

CENTRAL PARK

Bree Davis squinted up into the afternoon sun, following the flight of the ball he'd thrown, circling under it like a drunken sailor—forward a step, then back, right then left. Nick cringed, seeing disaster coming. He shouldn't have thrown the ball so high, but she'd challenged him, insisting that if Derek Jeter could do it so easily, then she ought to be able to do it with effort.

The ball came down, glanced off the fingers of her glove and bonked her on the head, right above the brim of her cap, knocking her on her butt. She sat in the grass like Raggedy Ann, her legs splayed apart, her head tilted a little cockeyed.

Nick jogged over. Bree, looking more shocked than hurt, gazed up at him in a daze. "I should have known there'd be a catch," she said.

"Or non-catch, as the case may be." Nick helped her to her feet, took off her cap and kissed the top of her head. "I hate to say this, but you not only throw like a girl, you catch like one, too."

"Well, duh. Haven't you noticed, Nick? I *am* a girl."

"Oh, I noticed all right."

She gave him a hug. "I think it's time for the seventh-inning nap."

They went over to where their blanket was spread out under a tree. They'd already had their picnic lunch and their exercise. With less than an hour left for relaxation before they had to hightail it back to the restaurant, their half day off was nearly over. After the week they'd had, it wasn't enough.

Dominick's California Cafe had become the hot new place

in town. Every day since the review had come out they'd run at full capacity, both lunch and dinner. The *Times* saw the potential for a human-interest story, sent a reporter over midweek, then ran an article in Friday's paper under the headline Disgraced Cop Makes Good as Chef.

Nick was pissed. "She sandbagged me," he complained to Bree, referring to the reporter as "a little sweet-as-molasses, Dixie bitch."

"That's what you get for staring at her boobs instead of paying attention to what you were saying."

Bree had watched the interview from afar, filing an after-action report replete with terms like "sneaky," "conniving," "blatant" and "hussy." Mostly, though, she didn't like the reporter's cleavage, which Nick had to admit was memorable. The woman had soft-soaped him for a story, twisting his words to make the tale interesting, if misleading.

But they discovered the truth to the old saying there's no such thing as bad publicity. Friday and Saturday night they could have filled Madison Square Garden, turning away as many customers as they served. "Disgracing yourself seemed to work well," Bree said somewhat snidely—his fumbling over the reporter not having been forgiven. "Now if you can just arrange to kill somebody, it wouldn't be long before you could buy out Donald Trump."

Bree wasn't one to hold a grudge for long, though, even as she'd revealed herself to be the jealous type. The baseball glove had helped—"a really sweet present"—plus there'd been a bottle of perfume and raises for her and Eddy. They'd taken on three more waitpersons. The main thing was Nick hired another chef, an Italian kid with skill, charm and restaurant experience in L.A. Aldo could cook and he had an eye for Bree. Nick put up with the latter because he needed the former.

But the goings-on at the restaurant had been put aside for the moment. This was their escape to the bosom of Mother

Nature—no busty Southern reporters, no Aldo, just the pale blue sky and a leafy canopy overhead, the twitter of birds, the yowl of half a dozen brats in the neighboring encampment, plus the usual traffic sounds on Central Park West.

Bree laid her head on his shoulder, her arm across his belly, intending, apparently, to sleep. Hidden in the excitement of the past several days was an intimate camaraderie between them that had the earmarks of romance, maybe love.

Nick worried about that, just as he worried about what was going on back home in San Francisco. His relationship with Bree could be dealt with in due course. Joe was his immediate concern, though his brother's woes were only the tip of the iceberg. There was a bevy of problems waiting for him back in good old S.F.

Nick had tried several times—always unsuccessfully—to reach his brother, neither connecting with him nor getting a return call. Clearly, Joe was avoiding him. What wasn't clear was whether he suspected Nick knew about the sixty-eight thousand that hadn't made it into the books.

Another concern was their father. When Nick hadn't been able to reach Joe, he'd bitten the bullet and phoned the nursing home, only to discover the old man had had a mild stroke. Tony was in no immediate danger, a nurse reported, but his speech had been impaired and communication was difficult. In a moment of weakness, he'd told the nurse to tell his father that he'd be out to visit as soon as he could. Having created the expectation, he'd have to follow through. But when? How long could he put it off?

The one person he'd talked to during the week was his sister-in-law, Gina, a sweet woman, devoted to her family, if a touch careworn and weary. In talking to her this time, he'd detected some anger, though she said nothing disloyal. Gina was the quintessential victim who seemed always to be at someone's mercy, in this case, her husband's. That didn't strike Nick as healthy for either of them. Not that he was an exemplar of wisdom when it came to women.

"I don't know where he is half the time, Nick," Gina had said of Joe. "Don't ask me what he's doing, because I don't know, but I can vouch for the fact that he's feeling the strain."

"How's his health, Gina?"

"You're talking about the MS?"

"Yes."

"Remarkably stable the last year or so. He uses a cane, but gets around well. The stress isn't good for him, but you know your brother. He won't listen to his doctor, much less me."

"Well, have him call me, will you, please?"

It hadn't worked. And it worried him. He hadn't wanted to say anything to Gina about the recorded message Mort Seidel had played, which meant that there was nobody he could talk to about it. Any way he looked at it, the pressure was building on him to make the long trek home.

Bree purred like a kitten and he realized she was dozing. He inhaled the flowered scent of her hair as the summer breeze washed over them. The warm sun took him back to another time in his life and another woman, a summer long ago in Siena. The woman—a girl, really—was named Julianna. He thought of that sunlit room with the view of the bell tower and the hills of Tuscany, the room where he and his lady fair would retreat after a morning of cooking classes to make love until dusk. He'd loved Julianna with a desperation known only to youth. Yet the memory stayed with him and, he suspected, always would.

Unhappy times, on the other hand, he tended to associate with his ex-wife, Cindy, though he knew that wasn't fair. There'd been good times, as well, but they were mostly forgotten, drowned in the bitterness, the recrimination and the alienation of love turned bad, of broken trust and wounded pride. No, it was Julianna he returned to when he wanted a happy memory.

"If she was so perfect, why in the hell didn't you marry her?" Cindy had said toward the end of their marriage. She'd divined that Julianna was the love of his life, though he'd never said so, keeping his feelings to himself, oblivious to the power of a woman's intuition.

He'd often wished he had married Julianna, though, of course, there was no guarantee that would have led to nirvana. There would have been problems to overcome. First, he'd been only twenty-one and Julianna twenty. Second, she spoke only a few words of English and his Italian was marginal at best. Third, her father was tyrannical and never would have permitted it, even allowing for the fact that Nick was of Italian heritage. And fourth, upon her return to Rome at the end of the summer, Julianna had been rushed into marriage to the boy she'd been unofficially engaged to since she was fourteen. The last Nick had heard, she'd had her fifth child. Another nasty turn of fate.

Or, so he'd thought until several years later when, over a bottle of wine, he'd told his old man what had happened during his magical summer in Italy. Expecting sympathy and understanding, he got what he least expected—disapproval. Not for fucking around, but for failing. "How much could you have loved her, Nicky, if you didn't go claim her? Maybe in fairy tales a man will send you his daughter and a check for fifty thousand dollars, but in my experience, you gotta go after what you want, including the woman you love. Everything worth having is worth fighting for."

Maybe. But wasn't there something to be said for pathos? Couldn't there be pleasure in the poignancy of tragic love? Couldn't a guy be happy riding the waves? What was wrong with packing up and moving on?

To which Tony would say, "There's two ways to get from here to the grave. You either let life happen to you or you make it happen for you. The choice is yours." Which was probably right. Every life had a pattern, Nick discovered, and the older you got, the harder it was to change that pattern. He'd made a career of taking the easy way out and, after thirty-seven years, he was beginning to see that had a price, as well.

But maybe the success of Dominick's had been his turn-around point. It had taken a hell of a lot of hard work, and Nick had reason to be proud. His personal life was more tricky, though. When it came to family and matters of the heart, he was still riding the waves.

Nick's cell phone, lying on the blanket next to them, rang.

"Oh, don't answer it, Nick," Bree moaned.

"Got to, babe, it could be the *Washington Post*."

"I knew it. The fame's gone to your head."

He picked up the phone. "Hello."

"Nick, it's Gina."

Before he could get out a word, his sister-in-law began to cry.

"Hey, whoa. What's wrong?"

"Joe's having an affair," she sobbed, only barely blubbering the words, "and your father had another stroke."

Nick sat bolt upright. A soccer ball with a gaggle of boys in hot pursuit went past their blanket. He let Gina cry for a second or two. When she seemed to have gathered herself, he asked, "How serious is it?"

"Joe's as good as dead because, I swear, I'm going to kill him. If he couldn't think of me, don't you think he'd have some concern for his children?"

Nick wasn't referring to his brother, but he didn't bother pointing that out. "What about the old man?"

"He's in the hospital. This was more serious than the last one, but not critical." She sniffled. "I hate to ask you to come home, Nick, but everything is coming apart. I don't know what to do." Again, she began to cry.

The sound of sirens came from across the park, probably Fifth Avenue. Gina was crying and New York continued with the hectic business of living. It was patently clear—he had no choice now but to go home.

TUESDAY SEPTEMBER 3RD

COW HOLLOW, SAN FRANCISCO

Billie Fox always had mixed feelings about her monthly lunch meeting with her ex. On the one hand, she welcomed the child support check he insisted on delivering in person, as well as the conversations they had about Emily. It helped that they remained on good, even friendly, terms, which Billie attributed to their respect for one another as professionals and their devotion to their child.

On the other hand, Sonny Culp was a living reminder of one of the sadder chapters of her life. In abandoning her, he'd broken her spirit, her confidence, her self-respect and self-image as a woman. For the most part, Billie had managed to move on, but seeing Sonny always sparked reminders of an inadequacy she couldn't fully rationalize away.

She arrived at the Balboa Café ten minutes late, but before Sonny, which was normal. Her ex was one of those people who simply tried to do too much, squeezing thirty-six hours of living into twenty-four-hour days. As a result, he always

ran late, though it had more to do with being prepossessed
with work than discourtesy.

"Hi there, Ms. Fox," the bartender called as she strode the
length of the bar, headed for the dining area at the rear of the
café. "Spring any bad guys out of jail today?"

"Tons, Pete. You can expect a crime wave any minute
now."

The bartender chuckled. He was a big, jovial political conservative—a rarity in San Francisco. She'd once debated gun
control with him until closing time, consuming three big
glasses of chardonnay in the process.

The café was long and narrow and, being situated on a corner, huge windows ran down the side of the room, lighting
the rich, dark paneling. The Balboa had a European flavor—
white linen tablecloths, crisply dressed waiters and a decent
wine list to complement the seafood and pasta bill of fare. It
was Sonny's home away from home. Her ex was a creature
of habit and very turf-conscious.

She was shown to the window table Sonny preferred. A
bottle of his favorite cabernet was already open and breathing, as per his instruction. He was not much of a drinker, except, it seemed, when he was around her. That should have
alerted her to potential problems in the relationship, but it
hadn't. It was only after the fact that Billie realized the anes-
thetizing effect of alcohol had been necessary for him to endure her company—her husband, as it turned out, was gay.

Their marriage had been mainly a union of spirit—needless to say, one that grew out of mutual respect, shared be-
liefs and zeal for their common purpose. That hadn't exactly
fallen by the wayside, but it had paled beside Sonny's love
for Martin Fong, the celebrated San Francisco politico and
Sonny's partner for four years, the man for whom he'd left
her.

What truly hurt Billie was the knowledge that her husband's feelings for her had never even come close to what he felt for Martin. At most, she had been the secretary of his heart, as she had once been the secretary of his law office.

But their marriage had been a learning experience. It taught her the danger inherent in compromising feelings and rationalizing needs. The importance of being loved was easily enough understood. Loving another was much more complicated. The trick, she'd learned, was figuring out how those two things went together. With Sonny they never had.

In time, Billie had come to understand that her husband's romantic preferences had nothing to do with her and everything to do with who *he* was. Once she'd passed that threshold, her primary concerns shifted to Emily. Ironically, Martin had proved to be a positive factor in that regard.

Sonny, while a serious and responsible father, had not embraced parenthood with joy or passion. He loved his child, but it was a love of the mind, not of the heart. Martin, on the other hand, had become the enthusiastic parent Sonny would never be. And, serendipitously, Emily was just as enamored of Martin, who soon became her great pal and unorthodox parent figure. How many little girls could claim to have a gay, Chinese, male politician for a stepmother?

Growing impatient, Billie checked her watch, then poured herself a glass of wine, deciding Sonny's tardiness justified her starting without him. She could hardly be angry with him, though. This was quintessential Sonny. Of greater concern was his state of mind. On the phone today he'd seemed down, his spirits no brighter than when she'd last seen him on Sunday. He and Martin had brought Emily home after their biweekly visit. Sonny and Emily had come to the door while Martin waited in his Mercedes.

"So, did you have fun this weekend?" Billie had asked her daughter as the child hugged her thighs.

"Uh-huh."

"This time we mostly stayed home," Sonny had said, "except to go out to dinner." He was considerate that way—always keeping Billie informed.

"We ate Chinese," Emily had piped up. "Me and Martin like Chinese."

"Martin and I, honey," Billie had corrected.

Sonny had listened, a sad smile on his face. After Emily had given him a hug goodbye and had gone inside to see her grandfather, Billie, sensing something was amiss, asked her ex if he was all right. Sonny replied that he was fine, but she hadn't believed him.

"You sure?"

"You know how I get emotionally involved in my work."

"Anything you want to talk about?"

Sonny shook his head. "Not now. Maybe Tuesday when we have more time."

That in itself was an indication of how upset Sonny was. He was one of those men who kept his feelings pent up inside, rarely sharing, no matter how much he was in pain.

Billie had just taken a couple of healthy gulps of wine when Sonny Culp appeared at the door. As usual he had his tattered briefcase in hand. It was so much a part of him that it was more an appendage than an accoutrement. Sonny was fair and ruddy, a balding strawberry blonde with wisps of hair going to white. He was a painfully serious man who smiled with reluctance, seeming eternally pensive.

Sonny Culp did not seem gay by outward appearance. His manner of dress was a touch sloppy; he lacked care and taste. The beautiful ties she'd bought him over the years rarely saw the light of day. Sonny lacked the grace and panache of most gay men, and his manner was without affectation. If there was any outward indication of his sexual orientation, it was in the fact that he had no discernible sexuality, at least to her feminine eye. There was no electricity in his look, only evaluation. Sonny was repressed, Billie had come to realize, a condition she'd wrongly attributed to his sober intellectuality.

Reaching the table, he put his briefcase on the spare chair, then mumbled his usual apology as he kissed her on the temple. "Sorry. Rough day."

Billie was never quite sure why the temple or forehead kiss survived their divorce, unless it was his way of saying she remained in good standing. Without another word Sonny took the bottle of wine, splashed his glass half-full and took a big slug, sloshing it in his mouth for a moment before gulping it down. There was a momentary smile of pleasure, then he reached into the inside pocket of his tweed sports coat, removed the letter-size envelope with "Billie" typed on it and dropped it in front of her.

"Your check, madam."

It was a ritual repeated monthly. Billie took the envelope and slipped it in her purse.

"Thank you, Sonny."

He took another drink of wine, then, for the first time, looked into her eyes and said, "So, how's everybody?"

Billie, as always, took that to mean, "How's Emily? How's your dad? And how are you?"

"We're fine," she replied. "Just fine."

"That's good."

There were times during these awkward moments when she would look at her former husband and try to imagine herself in bed with him. Though she knew perfectly well it had happened, for the life of her she had trouble picturing it. There was a certain amount of repression going on, to be sure, but she concluded the difficulty she had was due to the fact that they had never truly been lovers. Sex had been a ritualistic exercise, about as personal as an exchange of greeting cards.

"More to the point, Sonny," she said, "how are *you?*"

He turned his wineglass by its stem, examining the contents. "Work's been trying lately."

"So you said on Sunday. Anything in particular or just the usual stresses and strains of the holy war?"

"I guess I'm in a down phase," he said. "Every time I start feeling hope, the system lets me down."

"What do you mean?"

"Oh, nothing." He drank more wine.

"No, tell me," she said. "Something's obviously bothering you."

Sonny stared out the window at the street. "Are all the rest of them that corrupt, Billie, or are you and I just crazy?"

"Are we talking about heartless conservatives, conscienceless moderates or both?"

"Oh, I don't know," Sonny said with a sigh. "I'm just tired, I guess. Maybe I'm getting old, losing my optimism, my hope."

"That's a pretty serious indictment of something. I'm just not sure what."

"For your own good, it's better you not know, Billie."

The remark sobered her. "For my own good? What do you mean?"

"Nothing," he said, shaking his head. "I didn't intend to sound ominous. It's really nothing. Forget it."

"No, Sonny, you're in trouble, I can tell."

"I've been ruffling feathers again, that's all. You know how I'm regarded by my peers."

"I've never known Sonny Culp to worry about what people think of him."

"I *don't* worry. It's the stench coming off of them that gets to me. I don't like being disillusioned. But this is nothing to talk about before lunch. Are you hungry?" Sonny signaled the waiter, who approached.

"Are you ready to order, Mr. Culp?"

Neither of them had consulted the menus. It wasn't necessary.

"I think so," Sonny said, glancing at her.

"What's your freshest fish today?" she asked the waiter.

"Sea bass is excellent."

"I'll have that."

"Very well." He turned to Sonny. "Sir?"

"Caesar salad."

"Anything else?"

"No, that's it."

"Thank you." The waiter took the menus and left.

"Just a salad?" Billie said. "Are you feeling all right? Is that the problem?"

"No, I'm just tired. I got you riled up needlessly. Let's talk about something else."

She could see he didn't want to discuss whatever it was that was bothering him. She figured it was a professional matter or they wouldn't have gotten this far—unless it was a health issue, a subject that was extrasensitive for her.

Considering Sonny was gay, Billie worried about AIDS, though contacting the virus wasn't quite as ominous as it had once been. Even so, it could kill, the same as her cancer, making it a concern, whether Sonny was careful and responsible or not. The subject wasn't something easily broached, though, leaving her little to say except that her own tenuous health made it all the more important that Sonny take good care of himself.

Billie reached over and put her hand on his. "You know me," she said. "I'm not one to pry, but because of my cancer I'm always concerned about you. It's important to me to know you're okay."

"Billie, I *am*," he said, sounding sincere. "No need to worry. Anyway, you're in remission."

"But I'm vulnerable. It could come back at any time. I need to know that Emily would still have you. Just in case."

"You're being alarmist," he said.

"You aren't in danger of any kind?"

He hesitated only a moment. "No."

This time he did not sound sincere. He might not have health problems, but there was a threat of some sort. Then it hit her. His initial comment about others being corrupt, combined with this danger business, sent up a red flag. Sonny had never been shy about butting heads with the rich and powerful, and that did not make him a very popular fellow in some circles. Though he'd been threatened often enough, no harm had ever befallen him due to his law practice. But attorneys certainly weren't immune to physical danger, and someone like Sonny was among the most likely of candidates for that sort of thing.

"You're worried about your enemies," she said.

Sonny winced. "Billie, come on."

"That concerns me, Sonny. You've got a responsibility to Emily. Whatever it is you're involved in, don't push too hard. Survival is more important than being a superhero."

"You're getting yourself worked up over nothing," he rejoined.

"Easy for you to say."

Sonny sighed woefully. "Look, I'm not being cavalier. I'm trying to be supportive, just as I was when you were going through your ordeal."

Billie felt badly. She wasn't trying to lay a guilt trip on him. God knew, he'd been supportive. In fact, she'd found out later that he'd delayed asking for a divorce six months in order to help her get through her battle with cancer. He didn't have to do that, but he knew she'd had a full plate—an infant to care for, breast cancer, her career on hold. A husband leaving her on top of all that would have been too much to bear.

"On another subject," Sonny said, clearly wishing to move on, "how's your social life?"

Billie groaned. If her obsession was health, his was her romantic life, or lack thereof. The hardest part of the divorce for him, apart from Emily, was his fear that he'd spoiled her chances for finding happiness with someone else. Sonny wasn't above chastising her for not making a more concerted effort to find someone. "You're a wonderful person," Sonny would say. "I can't be the only one who appreciates that. Are you giving them a chance or being stubborn?" She'd roll her eyes and say, "Sonny, that's not your problem, so give it a rest, okay?"

"There's nothing to report," she said curtly.

"You aren't seeing anyone at all?"

"If you must know, Thursday I'm going out to dinner with a very eligible doctor. *Very* eligible."

Sonny grinned. "Hey, that's great! Why did you say there's nothing to report?"

"Because next time I see you, you'll be asking to see the ring and it ain't going to happen."

"Not if you're determined that it won't."

"Sonny, please. Let's just enjoy our lunch and set our respective fears and guilt aside, okay?"

Their meals arrived just then and Sonny nodded, as if to say, "Saved by the bell."

As they ate, the conversation moved in other directions. The balance of the lunch was cordial, but Billie remained concerned. She knew Sonny Culp. Something was troubling him. She'd find out what it was eventually, but not before some sleepless nights. Divorce and disease, she'd learned, were a deadly combination.

WEDNESDAY SEPTEMBER 4TH

UNION SQUARE, SAN FRANCISCO

The taxi pulled up in front of the St. Francis, and Elaine Chang, elegant in a Chinese-red-and-black St. John suit, handed the driver a twenty and slipped out of the back seat with the helping hand of the doorman. The wind rushed down Powell Street, threatening her elegant, silky-black coiffure. Elaine, twenty minutes late, hurried to the entrance in her spike heels, practically swept inside by a sudden gust of wind.

Having reached the relative calm of the lobby, she considered whether to repair to the ladies' room to check her hair and makeup, thus risking irritating Ken Lu even more because of her tardiness, or simply to appear at the table a touch disheveled and apologetic. She opted for the latter course, theorizing that her regret would seem all the more genuine.

The Compass Rose, the tearoom where she was to meet Lu, was to her left and up a few steps. Catching her breath, she mounted the stairs. As the maître d' approached, she glanced around and saw Ken seated at a front window table overlooking the square.

"I see my party," she said to the maître d', brushing past him.

Ken Lu, clad in one of his customary white suits and sunglasses, appeared serene, his hands·folded on the crisp white tablecloth, the table clear except for a single deep-red rose in a bud vase. But, considering what was at stake, he had to be anxious.

"I'm so sorry," she said in Cantonese as she slid into the chair hastily presented by the waiter. "I trust you will forgive me, though, Ken. I have good news."

"Do you really?"

His underwhelmed reaction was deliberate so as to emphasize the fact that she'd been stringing him along for days with promises and only one token check to show for his time and goodwill.

"I know you're upset about the delays and I can't blame you," she replied. "I am equally frustrated. But the end is in sight."

"Is *that* the good news?" he asked, arching an eyebrow from under his dark glasses.

"Tomorrow," she said. "We'll finalize the deal tomorrow."

"Can I rely on that?"

"The money is in the account. Joe's showed me because I insisted. The problems now are purely mechanical. It's a question of getting from point A to point B."

"His pocket being point A and mine being point B?"

"Essentially, yes."

"You say the problem is 'mechanical.' What do you mean?"

The waiter brought the menu. Elaine asked for a pot of typhoo without looking at the card. Ken ordered scotch, neat. When the waiter was gone she answered her companion's question.

"I'll be candid. The problem is Joe's lawyer."

Ken Lu's face registered alarm. "He opposes the deal?"

"No, he's advising Joe to be cautious, to *'have all his ducks in a row.'*" She said the last in English.

"Meanwhile, the hard-earned opportunity to claim a fortune is slipping away," Lu rejoined. "Mr. Sasso will not be the only one to lose out, Elaine. Because I trusted you, I, too, am at risk. And you, as well."

"Not to worry, Ken. Joe has promised that tomorrow he'll have it all worked out. He's asking that we meet with him and his lawyer in Tiburon to hammer out the details."

"I don't know why so much is being made of this," Lu replied. "It's really very simple. I need two million dollars to proceed."

"Yes, but you know these Americans. They like to 'dot all the I's and cross all the T's.' At least the lawyers do."

"Can we trust that this lawyer won't squelch the deal?"

It was the very question that had kept Elaine awake with worry the past few nights. When Joe first told her that he wanted to consult Sonny Culp in the matter, she'd been livid. "The utmost secrecy has been a condition from the very beginning," she'd warned. Joe was adamant, though. "Sonny can be trusted. He's helped me with the most delicate problem imaginable. I'd trust the man with my life." But Elaine was familiar with these American lawyers, the way they thought, though Sonny Culp himself, she knew little about. Professionally, that is.

"Joe has made it plain to the gentleman that he wants the deal," she explained patiently. "The lawyer has been given the task of determining *how*, not *if*."

Ken Lu maintained a stony silence. Tapping the tips of the fingers of each hand together, he gazed out the window, his jaw working. Outside, a cable car went gliding down Powell Street, past the hotel, its bell clanging.

"I wonder," Lu said after a while, "if this lawyer's thinking might be influenced by a cash payment, a contribution to his children's education."

Elaine smiled. "It's a worthy thought, however, the risk is very great. If he cannot be bribed then the deal will almost certainly be lost."

"What is our option, then?"

Their drinks arrived. Elaine lifted the lid off the teapot to see how much it had brewed, then replaced it.

"This is what I propose," she said, looking straight at Ken Lu. "We will wait and see what happens tomorrow. If for any reason the problems are not resolved and the lawyer causes a further delay, then I will move on to plan B."

"Which is what?"

"Ken, it's better if you don't know. Let me say this, though. Sometimes there are better ways to influence a man's thinking than an offer of money."

"I've seen ample proof of your charm," Ken Lu said, "but isn't it a bit risky to seduce your lover's lawyer?"

She laughed and poured herself some tea. "Sonny Culp would have no interest in me, regardless of the circumstances. Ken, he's gay."

Lu's eyebrow rose, then he grinned. "I see evil in your smile, Elaine."

"No, you see a woman fully determined. I will bend Mr. Culp to my will," she said, "or die trying."

THURSDAY SEPTEMBER 5TH

RUSSIAN HILL, SAN FRANCISCO

After making breakfast for her son, Gina Sasso, her jaw set, drove from Cow Hollow to the building on Russian Hill where her husband's mistress lived. Joe had not come home the previous night, nor had he called. As she suspected, his Mercedes was parked a few doors up the street, for all the world to see. His actions were so blatant that Joe must have concluded their marriage over. That brought tears.

When the detective she hired first told her about Elaine Chang, Gina was shocked. Oh, she'd had suspicions. At some level she'd known for months. But a woman didn't easily confront doubts about her worthiness as a wife. And, the closer the pain came to the surface, the sharper it became. She'd finally reached the point where reality could no longer be denied.

Joe had shown all the classic signs—he'd been distracted, he'd stayed out late, he was irritable, sometimes he didn't look her in the eye and they hadn't had sex in months. Gina tried talking to him, but it was not easy to broach difficult subjects with Joe Sasso. Instead, she'd been subtle, hoping to catch him with his guard down.

"You feeling okay, Joe?" she asked one Sunday morning.

He'd been lying in bed, staring off into space, while she'd dressed to take the children to Mass. "Yeah, I'm fine."

"You sure? Because I'm kind of I'm worried about you."

"There's no reason to worry, Gina. I've had a tough week, that's all."

She knew better than to ask why. Joe never discussed business. "That's for the office," he'd say. But despite his assertions to the contrary, he had been bringing his problems home—he just hadn't been discussing them with her. And Gina knew the issue wasn't his health, because that was the one thing he did share.

Joe Sasso's symptoms were so mild that people who weren't around him often probably didn't notice. Lately, though, he'd been more dependent on his cane, saying, "Sometimes I feel a little shaky, that's all."

"You sure the doctor hasn't said anything I don't know about?" she'd asked as she dug her rosary out of her dresser drawer.

"No, of course not. I'd tell you."

"Then why are you acting strange? If there's something you need to tell me, just say it."

"I've got nothing to tell you, Gina, except that I've had a rough week. A few rough weeks. Now, let it go, all right?"

But she couldn't. The night he'd come home with the smell of another woman on him was the last straw. The next day she'd hired Rolando Inocentes.

He was Filipino, her age, small with a full head of hair combed in the shape of a helmet. A week after hiring him, she got the report. They met in a coffee shop on Bush Street.

"The lady's name is Elaine Chang, Mrs. Sasso," he told her.

"Elaine *Chang?* What is she? Chinese?"

"Yes."

Gina was astounded. "What's she like?"

"Ms. Chang has a past. She's a former prostitute."

"Oh, dear God," Gina had said, making an abbreviated sign of the cross.

"Well, maybe prostitute is too strong," the detective said. "What's that term? *Kept woman,* that's it. She's been the mistress of many important men."

But Gina's mind was stuck on "prostitute." She'd been horrified. The father of her babies, her husband of twenty-two years. Hadn't she been a good, loyal wife who'd given him four wonderful children? What was Joe thinking?

Gina had gotten the woman's address from Inocentes, not knowing what she was going to do with it. For days she was catatonic, frozen with fear and hurt. Joe came home late and left early, sleeping downstairs in the guest room. She'd hardly seen him. When they did come face-to-face, Joe looked right through her, distracted, indifferent. Realizing the time had come to be assertive, she vowed to confront him that night. But he hadn't come home, leaving her frustrated and distraught. Clearly he was with his mistress again. Gina was ready to shoot them both.

Now, finding no legal place to park, she pulled over in front of a fire hydrant, a spot affording her a view of the entrance of the building. As she stepped from the car, who should come out the door but her husband, accompanied by the femme fatale.

Elaine Chang was pretty, her skin as pale and smooth as vanilla custard. She was in a sleeveless red top and matching skirt. The hem of the skirt was very short. She had on high-heel sandals. Gina did not feel hatred so much as she felt futility. This woman was everything she was not.

The lovers, much to Gina's surprise, were talking in rather animated fashion, their voices bordering on angry. She only caught an occasional word. Elaine Chang, clearly in a huff, put on a pair of sunglasses with a grand gesture and went stomping off toward the Mercedes. Joe limped along behind. All was not well in paradise, it seemed. This gave Gina a sense of morbid satisfaction.

Though he could have seen her if he'd bothered to look, her husband didn't glance in her direction. She got back in her car. Moments later, Joe and the woman drove past. He was red-faced but chastened, if she was reading his expression correctly.

Gina decided to follow them. For a while they were out of sight, but at California Street she got a glimpse of the Mercedes turning west. Gina pursued the lovers to Van Ness Avenue. Joe turned right and sped off. She followed, barely making the light at Lombard Street, where they turned west again. After a few blocks they jogged over to Chestnut and stopped next to the Moscone Recreation Center.

There wasn't room to stop behind them, so Gina continued on, parking farther up the block. She looked back in time to see Joe crossing the street. Elaine stayed in the car.

The buildings along that stretch of Chestnut Street were two- and three-story flats with small commercial and office spaces mixed in with the residential units. Joe entered a stucco building painted pale blue. Gina decided to have a look. After all, what did it matter if he saw her?

She crossed the street and walked to the blue building. The ground floor was an office. The sign in the window said Sanford P. Culp, Attorney-at-Law. Then it hit her. Joe was seeing a divorce lawyer.

Gina glanced across the street at the Mercedes. Elaine Chang sat in the passenger seat, looking at herself in the visor mirror, putting on lipstick. Gina glared, realizing that Joe might actually be planning to marry the woman, which meant Elaine Chang was going to be a part of her life—and her children's lives—for some time to come, whether she liked it or not.

What would she tell the kids? That their father found a better, younger, sexier woman? Anthony was twenty and attending the University of San Francisco. He and Joe didn't get along, so he wouldn't suffer, but Tina, almost nineteen and starting her sophomore year at U.C., Santa Barbara, would be hurt. The two still at home were the ones Gina worried about most. Both were in Catholic high schools, Shelly at Mercy High and Blake at Sacred Heart. Blake was sensitive. He'd be shattered by a divorce. No matter how Gina handled it, this affair of Joe's was going to destroy the family she'd worked so hard to nurture. And all for some prostitute! Gina was more than angry; she was incensed. Gina decided to confront him now, right in front of his lawyer, if need be.

Inside was a small vestibule with a staircase leading to the second floor. The entrance to the attorney's office was to one side. Stenciled on the glass door was a smaller version of the lettering in the front window—Sanford P. Culp, Attorney-at-Law.

Gina saw that the door was ajar. She heard voices inside.

"Goddamn it, Joe," a man said, "I can't leave now. Look at this place. It's been trashed. The bastards took my computer, my files."

"Sonny, I just need you for an hour."

"Can't you understand? They've destroyed or taken everything, even the firebox with my backup disks. It's them, Joe. This is what it's come to. I told you it was serious."

"Have you called the police?"

"Lot of good that would do."

"What *are* you going to do, then?"

"See what I can reconstruct, I guess. If necessary, I'll start over."

"Sonny, I don't care about that now. Elaine is all that matters."

"Well, this matters to *me!*" the lawyer shouted. "This is about a lot more than you."

"Listen, I know you're upset," Joe said, "but Elaine and I want to get going on this."

"You'll have to negotiate without me, Joe. I'm sorry."

"Can't you give me an hour? Please, this means the world to me, you know it does."

"Look," the lawyer said. "Go to your meeting, do what you have to do and come back tonight. I'll go over everything with you then. Bring Elaine, if you want, but now I've got to take care of this mess and salvage what I can. What if they come back?"

She continued to listen to them argue, but it sounded as if Joe was giving up. He made sounds like he was about to leave. Gina, confused, lost her nerve.

She decided to retreat, hurrying out the door. Elaine Chang, still in the car, was staring straight ahead. As Gina scurried along the sidewalk, she glanced through the window of the building. The office did appear to be torn up. She saw Joe wading through the rubble, headed for the door.

By the time she got to her car, Joe had come outside. He limped across the street, leaning heavily on his cane. He did not look happy. Gina was at a complete loss.

A moment later, the Mercedes went roaring past her. Gina started the engine and took off in pursuit of her husband and the dragon lady, having no idea where they were going or what she would do when they got there.

SAN FRANCISCO INTERNATIONAL AIRPORT

Igor Sakharov was relieved when the pilot began lowering the flaps. Soon they'd be on the ground, then maybe he'd be okay. It wasn't the flying. He wasn't airsick. Something inside him was wrong.

And it frightened him.

For the past few days, ever since Viktor Chorny's visit, he had not been feeling well. Sometimes he felt a pain in his chest, usually mild. At other times he felt light-headed. Occasionally he had to struggle to get his breath. He thought it was indigestion. But even after chomping down a whole roll of Tums, he felt no better.

He'd said nothing to Eve because he was certain she would accuse him of trying to get out of the job. "This is a godsend," she'd enthused when he told her about the deal Viktor had offered. "Iggy, we can continue our business without sacrifice."

Igor had hardly slept the past three days, lying awake, listening to the complaints of his body. That morning, he'd dragged himself from bed, showered and dressed. Eve had already packed his suitcase, including the disassembled 9 mm automatic, the parts of which he'd taped to a piece of sheet metal cut in the shape of an iron—the technique he'd devised to avoid detection by the airport X-ray machines. After feeding him breakfast, his wife had sat with him in the front room while they waited for Alexei to arrive.

"Iggy, I know you don't want to do this, but it means so much to us, and I'm proud of you for bucking up."

"Only for you would I do this."

"I know that," she said, patting his cheek.

The pain was noticeable even then, but Igor told himself it was the coffee, which he'd choked down against his better judgment. When he'd kissed his wife goodbye, an odd premonition went through him that he'd never see her again.

It wasn't until midway through the flight that the pain in his chest became severe. As the plane began its descent, he'd very nearly fainted.

Alexei, oblivious, sat next to him, reading the in-flight magazine for the second time, chewing gum with the subtlety of a popcorn popper. Every time the flight attendant went by, Alexei would lean into the aisle in order to bump her hip with his shoulder. Igor was surprised his brother didn't just trip her so he could see up her skirt. Alexei had made a game of harassing women from the age of fifteen. Several times, mostly when drunk—alcohol being another of his problems—he'd gone too far and gotten in trouble with the authorities. He had a perverse streak, and one day, Igor was certain, it, together with the vodka, would do him in. But Igor couldn't worry about his brother now. He faced a much bigger challenge—somehow pulling off this job and surviving.

By the time the plane touched down, Igor was soaked in sweat and his head was swimming. Breathing was a chore. Alexei, who was jumpy as a kitten with a ball of yarn, finally noticed.

"Чтó сдучи́дось? *What's wrong?*" he asked.

"I'm a little light-headed," Igor replied in English. "Too much coffee, I think."

Alexei nervously flipped a bottle cap from hand to hand. "Maybe you should stop drinking coffee, then."

"Good idea."

The plane pulled up at the gate and Igor did not immediately stand. He let the plane empty, telling Alexei the doors wouldn't open any faster just because they were at the front of the line. When he finally did get to his feet, he felt weak as hell.

Once through the gate and into the terminal building, he seemed to breathe easier, but now walking had become a challenge. What the hell was wrong with him? The trip to the car-rental counter became as arduous as a hike across the Urals. Halfway there he had to stop and sit on a bench. Alexei grew concerned.

"В чём дéл? *What's the matter?*"

Igor told him about the pain, the dizziness, the nausea.

"Maybe you should go to the hospital."

"No. I just need a few minutes. Why don't you go to baggage claim and get our suitcases?"

As Alexei went off, a deep fear filled Igor Sakharov's heart. He wouldn't see Eve again. Now he was certain.

***

As Nick Sasso disembarked at San Francisco International Airport, he felt like a fighter coming out for round one of a long-awaited rematch. The bruises may have faded from the first bout, but he could still feel the sting of his opponent's blows. Maybe what they said was true: you couldn't go home again.

Oddly enough, it had all fallen into perspective at JFK when he said goodbye to Bree. She'd smiled a bit sadly, and he found himself wanting to tell her that he loved her. Then it struck him. In running from his problems five years ago, he hadn't put the past to rest so much as he'd avoided facing it. He'd gotten on a big wave and he'd ridden it all the way to New York. And now he was back home, finding the place unchanged because he was unchanged, at least in the ways that mattered.

Nick realized he couldn't love Bree nor, for that matter, New York, until he'd put San Francisco behind him once and for all. The process probably had to begin with his father because the roots of everything in his life sprang from Tony Sasso.

Knowing that didn't make leaving New York any easier, though. Nick was concerned about his restaurant, the first great success of his career. He worried that the opportunity fate had given him would slip through his fingers. This dealing with unfinished business was grim duty, pure and simple. Yet, he sensed it was essential to his future.

"Don't worry," Bree had said when he'd gathered the staff at the restaurant the previous evening to give his final instructions. "Between Eddy, Aldo and me, everything is going to be fine."

Nick hadn't liked Aldo's grin. He was sure the bastard would try to move in on Bree in his absence. And though he didn't expect her to jump in bed with the guy, their relationship had been built on the thin ice of a good time.

New York, his restaurant, Bree, all the rest of it, was on the back burner now. Circumstance had made his family his top priority, and that was what he had to focus on. Home.

Airports were airports and there was no reason SFO should seem special, yet it did have the feel of home turf—even though he hadn't yet gotten a whiff of the maritime air, the foggy vapors that came rolling over the hills and oozing through the Golden Gate. August in San Francisco was head-lights at four in the afternoon, sixty-three degrees, the smell of crab pots, the bellow of a foghorn and the strident call of the gulls above the waterfront.

But San Francisco was also a courtroom at the Hall of Justice, spiced with cleaning solvent, dank air and the smell of humid flesh. It was the raw nerves of the street, the blurry glow of neon in the Tenderloin, bedsheets damp from love-less sex, a locker room pungent with sweat and dirt and leather. It was classrooms, wine bars, drag queens, bankers, churches, ferryboats, cops, strippers, hair salons, tearooms, halfway houses, tourists and street people. It was where he'd gotten spanked for the first time, laid for the first time, fired for the first time, married and divorced. It was where he'd tried to be Joe DiMaggio and failed, then tried love and failed at that, too. It was where he'd built self-respect and lost it. It was San Francisco. It was home.

He'd told Gina he'd call when he arrived, so he stopped along the concourse and got his cell phone out. She'd prom-ised to ask Joe if there would be a problem with him sleep-ing in the spare room at the Yankee Clipper, and Nick thought he'd better check first before heading to the restaurant.

The room he'd wanted to use was on the second floor, across from the office. It had a bed. The old man had used it primarily as a place to fuck the hostesses during the lull be-tween the lunch and dinner service. Between 1955 and 1996, Tony Sasso must have screwed thirty or forty different women in his retreat. Some were grandmothers by now, but even into his sixties, the old man preferred them young and firm. Tall was important, maybe because Tony was short.

When Nick was in high school and his grades were below standard, he would come to the restaurant, per the old man's orders, to do his homework. Sometimes Tony would still be in the spare room with the hostess of the moment when Nick got there. Early on he'd listened, especially when the girls were vocal, but after a while it turned into a bland ritual, like the monarch's *toilette*.

Tony Sasso wasn't an exhibitionist, but his guiding philosophy was that sex was an essential part of a man's mandate for existence. Better he live in accordance with his nature, even if it meant being corrupt at the edges. Maria Sasso, Nick's mom, only lived through the first half of Antonio Sasso's reign, mercifully having departed by the time the old man got to the point of embarrassing himself.

Nick dialed his brother's home number. His nephew answered the phone.

"Blake, this is your uncle Nick. How're you doing?"

"Oh, hi."

"Your mom there?"

"No."

"You expect her back soon?"

"I dunno."

Nick had forgotten the teenage mind, not having been around since Anthony, the eldest, was this age. "Did she leave a message for me?"

"Not that I know of."

"Hmm. Well, could you tell her I'm going to the Yankee Clipper to drop off my things before I go to see your grandpa?"

"Sure."

Nick wanted to make conversation, if only out of a sense of politeness, but he doubted he'd be doing his nephew any favors. "Thanks," he said. "See you later."

He hung up, shaking his head. Across the way some little drama was taking place. A man, looking pale as a sheet, was leaning against the wall, supported by another man who was trying to fan him with a magazine. Nick watched for a second or two, wondering if he should ask if they needed help, but then a security officer, a large black woman, came along. The man in distress did not seem pleased. As Nick continued on his way, he heard the woman saying something about a wheelchair. The matter seemed to be in hand.

MARIN COUNTY

They'd crossed the Golden Gate, gone through the Rainbow Tunnel and emerged from the fog as they descended the Waldo Grade. Gina stared at the Mercedes, only vaguely aware of Richardson Bay off to the right, sparkling in the bright sun. She had always liked Marin, but it made no impression on her now, not the elegant homes studding the green slopes of Belvedere Island, not the sailboats swirling off Sausalito like a flock of doves, not the clear blue sky nor the broad shoulders of Mount Tamalpais that warded off the fog and ocean breezes.

Watching Joe in the car ahead, Gina saw him turn to the woman from time to time. Were they still bickering, or had they settled their lovers' spat? More importantly, Gina wondered how she and Joe had come to this awful place where she needed to ask such questions of the man who had pledged to love her to the end of time.

Her friend, Arianne, told her she was lucky it hadn't happened ten years ago when she had four small children. Gina shuddered to think how devastating that would have been. Of course, there was never a good time for something like this, but she needed to look for the bright side. She would always have the love of her children. Before long there would be grandchildren, a large family to love and care for. Yes, it could be worse.

Gina was surprised that she was already looking back on her marriage as though it were history. It had taken over twenty years, but her mother had been proven right. When Gina had announced her intention to marry Joe Sasso, her family had been slow to embrace the idea. The Sassos had a reputation. The patriarch of the family had sown plenty of wild oats in his day—so many that her mother hadn't dared to relate some of the stories. "Think long and hard before you do this, Gina," was all she would say.

Being a good Catholic, she'd prayed hard, though not long. Joe was her prince in shining armor. Sure, he had feet of clay but adultery was so unlike him. In the past his deviant tendencies ran to gambling. Seven years ago, Gina had put her foot down about his trips to Reno and Las Vegas. But that was small potatoes compared to his wheeling and dealing in the business world. Her husband was obsessed with becoming rich, *very* rich. He had a weakness for schemes involving quick money. More than once his father had lectured him about his excesses, though Gina had only heard one conversation between them.

No question Joe was a promoter who knew how to make things happen. Once, before old Tony folded his tent and headed for the rest home, he'd taken her aside and said, "Gina, you've got a smart husband. He understands business, which is why I'm letting him take over the Yankee Clipper. But he don't understand his limits. You've got to help him keep his eye on the ball. Will you do that for me?"

She'd said she would, but it was an empty promise. Old Tony was used to the way it had been with his own wife. Before her death, Maria had been the power behind the throne, a moderating influence who helped her husband keep his priorities straight, if not his pants zipped.

Joe, for all his good intentions, didn't share his father's philosophy. He cherished his independence and he liked power. Whenever Gina tried to talk to him about what he was doing, he'd cut her off. "As long as I put food on the table and everybody's got a roof over their head, it's my problem, Gina. We've got a partnership, you and me, and what makes it work is a division of labor."

The Mercedes moved to the right lane, exiting the freeway at Tiburon Boulevard. Gina followed. What could they be doing? Joe had talked to the lawyer about a meeting. Tiburon was a strange place for that. Or was this trip about something other than business?

When they reached the village of Tiburon, Joe turned on Main, a tiny street lined with shops and restaurants bordering the waterfront. At the end of the first block was a parking lot, which Joe entered. Gina, fearless now, was right behind him, prepared to smile and wave if he looked in his rearview mirror. He didn't.

She did not park next to them because there wasn't a place. Once she did find a spot, Joe and the dragon lady were already headed for the street. By hurrying, she was able to keep them in sight.

Joe and Elaine Chang strolled ahead of her, he leaning on his cane, she with her arm linked in his. Apparently they'd made up. Gina's cynicism surprised her. Snide thoughts kept her from crying, but her heart pounded like crazy. Adventuress was not a role that came easily.

The commercial section of Main was small. It didn't take Joe and his companion long to reach their destination—Sam's, a bar and restaurant. It was famous for its large deck built over the water, next to the yacht harbor. Gina hadn't been to Sam's in years, but she knew it was a popular spot for Marinites to gather. Perhaps trysting lovers, as well.

Gina waited outside, trying to bolster her resolve. Okay, she'd come all this way. Now what was she going to do?

Wait until they were seated, then slip into a chair at their table and give Joe the what-for? A loud, shouting scene was not her style. She didn't relish the thought of a tearful lament, though she was afraid there would be tears. Why let that stop her, though? The question was, what could she accomplish?

At some level she wanted to humiliate and embarrass him. Revenge. That was at the top of the list. Make him pay. She also wanted to show him that she was tough, that she wouldn't roll over and allow herself to be bullied. She'd look him in the eye and tell him that he was a disgrace to his family and that she'd had enough. He could come home long enough to get his things and then never darken her door again. She'd say it just like that.

Drawing a fortifying breath, Gina pushed the door open and stumbled into the dark, boozy-smelling bar. There must have been a million neighborhood joints around the country just like it. The allure of Sam's was the glass-sided dining room and the deck, which offered a panoramic view of the San Francisco skyline. The bar served mostly as a holding area for guests waiting for a table.

Seeing they weren't in the bar, she made her way through the crowd and down the hallway leading to the deck out back. She stopped at the door and surveyed the sea of tables framed by the naked masts of sailboats in the marina beyond.

Then, in the far corner of the deck, beyond the hostess's podium and the crowded tables, Joe and Elaine Chang sat at a table with a middle-aged Asian gentleman in a white linen suit. He wore large sunglasses that masked his face. A tall glass with some sort of drink sat before him.

Gina hadn't expected this. Did she make her speech with a third party present? Would that deepen Joe's humiliation, or make her look like a fool? She supposed it would depend on what was going on. If the man was Elaine Chang's brother, for example, and they were discussing the terms of marriage, a dramatic intrusion might be just what the doctor ordered. On the other hand, if it was a business meeting, she'd simply come off as a blithering idiot.

Joe's back was to her, which meant she could get all the way to the table without being recognized. Elaine Chang probably had no idea what she looked like. When the people at the table behind Joe got up to leave, Gina saw her chance. She hurried down the ramp, past the unattended hostess podium, then wound her way toward the corner, plopping down at the recently vacated table, taking the chair nearest Joe, their backs to each other.

At almost the same moment, the Asian gentleman got to his feet. "Please excuse me for a moment," he said in heavily accented English.

As he left the table, slipping past her, Gina got a good look at him. He had a distinctive scar above his right eyebrow. It was half an inch long.

Elaine Chang, glancing over Joe's shoulder, watched the man for several moments, then leaned close to Joe, saying something Gina couldn't hear. But she was able to make out her husband's response.

"This Buddha is going to be the death of me," he said. "Figuratively and maybe literally."

Gina couldn't make out the woman's response.

"Well, everything I have is riding on this," he said, "most especially my children's future."

Joe's words entered her heart like a dagger. Gina felt herself choking up. The reference to their children was too much for her. Tears gushed. Her courage abandoned her, leaving her no choice but to get up and run. She didn't stop until she reached her car. She was still crying when she got to the freeway. Wiping her tears, she wondered if maybe the best solution was to kill them both.

BURLINGAME

When they got to the entrance to the hospital parking lot, Igor Sakharov told his brother to pull over and stop.

"What now?" Alexei said.

"I don't know if I can go in there."

"Igor, you're either sick or you're not."

"У меня болит *I have a pain*," he said, rubbing his chest, "but that's not the issue. Maybe I'm better off sick than dead."

Alexei groaned. "You're afraid."

"I'm not afraid," he snapped. "I don't trust them, that's all."

"Igor, these are American doctors. Everything in America is perfect, you know that."

"Don't ridicule me, Alexei. I am your elder brother."

The younger Sakharov shook his head. "Хорошо. *All right*. So, what do you want to do?"

Igor was torn. And afraid. With the monolith of Peninsula Hospital rising before him against the backdrop of a blue-gray sky, Igor Sakharov wondered if this was what his prescient mind had foreseen. He'd never even heard of Burlingame, California, before now. Its principal virtue, as best he could tell, was that it was near the airport. How could the Fates have chosen this place for his death?

"Igor," Alexei said, drumming the steering wheel, "we don't have all day. We've got two people to kill. Do you want to go inside or do you want to go to San Francisco and do the hit?"

"I'm not sure."

Alexei was clearly exasperated.

"Perhaps if I look inside the building," Igor said, "I'll be able to tell if it's best to stay or go."

Alexei started the engine without waiting for further instructions. Igor could tell his brother was losing his patience. His brother was so excited to be doing a hit, he could barely contain himself. He was like a schoolboy on holiday.

Over the past few days, Igor had given him a crash course in assassination. They'd discussed principles and technique. Igor had hammered at the fundamentals, quizzing him relentlessly. They'd spent an afternoon at the shooting range, at the end of which they'd driven out to a remote spot in San Bernardino County where Igor, fighting his dyspepsia with Tums, schooled Alexei on execution techniques, having him pump rounds into watermelons they'd purchased at a roadside stand.

"The first and most important thing is to remind yourself that this is not recreation," he'd told his brother. "This is done for money, not fun."

"What difference does it make?"

"When you do things for pleasure, like fucking, for example, you tend to get careless because your mind is on the sensation. A job done professionally is done with precision. Don't enjoy this work, Alexei. It is unhealthy."

His brother had begun to laugh. "It's definitely unhealthy for the victim."

Igor had given him a look. "Assassination is not a laughing matter."

Alexei had sobered up after that, but Igor was still concerned. His brother was too frivolous to be a professional killer. Plus, he remained unproven under pressure. Watermelons were not people, after all.

Alexei pulled the rental car to a stop at the entrance to the emergency room. "Do you want me to go inside with you?"

"No, stay here. I'll be right back."

Igor climbed out with difficulty and walked unsteadily toward the doors, which slid open. Once inside, he inhaled the distinctive smell of the place. Rubbing alcohol? Disinfectant? Blood? Suddenly the walls began to spin and a pain shot through his heart. Even before he could cry out, he felt himself collapsing. Igor Andreyevich Sakharov was unconscious before he hit the floor.

NORTH BEACH

Nick pulled his rental car to the curb in front of the Yankee Clipper and got out. It felt funny to be standing before the mother church after all this time. The Clipper, venerable and proud, looked a little shabby to his polished eye—he was, after all, a New York restaurateur, the proprietor of the hottest new joint in Manhattan. But he was also Nicky Sasso, the younger son, the kid, the shortstop, the hotshot who'd gotten Tina Arigoni's cherry on his father's bed in the spare room while the old man was downstairs drinking Chianti with her uncle Giancarlo. He was the favored son, the lover, the cook, the cop, the schlemiel, the misfit, the bad egg. And he was home.

The parking valet, a kid Nick had never seen before, gave him the claim stub without comment and climbed in behind the wheel. Nick, his briefcase in hand, watched him drive off, then went inside. The hostess wasn't up front, but the revered old fixture in the dining room, Gennaro Ravara, happened to be passing by with a plate of spaghetti in his hand. He stopped in his tracks, the little serving cloth on his forearm giving him an air of starched formality. He stared at Nick, his eyebrows making an inverted V, his hooked nose—larger and drooping more each year—hung over his lips like a failing erection.

"Jesus Christ, you came," he muttered. There was no smile, but that was no surprise. Gennaro never smiled.

"Hi, old buddy," Nick said.

"This a visit or are you here for lunch?"

Nick shrugged.

"Go sit in Benny's booth," he said, tossing his head toward the back, "and I'll bring you a bowl of minestrone while you think about it." His instructions imparted, Gennaro went off to serve his customer.

Before Nick managed to uproot himself, a tall, full-bodied but curvaceous middle-aged woman with blond-streaked hair came walking toward him from the back. She was in a black-and-white polka-dot silk dress with a scooped neckline showing lots of cleavage. She couldn't be the hostess, Nick told himself, yet she looked familiar the way a person's grammar-school teacher looked familiar, twenty years after the fact.

"Lunch?" she said, smiling with rubescent lips. Then she paused the way people do when in discourse with the past. A little frown, then, "My God. Nick?"

The way she said "Nick" brought it all back in a sudden rush. Linda Meyer had been a hostess at the Clipper years ago—it had to be twenty or more. Yeah, he was what at the time? Seventeen? Talk about a face from the past...and a body, too. Linda had not just been his father's girl. She'd gotten her hand in his own pants on several occasions, and he in hers.

"Linda Meyer? Are you working here?"

"Believe it or not," she said with a laugh. Then she gave him a big, ferocious hug, pressing her large, soft breasts against his chest, her scent erotic-familiar, in spite of the passing of decades. Taking him by the shoulders, she stepped back to look him over, smiling. "Your brother, sweetheart that he is, gave me a break. I was a reentry worker, without skills. What got me this job first time around had either gone to seed...or started sagging," she added with a laugh, "but Joe said there was a new management philosophy at the Clipper, that hiring was based on qualifications and experience, not age. It wasn't a requirement, but I told him I was going to join a health club and lose thirty pounds, anyway." She turned her body from side to side, showing it off. "Twelve pounds down and eighteen to go. What do you think?"

"You look great, Linda."

"You know, honey, so do you. A little more mature than the teenage boy I remember."

"Birthdays do that to you," he said.

"It's not Linda Meyer anymore, by the way. It's Linda Nassari."

"Oh?"

"Married and divorced. He was Iranian, in case you're wondering." She lowered her voice and leaned close. "And a fucking sonovabitch, if you want to know the truth. Talk about chauvinist pig... But that's all in the past. I'm a single working girl again. No kids, thank God. Kept the name because I was used to it and kind of liked it. I think it's kind of exotic, Hormoz—the asshole—notwithstanding."

"God, Linda, this is a surprise."

She glanced over her shoulder, then said in a confidential tone. "I hope you don't feel uncomfortable with me here...considering we have a past."

"No," he said, shaking his head, "not at all."

"That's good, because Joe doesn't know...about me and you. Your father and me...well, that's another story. Tony had very few secrets. I gotta tell you this, though, your dad, bless his heart, was a little guy, but he was a man." She sighed the sigh of someone looking back and recalling the good times. "But never mind all that," she said, looking him up and down. "So, what are you doing in town? I heard you live in New York now."

"I do. I'm here on business for a few days. Just got off a plane."

"Are you here to see Joe?"

"Among other things. I was hoping he wouldn't mind if I bunked upstairs."

"I don't know why he would, but I guess I shouldn't speak for him."

"He's not here, by any chance?"

She shook her head. "Haven't seen him for a few days."

"If he should call in, tell him I'd like to see him, would you?"

"Sure. Meanwhile, want some lunch?"

Gennaro came up to them and, leaning his hunched frame

around Linda, said, "When the hostess is through making goo-goo eyes, maybe she'd be kind enough to tell Mr. Sasso that his minestrone is at his table, getting cold."

"Thanks, Gennaro," Nick said.

Linda gave Nick a weary look. "The old fart hasn't changed in twenty years, except that he's slower and more grumpy."

"I'll go appease him."

"Well, don't be a stranger while you're in town," she said, giving him the smile of a happily divorced woman.

"I won't."

Nick went back to Benny's booth where DiMag, Marilyn and baby Vince looked out at him from a world frozen in time, a world that had been both innocent and heroic, a world of nuclear bombs, blond bombshells and the Bronx Bombers. None of it had been a part of his own life experience, but it was in his blood as much as his old man was.

Funny how strong the forces were that pulled you back in time. He was just a kid when the Simon and Garfunkel song was big, but the words had stayed with him. How did they go? "Where have you gone, Joe DiMaggio? The country turns its lonesome eyes to you?" Somethin' like that. As the old man might say—that's more true today than ever. Yep, the world missed DiMaggio, Marilyn and all the rest, more than they could know.

Gennaro set a basket of bread on the table.

"So...Joe hasn't been around, huh?" Nick asked, taking the napkin.

"You kidding? He gave up running this place for Lent. We never see him."

"Never?"

Gennaro shook his head, his pate shining through the pencil lines of hair that ran from the crest of his forehead to his collar. "I've already said too much. I'm not saying no more. Want a menu?"

"Just bring me a side of the best pasta in the kitchen."

Gennaro shuffled off and Nick took his cell phone from his briefcase. He called his brother's home. Blake answered again and they exchanged grunts.

"Your mom home yet?"

"She just got here."

"Could I speak to her, please?"

Gina came on the line. "Hi, Nick."

"Hi. I'm at the Clipper. You didn't find out if the studio is available, did you, by any chance?"

"No, I'm sorry. I haven't talked to Joe. And frankly I don't expect to. You'll have to deal with him."

Nick could hear the strain in her voice. "Gina, what's wrong?"

"Just a second. Blake," she said to her son, "will you go in the kitchen and get a frozen pizza out of the freezer?" She came back to him. "Nick, it's all over between me and your brother."

"All over?"

"I'm ready to kill him. Seriously."

"His affair?"

"I saw her today. Her name's Elaine Chang. She's a professional mistress or prostitute, whatever. All I've got to say is, I've had it. Somebody had better come over here and take Joe's gun, because I swear, the minute he walks in the door, I'm going to use it on him."

"Should I come now?" he asked, sensing her words might not be hyperbole.

"Have you seen your father yet?"

"No."

"Go see him first, Nick. Then come by."

"All right."

He had an ominous feeling. It didn't happen often, but when it did, some disaster inevitably followed. Nick needed to talk to his brother real bad. That much was certain.

BURLINGAME

Vaguely aware of the doctors and nurses working on him, Igor Sakharov drifted in and out. He wasn't sure how much time had passed, but some hours later he found himself in a hospital bed, hooked by wires to a battery of blinking, purring machines. It was in a room like this—not so shiny or fancy, granted—that his father had died.

A smiling nurse, a woman somehow plain and pretty at the same time, was at his bedside. "How are you feeling, Mr. Mason?"

Igor blinked with confusion. What did she call him? Then he remembered. His alias. He'd worked under various names over the years. Tom Mason was among his favorites. "What happened?"

"You've had a heart attack. The doctor thinks not a severe one, but we can't be sure until you undergo more tests."

"Heart attack?"

"The doctor will be in to see you in a while and he'll answer all your questions."

"Where is...uh..."

"Your associate, Mr. French? He's in the waiting room. If you'd like to see him, he can visit for a few minutes. The main thing is for you to rest."

"Why am I so woozy?"

"You've been sedated. Would you rather sleep for a while?"

"No, let me talk to...Jerry, please."

Igor was lucky to remember his brother's alias, Jerry French. Alexei thought it sounded sexy. "What a team," he'd said with a laugh. "Tom and Jerry!"

The nurse was all business. "I'll go get him," she said.

A few minutes later Alexei was at his bedside. As usual, they spoke in Russian, but softly, so no one would hear.

"So," his brother said, "the airplane food got to you."

"Alexei, you've got to get me out of here."

"You've had a heart attack, Igor. There's no way."

"But I can't stay here."

"You have no choice. You're going to be fine. At least, that's what they're telling me. The doctor said it's a warning."

"What kind of warning? That I'm at death's door?"

"No, you have to take it easy from now on and watch your diet. No more stress."

"Why are you sounding so happy about this?" Igor asked, suspicious.

"Because you have the excuse you need and so do I."

"What do you mean?"

"I'm going to do the job so we can get paid."

"No, Alexei, you can't."

"Why not?"

"Because you aren't ready."

"Well, we don't really have a choice. So, that makes it easy."

Igor shook his head, seeing disaster ahead. "Don't be foolish. Go to the hotel. As soon as they release me, we'll fly back to Los Angeles."

"Yes, Igor, but not until I've done the hit."

"Oh, my God," he said, realizing there was nothing he could do to stop him.

Alexei took Igor's face in his hands and kissed his forehead. "Relax and leave everything to me. The sword has been passed, big brother. You can play matchmaker now to your heart's content." He chuckled at his own pun.

But Igor did not smile. This whole affair was going to end in tragedy. He knew it.

THE MARINA

Elaine Chang had always prided herself on being decisive, so it was unlike her to circle the block three times before stopping and parking a few doors from the lawyer's office. She'd done her homework and was fully informed about Sanford P. Culp, Esq. Between her friends in the gay community and spreading a little money here and there, she had his story down cold. Names. Dates. Places. The question haunting her was did she use the information against him, or did she let nature take its course? There were risks either way.

Elaine's strength and her weakness were one and the same—she never left things in the hands of the gods. A passive woman could spend her life cleaning fish. So, too, could a careless woman. The trick, as always, was to know when and how to act, finding just the right balance of power and finesse.

As she sat in her Lexus, pondering her options, Elaine realized why Sonny Culp was giving her such fits. He was a man of principle. But, from all accounts, he was also a highly rational human being. What happened when those two things came into conflict was the nexus of the problem she faced.

How a person defined his self-interest was not easily determined when dealing with a man like Sonny Culp. She knew that money and power, the big two, were of negligible importance to him. That left self-respect and love. Figuring out how he balanced those two in his personal and professional life was the key. The plain fact was she didn't know. In time she'd learn more, perhaps, but she didn't have that luxury. If she was to affect the outcome of the deal, it would have to be now. Or never.

Elaine checked her face in the mirror, then, steeling herself, she got out of her car and walked up the sidewalk to Sonny Culp's office. She found the lawyer sitting at his desk, looking frazzled.

Culp was one of those Caucasian men who looked as if he'd been born and lived his entire life in snow. He was very pale, the only color in his skin flushes of red that invariably came and went with emotion. His eyes were a light blue-gray, his reddish-blond hair long since departed from the top of his shiny dome. All that remained was a longish fringe diluted with white. He had a young face, which belied his fifty-odd years. He was not fat, but his body was soft and paunchy. The top button of his shirt was undone and his tie loosened and twisted askew. For a gay man, his grooming and dress were, for want of a better word, relaxed.

As Elaine entered the reception area, Culp, seated at his desk in his private office, raised his eyes and stared at her through the open door. It took several seconds before her presence registered in his mind. She stepped into his office.

"Ms. Chang," he said at last, "what brings you here at this hour? We aren't supposed to meet until this evening."

"I thought perhaps things would go better later if we had a little chat first."

Only then did Sonny get to his feet. He did not invite her to sit. "I'm not sure that's a good idea," he said, running his fingers along each side of his head, collecting the errant strands of strawberry hair. "I think it's better if we wait until Joe is present."

"No, I would like to talk to you as his lawyer."

Culp seemed reluctant, but relented. He gestured for her to sit. "What can I do for you?"

"I would like to know if you're planning on squelching the deal I've negotiated between Joe and Mr. Lu."

"Well, you see, that's something I can't answer. I render my advice to my client and to him only. What he chooses to share is up to him. But without his authorization I can't discuss how I intend to advise him."

"Please don't give me that lawyer talk, Mr. Culp. I just want to know what you're going to do."

"I will advise my client to the best of my ability. Beyond that I can't say."

Elaine could see he intended to play it by the book. No surprise there. "Well," she said, "if you won't share your thinking with me, perhaps I can share mine with you."

"If you wish. But since we're speaking in regard to my client's interests, I will be obligated to share whatever you have to say with him."

"Do whatever you feel you must do, Mr. Culp."

"Okay, I'm listening."

"Joe and I have been working on this deal for months. We've made considerable expenditures of energy, time and money. I would hate that to go to waste because you pull the rug out from under us at the last minute."

"I'm aware that Joe wants the deal. But it's also my obligation to inform him of the risks inherent in the various courses of action he's considering."

"Joe told me you were reluctant to get involved."

"I've told him this is not one of my areas of expertise."

"Then why don't you bow out?"

"Look, Ms. Chang, there's no point in you and I discussing the nature of my relationship with Joe. With all due respect, it's not any of your business."

"Okay, then let me suggest that you stay out of the deal, not just for Joe's sake, but for your own."

He studied her. "That sounds very much like a threat, Ms. Chang."

"I wouldn't dare. Nor do I relish the thought of making Martin Fong aware of your midday excursions into the Castro, particularly the visits you make to a certain apartment on Collingwood Street."

Culp turned bright red. "That's blackmail!"

"No, it's not, Mr. Culp. You're going to do what you're going to do, but I, too, am going to do what I'm going to do. Martin isn't a friend, but I've met his parents and we have mutual acquaintances who care very deeply about Martin's well-being." She crossed her legs. "You seem like a nice man, but frankly, I wish you'd just go away. And I wouldn't be a bit surprised if you didn't feel the same way about me. Maybe we should do just that, go our separate ways. What do you think?"

"You realize you're committing a criminal act."

"Am I really? You mean by simply sharing what I know? I would think what I've said falls in the category of friendly warning. In your shoes, I certainly would want to be aware of the dangers lurking. But you're the expert. If you say it's criminal, then it must be." She studied him with a look of false desperation. "Please, Mr. Culp, give a poor innocent layperson the benefit of the doubt. Whatever I did that's wrong, I retract. I should have kept my mouth shut and let nature take its course."

Culp sat fuming. "I think you should go, Ms. Chang."

"If that's what you wish." She got up and went to the door, where she hesitated. "I hope this hasn't spoiled your day. If I had it to do over again, I wouldn't have come."

Culp didn't respond. But one look at him and she could tell he was calculating the consequences of the various alternatives. In a way, that was the best she could hope for. Whether or not she'd shot herself in the foot remained to be seen.

She left his suite, stepping into the vestibule. At the same moment a black woman in a wheelchair struggled to get in the front door. Elaine held it for her. The woman thanked her. Elaine was about to go outside when the woman gave her an imploring look.

"I hate to bother you," she said, "but would you be kind enough to hand this to Sonny Culp so I don't have to fight this door twice?"

Elaine was not eager to go back inside the lawyer's office, but she relented, taking the large manila envelope from the woman's hand.

"Bless you, ma'am. Wouldn't you think a lawyer working with the disabled would choose a building with better access for the handicapped?" With Elaine holding the door for her, the woman maneuvered her wheelchair outside.

Elaine went into Culp's suite. From the reception area she could see him, his head down on his desk and buried in his arms. She couldn't tell if he was crying or merely spent. Either way, Sonny was not a happy man. She took no special pleasure in that, but she was encouraged by the implications. Sonny Culp was wrestling with his soul. That meant she had a chance.

NORTH BEACH

After he'd finished lunch, Nick had the valet bring his suitcase from the car and take it upstairs. There was no sign of Joe, so he'd decided to exert his rights as a twelve-and-a-half-percent owner by moving into the studio. But before going upstairs, he decided to have a good look around to see how extensive the neglect was.

He was surprised to discover that things weren't too bad. The Clipper was much as it had been when his father opened it, during the Eisenhower administration. Sure, most of the fixtures and equipment had been updated, along with the furnishings, but the mood and the ambience remained old-time San Francisco in feel, with a distinctive baseball flavor. Joe—or maybe the staff—had kept it in decent shape.

Nick, feeling more nostalgic by the minute, decided to take a tour of the kitchen. On his way back, Linda Nassari stopped him.

"Your brother called a few minutes ago. I told him you were here."

"And?"

"He said he'd be in later this afternoon."

"He didn't say exactly when?"

"No."

Nick wanted to get out to Ingleside to see the old man, but he figured he'd better hang around to talk to Joe. Apparently, his brother wasn't hiding anymore. Maybe he'd even cleaned up his act. But after talking with Gina, Nick wasn't holding his breath.

"Do you think he'll show?"

She shrugged. "Joe's an odd duck. You never know what to expect."

"Yeah, I know. Thanks, Linda."

She went off, swinging her ass. Linda Meyer, the "older woman" in his life. The difference in their ages was only five or six years, but to a boy of seventeen it had been a lifetime. Linda Meyer had given him a sex education, made him a man. How ironic that she should be back at the Clipper now. Though he was hesitant to think in such terms, her unexpected presence smacked of "second chance." Pondering the vagaries of fate, Nick headed off to the kitchen.

It was late enough that the pace in back had slowed. He chatted with the staff, most of whom were new, but mainly he took in the smells, watched the plates being put up, tasted the creamed vegetable soup.

The current chef, a large, rotund man named Marco Falchi, was Italian-born, knowledgeable, competent, but in the end, Nick judged, a touch uninspired. They talked for a few minutes, but Nick mostly watched, enjoying himself, remembering. Of all the facets of the restaurant business, cooking gave him the greatest joy. He loved cuisine. As he saw it, the customers were just an excuse for creating dishes. And this was where it had all begun, right here in the kitchen of the Yankee Clipper.

Nick and his brother had been quite a contrast. As kids, from the first day they'd set foot in their father's restaurant, Joe had wanted to operate the cash register, whereas Nick had liked being in the kitchen where he sat on a stool, watching Carlo Cordoni, their longtime chef, orchestrate the creation of a dish. Once Nick was big enough, Carlo let him cut vegetables and stir sauces. The old "pasta maestro," as he called himself, told Tony that Nick had a gift. His father's proud response was one of Nick's fondest childhood recollections.

Where his desire to become a cop had come from, he couldn't say. In his youth, he'd had a penchant for trouble. But then, as the saying goes, the line between cops and crooks was narrow, so maybe his positive impulses had leaked over onto his dark side. Whatever it was, becoming a police inspector was a goal he'd set at an early age.

After high school he'd gone to city college to study police science. It had taken twice as long to complete his requirements as it should have because he hadn't stayed focused. Or maybe it was because his heart was in the kitchen of the Yankee Clipper.

Along the way there'd been that poignant summer in Italy, refining his cooking skills and discovering love. But growing up meant being serious, and becoming a cop had always struck him as a serious undertaking.

For reasons he still couldn't explain, marriage followed in short order. Maybe it had grown out of the conviction that a wife was a necessary ingredient to a serious life. The fact that Cindy's old man was a cop might have figured in, as well. But, even with a law enforcement career in the making, the Yankee Clipper remained an important part of his life.

When Carlo Cordoni retired, the old man asked Nick to become executive chef, a job he could handle on a part-time basis. Nick liked the idea because he wanted to keep his hand in. The restaurant business was, after all, in his blood.

Looking back on his twenties, Nick was struck by the fact that the hours he spent at the Clipper were the best. His marriage had gotten off to a rocky start and went downhill from there. Cindy had an abortion within weeks of their wedding, not even telling him about it until afterward. And she refused to discuss it, which perplexed him.

For several weeks prior to their marriage he'd been in Virginia, attending classes at the FBI Academy. By the time he and Cindy separated, Nick had pretty well figured out that the child hadn't been his.

Sleazy as the whole business was, Cindy's infidelity wasn't the root of the problem. Hell, with their relationship going south, he'd strayed himself. The real problem was they'd married for the wrong reasons—Nick out of some misguided sense of inevitability and Cindy on the rebound from her relationship with Terry Hughes, a cop she'd dated for over a year before Nick had come along.

Of course, the pressures of his job hadn't helped matters any, especially once he got involved in the case that proved to be his undoing. At the outset it had seemed so routine. A drug dealer named Noble Allard had shot and killed a teen addict over a drug deal gone bad. It was the sort of thing that happened all the time. Nick and his partner, Dickson Hong, had investigated the case, which soon turned into a nightmare. Nick had mishandled the evidence, then out of fear of blowing the case and his career, he'd tried to cover up his mistakes. The extent of the disaster hadn't become clear until the trial. In the end, it was Nick who was branded the wrongdoer and Noble Allard went free.

Then, with his career in shambles, Nick caught his wife screwing Terry Hughes. The double blow had knocked him on his ass. His solution, as in the past, was to climb aboard yet another pony and move on.

By that time Nick was enough his own man that he didn't fear his father's reaction—though he had little doubt there'd be one. Tony Sasso had felt his son's career in law enforcement had been a mistake, yet the old man had been more upset by Nick's domestic problems than his running afoul of the law. "I know these are different times," the old man said, on hearing Nick had filed for divorce, "with wives fucking around as much as husbands, but don't you feel just a little embarrassed?"

Tony Sasso knew all about pride, being a prideful man, but there was special irony in his remark. The old man had never cared for Cindy, if only because she wasn't Italian. Irish and Catholic—the latter in name only—weren't sufficient qualifications in his view. His philosophy was simple and he'd preached it from the day his sons first took communion—"Fuck blond and marry Italian."

Joe had taken the old man's advice, whereas Tony's "wisdom" had been lost on Nick. It wasn't the first time or the last that he hadn't heeded his father's counsel. He'd never quite figured out if that was a good thing or bad. But it was at that low point of his life that his relationship with his father went south.

Tony Sasso could have lived with his son's failings, but he couldn't handle it when Nick packed up and left town. The old man's disappointment turned to bitterness, which led to their estrangement. For his part, Nick simply wanted to forget and be left alone. It now appeared the decision was coming back to haunt him.

After his sentimental sojourn in the kitchen, Nick decided it was time to go upstairs to the "imperial suite." It was actually Joe who'd coined the phrase, and it was apt. For the better part of forty years Tony Sasso had run his business from the upstairs office. The bedchamber, converted from an old storeroom, had played an important role, as well. The old man hadn't been the best model for his sons, but Tony had fashioned a way of living that was rich, bawdy and filled with pleasure. By his own standards and the many who admired him, Tony Sasso knew how to live. Nick was still trying to figure it out.

If there was a victim in all this, it was Nick's mother, though to his knowledge Maria Sasso never complained about her lot in life or her husband's behavior. Tony, to his credit, always gave her her due. He was wise enough to seek her advice in business matters, recognizing the superiority of her judgment and instincts. His philandering never got in the way of his family obligations, which was probably in his pact with God, and Maria's bottom line.

Tony's other women—mostly the hostesses he hired— were generally as tolerant and accommodating as his wife. Though there must have been wounds along the way, "Tony's girls" were seduced not coerced. A few passed through the Yankee Clipper without ever sleeping with the old man, but his charm and his lavish ways made him hard to resist. Plus, Tony Sasso knew his limitations. He hired with his own prospects for success in mind, and he usually guessed right.

Nick was aware, though, that the Yankee Clipper now bore his brother's stamp as much as his father's. Shortly after Nick left San Francisco, Tony had retired, turning the operation over to Joe.

Nick climbed the stairs he'd so often ascended, both as a boy and a man. The office, he discovered, had been redone. Tony's photographs and mementos—mostly baseball-related—had been removed. Instead, the walls were covered with photographs and architectural drawings of the various buildings Joe owned. The shelves were filled with business books and journals. The furniture was new, as was the carpet and paint. There were few vestiges left of Tony Sasso.

This was his brother's operation now. Nick didn't relish talking to him about the missing funds, or anything else for that matter. In fact, the notion of calling Joe on the carpet made him feel like a pretender. His brother was, after all, the one who'd taken life seriously. Joe had striven, knocking himself out while Nick had played as long as it was fun, then, when trouble arose, he'd take the easy way out. Funny how clear that was to him now.

But whether or not Joe had blown it, Nick realized he couldn't ignore his brother's catalog of sins. If only for the sake of Gina and the children, it was incumbent on him to pull Joe back from the brink—assuming it wasn't already too late. Unfortunately, he wasn't well suited for the role of savior.

Nick noticed a light blinking on the answering machine on the credenza behind the desk. He had no business listening to his brother's messages, but after hearing the one Mort had played, he couldn't turn his back out of some false sense of propriety. The cop still in him made him go to the machine and press the play button.

There was only one call. It was from the same man who'd spoken in the message Mort had played.

"Joe, it's happened. My office was burglarized last night. They weren't after valuables, they were after my files. If this wasn't serious before, it sure as hell is now. Be careful, Joe. Be careful."

Nick plopped down in the desk chair, both worried and mystified. It *was* a good thing he'd come. And yet, he wasn't sure what he could do to help his brother. Finding out what was going on was probably the first step.

Staring blankly at the bookcase across from him, Nick noticed a small statue wedged among the books. Curious, he got up and went over to the shelf. It was a little Buddha, about eight inches tall, the sort you could find all over Chinatown, except it was painted a bright emerald-green. The color was strange enough, but stranger still was the fact that his brother would have it in his office. Joe wasn't into decorating.

Nick picked up the Buddha. On the bottom, written on the plaster with a marking pen, was "To J. from E." To Joe from...who? Then he remembered the Chinese mistress. Gina had said her name. What was it? Evelyn? No, Elaine. Elaine Ching or Chang, something like that.

He put the statue back on the shelf, wondering what the hell this was about. A gift from a lover? Nick had always considered his brother boring and predictable, but Joe was proving himself anything but. Was it a midlife crisis? Textbook, probably.

Nick stepped to the window, which overlooked the alley and the rooftops of the buildings behind. A gull winged its way across the gray sky, reminding him of the many hours he sat at his father's desk, staring out the window, fantasizing about baseball and pussy instead of doing his algebra.

Irresponsibility had been his biggest problem. And now, just when he seemed to be getting on track, his brother discovers Sodom and Gomorrah. "Joey," he muttered aloud, "what the hell are you doing?"

"No, the question is what are *you* doing?"

Nick spun around. Joe stood in the doorway, leaning on his cane. He was not smiling. He'd aged considerably, the lines on his face deeper, his eyes sunken. Joe, with flecks of gray at the temples of his dark brown hair, looked stressed, exasperated and not particularly happy to see him.

Nick said, "I figured we needed to talk."

"I gathered that." Joe made his way to the desk and sat down. "Take a seat," he said, gesturing toward the wooden guest chair across from him.

Nick sat. The fact that there were no hugs was not a surprise. Joe had always been somewhat standoffish and aloof, slow to engage. Their mother had been kind and loving toward him, but Vince was her firstborn and Nick, the baby, had been the clear favorite of both their parents. The fact that Joe hadn't offered Nick his hand was a pointed indication of his displeasure with the intrusion.

"There was no need for you to come," he said, steepling his fingers, looking solemn and tired.

"Communication by phone didn't seem to be getting results."

"I'm sorry about that," Joe said, actually sounding contrite. "My life has been hectic the last few weeks. I'm in the middle of some major, major things."

"So I gather, big brother."

Joe looked as though he wasn't sure what he meant—what issues or evidence he was alluding to—but didn't ask. He ruminated for a second or two, then said, "So, what's on your mind, Nick?"

"How blunt can I be?"

"As blunt as you want. It couldn't have been cheap flying out here."

"Well, the Clipper's books seem to be screwed up and some money missing from the accounts. You're not a sloppy businessman, Joe. The old man was concerned. And, frankly, so am I. Are you in some kind of trouble?"

"You flew all the way to San Francisco for that?"

"Sixty-eight thousand is not a fortune, but it's not nickels and dimes, either."

Joe said, "I've borrowed and I've been sloppy about it, yes. But it wasn't something I was going to take to Dad. He's out of the loop and is easily upset. I wouldn't have been doing him any favors. And I didn't think you'd care to discuss it, Nick, to be honest. You've called me, what, once in five years? And that was to get money."

"Yeah, I sold you half my interest in the Clipper. It was all aboveboard. I didn't ask for anything under the table."

Joe flushed. "What, exactly, are you accusing me of?" he asked, his voice shaking with anger.

"I'm not accusing you of anything. I'm asking for an explanation. Maybe my twelve and a half percent doesn't entitle me to an awful lot, but you do have a fiduciary obligation to the old man, not to mention justifying what you do to the IRS."

"The IRS is my problem, not yours. But you're right about the money I borrowed. I'll have a note drawn up and I'll send you a copy. In a few months it'll all be paid back with interest. *Mea culpa.* Now, is there anything else, Nick?"

Nick could see this wasn't going well and they hadn't even discussed what was really important. How did he raise the subject of Joe's marriage, the danger he seemed to be facing, his shaky personal finances and the rest?

"Look, Joe, I've not done this well. It isn't the money I'm worried about. It's you."

"*You're* worried about *me?*"

"I know how ironic that seems, but the rumors of your problems got all the way to New York. People are worried about you, Joe, me among them."

"I'm not interested in rumors."

"I'm not, either, but I do know that your finances are falling apart, not to mention your marriage. Unqualified as I may be to counsel anybody about marriage and business, your wife and our father have nobody to turn to but me. And since I care about you, too, I thought the decent thing to do was offer you my hand. Whether you're willing to take it or not is up to you."

His brother sat silently, not looking him in the eye as he considered his response. Then he said, "I appreciate your concern." His tone was measured. "I need to talk to Gina, it's true. We have some issues that need to be resolved. As far as finances are concerned, I have been shuffling resources, and some of my investments have suffered because of it. I'm working on something very big. It's huge. I've devoted all my time and energy to it at the expense of other things. Again, *mea culpa.* The point is, there's nothing for you to do, Nick. You've alerted me to the fact that I've been neglectful.

I appreciate that. I think, though, if you're going to worry about anybody, it should be Dad. Have you seen him yet?"

"No."

"Then don't waste your time with me. I've been through more wars than you'll ever know."

"Joe, what about the danger you're in? You can't brush that off."

"What are you talking about?"

"Your answering machine." Nick didn't want to tell him that Mort had played a message, but the one on the machine now would illustrate his point equally as well. It was brazen, maybe, but the situation called for strong measures.

Without a word, Joe turned around his chair and played the message. When it was over, he turned again and faced Nick.

"That was private. I don't appreciate you listening to it."

Nick felt himself losing his cool. "Never mind that, Joe. What the fuck is going on?"

His brother's face grew dark. "I think we've talked enough. Your twelve and a half percent entitles you to sleep in the spare room. Here's a key to the front door." Joe opened the desk drawer, took out a key and flipped it to him. "Be my guest. But stay the hell out of my office, all right?"

With that, Joe struggled to his feet, his glare as unkind as any Nick had ever seen. It was clear he intended to walk out. Nick got up. Joe started for the door.

"What about Gina?"

"What about her?"

"She knows about your Chinese mistress."

Joe's eyes narrowed. "I'm going to give you the best advice you'll ever get, little brother. Mind your own fucking business." With that he left, leaning heavily on his cane.

Nick stood there in the quiet of the empty office. He'd certainly screwed that up. What was worse, Joe had made him feel like a fool for sticking his nose in. And, for all his de-

fensiveness and invective, maybe Joe was right. Nick wasn't
his brother's keeper, whether Gina and his father wanted him
to be or not. Even so, he'd probably done the right thing by
trying. Coming all this way to be rebuked was an expensive
gamble, but if nothing else, he'd be able to see the old man.
Sad as it was to say, there may not be many more opportunities. Nick figured he had to content himself with that.

THE TENDERLOIN

Alexei Sakharov had been driving in circles for an hour,
so uptight that he felt he was going to explode. He wanted a
drink in the worst way, but figured that was the last thing he
needed—to get drunk and blow everything.

It was hard to say what was worse, his nerves or his frustration. He'd gone by the lawyer's office, but nobody was
there. Then, to kill time, he'd cruised by Sasso's house and
the restaurant, if only to get the lay of the land. No sign of
the guy, though he could have been inside either place. Alexei
sure as hell wasn't going to show his face in public.

So here he was, cruising the Tenderloin, thinking about
vodka, something he knew he couldn't have. The next best
thing was a piece of ass, but that could be awkward, too. Truth
be known, he was as addicted to pussy as he was to booze.
But the thing about pussy was that it didn't keep you from
shooting straight. Maybe a piece of ass would calm his nerves.

Sex on demand meant a hooker, but there were risks, not
the least of which was intervention by the cops. Even so, he
was checking out everything on the street, his resistance slipping by the minute.

The advantage of a streetwalker was that the encounter
was anonymous. A call girl would be too risky. They weren't
into faceless fucks. Alexei knew the game well—he was on
a first-name basis with half the call girls in L.A.

It was hard to say why, but prostitutes had always been a turn-on for him. In Moscow, even when he was married to Ludmilla, he'd pay for sex. An affair had no appeal. Seduction was a terrible waste of energy. It existed for women, not men.

On Polk Street, Alexei stopped at a light. There was a convenience store on the corner. Glancing over, he noticed a group of kids inside the door, teenagers, maybe early twenties. Most were boys. They were laughing and clowning. A girl with stringy blond hair and a wraparound denim miniskirt stood in the middle of the group. Despite the cool temperature she had on a halter top and loose denim jacket pushed back off her shoulders. Seeing Alexei look her way, she waved and he waved back. Then she lifted her skirt above her waist. For a second he thought she was naked, but then he could see she had on thong panties. Giggling, she doubled over with laughter as the boys howled. Druggie, he thought. The light changed and Alexei drove on.

There were a number of hookers on the streets, as many male as female. Some were transsexuals. Toss-ups. Nothing looked good to him and, worse, he was getting more frustrated. Circling, he found himself on Geary Street, headed east. He'd just about decided to flick it in and head back to the Marina when he spotted a black girl in a gold micromini dress at the corner of Hyde. She had on some kind of little white jacket over the dress, a feather boa and four-inch heels. Alexei pulled to the curb and stopped. He lowered the window on the passenger side. Bending over slightly, she peered at him. She looked wary and uncertain. Alexei had an instinct for women. This was no pro. If he had to guess, he'd say she was fairly new at hooking.

"Hi," he called.

The girl took a step toward the car, bending lower, squeezing the boa closed at her neck. "Looking for a date?"

"Maybe I am," Alexei said.

"What do you have in mind?"

"I could get a hotel room. We could party."

The girl moved right to the window and took a close look at him. "What kind of accent you got, anyway?"

"Does it matter?"

"Matter to me."

Alexei considered himself an American now and didn't like people making reference to his speech or asking about his national origin. Sure he had an accent, one much more pronounced than Igor's, who'd been trained in language. But his English was fluent. That ought to be good enough. "German," he said sarcastically.

"Tourist?"

"Businessman. Look, you want to party or not?"

"That depend. You thinkin' an all-nighter or a quick trick?"

"How much fun are you, sugar pie?"

She gave him a look of uncertainty, glancing back up the street. "A head date is a hundred. Two hundred for full service. You want an all-nighter, it'll cost you four."

"*Four*? That's call-girl prices."

"Look, if you don' know what you want, what say you drive around the block and think about it," she said, moving back up onto the curb.

Alexei checked her out thoroughly. She looked clean, had a certain freshness about her. She didn't seem like a street tramp. It made him wonder. A diamond in the rough? Or a cop?

He knew the smart thing was to drive on, but he had a funny hankering for this girl. He decided to test her. "A hundred and fifty to get laid," he said.

She considered it.

"I won't go any higher," he warned.

The girl stepped over to the car, opened the door and slid in beside him. She did not close the door, leaving one foot in the street. They looked at each other with mutual distrust.

"I don't want no rough stuff," she said. "You a gentleman?"

"A perfect gentleman."

"I'm serious."

"You're awfully particular, sugar pie. Must mean you aren't a druggie."

"I don' do no drugs."

"Let me see your arms."

She gave him an indignant look.

"If you're clean, what does it matter?" he said.

She glared, but held out her arm. Alexei ran his fingers over the inside of it, feeling for bumps in her veins. It was nearly dusk, the light poor enough and her skin so dark that it would have been tough to see needle tracks.

"Let me see the other one."

She held out the other arm. "You lookin' for a Girl Scout or what?"

"Just clean fun."

"What hotel?"

"Thought I'd get a room down on Lombard."

She remained uncertain.

Alexei said, "Close the door."

She did. He took off up the street.

After he'd gone a block, he said, "What's your name?"

"Jolie. What's yours?"

"Jerry."

"You sure you're German?"

"Why?"

"Say some'in'."

Alexei knew a bit of German and rattled off a few phrases. Jolie gave a derisive snort.

"What?"

"I lived in Germany for two years," she said. "You ain't German, mister."

"You're a smart girl."

"What else you lie about?"

"Want me to pull over and let you out?"

She thought for a moment, then said, "As long as your money's American, I guess it don' matter."

"As American as apple pie," he said with a laugh. He glanced at her tits. "You give me an especially good time, Jolie, and I might buy you for the night."

"It your birthday or some'in'?"

"In a way it is, yes."

"Then happy birthday."

"Thanks. You like vodka, by the way?"

"Don' drink while I work."

"Yeah? Well, you don't have a problem with running into a liquor store and getting me a bottle, do you?"

"Guess not."

Alexei reached over, put his hand on the inside of her knee and drew it up under her skirt. He gave her thigh a squeeze. "I guess we'll find out if it's going to be a happy birthday or not, won't we?"

INGLESIDE

The drive out to the nursing home was long, especially during rush hour. Nick didn't mind, though; it gave him a chance to think. His return to San Francisco was going no better than his departure five years ago—at least the gods up on Mount Sutro seemed not to be looking upon him with any greater favor than before. Maybe he was jinxed.

While sitting at a light on 19th Avenue, Nick decided to call New York and see how things were going at Dominick's. Eddy answered the phone.

"What kind of night did you have?" Nick asked.

"Good for a Wednesday. Down a little from tonight, but still good."

The words *down* and *good* instead of *up* and *great* put a shot of anxiety in him. "So, what do you think? Normal fluctuation or is the bloom off?"

Eddy laughed. "Nick, things are fabulous compared to before."

"I guess I'm greedy. Either that or paranoid. Is Bree there?"

"No, she took off a while ago."

Nick checked his watch. It wasn't all that late in New York. "How about Aldo?"

"Sure, who do you think is cooking?"

"Yeah, well, good. Tell them I said hi."

"Will do."

Nick was mildly ashamed. Jealousy was not becoming. It was his mood. He was sorry now he'd made the trip. No good deed goes unpunished, it seemed.

He was only minutes away from the home and feeling uneasy. He wasn't sure whether he was prepared to see the old man in a state of deterioration. Tony Sasso, for all his faults and failings, was still to Nick the father god, the Little League parent, the fulminator against errant behavior and the dispenser of favor. The old man was more than a person. He was an idea, a force, the creator. The last was what gave him his power.

From the age of fifteen on, Nick hadn't feared his father—not in a physical sense—but he'd continued to revere him. And because he revered him, he tested him, at times pushing things to the limit. If Nick had a strong ego, it was due, at least in part, to the fact that he'd never been able to destroy his father's love. The old man had endured a lot at Nick's hands, passing every test. What bothered him most was that he wasn't sure he deserved it. But then, what man had walked the earth without at least a nugget of self-doubt in his heart? The strong learned to breathe life into dreams and didn't let go until they came true. His old man had taught him that, though Tony's language was a bit more colorful than Nick's—

"If there's something you want real bad, kick ass until it's yours." It was a work in progress.

The ocean, a dozen blocks away, had covered Ingleside in a briny fog spiced with eucalyptus. The streetlight in front of the nursing home, a flat-roofed structure, wore a halo, and the windshields of the cars parked in the street glistened with moisture. Nick drove around looking for a spot and was two blocks away before he found one. The walk back in the fog brought on myriad memories: screwing under a blanket at Ocean Beach; drinking tequila in a convertible up on Twin Peaks, the fog so thick you couldn't see the hood ornament; stealing a tombstone from the cemetery in Colma and putting it in Saint Ignatius's dugout before the championship game; burying Maria Sasso in the same cemetery in Colma and wondering if some asshole was going to steal her memorial as a prank; saying goodbye to the misty skyline of San Francisco through the window of a taxi headed for SFO. The fog was as much a part of his growing-up experience as his mother's spaghetti and his father's sermons on living.

The nurse doing paperwork at the reception desk pointed him down the hall to his father's room. As he passed by, Nick glanced into the rooms of the inmates. He saw old folks propped up in bed or sitting in wheelchairs, their chins tucked to their chests or their heads listing at forty-five degrees. There was a low rumble of sound in the wing—TVs, sobs, a rambling monologue, moans, but no laughter. What Nick saw was the trailing edge of humanity clinging to the skirts of a society that wouldn't, or couldn't, notice. These were souls abandoned by time, real people in an unreal state of suspension. Knowing his father was among them was enough to choke him up.

The prelude should have prepared him, but it didn't. Tony Sasso, the man who had cursed and nurtured him, fought and loved him through all those tumultuous early years of life, now waited for him in a dimly lit room, a shriveled afterthought of the someone he'd once been. Nick stared into the room from the doorway, seeing what every man alive dreaded—his own mortality.

The fact that the old man did not see him was a blessing. The well of self-pity Nick felt was enough to drop him crying to his knees. Ultimately the saga of a parent was about one's self. He saw it clearly now. More than approval, more than love, more than the air he breathed, he needed forgiveness.

Nick ventured into his father's room with the same trepidation that he'd approached his mother's casket at her wake. That had been his first up-close encounter with the dead. This was his first up-close encounter with the impermanence of his own existence.

He was at the old man's side, but Tony didn't see him. "Dad..." he said, taking his father's cool, parchment-dry hand.

The old man's gray eyes slid across narrow slits, almost, but not quite reaching him. Nick took a half step closer to the bed, more in line with Tony's field of vision. "How are you feeling?"

The old man focused on him. There was a spark of recognition. His lip, sagging grotesquely at one corner, quivered slightly, but there was no sound. Nick leaned over and kissed his father's forehead. Tony wheezed in response, but that was it.

"I heard you weren't feeling up to snuff," Nick said, "so I hopped a plane to come out and give you the what-for. So tell me, is this a bid for attention, or what?"

The old man's lip twitched, but it was barely perceptible. There was a dewy glimmer in his eye.

"Let me cut right to the chase," Nick said, sitting on the edge of the bed, still holding his father's hand. "I've been checking out things at the Clipper and it's really not so bad. The operation's running smooth, Marco's on top of the kitchen and Joe's got the business side in order now. There was a glitch, but we talked about it. He's going to draw up some paperwork and send me a copy. The books will be rectified and everything should be all right soon."

Nick felt a pulse go from his father's hand to his.

"It won't be perfect, of course," he continued, "but nothing ever is. Mainly I wanted to put your mind at ease because I know you've been worrying."

He glanced around the room to give the moisture in his eyes time to dry. It was then he noticed the photo of DiMag, Marilyn and his infant brother, prominently displayed on the wall with all the reverence of the Holy Family. Only the halos were missing. Nick's eyes continued to move about the room.

"Pretty Spartan digs you got here, Dad. What's the allure?" He leaned closer and, in a confidential tone, said, "Is it the nurses?"

There was another glimmer in the old man's eyes. Nick nodded.

"That's what I figured. So, I guess you're wondering how I'm doing. My restaurant's finally making money, enjoying a boomlet of popularity, I guess you could say. And the girls in New York aren't bad, but a straight guy's got a hell of a lot more competition there than here, if you know what I mean." He laughed, thinking, hoping, that maybe deep down his father was laughing with him.

Nick looked at the man who'd given him life. Tony Sasso was hanging on, refusing to let go. Then he saw the old man's lip quiver, his chin straining as if to speak. Nick leaned close, but all he could hear was a rush of air from the old man's throat.

"You want to say something, don't you, Dad?"

Tony managed a nod.

"Can you write?"

The old man's eyes widened slightly. Understanding, Nick looked around the room, finally finding a pad and pen in a drawer. He brought it to the bed and slipped the pen between Tony's fingers. The old man couldn't lift his hand, so Nick lifted it for him, holding the pen against the pad. His wrist and hand trembling, Tony managed to carve a series of wiggly lines onto the paper. When the hand dropped to the bed, Nick removed the pen and looked at the pad. The squiggles looked like a kindergartner's rendering of the alphabet, a map of Lombard Street. But there were two discernible words on the page—"D-O-N-T Q-U-I-T."

Nick looked at the paper, then at his father, and back to the paper again. The letters he saw were all the more powerful for the desperation of their making. This, he realized, was more than fatherly advice—it was a cry for help. The old man was asking him to see things through for all their sakes.

At his father's sickbed, Nick Sasso had come to a fork in the road, a place where the questions of a lifetime coalesced into one profound and fundamental question of being. Did he stay and see this through, or did he go back to New York and get on with his life? More importantly, perhaps, was whether the time had come to look the past in the eye, or simply punt and live on to deal with it another day. When was the time ripe for a man to look deep into own his soul? For his father's sake, if for no other reason, Nick wanted to say the time was now.

Folding the piece of paper neatly, he looked in the old man's eye and said, "I won't quit, Dad."

Maybe it was projection on his part, but he thought he saw relief on his father's face. Leaning over, he kissed him on the forehead again, then looked for some distraction.

"I see you got a TV set. Hasn't anybody asked if you wanted to see a game? These nurses must not know they've got a baseball fan in residence. Let's see if I can find something."

He turned on the set that was mounted on the wall. Flipping through the channels, he found an A's game. They were playing Detroit, not the Yankees, but what the hey, it was the American League.

The two of them watched the game for maybe fifteen or

twenty minutes until Tony drifted off to sleep. Nick turned off the set, kissed his father again, then slipped from the room. This time as he walked down the corridor he saw little but the winding course through the laundry carts and wheelchairs, the pill wagons and mop buckets. The only cry he heard was the plaintive wail of his own heart.

THE MARINA

Alexei Sakharov, craving a drink more than life, parked around the corner, slid Igor's 9mm automatic out from under the seat and weighed it in his hand. The hooker, Jolie, was installed back in the motel room with halves of the four hundred-dollar bills he had torn in two. He'd put the other halves in his pocket, warning her not to start on the booze until he got back.

"Where you going, anyway?" she'd asked.

"None of your fucking business."

"This is kind of crazy, bringin' me here and takin' off, ain't it?"

"What do you have to worry about? You're getting paid for a night, aren't you? And instead of spreading your legs, you get to lay here watching TV, eating bonbons...at least until I get back." He chuckled, twitching his arched eyebrow. "That's when you better hold on to your hat, sugar pie."

Alexei had set up a reward for himself—do the hit, collect the reward. God in heaven, was he ever looking forward to it. A sweet black girl and a bottle of vodka. America and Russia. The best of both worlds.

Reaching under his coat, he slipped the gun into his belt, then got out of the car, walking as unobtrusively as possible back to Culp's office. He was a bundle of nerves, but he told himself his future was on the line, indeed, his whole life. He had to get over this hurdle, and once he did it would be a piece of cake from here on out.

When he got to the building, he saw that the front blinds were drawn but there was light coming from inside. After glancing up and down the street, he stepped to the entrance to the building and opened the door with a gloved hand.

Muttering an expletive in Russian for courage, Alexei Sakharov entered the vestibule, removing the automatic from his belt. The lettering on the door to his right read, Sanford P. Culp, Attorney-at-Law. Testing it, he found the door unlocked.

Alexei took a couple of deep breaths, thought about the watermelons and the money awaiting him, then quietly slipped inside.

NORTH BEACH

By the time Nick reached the Yankee Clipper, the height of the dinner hour was over. He was surprised to find Linda Nassari and Gennaro Ravara still there. "What's with you two?" he said to Linda, who was standing at the podium when he came in the door. "Don't either of you have a life?"

"The evening hostess called in sick," she told him, "and since I want to buy a new sofa, I volunteered to stay and make a little extra moola. Gennaro works a split shift three days a week. Says once he's out of bed he doesn't mind a long day. That way he gets more days off."

"Incredible. The guy's a man of steel."

"A good quality in a man," she said with a wink.

Nick rewarded the quip with a smile. Linda looked at him the way women do when they're sizing a man up. He suspected she was thinking back on their times together with fondness.

"You hungry?" she asked.

"Not especially. I had a late lunch, plus two meals on the plane."

"It's been a long day for you, hasn't it? How about something light? A salad and a glass of wine?"

"Actually, a glass of wine would be nice. And a salad, too. Good idea."

Linda led the way back to Benny Vocino's booth, swinging her ass like before. He plopped down on the banquette and Linda signaled Gennaro. Nick thanked her and watched her return to her place up front. A woman on the loose, sending signals, was hard to ignore. He weighed the pros and cons. Getting involved with a ghost from the past was the last thing he needed at a time like this. But he couldn't deny the allure.

When Gennaro came by, Nick told him what he wanted and then sagged against the banquette, taken by exhaustion. He was wrung out emotionally, yet, in an odd way, he felt renewed. He'd come home more out of obligation than anything else, but now he had a sense of purpose that transcended more financial success. Maybe the old man had given him a gift as well as a burden. He wanted to think so.

His first, and perhaps greatest, challenge was to save someone who seemingly had no desire to be saved. Joe and Gina were both a worry.

After leaving the nursing home, Nick had gone by their place, but nobody was home—or they wouldn't answer the door. He hoped to hell Gina's remark about wanting to shoot Joe was hyperbole. She wasn't the violent type, but high emotion did strange things to people, especially in the face of infidelity. Nick could attest to that.

Gennaro brought him a bottle of the old man's favorite Chianti. In a way, it was fitting. As much as anytime in his life, Nick felt like Tony Sasso's son. Having a glass of Chianti in the Yankee Clipper and ogling the hostess was how the old man had spent his life. And the sad reality was that Tony was at the end of the line. Nick knew it when he saw him. And the old man knew it, as well. But in spite of that, or maybe because of it, there was one last battle to be waged. Nick had been anointed protector of the family standard. Whether he was up to the task, whether the ghosts of the past were to be vanquished, remained to be seen. But he was determined to give it his best shot.

Nick checked the time. It was late in New York, nearing midnight, but he felt a strong urge to talk to Bree. He wanted a nostalgic glimpse of what he was giving up, at least for a while. There would be life after this was over, he told himself. He wanted what he'd found in New York to wait for him. If it would, it might find him returning a better man.

He dialed her number in Brooklyn, prepared to apologize for waking her. But she didn't answer. He left a message on her machine, mainly to see if she might pick up the phone, but she didn't. "Just wanted to see how things are going," he said. "Looks like I might be tied up here a little longer than I thought. Don't burn yourself out at the restaurant. Take time off and have some fun." He waited and, when she didn't pick up the phone, he hung up, disappointed. She probably went to a movie or something.

Nick took a big gulp of wine and had a few bites of salad. He thought of Bree the day they'd gone to Yankee Stadium—the reaction she'd gotten from men on the subway and in the stands—and asked himself if he could consider marrying a woman like that. The answer that came to him with clarity was no—not until she'd grown up and, maybe more to the point, not until he'd grown up, as well. The good news was that his dear old dad had given him a push in the right direction.

An emergency vehicle went down Columbus Avenue, its siren blaring. Nick shivered, once again gripped by an ominous feeling. Then, as though the siren had been his cue, Donny McCabe came walking in the door.

The ghosts were coming at him fast and furious now. Not yet in town twenty-four hours and already he'd encountered reminders of every shameful thing he'd ever done. Who would be next? His truant officer?

Donny McCabe had not been a central figure in Nick's life, but he'd been a pal of Terry Hughes, Cindy's lover and her unindicted coconspirator in adultery. More importantly, perhaps, Donny had been a brother cop, another inspector in Homicide during Nick's tenure in the section. While not directly involved in any of Nick's woes, Donny had seen it all: Nick brought to his knees by the forces of justice and his own stupidity, costing him his career in law enforcement.

Donny McCabe had also witnessed the destruction of Nick's marriage. Despite all that, he'd been one of the most tolerant and understanding players on the scene, giving him more slack than most. They hadn't been friends, but neither were they enemies.

McCabe talked to Linda up front. She shook her head several times. Donny looked unhappy. Then she pointed back in Nick's direction. McCabe squinted to see. Nick recalled that he had vision problems—hated wearing glasses and couldn't tolerate contact lenses. Donny was a tall guy, long and lanky. Had he been a ballplayer, they might have called him the Junior Big Unit because of his resemblance to Randy Johnson.

Not surprisingly, Donny McCabe left Linda and made his way back toward Benny Vocino's memorial booth. Nick was not particularly thrilled, but he was loath to show it. He got to his feet, hoping for a quick "Hello, how you doing?" then be done with it.

"Well, I'll be damned," Donny said. "Didn't expect to find you here."

"Hi, Inspector McCabe."

They shook hands.

"It's no longer inspector," the visitor said. "I resigned from the force a couple years ago. Now it's Vice President McCabe."

"Vice President?"

"Yeah, I'm vice president of security for Western Pacific Bank."

"Well, congratulations."

McCabe shrugged. "The title's impressive, the salary not so much so. What brings you to San Francisco, if you don't mind me asking? I heard you were living back East."

"Yeah, New York. I'm here on family business."

"I am, too, in a manner of speaking. Actually, I'm looking for your brother. Haven't been very successful tracking him down in daylight hours, so thought I'd try evening."

Nick could see this might be going somewhere so he asked McCabe to join him.

"Maybe for a minute or two," Donny said.

They sat in the booth.

"Glass of wine?" Nick asked.

"No, thanks. Coffee maybe, if that's not too much trouble."

"Not at all." Nick stopped a busboy who was passing by and told him to bring McCabe a cup of coffee. "So, what do you need to see Joe about, assuming it's not confidential?"

"It is and it isn't. But, considering you're family and a former owner of this place, you'd be interested and maybe you can help."

"What do you mean, *former* owner? I still have an interest in the Yankee Clipper."

"No shit?"

"Yeah. What makes you think I didn't?"

"Joe told us he bought you out."

"He bought part of my interest, but not all."

"Christ, this is worse than I thought," McCabe said, putting his head in his hands.

"What's this about, Donny?"

"The details of a bank's relationship with its customers is confidential, not that I know all that much. They tell me what they figure I need to do my job."

"Don't stand on ceremony," Nick said. "This is a family

operation and you're talking to family. Anyway, you can deny telling me anything. Who would they believe in this town? You or Nick Sasso?"

"You got a point."

Nick would have preferred McCabe not to be so quick to agree, but he could hardly complain. The busboy brought the coffee, but the V.P. of security for Western Pacific Bank ignored it.

"Okay," Donny said, "off the record." He lowered his voice. "Several months ago Joe borrowed a large amount of money from the bank."

"How large are we talking?"

"Mid six figures."

Nick felt his stomach drop.

"So, anyway," McCabe went on, "Joe put up a couple of his buildings and the restaurant as collateral. Because of his strong financial statement, not much checking was done, but our loan department found out later that the buildings had already been leveraged to the hilt. No equity. Things got real bad when Joe never made a scheduled payment on the loan. Our people tried to talk to him, but he wouldn't cooperate. The bank decided to come after the restaurant, figuring that would put the fear of God in him. Even though he has a power of attorney for your father and signed loan documents for him, we notified your dad of our intention to take over the restaurant."

"Donny, when was this?"

"They sent him a letter the end of last week. Tony came unglued, apparently. Called up, claiming he hadn't signed any power of attorney and that the bank was full of shit. They sent me to see him on Tuesday, after the holiday weekend, but he was in the hospital by then."

"I wonder why?"

"Hey, don't go blaming me, or for that matter the bank. We're going by what Joe told us. We got a signed power of attorney in our file. What I'm trying to find out is if it was forged, because if it was we're turning this over to the police.

"Let me get this straight. Your bank intends to take possession of the Yankee Clipper?"

"The powers that be are going to do whatever is necessary to protect the loan, let's put it that way. I'm trying to find out what the hell is going on. Meanwhile, our lawyers have gotten into the act. I've got legal papers in my pocket, which I'm going to serve your brother, if I can ever find his ass."

Nick couldn't imagine a worse scenario. He had a sudden headache and pressed his temples. He pictured his father's beseeching eyes, his voiceless desperation. The phrase "don't quit" took on new and deeper meaning.

"I can see this is coming out of the blue," Donny said. "I'm sorry, but the guy you need to talk to is Joe."

"Yes, I know. And I will. You won't be surprised to hear that my brother's got other problems. But he's also got a plan for cleaning everything up. I know that's not going to calm the bank, but that's what he's told me."

"As the boys in the loan department would say, 'Show me the green.'"

Donny McCabe picked up his coffee cup and took a long drink. "So, how are things going for you, Nick? I guess you went back East to get a fresh start."

"Things are fine...in New York. My problems at the moment are right here."

"The more things change, the more they're the same, huh?"

"Yeah, right."

Nick couldn't have put it any better. The only difference now was that, instead of being the one fucking up, he was the one cleaning up. Of course, this was only his first day in town. There was plenty of time to find some trouble of his own.

Meanwhile, he saw McCabe's visit as an opportunity to

catch up. "Tell me, Donny, what's been happening in the City by the Bay? I literally haven't heard a thing outside the family for over five years."

"Your ex and Terry got married finally, I guess you heard that."

"No, but I'm not surprised. The man has my sympathy."

McCabe chuckled.

Nick said, "What do you hear from the boys in Homicide? Do you keep in touch?"

"You really want to talk about that?"

"I take it you don't."

Donny McCabe shrugged. "Your jersey isn't exactly hanging on the wall down there, Nick."

"I don't suppose it is. How about Dickson Hong? He retired yet?"

"No, but he's getting close."

"Still in Homicide?"

"After what happened, they weren't going to make him lieutenant. I think he's just thankful they didn't put him on the street out at Hunters Point."

Of all the consequences of his fall from grace, the damage done to Dickson Hong's career was probably the thing Nick regretted most. Dickson had stood by him right up to the end, when Noble Allard had gone to trial. Hong had taken the stand, having no idea what was about to hit him. The defense counsel, Sonny Culp, had torn them both limb from limb, torpedoing the state's case, embarrassing the department, the D.A.'s office, everybody. Nick deserved what he got. Dickson didn't.

Though more than half a decade had passed, Nick could still hear Culp's voice rising in the courtroom. "Isn't it true, Inspector Hong, that you were the lead investigator at the crime scene?"

"Yes, sir."

"And as such, it's your responsibility to make sure that the other officers are performing their duties correctly."

"Being senior, that was my responsibility, yes."

"Then why is it that you took Inspector Sasso's word for it that the alleged murder weapon had been in his custody during that critical first hour of the investigation at the crime scene?"

"I've never known Inspector Sasso to be untruthful, Counselor."

"But he was, wasn't he? Inspector Sasso lied to his superiors, filed fallacious reports, altered records—"

"Objection," the prosecutor said, jumping to his feet. "Counsel's being argumentative."

"Sustained," the judge said. "Mr. Culp, please direct your questions to the facts of the case."

"Thank you, Your Honor." Sonny Culp had walked in a large slow circle in front of the witness stand, then stopped and said to Dickson Hong, "There has been testimony, damning testimony, about Inspector Sasso's lies and misdeeds. My question, Inspector Hong, is why these irregularities—dare I say criminal acts—escaped your notice? Was the truth inconvenient to the police, Inspector, or were you simply derelict in the execution of your responsibilities?"

"I wasn't as diligent as I should have been, Counselor."

"You weren't diligent, you say. And here sits a man accused of murder, his life on the line, while one officer has been shown to have tampered with the evidence against him and the officer in charge, you, Inspector Hong, admit that you were not as diligent as you should have been in discovering this wrongdoing."

Sonny Culp then walked slowly and deliberately to the jury box, running his hand over his bald pate. "Tell me, Inspector," he said, looking into the eyes of the jurors, "who should these good people feel compassion for? A man whose life is hanging in the balance or a police force that is negligent, incompetent and lacking in diligence?"

"Objection!" the prosecutor screamed.

Sonny Culp lifted his hands in surrender, turned and

walked back to the defense table, shaking his head. "No further questions, Your Honor."

Nick could not think of the trial without cringing. He'd apologized to Dickson Hong that day and the day he'd gathered his things from his desk and left the department. Each time Hong had sat stoically, listening. His one comment to Nick was, "I made a mistake in judgment, too." What he'd meant, of course, was that he'd trusted his partner when he shouldn't have. It was the cruelest, most cutting indictment of all. But it was deserved. Nick had no grounds for complaint. The greater victim, in a sense, had been Dickson Hong.

LOMBARD STREET

Jolie Hays lay on the bed, staring at the faded drapes, wondering what kind of bullshit her honky john was up to. He'd been gone an hour and she thought maybe he wasn't coming back. True, he did tear those hundreds in half but, if they didn't do him no good, they didn't do her no good, either.

Jolie was new enough at this business that she didn't have it all figured out yet, but she was learning, and more importantly, she was making money. Tough way to do it, that was for sure, but it was only temporary, if her plans worked out.

As far as this john with the funny accent was concerned, Jolie didn't know whether to be worried or not. If he had something bad up his sleeve, seems she would know by now. That was what a girl on the streets had to worry about—the crazies. This one was strange, but so far he'd treated her right...*if* he showed up with the other halves of those hundred-dollar bills.

Just then she heard some fumbling outside the motel-room door, then the sound of a key in the lock. The door opened. Jerry appeared, a big grin on his face.

"You ready to par*tee,* sugar pie?" he asked, slamming the door shut behind him.

Jerry French—she didn't believe for a minute it was his real name—had rosy cheeks and bright eyes with a funny look about them. She couldn't say in what way. Maybe dangerous.

"You remember the other half of the money?" she asked, wanting to get that settled right up front.

Jerry slipped his hand in his pocket, extracted a torn bill, crawled across the bed to her and poked it between her breasts. Jolie pulled it out and looked at it.

"How about that," he said. "I've only been in the room thirty seconds and already you're a hundred dollars richer."

"Yeah, and I've been sittin' on my ass for over an hour, too."

"Well, why don't you get out of your clothes then, and let's make up for lost time."

Jolie scooted over to the edge of the bed and stood. Jerry took off his jacket and hung it on a chair. Jolie pulled her gold lamé dress over her head, folded it and laid it on the top of the dresser, leaving her in nothing but her panties and bra. Jerry turned to watch, grinning again and flicking his eyebrows.

"You sure in a fine mood," she said. "Getting laid that much fun?"

"Sugar pie, I just made the easiest hundred thousand I'll ever make in my whole damn life."

"You say what?"

"I'm a rich man, Jolie."

"What you do, anyway? Rob some bank or some'in'?"

"That's not your concern, honey. Your job is to open your legs so I can fuck your brains out. I sure hope you're ready."

He went over and grabbed the bottle of vodka from the table where he'd left it. After pouring some in two glasses, he brought one to her. Jolie had her bra off. Jerry took one of her breasts in his hand, leaned over and ran his tongue around her nipple, sucked on it a couple of times, then took a little nip with his teeth.

"Ow!"

He laughed. Then, touching his glass to hers, he tipped it

up and swallowed the vodka in three or four gulps. Jolie, amazed, took a little sip from her glass and put it down the dresser. Jerry patted her on the butt and said, "Now take off those panties."

NORTH BEACH

It did not appear to Nick that Joe had been using the studio in the same fashion as the old man. To the contrary, it didn't look as if the room had been used much at all. Somebody had stacked boxes of supplies in the corner, including two huge cartons of toilet paper. The bed remained as in his father's day, and there were neatly folded sheets lying on the corner of the mattress. The place was dusty, further proof that it hadn't seen much action.

The bed was modest and the bath and a half off the office not exactly luxurious, but they were adequate. Anyway, after the expense of a last-minute plane ticket, Nick was glad to spare himself San Francisco room rates.

The first thing he did was take a nice hot shower. When he got back to the room, wearing his bathrobe, he found Linda Nassari. She'd made the bed and was sitting on it, her legs crossed and her skirt fanned out on the blanket.

"I took the liberty of getting the place a little more hospitable," she said. "There's another glass of wine on the table. And the rest of the bottle."

He could see what was happening. The question was, did he want to go there? "Very considerate. Thank you."

"My pleasure."

Linda's appeal was that she was friendly. So far, he'd been hammered by everybody he'd talked to, and the prospect of a soft hand and an open heart was inviting. Linda had already shown compassion, and she remained one of the more positive experiences of his teen years. Sure, their relationship had been illicit, criminal even, with shades of Oedipal high jinks, but she'd made him a man. That was worth an awful lot.

Earlier, after Donny McCabe had left, she'd come to the booth and sat down with him. "Everything all right, Nick?" she'd asked.

"Actually, no."

"Anything you want to talk about?"

"Let's put it this way. I've come to realize that sins of the past die slowly and that when somebody screws up, the innocent suffer as much as those who deserve it."

"Huh?"

"Frankly, I don't want to talk about it," he'd said. "If the past has to be dredged up, better I think of the things I did as a naughty seventeen-year-old. At least that was fun."

Linda had blushed. "It was, wasn't it?"

Nick, now more chastened, but freshly showered, at least, went over to the table. "Only one glass?"

"I thought coming up here was pretty presumptuous already," she replied.

"Not among old friends." He sat on the bed next to her. "We can share," he said, handing her the glass.

Linda tossed her streaked blond hair back in a seductive way, then took a sip of wine. She gave him back the glass. "This is an odd time to ask, I know, but I take it you're unattached."

"I have a girlfriend, but it's a casual relationship."

"It's not serious?"

"I took her to a Yankees game the other day. I don't know if you consider that serious or not."

She took the glass from his hand and took a bigger sip. "I did the married-man thing in my youth," she said. "I vowed not to fall into that trap this time around. Fiancées, either."

"It's not that kind of relationship."

"I like to ask *long* before anything happens."

Nick could see that assumptions were being made right

and left. And, while he hadn't planned on hitting on Linda, here they were in the royal bedchamber, sharing a glass of wine and talking about the rules of the game. She put the glass back in his hand.

"Mind a personal question?" he asked.

"No."

"What's it like being in this room, twenty years after the fact?"

"You and I didn't do it here, Nick. It was always at my apartment. Don't you remember?"

"I wasn't referring to us."

"Oh, you're talking about Tony." She glanced around the room. "I couldn't help thinking about it, to be honest. In fact, my second or third day back on the job I sneaked up here to have a peek."

"Fond recollections?"

"I was taking a walk down memory lane, remembering what it was like to be young. But I wasn't just young back then, I was naive and stupid, too."

"*You* were young?" Nick said, taking a long sip from the glass.

Linda nodded, her smile knowing. "They'd probably throw me in jail nowadays. But I've got to be honest, I do have fond memories of those times."

"Tell me, what was it like having a father and son...unless that's too personal a question?"

"I was role-playing. Like most kids, I was self-possessed and frivolous. Tony was the boss, sort of a sexy father figure. I liked him. He could be really sweet. He knew how to make a girl feel good. Tony was fun, made sex a game. He gave me flowers. It was all so kitschy and old-fashioned, but I was lonely and didn't have anything else going on in my life. I figured it wouldn't last more than four or five months, and it didn't."

It was the first time he'd had a glimpse of the old man

through the eyes of one of his women. Back when he and Linda were intimate, she hadn't talked much about "the boss," other than the occasional comment or to answer a question— not that Nick himself had been particularly eager to discuss his father. He'd certainly been aware of the implications of his conquest, though—the king is dead, long live the king. The mantle of manliness had been passed.

Nick drank more Chianti. Linda got up, went to the table, refilled the glass and returned.

"Are you wondering why I seduced the boss's son?"

Nick shrugged.

"First, because you were cute and very mature for your age. And second, because it gave me a feeling of power. With Tony, he was very much in charge. You were like my student. I guess a lot of people would say that's sick, but..." She drank some wine. "Never mind me, how was it for you, screwing your father's mistress?"

Nick pondered how he'd felt. "To tell you the truth, I don't know if I was being my own man, or if I was trying to be him."

"Maybe it was a little of both, Nick."

He thought about that. He thought about the whisper of Tony Sasso he'd seen at the nursing home that night, the passing of the torch from father to son, the charge he'd been given. Linda gave him an even greater awareness of the fact that he stood in his father's shoes.

She reached over and wiped away the tear running down his cheek with her thumb. Another tear came. She put her arm around him and rested her head on his shoulder.

To Nick it was more than being seventeen again, revisiting an earlier time in his life. A lot of shit had been packed into the memory banks in the interim. Hell, he and his teacher had both done a lot of living since she'd taught him all the marvelous uses of an erection. And there had been transformations, as well, a pivotal one having occurred just that evening.

"You been to see your father?" she asked him.

"Yeah, tonight."

"How is he?"

"Dying."

She patted his bare thigh. "I'm sorry, Nick." She gave his leg a squeeze. "Life is not a bowl of cherries. There are always pits. Tony used to say that."

Nick nodded. Damn, if another tear didn't roll down his cheek.

He had a very strong desire to screw Linda Meyer just then—not Linda Nassari, Linda Meyer. He wasn't sure why, whether it was to embrace his youth or vanquish it. Sex, they say, is an abbreviated form of death, the ultimate release. That could explain it. "Make me a man, Linda," his soul seemed to be pleading, "Make me a man, like you did before."

Their cheeks touched first, then their lips. Her hand slid under his robe and grasped his cock.

Two minutes later they were naked, at the end of the bed, she on her back with a pillow under her derriere, her calves wrapped around his neck. Nick rubbed his cock against her moist crease, not as hard as when he was seventeen, but doing a credible imitation. She'd taught him this somewhere around lesson five.

Nick took Linda's broad, white hips in his hands, and leaned into her until he reached bottom, making her gulp, just the way she had twenty years ago. He began undulating, and she caressed herself, their common rhythm building in harmony. They were both at the point of orgasm when there was a sudden loud rap on the door. It flew open. They both turned their heads. There stood Gennaro Ravara, the same frown on his face as always.

"I know this isn't the best time," he muttered, "but I've got bad news."

Nick, frozen with incredulity, didn't have it in him to ask what.

"It's your brother," the old waiter explained.

"What about him?"

Gennaro drew a long breath, then spit out the words. "Nick, Joe's been murdered!"

LOMBARD STREET

By the time the john finally got his rocks off for the second time, Jolie Hays felt as if she'd been drilled and then some. She'd had men who fucked with enthusiasm, but this Jerry was a maniac. He rolled off her, leaving her soaked in their sweat.

Two or three minutes passed before he said, "Bet you a hundred dollars you can't drink a shot of vodka for every two of mine."

Jolie blinked. They'd already drunk a third of the bottle. "I know your game. You tryin' to get me drunk so you can steal my money."

"No, soon as you pass out, I'm going to fuck you in the ass."

"No way. You done me twice already. How you going to get it up again? Never happen."

"A hundred dollars says you're wrong, sugar pie," he'd said.

"Let me see your money. No more of this half-bill shit."

Jerry got up and took five twenties from his wallet and dropped them on her wet stomach.

"You serious."

"Damn right."

"You drink two, but I only have to drink one."

"That's it."

"Shit, man, that like stealin' candy from a baby."

"Want me to go first?"

"Be my guest."

Already half-drunk, they sat side by side on the sagging bed in a motel room filled with blond furniture, and started downing neat shots of vodka. By the time the fifth shot was in her hand, the room was spinning so bad she had to hold on to the headboard with one hand. "Your fuckin'...stomach, made of iron...motherfucker."

"Give up?" he said with a grin.

"Fuck...you...Jerry."

With that Jolie downed the shot. She was only conscious another thirty seconds. When she came to he was riding her ass, fucking the bejesus out of her. Somehow she got her face to the edge of the mattress and threw up on the floor. Jerry kept laughing and humping, not slowing down a bit.

"Goddamn, but I'm good!" he shouted, going at it. "Just be glad you're only getting your brains *fucked* out. Those other two sons of bitches got them *blown* out! Yippee! I'm rich!"

She was aware of him collapsing on her, hanging on before he rolled off. She could hear his labored breathing.

"Я дюбдю вáс," he muttered.

Amazingly, out of the swirling confusion of her brain, she formed a semicoherent thought. That was Russian, she told herself. She'd heard people say it in Germany. It was one of the few Russian phrases she knew. The motherfucker had just said, "I love you."

RICHMOND DISTRICT

Billie Fox hated men so much she could scream. Actually, that wasn't true. She didn't hate men, she hated vetting them—separating the goats from the sheep, the creeps, the morons and the egoists from the occasional mensch. The undeniable fact was there were far too few decent guys in this world, and the genuinely nice ones seemed either to have bad breath or a wife.

And so, as the evening came to an end—the finale of her first date in four or five months—Billie was not in the best of moods. Roger had barely brought the little sports car to a stop in front of her house, than she was out on the sidewalk. Knowing she had to go through a good-night ritual of some sort, she braced herself to shake his hand.

The streetlight was bright enough for her to see his determined expression—that look that said, "Somehow, someway, I'm going to score." Since it was their first date, the chances were he'd set his sights on a good-night kiss, a bellwether signal for dates to come. The thing was, Billie had already decided there'd be no more dates. This was it. *Nada mas.*

Not that he wasn't a nice man. Granted, he was boring, but that could be forgiven, considering this was his first time out of the chute since his divorce. The guy hadn't played the dating game for twenty-five years, and her tolerant side reasoned he deserved some slack. But the simple fact was, Billie Fox didn't have the nurse mentality, the patience. She was a scrapper, a gunslinger, a tough broad—some might argue a bitch—and she was too busy, by a damn sight, to waste time soothing a bruised ego, building a guy's self-confidence, helping him back to social and emotional health. Besides, the good doctor, eligible though he may be, wasn't her type.

"Well, Roger," she said in her best and most commanding courtroom voice, "I had a good time. Thank you for a very nice evening."

Dr. Roger Barlow, if a bit rusty, was no fool. He read the message in her tone loud and clear. Clearing his throat, he said, "You aren't going to let me walk you to the door?" The guy had the kind of throbbing baritone that could produce goose bumps—a major reason she'd agreed to the date in the first place—but he was more promise than performance. A fifty-year-old physician with a new sports car, a new penthouse apartment, an old wife still in the family home out in St. Francis Woods and two kids in college—USC and Pepperdine—was so loaded with baggage that her little canoe simply wasn't up to the task.

"My legs might be skinny," she said, "but they'll get me up the steps."

Roger Barlow assumed that complacently benign, but dutifully kind expression that doctors wore like stethoscopes. "I think you know what I mean, Billie."

"We're being frank, are we?"

"I prefer it."

"All right," she said with a sigh. "You're a nice man. A very nice man, and I mean that sincerely. But you're also newly divorced. A person in your circumstances—*anybody* in your circumstances—is a danger, especially to themselves. The long and the short of it, Roger, is this—you have a lot of crap to work through and I don't have the time, the energy or the inclination to go through it with you, nice though you may be."

"You're a brutally honest woman, Billie."

"Hey, when you spend your days dealing with soulless thugs and crusty cops and cynical judges, you develop a habit of telling it like it is."

His smile grew more benevolent. "Let me ask you this. You knew my circumstances going in. Why did you agree to go out to dinner with me?"

"We're still being honest?"

Roger smoothed his thick silver hair with an elegant sweep of his hand. "By all means."

"One, you're not chopped liver, no matter how you cut it. Two, the voice. Three, I think everybody has a secret desire to be proven wrong on something they know to be true."

"Evidently I didn't quite cut the mustard."

"I'm forty-three, Roger. I'm a cancer survivor and I'm divorced. Neither people nor life surprise me much anymore. But I still indulge myself occasionally. Believe me, you done good tonight by any standard. When the moment of truth comes, though, it's always best to go with what you know in your gut to be right, and that's what I'm doing."

"Might your feelings be different, say, a year from now?"

"Possibly. Who knows? But my prediction is you'll be otherwise occupied. I don't need to tell you how eligible you are."

"And, of course, that makes me want you all the more...which you fully realize, I suspect."

"Know this about me," Billie said. "I don't play games."

His smile reflected his amusement. "I had a very nice evening, Ms. Fox, including this conversation. Thank you." With that, he kissed her on the cheek and returned to his Mercedes sports car. He gave a little wave before climbing in and driving away.

Billie's gait as she climbed up the long flight of steps to the front door was more gimpy than it would have been had Roger Barlow, M.D. still been standing on the sidewalk. It was partly because of her bunion and partly because of her state of mind. She really didn't like dating, but she went out from time to time, anyway, if only to prove she wasn't a nun in civilian clothing. And, despite what she'd said to Roger, deep down she believed that lightning did occasionally strike in unlikely places. The odds notwithstanding, somebody *did* win the lottery, didn't they? Of course, she never played unless the prize went over fifty million, which showed that bigger stakes produced bigger fools. In her experience, the same thing applied to socializing with men.

Billie got her keys out of her purse and let herself in. Closing the door behind her, she leaned hard against it, her shoulders slumping. She played back Roger Barlow's voice in her mind, not so much for the words as the sound, wondering without conviction if she'd been precipitous. Second-guessing, she knew, was an important part of the ritual.

Gathering herself after a moment, she went into the front room where she found her father snoring away—or, more accurately, wheezing, he didn't snore—in the big brown leather easy chair he'd brought with him from Fresno, the late news purring just loud enough for a person to catch every third word. Once Emily was in bed, her grandfather would turn down the sound so as not to disturb her. "Dad," Billie once told him, "six-year-olds sleep like the dead. An earthquake eight points on the Richter scale wouldn't wake her."

"It's not just sleep that matters," her father replied in the patient but instructive tone of the schoolteacher he'd been, "it's the *quality* of the sleep." That was Mel Fox, as devoted to his granddaughter as he'd been to his daughter. A more saintly and selfless man had never lived.

As to his addiction to TV, Mel would only say, "Everybody's got something and you have to admit this habit's more harmless than most." Billie figured that at first her dad used TV as an antidote to loneliness. It was a way to be *of* the world without really being *in* the world. Once she'd moved out of their home in Fresno to make a life in the big city, Mel Fox had been left without purpose. He'd continued teaching sixth grade, but the heart of his existence had been ripped out. He'd devoted nearly twenty years to being both Billie's father and mother. And, just as importantly, he'd been determined to compensate spiritually and emotionally for the abandonment Billie felt when, virtually without warning, her mother, Betty, up and left them. Billie was not yet five at the time.

She could not look at her dad, whether he was awake or sleeping as he was now, without feeling tremendous love and gratitude for what he'd done. Most amazing of all, Mel Fox had never asked for anything in return. Loving service contained all the reward he needed. How many men were like that? And why couldn't she find one who loved her with the same unyielding devotion as her dear old dad?

During her visits to Fresno, Billie would tell him that he needed to make a life for himself, that it was long past time to get a little selfish. He'd demur, saying that he had his students and a few friends. That was all he needed.

Despite his denials, Mel had a hole in his life that TV and volunteer work couldn't fill. It was three years after he'd retired from teaching that Billie and Sonny split up. She didn't even nod in the direction of the single-working-mom routine. Sonny wasn't out of the house a week before Billie called her dad and said, "How'd you like to raise another little girl?"

The arrangement, now nearly four years old, had been a godsend for them all. Billie could concentrate on her law practice without guilt, Mel had another shot at his true life's calling—parent and homemaker—and Emily had a doting, devoted parent figure always at hand, ready to care for her, guide her and love her unconditionally.

Slipping off her shoes and flexing her swollen feet, Billie picked up the remote control from the floor beside her father's chair and turned off the TV. "Come on, Pop," she said, gently shaking his shoulder. "Time for bed."

Mel awoke with a start, blinking. "Oh, Billie, you're home. Didn't even hear you come in."

"How could you over the roar of the TV?" she said, giving him a wink.

Mel, still spry at sixty-eight, but far too sedentary even by his own admission, sat upright, rubbing his eyes. "How was the date?"

"Let me put it this way, I'm glad Roger did the bypass on you last month and not next week."

"He acted like you owed him just because he saved my life?"

"I wouldn't say that," Billie said, taking off her black gabardine jacket and laying it over the arm of the sofa. "More than anything we just didn't click." She dropped onto the cushion.

"That's too bad, honey. He seemed to have a lot going for him."

"Looks, money, success, intelligence...yeah, the foundation was there, all right."

"But your heart didn't go ping."

"Pop, my heart stopped going ping when I was sixteen. What I hope for now is some kind of convergence—friendship with a dollop of chemistry." She reflected. "Hell, I'm not looking for anything, truth be known. I just go about my business and let fate come to me. My work is all I need."

"You're still young, Wilhelmina."

Her father rarely called her by her given name, and when he did it was to signal serious intent—he was too considerate to lecture or pontificate. That had enabled them to have adult conversations back before she was a teenager. "Early middle age, Pop. I ain't no spring chicken."

"From my perspective you are."

"Thanks."

"I guess you won't be seeing Dr. Barlow again."

"You know, Dad, I'm surprised the good doctor wanted to go out with me in the first place. I may be seven years younger, but that's a far cry from the thirty-five-year-olds men his age go for when they're fresh out of the cage. Granted, I'm not fat, but I'm too tall, I'm several degrees shy of pretty and I only have a boob and a half. Do you think he figured I'd be desperate?"

"He saw you for the lovely person you are, Billie."

"Dad, I wish you wouldn't do that."

"What?"

"Exaggerate."

"It's the truth."

"I want you to know I was the only person at the first dance I went to back in the seventh grade who thought I was pretty. It shocked me when Mr. Adamson was the only person who asked me to dance."

"That was because you were six inches taller than all the boys and you were as fearless then as you are now. How many thirteen-year-old boys are equipped to deal with that?"

"See, thirty years later you're still trying to make me feel good about a disastrous seventh-grade dance."

"I have to stay in practice for Emily," her father said with a crooked smile.

Billie reached over and patted his knee. "I think I'm going to call it a night."

"I hope you at least had a nice dinner."

"Yeah, it was great. I especially liked the Caesar salad," she said, pointing to the spot on her taupe gabardine slacks where a leaf of lettuce had taken the plunge from her fork to her lap. "These babies are headed for the cleaners."

Billie was always amazed how undone she felt after a date, as opposed to how crisp and pristine she felt when gazing into the mirror at the beginning of an evening. That seemed to be true whether a little rolling around on some guy's couch was involved or not. Amazing what six hours of sleep, a shower and a fresh blouse could do for a girl, however.

Removing her pearl stud earrings—the only jewelry she wore—Billie got to her feet and offered her hand to her dad. Mel grasped it and she pulled him out of his recliner. In her stocking feet, she looked straight across at him, though not that many years ago he had an inch or two on her. The ravages of time.

Just then there was a knock at the front door. Billie and her father looked at each other. Surely Roger hadn't returned to make another stab at a good-night kiss. She'd been ready to bet her eyeteeth that Roger Barlow was destined never to darken her door again, whether as friend or foe.

Billie went to the door and looked through the peephole. It wasn't Roger. No tall, patrician-looking silver-hair chap on her stoop. This guy was short, slender, dark-headed. His back was to the door as he peered out at the street. Whoever it was probably was no match for one of her better roundhouse rights, but knowing the lowlife of the city, Billie tended to err on the side of caution.

She turned on the porch light and called, "Who is it?" through the door.

The man turned and she saw that it was Martin Fong. "It's me, Martin," he called back.

Billie, surprised, opened the door. "Martin..." Seeing tears streaming down his face, she stopped before anything more came out.

His face crumpled.

"Martin, what's wrong?"

"It's Sonny," he blubbered. "He's been murdered."

A bolt went through her. *"What?"*

"Shot and killed in his office, along with a client. Half an hour ago the police came and told me." He shivered.

Billie's heart nearly stopped. She couldn't believe what she was hearing. "Who...what..."

Martin shook his head. "They don't know who did it." He choked out a sob, wiping his eyes with thin hands. "I pray to God it had nothing to do with me."

Billie blinked. "What do you mean?"

"You know what my life is like. Politics can be hell."

"But why..."

Martin shuddered. "I don't know. I'm just talking. I...I...I'm in shock."

That was certainly understandable. She was, too.

"Well," Martin said. "I felt it was my duty to let you know...because of Emily. I didn't want you reading it in the paper. I thought you should be prepared."

Billie was too stunned to speak. Sonny? Dead? She shook her head as tears filled her eyes. "Do you want to come in?"

Martin equivocated for a moment. "No," he said in a small voice, "but thank you for asking. I'm going now. I...I...just had to come," he sobbed, "because of Emily. Billie, I love her so much...I...I..." Then, shaking his head as if to say he couldn't deal with it, Martin ran down the steps to his car.

She didn't move until he'd driven off. Then she closed the

door and turned around. Her father stood not far away, obviously having heard everything.

"I'm so sorry," he said.

Billie turned the events of the last few moments over in her mind. Despite whatever else Sonny Culp was, he had been her mentor and her friend, the architect of her career. Losing him like this was, in a sense, more traumatic than Sonny's infidelity and their divorce. Her worst fear had been realized—Emily was down to one parent, a cancer survivor at that.

MARINA DISTRICT

The cool, damp wind blew through the Golden Gate and across the open fields of the rec center, cutting as deeply as the icy East Coast gusts that came down the Hudson in, say, late November. The numbness he felt was the kind that accompanied tragedy that was too big for ordinary comprehension. Nick knew with his head that his brother was dead, but not with his heart.

He was also struggling with the fact that the second victim was Sonny Culp, the one human being apart from Nick himself who was most responsible for his demise. Moreover, Nick couldn't imagine what Joe and Culp would be doing in the same room, much less ending up as the victims of a double homicide.

The patrol officer who'd brought Nick to the crime scene wasn't sure which inspectors were on the case. "I heard somebody mention Carl Plavec," he'd said, "but I don't know the guy." The name meant nothing to Nick, but then it *had* been five years. A third of the Investigation Bureau must have turned over since his departure.

The officer had gone into the building to see when one of the inspectors might speak with him, and Nick had gotten out of the patrol car for some air, having forgotten that August in San Francisco was not August in the Big Apple. Despite his sports coat, he shivered, but his attention wasn't on the weather. He focused on the cordoned-off area across the street, the pastel faces of the buildings tinged red by the flashing lights of the emergency vehicles. The place where his brother had died.

The fear in his heart and the emptiness in his gut had been with him almost from the moment he'd heard about the killing. He worried that Gina was somehow involved. She'd said she wanted to kill Joe. She'd even mentioned his gun. Lord, that would compound the tragedy. Yet he couldn't believe she'd actually do such a thing. Not Gina. Not timid, quiet suffering Gina. And yet...

He began to pace, yearning for a cigarette for the first time in a decade. He tried phoning his sister-in-law again on his cell phone, getting no answer. Not a good sign. The police, he'd heard, had gone by the house to impart the news but no one was home. Nick began to fear the worst. At what point did he say something to the investigators? After he'd spoken with Gina?

Then there was the old man to consider. He'd eventually have to be told, but clearly, this wasn't the time, not in the condition Tony was in. Nick pictured his father's stricken visage, the worry in his eyes, the helplessness. And now old Tony had lost another son. It added a whole new dimension to his plea for Nick to hang in there, not to quit.

As he watched the comings and goings, Nick thought of his brother in another context—as he'd been at their mother's funeral. The depth of Joe's grief had surprised him, the deep sobs shaking his hulking but fragile frame. Their mother had died slowly, and Nick had mourned her in life, during those long months as she failed. Joe, who'd kept an emotional distance as she'd gradually slipped away—whether out of fear of pain or fear of feeling—completely lost it when she'd finally passed. Nick wondered if some similar, unexpected reaction would hit him now. But so far all he felt was numbness and distance. It was the distance that troubled him.

It wasn't long before a solitary figure emerged from the beehive of activity, an unassuming gentleman in a coat and tie, his shoulders slightly rounded, his carriage and gait familiar. He disappeared behind an ambulance, then reappeared, crossing the street now, his attention vaguely focused on Nick. It was Dickson Hong.

The unexpected appearance of his former partner was disquieting. For a moment Nick wondered what he could possibly have to say to him, only then realizing Hong was most likely investigating the crime. Nick waited on the sidewalk until the inspector reached him.

"Hello, Nick," he said.

"Dickson."

"I'm sorry about your brother."

Almost as an afterthought, he extended his hand. Nick took it. Hong's grip had never been firm, nor was it limp. A handshake to Dickson Hong was a substitute for eye contact, something he effected only intermittently. The veteran inspector often spoke to your shoes, your tie or the wall behind you. But when his eyes did meet yours, they penetrated right through you. In an interrogation Hong could be deadly as a cobra lulling its victim into complacency.

"Thanks," Nick said after waiting unsuccessfully for Dickson Hong's eyes to meet his.

There was an awkward moment, then Nick said, "You're handling the case, I take it?"

"My partner, Carl Plavec, and I were on call when it came in."

Hong had a rather flat face and teeth that needed whitening. Part of the problem was he was a smoker. Whenever he was outside he always seemed to have a cigarette pinched between his thumb and middle finger, as he did now.

The inspector's dress was understated, his choice of colors running mostly to browns. He liked tweeds and clearly had his favorite jackets. The sports coat he wore now was somewhat worn, a consequence of too many years in the closet and too many trips to the dry cleaners. Nick remembered when it was new.

The two of them stared at the building. Hong took a drag on his cigarette, grimacing. He always looked as if he was sucking on a lemon when he smoked. As was his habit, he tucked the hand with the cigarette behind his leg, sort of hiding it.

Nick said, "I don't suppose you have any idea what happened."

"Not yet. Culp was shot in the chest at fairly close range, your brother in the back, probably trying to flee."

"Motive?"

"Nothing obvious. There are several possibilities. I don't think it was incidental to a burglary or robbery, anything like that. No break-in. Valuables remained on the bodies. One odd thing is that there isn't much in the way of office equipment in the suite. No computers."

"I think I may be able to explain that."

"Oh?"

Nick told him about the messages on Joe's answering machine, the one Mort Seidel had played for him over the phone and the one Nick had heard at the Clipper, especially the reference to the office being burglarized. "The caller didn't identify himself, but given what's happened, Culp is a likely candidate."

"Yeah, could be. I appreciate the information. I'll check to see if a burglary was reported."

"It might not have been," Nick said. "Assuming the voice on the those recordings was Culp's, he expressed a distrust of the police."

A faint smile flickered over Dickson Hong's mouth, but he refrained from commenting. Instead, he said, "We'll talk to the accountant and listen to what's on the machine, maybe come by tomorrow."

"I'm staying in the little studio above the restaurant, so I'll be there."

"Good. Let's make it first thing."

"Fine."

"Of course, we'll want to talk to Mrs. Sasso, too."

"Gina might like it if I'm there when you speak to her, if that wouldn't be a problem for you, Dick."

Hong gave a half shrug. "You wouldn't know where she is, would you?"

Nick told him about speaking to his sister-in-law on the phone and her anxiety over Joe's affair. He didn't mention her comment about Joe's gun and wanting to shoot him. No sense in creating what could be unwarranted suspicion. It would get sorted out soon enough. Dickson, as would be expected, asked about the affair.

"About all I know is the woman's name and the fact that she's Chinese. Elaine Ching or Chang, something like that."

Hong nodded, processing.

"She could be helpful," Nick said as though the obvious hadn't occurred to Hong, though it surely had. Then, "Do you know her?"

"If it's who I'm thinking of, I know who she is, but not a lot more."

More silent reflection on both sides.

"Who found the bodies?" Nick asked.

"Woman in an upstairs apartment. When she came home, she noticed the law-office door ajar and peeked in, saw the bodies and called 911."

Nick stared at the reflection of the emergency lights in the window of the ground-floor law office, knowing his brother's body was inside. Even so, Joe's death remained an abstract notion, information without complete emotional content.

"I don't suppose you have any theories," Hong said in an offhanded way.

"Not really. Joe's been having financial problems and was under a lot of pressure. I know that. If he was feeling the heat, other people obviously were steamed, but I can't give you a specific name."

"Hmm." Hong tapped the ash off his cigarette. "What are you doing in town, if you don't mind me asking?"

"I'm here mostly because of Joe. Gina was upset over his affair, and his financial problems were impacting the restaurant, upsetting my father, so I flew out. I just got here this morning."

Hong nodded. "We'll have to talk about that in more detail tomorrow. When people have problems, they see lawyers. That could explain what he was doing with Culp."

"Still, Sonny's an odd choice."

"Tell me about it." Hong sucked on his cigarette. "Do you think your experience with Sonny Culp would affect your brother's feelings about him?"

"Now that I think about it, I guess not. Joe was aware of Culp's role in the Allard case, the way he decimated me, you and the prosecution. But knowing my brother, he might have considered it a positive—proof that he was hiring the best shark to be had. Even so, when I heard Joe died with Sonny Culp, it about knocked me on my butt."

The reference to the Allard case caused Hong's eyes to glaze over. He refrained from direct comment, though. "It'll be interesting to find out what did bring them together."

Nick could see past events weighed on Dickson like an unpleasant refrain. Turning his attention to the activity across the street, he wondered when the bodies would be brought out. "Did it look like my brother suffered?"

Hong shook his head, seemingly pleased with the change of subject. "Appeared to me he went right away. The round must have pierced his heart, severed an artery, something like that. Couldn't have been conscious long. Seconds at most."

Hong's words might have sounded insensitive to a casual observer, but Nick understood that it was the way comfort was bestowed among those who routinely face life's harsher realities. There were better deaths and worse deaths. Dickson Hong endeavored to place Joe's in the former category, a gesture for which Nick was grateful.

He thought again of his sister-in-law. "That's good," he said to Hong. "If Gina or the kids ask, it's better to be able to say that he died quickly."

"You plan on talking to her?"

"Yes, I'll probably swing by after I leave here."

"Let her know that we'll be paying her a visit, would you? But if she has something hot, contact me or my partner right away."

"Sure. Who's Plavec, by the way? Somebody new?"

"Yeah. Big Polish kid. Like all the young ones, he's determined to climb to the top. Preferably by next week. They never learn there are no shortcuts to success."

Another indirect reference to the past. Dickson Hong was subtle, always subtle.

"Carl's a good guy, though," he went on, "a serious cop. Like them all, he has a lot to learn."

Nick wanted to say, "He couldn't have a better teacher," but almost anything he said would be irony in his mouth. It was bizarre that they were even talking, when you stopped to think about it. Were it not for two deaths, they wouldn't be.

Exactly what Dickson Hong was thinking about the situation, Nick had no idea. The man was above all a dedicated professional. Whether time had tempered his emotions, only he knew. But knowing Dickson as he did, Nick was aware it could remain this way indefinitely. Subsuming his ego, detaching himself from the objective facts, was Dickson Hong's way. It wasn't Nick's way, though. He felt the need to bring things closer to the surface.

Taking a chance, he decided on a backdoor approach. "You must feel a little odd, investigating the murder of Sonny Culp."

Hong took a deep drag on his cigarette, grimacing. "At this point he's a corpse and, as you know, there's no such thing as a conflict of interest with the dead. Anyway, it doesn't matter how I feel. Culp won't know whether I succeed or fail."

"What about me, Dickson?" Nick said, taking the plunge. "That's my brother in there and, for the moment, anyway, I'm alive and kicking."

Dickson Hong's eyes settled on him, cobra fashion, though his words remained gentle. "I'm not doing my job for you...except to the extent you're a taxpayer."

"What I meant was, I wouldn't want the past to get in the way."

"Of what?"

Nick pondered how to respond. "Maybe the problem—if there is one here—is in my head."

Hong's eyes hooded. "That's nothing new." He let the barb hang, then drew deeply on his cigarette, letting the smoke stream from his mouth and drift into the San Francisco night.

Those three words, uttered ever so softly, had said it all. It explained what had gone wrong with Nick's law enforcement career and the case that had been not only his downfall, but Dickson Hong's, as well. It explained how taking the easy way out could destroy careers, maybe lives, robbing a man of his dignity and self-respect.

At the nursing home that evening he'd faced the failures of his personal life and here, on a cold and windy San Francisco street, he faced the failures of his professional life. Hong didn't know much about Nick's family situation, but he knew about Cindy and Terry Hughes. He knew that Nick had lived a life of empty commitment and shallow principle, a life filled with gestures that always seemed to fall short.

Seeing Dickson Hong this way, on the heels of his epiphany with his father, made him crave redemption as he never had before. He wanted to take the little rumpled time-worn inspector by the shoulders and shout into his placid face that he was a better man than Hong realized, that he might have fucked up, but it wasn't because he was evil—stupid maybe, lazy, cowardly, naive, even arrogant, *but not evil!*

Bending over, Hong crushed the ash of his cigarette on the curb, then slipped the butt into the side pocket of his jacket, a habit that drove his wife nuts. Nick, still flushed with emotion, realized his former partner was about to take his leave. He hadn't yet earned the right to say what was on his mind, to plead his case to the only person who truly mattered, but he couldn't resist reaching out and trying to connect one more time.

"How's Suze doing, Dickson?"

Hong stared up the street. "Living and dying with the Giants, if that gives you any indication."

"A tough life, considering they haven't won a world championship in, what? Fifty years?"

"I won't tell her you said that." Dickson's eyes focused in from some distant point and he said, "I'm sorry about your brother, Nick. And I want you to know that Carl and I will show you the courtesy due any former officer. We'll keep you informed of our progress. It wouldn't be right if you had to read it in the paper."

"I appreciate that."

"But there's a condition."

"Okay."

"Don't get in my way. I don't want to be responsible for another blown case." With that he gave a casual half salute, turned and crossed the street.

Nick stood there, eviscerated—the shortstop who couldn't hit, the prodigal son disgraced, the husband who didn't know his wife's heart, the cop who tried a little too hard and ended up shooting himself in the foot. The pain Nick felt was fresher than it had been in years. Only then did he realize how badly he wanted to get away, how desperate he was to find a pony and get his ass out of there. But he'd made his father a promise. And even though he already regretted it, he wasn't going to cut and run. This time, if only for the sake of his father and Gina, he'd see it through.

VAN NUYS

Eve Adams sat on the edge of her huge California king bed, listening to David Letterman while she painted her toenails seashell pink. She was naked because Iggy loved seeing her naked, and going around the house without clothes on had become a habit for both of them. In the summer, when it was warm, there were days when they put nothing on at all. "That's what growing up in Siberia does to you," Iggy had said.

Her dear, sweet Iggy. He'd scarcely been gone twelve hours and already she missed him. He could be thickheaded, and at times he exasperated her, but there was no question he was the love of her life. She adored him as much as he adored her. She did worry about him, though. Iggy had not been himself of late. There was a time when he'd been driven, full of energy, but recently he'd been lethargic, mopey. He'd lie on the sofa for hours on end. Even his sex drive, which was strong by most standards, had waned. He still grabbed her and kissed her all the time. And he talked about sex, but more often now it never went further. Eve knew she had to get him to a doctor. It would be a challenge, though. He wasn't rational about matters of health.

She'd just finished her last toe when the doorbell rang, startling her. Eve glanced at the clock. It was practically midnight.

She was instantly wary. Though they lived in a decent neighborhood, there were flakes everywhere and you just never knew. Still, she had to investigate.

Eve got her white terry robe from the bath and padded through the house, pausing in the family room to make sure she'd closed and locked the slider. Reaching the front hall, she turned on the porch light and looked through the peephole. She could see no one on the porch. Maybe it was some kid playing pranks, running down the street, ringing doorbells.

She wasn't about to open the door and investigate. If it happened again, she'd call the police. Turning off the porch light, as well as the light in the entry hall, Eve made her way back to the master suite. Removing her robe, she took it to the bathroom and hung it on the hook behind the door. Then she sat on the toilet and peed. Afterward she washed her hands and face. As she peered into the mirror, applying moisturizer to her skin, it occurred to her she couldn't hear the TV in the bedroom. She didn't remember turning off the set, so, putting down the bottle of moisturizer, she stepped to the door. Sure enough, the set was off.

That sent a little jolt through her. What was going on? Was she losing her mind?

As she stood there, more wary by the moment, she heard something in the front of the house. Cocking her ear, she realized it was music. She hadn't put the stereo on. Was somebody in the house? Her heart began racing.

Then it occurred to her. It was Iggy! The bastard had finished the job early and come home. But what was he doing, sneaking into the house? Was it some sort of sexual game?

Amused, Eve decided to play along. She stole through the dark house quietly. Yes, the music was coming from the stereo in the front room. It sounded Russian. Iggy had a few recordings of Russian music, but this did not sound familiar. Had he bought something new, perhaps?

The front room was completely dark. Eve strained her eyes, but could see nothing but vague shapes.

"Iggy, what are you doing?"

No response.

"Iggy, this is not very funny. You scared the crap out of me."

Still he said nothing.

She didn't know what he was up to, but the game wasn't very amusing and she definitely had no patience for it. Feeling her way to the closest table lamp, and nearly knocking it over in the process, Eve turned on the light. Squinting, she peered about the room. It looked empty.

"Igor Sakharov!" she cried. "This isn't cute!" She marched over to see if he was hiding behind the drapes. He wasn't. She looked behind the sofas. Not there, either. "Iggy!" she screamed.

This time she got a response. Laughter. But it didn't sound like her husband.

Her heart already pounding, Eve nearly died when a huge blimp of a man stepped from the hall into the front room. Viktor Chorny.

Eve shrieked and dived behind the sofa.

"Viktor!" she screamed. "What the fuck are you doing in my house?" She peeked over the top of the sofa at his ruddy face.

"I was in the neighborhood," he said in his thick, Russian accent. "I thought, perhaps Eve is lonely. Perhaps I can comfort her."

"How did you get in here?"

Viktor laughed so hard his huge belly shook. Eve could smell the vodka on him clear across the room.

His expression grew serious. "Madame Sakharov, give me the tools and the time and I can be in the president's bedroom at the White House. I am most accomplished at such things."

"You broke into my house?"

"Broke? This is not the right word."

"Well, I don't care what the right word is. *Leave,* Viktor. You're drunk."

"I have had a little vodka, this is true. But I brought also cherry vanilla ice cream. It is in the freezer. Shall I get a bowl for each of us?"

"This is not the time for nonsense. I want you out of here. *Now!*"

"Eve, my darling, you are showing very poor hospitality."

"Iggy would kill you if he were here. You know that, Viktor."

"Yes, my pet, but Igor Andreyevich is not here. Alas, there is no one in the house but you and me."

"Viktor, leave this instant or I'm calling the police!"

"The police? That is a curious choice." He began walking toward the sofa.

"I'll tell Iggy," she warned.

"Tell him what?"

"That you came into the house uninvited and scared me."

"Are you frightened, little one?"

He was opposite her now and stretching his neck to see over the couch. Eve hunkered down. She was scared shitless, uncertain about what he intended to do. Surely he wouldn't hurt her. He and Iggy had been friends and colleagues forever.

"You are embarrassing me, Viktor," she said firmly. "If you leave now, all is forgotten, so go!"

He chuckled. "But I don't want to go, my love. In fact, I hoped most strongly that you would receive me with pleasure."

"You're out of your ever-loving mind. In the morning, when you've sobered up, you'll be mortified."

"You will never know how often I dream of being alone with you, my pet. Don't you see it? This is our very chance!"

"My God, what can you be thinking? I'm married to your friend. I love my husband. I don't want you."

"How can you know this if you have never tried?"

Eve could see he was determined. He could easily overpower her...*if* he could catch her. She realized that was her best hope—to flee. Out the front door, if necessary. Anywhere.

"Okay," she said. "I'll have a bowl of ice cream with you."

"Excellent. Come, let's go to the kitchen."

"You get the ice cream, Viktor, and I'll get dressed."

"Ha! You take me for a fool, do you? I may have drunk some vodka, but I'm not easily deceived. We will go together. Come, my love, give me your hand." He extended it over the sofa.

"I don't want to. I want to go get dressed."

"But you are much more pleasing to the eye as you are."

Eve could see he was blindly determined to do something—probably fuck her—which meant she had no choice but to run. She pondered a way to distract him. All she needed was a second or two to dash past him.

Eve boldly stood, exposing herself. "Is this what you want, Viktor?"

His fat lip sagged open as he gaped at her. "Ah, a dream, a vision!"

"Take off your clothes, then, and let's get it over with."

He smiled. "Very well. Come around the couch."

"After you're undressed."

"Tsk, tsk," he said, shaking his finger admonishingly. "You come to *me!*" His tone became commanding as his beady eyes narrowed and his wet, pink skin turned purply red.

Eve had heard stories about Viktor Chorny's brutality. And she knew him to be a womanizer. She thought that was all in the past, but realized now she was wrong.

Chorny extended his hand across the sofa. Eve tentatively

extended her hand toward his. Their fingers were six inches apart when Viktor seemed momentarily to lose balance. Eve saw it as her chance. She quickly dashed toward the end of the sofa, hoping to make it across the room before he could recover. But she slipped and nearly fell to the floor. It slowed her up just enough that Chorny was able to right himself and lumber over, cutting off her route of escape and snatching her arm at the last second.

He yanked her back, slamming her against his mountainous body. Eve flailed at him, twisting to free herself, but his grip was viselike. He moved behind her, enveloping her with both arms. She was surrounded on all sides by flesh, arms bigger than her thighs. A fat palm pressed down on her breasts, the other on her stomach.

"In my youth I played soccer," he said. "I was very quick on my feet." He began to knead her breasts. "Ah," he said, his boozy breath washing over her, "how long I have dreamed of this moment."

"Iggy will kill you."

"Perhaps. We shall see."

Desperation welled. "Please don't, Viktor."

"What, my love? Only minutes ago you were so willing."

"I don't want this," she cried as the tears began to flow.

"Tsk, tsk. How can you know?"

"I do, I really do. Oh, please, Viktor..."

"Come," he said, ignoring her, "let's go to the bedroom where we will be comfortable."

FRIDAY SEPTEMBER 6TH

LOMBARD STREET

Jolie Hays awoke with the worst headache of her life. Every orifice burned or hurt. The previous night was an alcoholic blur except for their bet and the consequences, which she recalled all too well, along with the john's rumbling, drunken monologue. She remembered him ranting about somebody named Ludmilla and how much better the women were in America.

Jolie also had a hazy recollection of talk of killing and murder, of men being shot. What could that have been about? She lifted her head from the pillow and took a good look at the man beside her, as though the explanation might be found on his face, but there was nothing there but his open mouth and the sound of snoring. She pushed his leg off her and sat up with some difficulty. There was dried blood on her thighs and on the sheets. She felt as if she'd been fucked by a telephone pole.

The john himself told her she was green. "You broke every hooker rule," he'd said at one point. "You're goddamn lucky

I'm a gentleman, sugar pie. You can't let your guard down. One night some psychopath's going to slit your throat."

Jolie got to her feet, but the room seemed to turn and she lost her balance, nearly falling back onto the bed. She managed to gather her clothes, then stagger to the bathroom. Washing herself was a painful experience and she vowed right then never again to drink while she worked.

When she came out of the bath several minutes later, she found Jerry on the edge of the bed, holding his head, his uncircumcised penis pointing at her like a rapier. She quailed at the thought of more sex. Surely he'd had enough.

The john glanced up at her. His queasy expression told her she was probably safe.

"Did you have a good time, Jolie?" he asked, rallying.

"I'll tell you when I got the rest of my money."

Jerry went to the dresser where he'd put his wallet. "Hookers usually want to be paid up front," he said.

She was embarrassed by how he'd thrown her off her game. "Yeah, well, you is a gentleman, right?"

He put a half of a one-hundred-dollar bill in her hand.

"We agreed on four hundred, man."

"You got one hundred when I got back, five twenties and this makes three hundred."

"What about the other hundred?"

"You lost our bet, remember?"

"You fucked me in the goddamn ass, ain't that enough?"

"A deal's a deal. Now give me the other halves of my hundred-dollar bills."

"You're a motherfuck, know that, Jerry."

He smiled, but she gave him the bills, which they laid out on the bed, to make sure everything matched. She was pissed. All that for three hundred dollars.

"What's the matter, Jolie?" he said. "You don't look very happy."

"Mister, you fuck like a wild man, tear me to pieces, and this all I get. Only man I know worse than you was my step-daddy."

"Your stepfather?"

"Not really, but he live with my mama while I growin' up. He fucked me and my sister whenever he want and don' give us nothin', not even an ice cream."

"Now that's a sad story. Tell you what, sugar pie, I'll give you a chance to make another hundred, so you'll have your four."

"Oh, no. I ain't fuckin' no more. Not until tomorrow. Maybe the day after."

"It's not for sex," he insisted.

"Then what?"

"I want you to tell me everything you heard me say last night," he said, holding the two halves of one of the hundreds between his fingers.

"That all?"

"But it's got to be the truth. The whole truth."

"I don' remember much."

"Let's hear what you do remember."

"You talk about somebody name Ludmilla."

"What did I say?"

"Maybe she a fucking bitch, some'in' like that."

"That could be true."

"Who she?" Jolie asked, her feminine curiosity getting the better of her.

"My wife. Ex-wife, actually."

"That explain. What happen, if you don't mind me askin'?"

"I caught the bitch fucking the old man in the flat across the hall. The sonovabitch must have been sixty, if you can believe it."

"Where that?"

Jerry smiled. "Berlin. I all but beat her to death, which is one reason I'm here and not there."

"Yep, Jerry, you a hard man."

"What else I say?"

"Nothing."

"Come on, honey. I said a lot more than that."

"I too goddamn shit-face, man. How I supposed to know?"

"You got to work harder for a hundred than that."

"I guess you talkin' about some mens."

"What about them?"

"Something about them dead. I don't know exactly, 'cept that you was pretty damn glad. That's all I hear. Honest."

"You sure?"

"Swear on my mama's grave."

Jerry gave her half the bill.

"What's this? Don' do me no good."

"You're holding back half, so I'm only giving you half."

"You a sonovabitch motherfucker, Jerry."

"I play by the rules."

"What I suppose to tell you?"

"About the men."

"Nothin'. I don't know nothin'."

"Okay, you can go, then. Beat it."

"Asshole."

Jerry shrugged and tossed his head toward the door.

"I only remember one other thing," Jolie said.

"What's that?"

"You said, 'I love you,' in Russian."

"How do you know it was Russian?"

"I been to Berlin."

Jerry got a big, wide-ass grin on his face. "You're an honest woman, Jolie. I like that."

"So, I get the money?"

"Tell you what. I come to San Francisco sometimes. You were a damn good lay. Maybe I'll give you a call. Beats picking up a john on the street."

"You do that, then," she said, holding out her hand for the other half bill.

"Can't call you unless I know your telephone number."

"Give me some'in' to write with."

Jerry got a pencil and pen from the nightstand next to the phone. She wrote down the number of DeLon Pitts, the pimp who'd been hustling her for a week. DeLon told her to use his number if she ever got in a jam. This seemed like as good a jam as any. Jerry gave her the other half of the hundred and patted her ass.

Jolie hightailed it out the door.

NORTH BEACH

Nick Sasso woke to the sound of a garbage truck in the alley and the glare of the sun coming in the dusty window. Shit. It all came crashing into his consciousness with the subtlety of an express subway train rocketing through a station. His brother, Joe. Sonny Culp. The homicides. Dickson Hong. The painful hours he'd spent with his sister-in-law and his nephew, Blake.

Nick hadn't gotten back to the Clipper until 3:00 a.m. Gina and her youngest had gone out for dinner and a movie. They'd only been home fifteen minutes when Nick arrived with word of Joe's death.

Gina was shocked and it seemed genuine. Almost immediately Nick had discounted the possibility that she was responsible. Her initial energies were devoted to her son. Still a few years shy of being a man, Blake had cried, gotten angry, and finally withdrawn into his shell. Gina must have spent an hour with him in his room. Nick had occupied himself trying to track down his other nephew and his nieces. Shelly was up at Tahoe with the family of a girlfriend, Tina was already at school in Santa Barbara and Anthony was in Mexico with a couple of buddies. He was able to reach the girls, but Gina wanted to be the one to tell them, so he called her down to impart the tragic news. It was grim duty all around.

When Nick recounted how she'd have to speak to the police, Gina said that was fine, so long as she could be home when her girls arrived. And she wanted to continue to try to track down Anthony. When Nick had made to leave, Gina walked him to the car so that they could talk in private.

Standing on the sidewalk in a long bulky cardigan that swallowed her hunched frame, his sister-in-law told him that she had nothing to do with her husband's death, unless wishing it had done the trick. "I know I said some harsh things, but it was just talk, Nick."

"That's what I figured."

"There is something else," she said. "I think I know why Joe and that lawyer were killed."

Her comment brought him to full attention, even in his state of exhaustion. "Why?"

"Yesterday morning I followed Joe and his girlfriend to the law office where the murders took place. She stayed in the car but I overheard the men arguing about her."

"What did they say?"

"Joe wanted the lawyer...what's his name again?"

"Culp. Sonny Culp."

"Yes, Sonny. Joe wanted Sonny to go to some kind of meeting, but he said he couldn't because his office had been burglarized. The long and the short of it was that they were going to get together, there in the lawyer's office, last night. Sonny told Joe to bring her, if he wanted to. Nick, I think she killed them."

"Why?"

"Because she and Joe had been arguing and Joe gave the impression he was anxious about her when he spoke to Sonny. There was a lot of high emotion among the three of them, I can tell you that."

"They didn't say what the meeting was about?"

"No, but after Joe and the dragon lady left the lawyer's office, they went to Tiburon and met with a man. I don't know who, but he was Chinese. That was probably who Joe wanted the lawyer, Culp, to meet. But that Elaine Chang is right at the heart of things, Nick, I know she is."

"What do you know about her?"

"Only that she's a prostitute turned businesswoman. I don't know what was going on, but Joe and Sonny Culp probably died because of it, whatever it was."

"You have to tell all this to the police."

"Yes, I intend to," she said with a shiver, hugging herself.

From his current perspective of the morning after, things seemed clearer, his mind sharper, not dull with fatigue and shock as it had been when he stood in the street talking to his sister-in-law. He realized that Gina might very well have found the key to her husband's death. But he also realized there was a flip side. If her story was true—and he had no reason to think it wasn't—Gina knew that Joe would be meeting with Culp in his office. She also knew that Elaine Chang was involved, which would make Elaine a ready scapegoat. He didn't want to think his sister-in-law was that Machiavellian, but she *was* a woman scorned and Elaine Chang was her rival.

Last night hadn't been the time to pursue the matter. Gina had been in need of compassion. He'd tried to be supportive. "I'm sorry that Joe failed you in the end, Gina," he'd told her.

"Right now all that matters is the children."

Nick had hugged her, and Gina cried for a minute with her face buried in his shoulder. Then she went inside to be with Blake. On his way back to the Yankee Clipper, Nick had shed some tears. His brother's death had finally begun to sink in.

When he got home, he'd crawled into bed, wrung out. But sleep eluded him. His last conversation with his brother—especially Joe's angry rebuke—haunted him. Could he have done something to prevent the murder? Had he allowed himself to be too easily deterred?

Other than regret, Nick felt more pain than anger. There was no one to blame, to hate yet. That would come later. Until he could convince himself otherwise, he'd assume responsibility.

Nick also worried about his father. The nurse at the home had said improvement could come in a matter of days, which meant he'd have to tell him about Joe soon. And, once his brother's body was released, there'd be the funeral to get through. After that, he'd face the task of straightening out the mess Joe had left behind. The family was in jeopardy of losing the Clipper, and given the state of Joe's finances, Gina and the kids could end up on the street. The burdens were piling up.

Though he'd only had a few hours' sleep, Nick decided to get up. Dickson Hong would be coming by later. Hong and his partner would want to talk to Gina, especially after what Nick had learned from her last night. Meanwhile, back in New York, life went on without him, his destiny, at a crucial juncture, waiting for him. How odd Dominick's California Cafe didn't seem quite so important as it had just hours ago.

Amid the turmoil of his thoughts, Nick heard a loud sound downstairs, perhaps a door slamming. It seemed early for any of the kitchen crew to be arriving, so he decided to investigate. Putting on his robe, he went to the door then stopped, hearing voices—people speaking in what sounded like Chinese. He crept down the staircase, wondering what the hell was going on.

Reaching the bottom of the stairs, Nick glanced at the dining room. A restaurant before opening time was like a woman without makeup. The bones were blatant, the blemishes glaring. You noticed the gashes on table legs, the bread crumbs on the floor, the unventilated air, the empty quiet.

Later, when they were open for business, the tablecloths and flowers, cooking smells, the murmur of the clientele, the clatter of dishes and the bustle of the staff would make the place come alive. A good restaurant was seductive that way. Asleep, it wasn't a pretty sight, however.

Nick's attention was taken by an angry shout in the kitchen, followed by more subdued conversation. He couldn't understand a word, of course, but he sensed anxiety. A debate over who'd wash the lettuce? If he were dressed he'd have gone in and asked what was going on, but since he wasn't, he chose a more subtle approach. He went to the kitchen door and pushed it open a crack.

He saw two Asians arguing. They were young and tough-looking, more the ilk of thugs than kitchen workers. He pushed the door open a bit, his suspicion growing. He was able to see out the back door and into the alley. Another guy, also Asian, this one with long hair, was opening the side door of a light blue van. It was empty, which meant this wasn't likely a delivery. It then occurred to him that it might very well be the opposite. They might be burglarizing the place.

Deciding a strategic retreat was in order, he headed back upstairs to call the police on his cell phone. He'd gone up halfway when he heard the kitchen door open. Judging by the voices, the men were on their way upstairs, as well. Nick just got in his room when the guys jogged up the steps, talking to each other. He heard a door opening. They were checking the office and would probably be coming into the bedroom next.

Nick managed to get behind the door just as it opened. An anxious moment passed. Then, apparently satisfied with a quick look, the intruder retreated across the hall, leaving the door ajar. Nick quietly crossed the room, retrieved the cell phone from his jacket pocket, only to find the battery was dead. Shit.

Peeking out the door, he could see that three of them were

searching the office. He couldn't use the phone in there, so he'd have to slip down the stairs and get to the one at the front of the dining room. After debating whether to take the time to put on a pair of pants or save every moment he could, he chose modesty over expediency and put on his jeans, though he didn't bother with a shirt and shoes.

The boys across the hall seemed fully occupied, busily going through drawers and disconnecting Joe's computer. Nick slipped silently out and started down the stairs, only to be brought up short by the sound of a woman's voice in the office. "Joe," she said in lightly accented speech, "why don't you go to the meeting alone and drop by my place afterward? I'd rather not be part of the discussion, to be honest. Call before you come."

Nick realized it was the voice he'd heard on the tape Mort Seidel had played during their crosscontinent conversation. Elaine Chang. The intruders must be playing the answering machine.

"In fairness, you should know," Elaine continued, "that it's tonight or never. We need your final decision. I have—" Nick heard a clunk and the recording abruptly ended. He figured the boys had ripped the cord out of the wall.

As Nick started back down the stairs, he heard footsteps below. Another desperado came around the corner and went up a step or two before he saw Nick. They both froze for a moment, staring at one another. Then, gathering himself, the kid sounded the alarm, shouting to his friends.

With three guys behind him and only one below, Nick decided to charge the lone ranger at the bottom of the staircase. Not as spry as he'd once been, the adrenaline nevertheless carried him down the stairs at a rapid clip. The kid, who must have felt as if he was in Pamplona for the running of the bulls, jumped back, reached under his leather jacket, fumbled, but managed to pull out a gun.

Nick got to him before he could raise it and fire, knocking both the guy and gun to the floor. Unfortunately, Nick went down, too. That gave his adversary time to scamper to his feet. Nick tried to get up as well, but didn't make it before the rest of the Mongolian horde descended upon him. They seemed to come at him in waves—karate kicks and punches in profusion.

It didn't take long to overwhelm him. Between the flying fists and feet, he had glimpses of his adversaries, but they were fleeting glimpses at best. One of them was a larger, heavyset guy with a round face and hands that were like bricks. The other two were the ilk of the kid with the gun— smaller and slight. The one with the long hair was especially young-looking, but he kicked like a mule. No more than thirty seconds passed before everything went black.

He probably was out less than a minute, but it was long enough for them to tie his wrists behind him and bind his ankles. As he came to he saw them carrying the computer and boxes of files down the stairs, through the kitchen, and presumably to the van.

Eventually the thug with the gun came back into the dining room, walked to the spot where he lay, drew the automatic from his belt and aimed it at Nick's head. In that split second where one's life was supposed to pass before one's eyes, Nick saw only one thing—that he was about to get a bullet in the head.

The kid, who probably had still been in diapers when Nick was taking ground balls in the Babe Ruth League, cocked the hammer and looked coldly into Nick's eyes as his finger begin to squeeze the trigger. Then it happened. First the crash, followed by the gun going off, his head bouncing on the floor, the sound of running, the kitchen door being shoved open and banging the wall, shouts, a car-door slam, the roar of an engine, screeching tires.

He was either dead and watching it all from heaven...or hell. Or maybe he was like a dying chicken, functioning for a while after his nervous system had been destroyed—a sort of mocking, but temporary, denial of death. He smelled the blood all right, but his eyeballs continued to sense light and his ears caught sounds. He even had feeling. The bindings on his wrists hurt like hell.

"Christ Almighty!" It was a woman's voice and it seemed to be coming from the front.

Still confused and uncertain whether he was alive or in the middle of some sort of cynical joke of nature, he turned his head to get a view of the front entrance, his cheek sliding over a slimy pool of blood as he craned his neck. In the glare of the morning light he could see a figure outside the large plate-glass window up front. She was standing at a gaping, jagged hole in the glass.

"Hey!" she called. "You all right?"

This struck Nick as a rather inane question. Not that he thought the answer was evident. But rather because it seem absurd to assume he would know.

"Hello?"

"Yeah," he called back, encouraged by the fact that he had a voice, although it did occur to him this still might be some sort of demonic sleight of hand. If he was a ghost, for example, she might not hear a thing. He could be dead as a doornail and just *think* he was alive.

"Hello?" she called again. "Can you hear me in there?"

Shit, he thought. I'm a corpse and I don't even know it. I'm just imagining I can hear and see and feel.

"Don't worry," she called to him. "I've called for the police and an ambulance."

Worry struck him as an odd word. Then, when he felt things starting to fade, a well of panic overtook him. Maybe death was finally catching up with him. Maybe the headless chicken was finally running out of gas.

LOMBARD STREET

Jolie Hays stood on the sidewalk outside the motel, waiting for the taxi. She didn't know which hurt worse, her head, her ass or her pride. In any case, she knew she screwed up bad. Her first mistake was agreeing to go with the motherfucker. Her second mistake was drinking the vodka. But after three nights of forty-dollar blow jobs, the prospect of all that money had seemed like a good thing. Now she wasn't so sure. *Never trust nobody,* Jolie told herself. A lesson learned.

About the time she started thinking maybe she should go find someplace to sit down while she waited, who should come cruising up to her in his BMW convertible but DeLon Pitts. He pulled up to the curb

"What?" she said to nobody in particular, except maybe God.

DeLon's smile was so wide she could have nailed all his teeth with a baseball bat. "Well surprise, surprise," he said, the gold chain around his neck gleaming in the morning sun. DeLon was a skinny little guy, but he knew how to style. He pushed his sunglasses up into his hair. "By gum, mama, you still alive."

Jolie smirked, looking past him at the slopes of Pacific Heights.

"You lucky, you know that, Jolie. That honky could have killed your ass."

Still she ignored him.

"If you smart, you get somebody like me lookin' out for your backside. But nothin' I can do if you won't be my whore. Mark my words, girl, one of these motherfuckers goin' to kill your sweet ass some night."

All Jolie could figure was that he'd followed them.

"You was boozin' with him like a dumb bitch, wasn't you?"

"It's none of your fuckin' business, DeLon. Why don't you take your pimpmobile and get your sorry ass out of here?" It scared her that he seemed to know everything she'd done. He must have been listening outside the door. But she was determined to act as if she didn't care.

"I promise you, Jolie, there'll be a day soon when you'll cry with joy to see my sorry ass."

She lifted her chin. Out of the corner of her eye she saw DeLon shake his head.

"Come on, baby, get in the car and let me buy you breakfast."

Jolie felt something rolling down her leg, probably blood. And she hurt real bad. She grimaced, wanting the taxi to come.

"Don't a nice big breakfast plate and a glass of buttermilk sound good?" DeLon persisted.

"No."

"You say no, but I hear your heart sayin' yes."

"Fuck you, DeLon."

"Come on, baby, you know I'm good for you. Without me, who's goin' to care?"

Jolie hated the sonovabitch, but maybe not as much as she hated the john who fucked her. It was hard to say who was worse.

"How's it goin' to hurt gettin' a free ride home?"

"I don't mind takin' a taxi."

"But mama, you smarter than that. Get your sweet little ass on this nice leather seat here beside me. Let me be your man."

Jolie knew if she didn't get in, she'd start crying. She got in the car.

DeLon brushed her cheek with the back of his manicured fingers. "How much the man give you?"

"Five hundred."

"Let me see."

She whipped her head toward him.

"I'm not going to take your money, babe. If I don't give service, you don't pay. I just want to see."

"Well, maybe four hundred."

"That okay. Whatever is, is."

Jolie took the money she'd gotten from the john and fanned it out on her lap, placing the halves of the torn bills in their proper places.

"That cool. The bank don't mind Scotch tape. What you two do, anyway? Play strip poker and run out of chips?"

"Fuck you, DeLon."

"Listen to me, Jolie."

She stared straight ahead, biting her lip. DeLon took her chin and gently turned her head to him.

Looking her right in her teary eyes, he stared at her hard and said, "With me managin', that'd be six or seven hundred in your hand. Five hundred for you and one or two hundred for me. I'm tellin' you, you're givin' it away, girl. You prime stuff, Jolie. There ain't nothin' like you on the street. You need a manager bad. I serious."

"Are we going to get something to eat or not?" she said, putting her money back in her purse.

DeLon Pitts smiled. "Yes, Jolie, we go in a minute. But first I want to tell you some'in'. You so fucking green, you don't even know who that was you fucked last night."

"What you mean?"

"That honky fuck was a killer."

"How you know that?"

"Because I heard him tell you he was. Didn't you hear?"

"Maybe."

"No, you too fucking drunk to know what he say. But it's proof that I's right. Think about it, girl. You come that close to a visit with Jesus." With that, DeLon put the car in gear and drove off.

NORTH BEACH

Nick was actually conscious before he felt the damp cloth on his face. Maybe it was her perfume that brought him to or the sensation of his hands and feet being untied. It took a little effort to open his eyes, but there she was, hovering over him, not exactly an angel of mercy, perhaps, but a concerned citizen at the very least. He had no idea who the hell she was.

"Hi," she said, her frown melting into a smile. "You had me going there for a minute."

"Who are you?"

"Billie Fox."

The name meant nothing. He blinked, taking in her unfamiliar features, the wavy auburn hair framing her long face. She wasn't a scintillating beauty, but her mouth and big brown eyes were expressive, and curiously calming. He was still skeptical about the authenticity of all this, but with each passing moment, weird though they seemed, he was beginning to think this was actually for real. Even so, his brain refused to move faster than half speed. "What...what..."

"Happened?"

"Yeah," he said, relieved she'd supplied the word.

"I was supposed to meet Dickson Hong here," she said, "but when I arrived, the place was locked up. I looked through the door and I saw you on the floor. It was so dark, I couldn't see what happened to you, whether you'd fallen or what."

"I think I was shot and killed," he said, letting his eyelids rest in the closed position for a moment or two.

Billie chuckled. "That came later."

Nick opened his eyes, wondering if he was about to be told he was indeed dead and that this was in fact the postmortem, God's version of the instant replay complete with expert analysis.

"When I saw the man with the gun getting ready to shoot you, I threw the valet-parking sign through the window to distract him. It must have worked because he missed...or, I guess just grazed you. The bullet tore your cheek. That's why all the blood. I've slowed the bleeding, though."

She wasn't talking fast, but Nick had to struggle to keep up. He was pretty sure he'd gotten most of what she'd said. "Are you saying you saved my life?"

She smiled. Her teeth were nice.

"Either that or your friend was a piss-poor shot," she said, pressing the cloth against his cheek, which had begun to throb. "You did get a nice little dueling scar for your trouble."

They heard a siren up the street.

Billie turned toward the front. "That would be the police. Can I open the door from the inside? I had to come in through the alley."

"No, you need a key."

"Where would I find one?"

"In my pocket."

A police car pulled up in front, two officers emerging with guns drawn. Nick tried to sit, but was overwhelmed by dizziness and fell back down.

"Let me get it," Billie said, patting his pockets to find the right one.

The cops pounded on the door and shouted, "Police!"

"Hang on, Officer," Billie called. "I'm getting a key."

Nick, woozy as hell, turned to give her better access to his pocket. Billie slipped her hand down through the folds of fabric.

"Please be advised that I only grope men when there's a medical emergency," she said.

He somehow found the strength to laugh. Billie extracted the key, shaking her head.

"Purses are so much more practical."

Nick watched her get to her feet and head for the door. Though she was on the lanky side, she seemed to have a nice ass, though with the loose pants, it was difficult to be sure. He wondered why it mattered, why he would even notice.

The cops came in, escorted by Billie Fox, who was giving them a summary of events. Nick, who continued to struggle with words, was glad to have an interpreter. More than that, he was glad to have someone with the presence of mind, the moxie and the strength, to hurl a sign through the window. She really had saved his life.

Over the next few minutes, more cops arrived, followed by paramedics—everybody, it seemed, but the mayor. At first they treated Nick where he lay, but when the haze in his brain began to burn off like coastal fog on a hot, sunny day, they let him move to Benny Vocino's booth. Somebody got him a shirt from upstairs, and Billie Fox joined him once he'd been patched up, sliding into the banquette across from him.

"Feeling better?" she asked.

"Much."

"You look better. You were a pretty spacey guy when I first got to you."

They'd told him he had a concussion and that's why he felt so disoriented. "If I haven't already expressed my appreciation for what you did, Billie, please accept my thanks."

"Hey, don't mention it."

She blushed and Nick found that endearing. They looked at each other, she shyly, which, considering her credentials as an action hero, struck Nick as a touch incongruous. Nice, nice lady, he thought.

He tried casting his mind back into that fog from which he'd only just emerged, recalling her saying something about meeting Dickson Hong. "Forgive me for asking a stupid question," he said, not knowing how else to phrase it. "Who, exactly, are you, anyway?"

"Sonny Culp's wife," she said. "Or, more precisely, Sonny's ex-wife."

BURLINGAME

Igor Sakharov wondered what the hell had happened to his brother. He hated being in the dark, almost as much as he hated not knowing whether he'd live or die. All he knew for sure was that he'd had a bad feeling ever since Viktor Chorny had shown up with the offer for this job.

Igor should have followed his instinct and turned down the deal. If he had, he wouldn't be in this hospital now, hooked up to machines, wires running everywhere. Maybe he wouldn't have had a goddamn heart attack. He'd taken on one too many jobs. That's what had happened. One too many.

He was as worried about Alexei as he was about his health, though. His brother was a loose cannon, unpredictable. God only knew what had happened to him. He could have been arrested, maybe killed. Or he might have had trouble tracking down the two guys and was still on the prowl. Anything was possible and very little of it was good.

Igor debated whether or not he should call Eve. In the past, he never contacted her in the middle of a job. Too risky. But he'd never been sick like this before. Hell, he could have another attack and die at any moment. Maybe it *was* worth the risk. Eve would bring him comfort. She was a tough woman, but also an angel.

He decided to take a chance. Putting the bedside phone on his lap he dialed his home in Van Nuys. Eve answered, sounding numb, like she'd been asleep. He'd forgotten it was still early and Eve did like her beauty rest.

"Oh, Iggy!" she cried when she realized it was him.

He thought he heard a sob. "Darling, what's the matter?" he asked.

"Nothing. It's just that I miss you. When are you coming home?"

Igor got a lump in his throat. Her voice was enough to elicit the image of her soft breasts, and he had an overwhelming desire to press his face into them and sob. Eve was his refuge from life and had been since the day they'd met.

"I'm sick, honey," he said, modulating his voice as best he could, keeping his emotions in check.

"What do you mean, sick?"

"Well, I'm in a hospital. I had a little...problem."

"Iggy, what kind of problem? What's wrong?"

"Heart attack," he said.

"*Iggy!* Oh, my God!"

"I thought maybe you should know."

"Is it serious?"

"Unfortunately, yes."

"Oh, *no...*"

Igor could picture her face. The shock. The concern. In a strange way it was a comfort to him. "Don't worry, though. I'm not dying. At least not yet."

"Where are you?" she asked, her voice dropping, the tone becoming resolute.

"In a place called Burlingame. It's near the San Francisco airport."

"When did this happen?"

"I didn't feel well on the plane. We came to the hospital. That's when I had the attack."

There was a horrified silence, then Eve said, "Is Alexei with you?"

"No, he left last night to take care of the business. I haven't seen him."

"Then you're alone."

"Yes," he said, his voice shaking.

"I'm coming up there," she said.

"It's not necessary." He said it without conviction.

"What's the name of the hospital?"

Igor gave her all the pertinent information, including the

alias he'd used. Having set the wheels in motion, he felt much better. Eve was his salvation and always would be. He was a strong man in most respects, but he had this chink in his armor. Eve knew how to deal with it. They were partners for life. He adored her.

"Don't worry about a thing," his wife said. "I'll be there as soon as I can. And you cooperate with the doctors, Iggy." She knew how he felt about the medical profession.

"I will," he said, his eyes filling.

"I love you."

"Yes, I love you, too." He put down the receiver as a sob bubbled out of his throat.

NORTH BEACH

They wanted to take him to the hospital, but Nick declined the offer. "I'll go later," he told the paramedic. "I need to talk to Inspector Hong."

Two guys from the Burglary Investigation Section arrived first, a lumbering Irishman, Mike Doolan, and a guy with a pockmarked face by the name of Bomberg. Nick didn't know them. They took charge of the scene, which warranted special attention because of the attempted murder, not to mention the possible connection to the double homicide in the Marina the night before. Dickson Hong and Carl Plavec were on their way. It turned out that Billie Fox was an hour early for her appointment with the detectives.

"Damned lucky for me," Nick said.

"I guess I was in a fog when I talked to them last night and screwed up the time."

"Homicide's not pleasant, even when it's a former spouse."

"Actually, Sonny and I got along okay," Billie said. "It's been four years since we split, long enough for emotions to settle. And whatever else Sonny is, he's the father of my daughter."

They were still sitting in Benny's booth, talking over glasses of water. Nick held an ice pack, which the paramedics had given him. He pressed it to the various hot spots on his head and body on a rotating basis. In addition to the grazed cheek, he'd gotten smacked in the nose—the cotton stuffed up his nostrils took care of the bleeding—a lump on the side of his head, plus a variety of bruises, contusions and possibly a cracked rib.

"Why did Dickson want to meet with you here?" Nick asked, the growing clarity of his mind starting to produce logical questions.

"He thought that between us we could figure out what Sonny and your brother were mixed up in. Dickson also said something about you having what might be Sonny's voice on a recording. He thought maybe I could identify it."

"Assuming the gangbangers didn't take the machine. From what I could see from my vantage point on the floor, they pretty well cleaned out Joe's office."

"By the way," Billie said, "my condolences for the loss of your brother."

"Thanks. And mine regarding your ex."

Billie's smile was a touch sad. "I don't suppose you're heartbroken over Sonny's demise."

Nick studied her. "You know about him and me?"

"I know about the case."

"Oh, really."

"In fairness I should probably tell you I was tangentially involved. I'm a lawyer myself, in case you didn't know, and at the time, Sonny and I were working together, though I didn't have my ticket yet. The chain of custody attack on the prosecution's case was my idea, as a matter of fact."

For a second he didn't believe her, thinking it was a joke. But then he saw she was serious. "Oh, so then I really have *you* to blame."

"Yeah."

For so long Sonny Culp had been his executioner that it was hard to picture someone seemingly so benign in the role. Did Billie Fox appreciate the consequences of her actions? he wondered. "Your legal brilliance got me tarred and feathered and run out of town, you know."

"No, Nick, I would say you have yourself to thank for that. I just figured out a way to use your mistakes against you."

"You're right. I was my own worst enemy." He'd known this all along, of course, but hadn't had occasion to admit it to someone who'd been involved—other than Dickson Hong, that is. It surprised him how good confessing it felt and figured it was probably part of the redemption process he'd begun last night with his father. He gently held the ice pack to his throbbing nose, looking at her over the top of it.

Billie Fox struck him as a very unusual woman, a *rara avis*. She was no kid—fortyish by his estimation—yet vital, bright, strong, tough. Not a delicate flower, certainly, but there was a softness and innocence about her. She seemed real in a way that few people did.

He shifted the ice pack to the bump on his head. It was unfortunate that she knew how he'd disgraced himself, bungling the Allard case. Then it occurred to him that if Billie Fox was conversant with the downside of his actions, she ought to know it wasn't the whole story. He found himself *wanting* her to be aware of the rest of it. He wanted her to know that he wasn't as awful as she thought.

"You know, Billie, you're right that I totally screwed up the investigation and I probably deserved what I got. But everybody seems to forget that the sonovabitch was guilty as hell. For all my stupidity, my intentions weren't bad. I wasn't trying to hang an innocent man. I hope you're aware of that."

"That's always the way cops think, Nick."

"Is it wrong?"

"The sentiment is fine, but we have rules for a reason. Otherwise, we could just let the cops round up guilty criminals and hang them. Sonny used the law and the jury's sense of fair play to punish you and protect the public in a different sense."

"And, in doing so, set a murderer free."

"Everything has its price."

"Oh, now I see why you married Sonny Culp."

"Actually, you don't."

The sternness of her tone gave him pause. "I'm sorry. I didn't mean to be flip...not with the woman who saved my life."

"No offense taken. We're having a philosophical discussion."

"Yeah, philosophical maybe, but it's pretty real to me. I don't expect any sympathy, but it wouldn't hurt if people acknowledged that a guy can screw up but still have good intentions. It's better than bad intentions. At least that's my contention."

She smiled. "I sometimes forget I'm not in a courtroom."

Nick found himself in the curious position of wanting her approval even though—or maybe because of the fact—that she'd been in league with Sonny Culp. Odd how his past and the woman before him were connected. "Philosophy aside, there's the human element," he argued. "Cops are people, too."

"Are you looking for forgiveness, Nick?"

"No, I'd settle for understanding."

"Courtrooms are dangerous places," she said, giving him a benevolent smile. "You had the misfortune of becoming the issue in that case. From my perspective, it wasn't personal."

He took that as a peace offering, though they hadn't really been at war. If there had been conflict, it was between two sides of himself, with Billie Fox as the pawn.

She looked toward the front of the restaurant as one of the crime techs came back inside from a trip to the lab truck. "I wonder where Hong is."

"Are they late?" he asked.

"A couple of minutes."

"They'll be here. Dickson was always punctual." Nick leaned back, shifting the ice pack to his ribs. "So, you're a lawyer and a mother."

"Among other things."

"Like what?"

Billie shrugged. "Baseball fan."

"Oh, really? Me, too. What's your team? The Giants?"

"Who else? How about you?"

"Yankees," he replied, pointing up to the picture on the wall above them. "It was about as automatic in my family as getting baptized."

"Of course. What am I thinking? This *is* the Yankee Clipper, after all."

"What else are you besides a lawyer, a mother and a Giants fan, if you don't mind me asking?"

"How about cancer survivor?"

"Really?"

"I had breast cancer several years ago."

Her words were sobering, first because they were so unexpected, and second because his mother died of cancer. The subject had a lot of emotion associated with it. He studied her, wanting things to be all right. "But you're okay now?"

"I'm in remission. My fifth anniversary is coming up in a few months."

"I take it that's good."

"It's a critical milestone if you're going to survive breast cancer."

Nick noticed a subtle flicker in her otherwise serene countenance, or was he projecting? A woman couldn't help but be affected by something like this. After seeing his mother go through it, he'd been sensitized to the issue, but he felt better, knowing Billie was in remission. He picked up his water glass. "Well, here's to your good health."

Billie smiled. "Thanks." She looked away.

One of the uniformed cops came over to the booth. "Ms. Fox?"

"Yes?"

"Inspector Plavec just called. He and Inspector Hong got tied up and said they'd be half an hour late. They wanted to know if that's all right or if you'd rather reschedule."

"Wouldn't you know it," Billie said to Nick. "Cops and doctors. They always make you wait. I've considered billing them for my time but somehow I don't think I'd get the city auditor to buy it." She sighed. "Fortunately my briefcase is in the car. You wouldn't mind if I ran my law practice from one of your booths for a while, would you, Nick?"

Actually, the notion rather pleased him. "Not at all. Be my guest."

She turned to the cop. "Would you let Inspector Plavec know that I'll be glad to meet with them in half an hour?"

"Yes, ma'am." He left.

Billie looked weary. "If I'm beat, you must be dying."

"I've felt better."

"Why don't you rest? I need to make some calls."

He would have preferred to talk to her some more, but he did feel like hell and some rest was probably a good idea. "Maybe I will lie down for a while."

"I'll get my briefcase."

Billie got up and headed for the door. Nick watched her go. There was a bit of a swing in her walk. Nothing like Linda Nassari, but she had a little sass to her. Nick liked that. He liked her mind, too. Her sense of humor. Her strength. She had an

appeal that was as unorthodox as it was hard to describe. Maybe
it was as simple as she made him want to know her better.

BURLINGAME

Olga Diachenko rolled her mop bucket and cleaning supplies into the hospital room as quietly as she could, glancing
at the man in the bed. His eyes were open and he stared at
the ceiling, tears running down the sides of his face. He
seemed oblivious to her presence, perhaps in too much pain
to notice her. As she crept toward the bathroom, she heard him
cry out, imploring God for mercy. That, in itself, was not unusual. What did amaze her was that the words were in Russian.

Olga was Ukrainian herself, two years in the States. Her
Russian was not the best, maybe not so good as her English,
now, but like most Ukrainians of her generation, she spoke
it well enough.

Hesitating, Olga considered speaking to the man—perhaps
no more than a simple, "God be with you," but she didn't. One
never knew when offense might be taken, especially by a Russian.

It was unfortunate, because there were so few reminders of
the old country, though the Russian connection was hardly one
of her favorites. Olga had a few Ukrainian friends in San Francisco, and, of course, there was her family—Elena, her daughter, Sam, her American son-in-law, and their two children.
Olga lived in the family's basement apartment. When they
were alone, Olga and Elena spoke Ukrainian, but when others
were present, it was usually English. There were so few opportunities to speak her native tongue; too bad the patient
wasn't Ukrainian. It would be nice to chat with somebody
about home.

Proceeding into the bath, Olga turned on the light and

began to scrub the toilet. Moments later she heard another voice in the outer room. Another man had arrived and he was speaking Russian. She stopped to listen.

"Why the long face?" Alexei asked Igor. "You're alive. What could be better than that?"

"I've worried about you, Alexei. I was sure you'd been captured by the police. Or worse."

"Почему? *Why?* You don't trust me to do a job?"

"It's not a question of trust. It's a question of experience. So, tell me. What happened?"

"It's done."

"The two of them?"

"Both. At the same time and same place. Two more corpses to grow vegetables." Alexei dusted his hands. "I'm no longer a virgin, brother dear. I'm a professional assassin, the same as you."

Igor frowned, glancing toward the door. "Alexei, please. Watch what you say."

"Posh," his brother said, dismissing him. "You are no longer in the KGB, Igor Andreyevich, and the FBI couldn't care less about you these days. There are no hidden cameras and microphones here."

"Yes, but this is no place to discuss our business."

"How many doctors and nurses speak Russian in this country? If there are three, how many are listening to us?"

"I told you, Alexei, in this business discretion is everything. Your very survival depends upon it."

"Okay, fine," his younger brother said, dropping into the chair by the bed. "We'll speak no more of it." He took out a handkerchief and mopped his forehead.

"You're all right, are you?" Igor asked.

"You don't see any bullet holes in me, do you?"

Igor grimaced. His thickheaded brother just didn't get it. But at least he was in one piece. And successful, if he was to be believed. Igor studied him. "You look tired. Did you sleep well?"

"Like a baby."

Igor knew his brother had been drinking. He was sweating vodka from his pores. "You've been partying," he said.

"I had something to celebrate."

"You must return to Los Angles immediately, Alexei. Never stay over after you've completed your business. I should have made that clear."

"What about you?"

"That's another issue. Eve is coming. Between us we'll handle things. Go to the airport and get on the next plane."

"You know what your trouble is, Igor? You have no joy."

"Alexei, you've forgotten what I told you. This is not a business you do for fun. Break this rule and you will pay, perhaps with your life."

His brother got to his feet. "I am glad you are feeling better, Igor Andreyevich. *That* brings me joy."

Just then, there was the sound of a flushing toilet. The partially closed bathroom door opened and a short, heavyset woman emerged, pushing a mop bucket. In her other hand she carried cleaning supplies.

"Excuse, please," she said in English, scarcely glancing in their direction.

The two brothers exchanged surprised looks. Only then did Igor conjure up a vague recollection of someone having entered the room, minutes before Alexei's arrival.

After the woman had disappeared down the hall, Alexei shrugged and said, "It was only a stupid cleaning woman."

Igor did not dispute the fact. Nor did he make note of what he'd observed. The woman was some sort of immigrant. Though she had on a hospital uniform, she also wore a scarf over her gray hair, in the manner of an Eastern European peasant. Her physiognomy, demeanor and carriage were consistent with that analysis. Igor had been trained to note such things. Had he engaged her in conversation, he would have been able to identify the accent, perhaps down to country and region. The two words she'd uttered were insufficient for such a determination, however. Naturally, he considered the disastrous possibility that the woman spoke Russian.

Alexei, oblivious, lingered a moment. "Well, I guess I'll go, then. Not much I can do here."

"No, you've done what you came to do." Igor could see his brother's disappointment and felt badly. "Most impressive considering it was your maiden voyage."

Alexei brightened some at the remark. "Viktor will be pleased."

"I'm sure he will."

"Take care of yourself, Igor," Alexei said with a touch of warmth.

"And you have a good flight home."

Alexei hesitated, then came over, took Igor's face in his hands and kissed him on the lips. "Get well, soon, big brother."

"I will, Alexei."

Igor Sakharov watched his brother walk from the room. Whatever had happened, had happened. Alexei was confident, but it was possible he'd made a disastrous mistake. But Igor had made one as well. He'd seen the cleaning woman enter his room and promptly allowed it to slip from his mind. Yes, he was definitely getting old.

NORTH BEACH

Nick ran through the nursing home naked, hotly pursued by a platoon of Ninja warriors brandishing swords. Things were getting tense when he became aware of somebody saying his name. "Nick. Nick. Are you all right? Nick, wake up." He felt something cool on his face and that brought him to. Opening his eyes, he saw a woman. She seemed familiar, especially looking down on him as she was. Then he remembered. Billie Fox.

"Uh?" He tried to lift his head.

"Hey, you were in a pretty deep sleep," she said. "I don't think that's good, coming on the heels of a concussion." She looked square into his eyes. "Are you okay?"

His brain did seem to be in a fog, but he was coming out of it. "Yeah. Dickson here? Is half an hour up already?"

"More like an hour. That's a hundred and seventy-five bucks at my rate, but two doughnuts at theirs. No big deal."

Nick smiled, but it hurt his nose and his cheek. "Everybody's waiting for me, huh?"

"They sent me up to get you, I guess figuring the job required a woman's touch. If you don't feel up to it, Nick, don't come down. In fact, this might not be a bad time to go to the hospital and get checked out."

"I will later."

He sat up with Billie's help.

"Just need to get my sea legs."

"You sure you want to do this? You can talk to them anytime. I really think you shouldn't push it."

"I don't know what kind of a lawyer you are, Billie, but you make a hell of a nurse."

"You could have gone all day without saying that."

"I offended you."

"No, I groove on sexist comments. But that's all right. You've had a severe blow to the head. I'm sure you're not yourself."

"Thanks for making excuses for me." He stretched his sore body. "Maybe I'll go to the bathroom before I come down."

"That's where I draw the line," she said. "I'll see you downstairs." With that, she got up and left the room.

Nick remembered why he liked her. But they did have serious business to conduct. He went into the bathroom.

The face that greeted him in the mirror was enough to cost

him his appetite. He took the cotton out of his nostrils and examined the nose. The last time it had looked this bad was when he got clobbered in the puss by a left-hander's big, sweeping curveball. It had taught him to turn away from a pitch rather than into it. Life's lessons could be painful. That hadn't changed.

Downstairs he found Billie in Benny Vocino's booth. Dickson Hong was up front, talking to a group of cops. Nick sat down across from Billie. She began putting away the legal documents that had been spread out before her.

"I've rounded up my witness, now the judge has disappeared."

"Hong's up front."

Billie turned. "Dickson, let's get this show on the road!" she called. "Hard as it is to believe, I've got only so many hours I can devote to my country."

"We'll be right there, Ms. Fox."

Billie looked at Nick and smiled the smile of a martyr.

"It doesn't bother you that he's investigating Culp's death?" Nick asked.

"Dick and I know each other pretty well. I do mostly criminal defense work. Usually, when he and I see each other, I'm taking him apart on the stand, but I don't think he takes it personally. What about you and him? Weren't there some hard feelings after that trial?"

"On his part, I'm sure."

Hong came walking toward the back of the dining room, followed by a large, ruddy-faced guy, presumably Carl Plavec. Hong's partner had the look of a plow horse on his way to the fields. They reached the booth.

"My apologies to you both," Hong said. He took a good look at Nick. "So they shot you, too."

"Thanks to Ms. Fox's timely objection, the gunman was slightly off target."

"The Sassos are having a bad week," Hong said, more with sorrow than wit.

He introduced his partner. Nick shook Plavec's hand.

"How many were there, Nick?" Hong asked.

"Four."

"Can you ID them?"

"The one who tried to shoot me I got a very good look at. Of the other three, one was big, one had long hair and the other was small, nondescript."

"The guys from Burglary ask you to look at pictures?"

"Yeah. I'm supposed to go to the hospital first, but we'll see. I wanted to stick around and update you. Have a seat."

The two inspectors sat down—Hong next to Billie, Plavec beside Nick.

"So, have you solved the case?" Hong asked, directing his question to Billie.

"No, we've been waiting for the master investigator."

"It's awfully early in the morning for flattery, isn't it?"

Billie said, "Actually, if Sonny had to pick somebody to go after his murderer, it would be you, Dick."

"Thank you."

"I'm sure Joe would feel the same," Nick added.

Dickson Hong, looking embarrassed, nodded.

"Any chance of getting a cup of coffee?" Plavec said, running his hand through his thin blond hair. He was thirty—give or take—and losing his hair early. Though his face was round, his features were pinched, his pale eyes narrow-set. When he smiled, his grin seemed to wrap around his nose.

"Anybody else?" Nick asked.

"Not for me," Billie said.

Hong shook his head. "No, thanks."

Nick told one of the kitchen workers to bring coffee to anyone who wanted some.

Hong steepled his fingers. "So, you two are getting along okay?"

"Yeah, can you believe it?" Billie said. "Me and a Yankees fan?"

Hong allowed himself a mild grin. Nick shook his head.

"What's wrong with the Yankees, anyway? They're the best team in baseball. Look at the record."

"To me the Yankees are arrogant," Billie said. "Like Republicans." She glanced around the table at the three men. "Now that I've already opened my mouth, I suppose I'm in the company of three Republicans."

"Independent," Hong said.

"Me, too," Plavec chimed in.

She gave Nick an inquiring look.

"I voted for Reagan, does that qualify me?"

"For something I shouldn't get into," she said dryly. "But never mind. We're here to talk about murder, not rape of the working poor."

Nick chuckled. The woman had a smart mouth, but he liked her. "How about that, Dickson," he said. "Ms. Fox saves my life and now she thinks she can get away with anything."

"If I'd known your politics, I might have thought twice before chucking that sign through the window," she rejoined.

Nick laughed. Hard enough that it hurt his ribs.

"Okay folks," Hong said, "let's get down to business. You're both experienced in criminal matters and you have ties to the victims. I consider that a resource. Do either of you have anything that would be helpful to the investigation?" He looked back and forth between them.

Nick gestured for her to go ahead. "Ladies first."

"I don't have much to contribute," Billie said. "Sonny and I mostly talked about our daughter, Emily. We seldom discussed our work. There were exceptions, though. Like earlier this week. Sonny and I met for lunch. He wasn't explicit but he hinted that work was getting to him. He was concerned and worried."

"About what?"

"He wouldn't say, but my impression was somebody was giving him trouble. He may even have felt he was in danger."

"But he didn't elaborate?"

"No, I tried to get him to talk about it, but Sonny played his cards close to his vest. He had a lot of pride and he took his clients' rights to confidentiality very seriously. I did get the impression though that his disillusionment was with the system, the legal system—lawyers, judges, the works."

"The man had a point," Nick said dryly.

Billie gave him a look, then, returning to her statement, said, "I suspect something was going on with a case that was an affront to his sense of fairness. That would be like Sonny. I've seen it before, but this had him more upset than usual."

"Do you think it could have something to do with the murders?" Carl Plavec asked.

"Quite possibly. Sonny tried to play it down, but I think he was afraid."

"Nothing has turned up in the search of his office," Hong said. "Is there any other way to find out what cases he was working on?"

"You could check his filings with the courts. He couldn't have had that many cases working."

"Good idea," Plavec said. He got out a notepad and wrote on it.

"Oh, and there's something else I might mention," Billie continued. "Sonny was heavily involved in Martin Fong's various political causes. Some were awfully controversial, which could also mean dangerous."

"Fong, the supervisor?" Nick said.

"Yes," Billie replied, "they were lovers."

Nick did a mental double take. "Your ex was gay?"

"Gay, bi...one or the other."

Nick was dumbfounded.

"I didn't divorce Sonny because I'm a bitch," Billie explained. "I divorced him because I didn't have the right plumbing to compete. It's the first time in my life I've ever felt totally and completely at a disadvantage just because I'm a woman."

"The lady's had a colorful life," Plavec said to Nick.

"So I see."

Plavec's coffee arrived. Nick asked Billie if she wanted something else.

"Maybe a glass of water."

"Bring some Pelligrino," Nick told the boy.

Hong, who'd remained silent and contemplative, asked Billie which causes Sonny and Martin Fong were involved in together.

"Gay rights, of course. Beyond that you'd have to speak with Martin. When I spoke with him last night he agonized over the fact that Sonny's death could be somehow connected with Martin's political causes."

"Oh?" Hong said.

"He didn't say anything about that to you, did he, Dickson?" Carl Plavec said.

"No. I spoke with him very briefly on the phone after they'd gone by to tell him about Sonny being killed," Hong explained to Billie and Nick. "He didn't say anything about having suspicions. But I'm sure he was still in shock and not thinking along those lines. We'll be talking to him, though. He's been advised."

"There's only one problem with all this," Nick said, lifting the ice pack from his cheek. "How does my brother figure in? I can guarantee you he wasn't involved in a campaign for gay rights or saving the whales."

Plavec guffawed.

"I have no idea how he was involved," Billie said. "I'm not trying to make a case for anything specific. I'm just giving you what my gut tells me."

Nick asked the inspectors if they were satisfied there was nothing in Sonny's office that would indicate what he and Joe were up to.

"Nothing so far," Carl Plavec replied. "A team's working over there as we speak, but as of the last time I checked, there's been nothing of consequence."

A big bottle of Pelligrino was placed on the table. Nick opened it and poured some water for Billie and himself. "Dickson?"

Hong shook his head. Nick handed a glass to Billie.

"Right from the source, guaranteed to cure all that ails you," he said.

"Thanks."

He'd no sooner said it than he realized his remark might have brought to mind her battle with breast cancer. He didn't want to appear insensitive, and was relieved to see nothing on her face to indicate she was upset. Maybe his experience with his mother made him overly sensitive. Hurting Billie was the very last thing he wanted to do.

Plavec's coffee cup was refilled.

"If you're searching Sonny's office," Billie said, "be sure to check his computer. Sonny did everything on it. Once I stopped doing clerical work, Sonny didn't bother replacing me. He did everything himself on the computer. Correspondence, pleadings, the works."

"There was no computer in the office when we got there," Hong said. "It was probably taken in the burglary."

"Sonny's office was burglarized, too?" Billie said.

"It seems so. Yesterday morning or the night before."

"And they cleaned out Joe's office upstairs," Nick said. "To me that says they not only wanted to eliminate the principals, they also wanted to destroy any evidence pointing to whatever it was Joe and Culp were into."

"You haven't given us your take on this yet, Nick," Hong said. "Have a theory?"

He put the ice pack down on the table. "I'm afraid I'm going to have to disagree completely with Ms. Fox. I think what got Joe and Sonny killed was some scheme, deal, project, investment that Joe was involved in with Elaine Chang. Because of the messages on Joe's answering machine, we know Sonny and Joe realized they were in danger." He turned to Billie. "That would explain Sonny's remark to you. Sonny also mentioned being followed, perhaps threatened. He warned Joe to be careful. Both their offices were burglarized and their files and computers taken. There was danger all right, and it involved a common undertaking."

"Who's Elaine Chang?" Billie asked.

"My brother's mistress."

"But not of the ordinary garden variety," Hong said. "Ms. Chang is a businesswoman of sorts. She brokers deals. Not all of them legitimate as she likes to think. We've long suspected she has contacts with the Chinese Triads, the criminal elements, but we can't prove it. The feds have had their eye on her, but haven't come up with anything solid. She's a smart cookie, a woman with friends in both low and high places."

"Why do you think Sonny would be involved in something with her?"

"Because my sister-in-law heard Joe and Sonny talking about Elaine."

"What?" Dickson Hong said.

"I found this out when I talked to Gina after I left you last night."

Nick then recounted the gist of what he'd learned from Gina, though he still didn't mention Joe's gun and Gina's comments about wanting to use it on him. "It all fits," he said. "Elaine and Joe were working some sort of deal. There's even an oblique reference to it in a message from Elaine on the answering machine upstairs, assuming it's still there. Joe had at least asked Sonny to advise him, maybe negotiate the deal."

"What kind of deal?" Billie asked.

"I don't know exactly."

"I can tell you right now I'm not buying this," she said, "but go on."

"Sonny wouldn't go to the meeting they talked about, so Joe and Elaine went without him. They met some Chinese guy at a restaurant in Tiburon. Gina had no idea who."

"We've got to talk to Mrs. Sasso," Plavec said to Hong.

Dickson Hong nodded, his eyes riveted on Nick.

"The other thing," Nick continued, "is that Joe and Sonny planned to meet last night."

"Your sister-in-law heard this?" Hong asked.

Nick could see the wheels turning in Dickson Hong's mind. But there was no point in him trying to protect her. Hong would be exploring every angle. "Yes, she heard them discussing it."

Hong got that expression on his face that Nick knew all too well—the look of a man putting pieces together in a puzzle. "Go on."

"There's not a lot more. In the brief conversation I had with Joe, he said he was working on something really big and that when he'd put it together he'd solve his financial problems."

"Did he give you any indication what type of thing it was?" Hong asked.

"No, but my gut instinct is that Gina's right. It has to do with Elaine Chang. At least she's heavily involved in whatever it is."

Carl Plavec shook his head. "None of this points to any suspects in the shootings last night."

"No," Nick said, "but if we can find out what deal Joe and Sonny were working on, we'll know what people were involved and that could lead us to the killers. This much I do know. My brother was a wheeler-dealer. He was always looking for the fast buck. Sometimes that meant getting involved with unsavory types. To be honest, I think it cost both him and Culp their lives."

Billie took a long drink of water. "I'm sure you're sincerely convinced of that, but I still don't buy it."

"Why not?"

"Because I know Sonny. He was passionate about justice, about doing the right thing. He considered himself the champion of the little guy. Sonny was not a shark. He had causes he believed in and he worked tirelessly on them. He would not be involved in a moneymaking scheme, even in an advisory capacity."

"But he *was* involved, Billie," Nick said. "I heard what had to be his voice on Joe's tape machine. My sister-in-law heard them talking about meeting with Elaine Chang, and Sonny did agree to meet with Joe last night. Presumably that was why they were together when they were killed."

Billie said, "Didn't you say Sonny declined to attend a meeting?"

"The first one. Unfortunately for them both, there was a later meeting."

"Sonny could have been placating him, but had no intention to get involved."

"You're reaching."

"Well, if Sonny was involved with Joe, it wasn't for the reasons you're suggesting. It was something else."

"This is all speculation," Hong said. "Why don't we listen to the answering machine? We have a recording of what may be Sonny and also Elaine Chang. Is that right, Nick?"

"Right."

"Carl, would you ask Doolan or Bomberg if the lab guys are finished with the office so we can listen to the machine?"

"Sure."

Plavec went off. Billie excused herself to go to the ladies' room, leaving Nick with Dickson Hong. The inspector's gaze drifted, never quite resting on Nick.

"This is a complicated one," Nick volunteered.

"For the moment." Hong steepled his fingers. "What's your sister-in-law like?"

"Salt of the earth."

"She capable of doing this?"

"The shootings?"

Hong nodded.

Nick could see Hong had already jumped three steps ahead. He shook his head. "I don't think so, Dick."

"Where was she last night?"

"She went out to dinner and a movie with her fourteen-year-old son."

Hong considered that. "Well, we'll talk to them."

"Why do you think it would be Gina?" Nick asked.

Hong reflected for a moment. "The shooter was not an accomplished assassin. If it was a hit, say, the result of a big drug deal gone bad, it would have been more professional in all probability. In Mrs. Sasso we've got a scorned wife. We've got a mistress. We've got a lawyer, maybe one handling a divorce action. Mrs. Sasso knew there was going to be a meeting that evening. There could have been a heated confrontation. Jealousy is a powerful motive. Plus, the wife doing in her errant husband is clean and simple. Mind you, I'm not accusing anybody. I haven't even talked to the lady. She's not a suspect at this point. But you asked."

"I don't think she is capable of murder, Dickson. Not any more than say, me."

"We haven't talked about that, either, have we? I mean,

you could have a motive for killing your brother. At this stage there are countless possibilities."

Nick was just paranoid enough to wonder if he was being baited. "I was here for a couple of hours before the cops came to tell me Joe had been killed. Donny McCabe came in and we talked for a while. And of course, the staff all saw me."

Carl Plavec returned and, seeing there was a serious conversation in progress, silently slipped into the booth next to Nick.

"We aren't certain about the time of death," Hong continued. "As you know, these things can range over a number of hours. Where were you before you were here?"

"I visited my father at the nursing home."

"Where was that?"

"Ingleside."

Hong's cobra eyes settled on Nick, but he said nothing.

"Yes, I know," Nick said, "I could easily have swung by the Marina on my way back here. But that places the shootings at the front end of the time frame."

Hong hunched his shoulders. "Like I said, there are any number of possibilities."

Billie returned to the booth. Dickson Hong stood to allow her to slide in.

"Did I miss anything?" she asked.

"A lot of guy talk," Nick replied.

"Really? Somehow I doubt that three such brilliant minds could be content talking about golf swings and jock itch. Are you sure I'm not being patronized?"

"Obviously, you're a feminist," Nick said.

"Duh." She drank some Pelligrino. "By the way, your ladies' room needs help."

"I'll see that it's taken care of."

"Seriously," Billie said. "What did I miss?"

"We were trying to determine whether I should be on the suspect list," Nick said.

"Oh. Well, that's cool. I can see how that might be. You kill your brother for the inheritance, Sonny for revenge, then you hire some guys to beat the shit out of you...or, you decide to save the money and simply throw yourself down the stairs, after inflicting a superficial gunshot wound. Yeah, I could sell that to a jury." She smiled. "But I'd rather defend you."

"Because of my charm and boyish good looks?"

"No, because I don't believe in the death penalty."

"Oh. Well, that makes me feel much better. What should we plead? Temporary insanity?"

"This is all very amusing," Hong said, "but Carl and I are on the clock. Could we get on with this?"

"Okay," Nick said, "but Billie raises a good point. Say the killer is somebody like Gina. Why the burglaries and the assault on me?"

"Like you said, Nick, it's a complicated case."

"Since we're throwing around names, why not Elaine Chang?" Nick asked. "She knew about the meeting at Sonny's last night and might have a motive."

"She's on our list," Hong said. "After you mentioned her name last night, we tried to get ahold of her, but nobody was home. There's a team headed to her place now."

"I'm starting to feel left out," Billie quipped. "Half of San Francisco is apparently under suspicion—or maybe I should say half the women."

"Criminal defense lawyers are immune," Hong said sardonically. "Without them, there's no fair trial. Plus, how could I do my job without you second-guessing me?"

"Dick, you make my day."

"Anybody interested in the answering machine?" Carl Plavec asked.

"Yeah, what did they say?"

"There wasn't one up there. The bad guys must have taken it."

"Swell," Nick said.

"Can't you tell us what was on it?" Billie asked.

Nick cast his mind through the fog encapsulating his brain, trying to conjure up the precise details. "The one that was on there yesterday was probably from Culp—at least that's my assumption. He told Joe his office had been burglarized and said the burglars were after files, not valuables. Then he warned him to be careful." He gave Billie a wan smile. "Like I said before, this just doesn't square with your theory about the murders being connected with some cause Sonny and Martin were mixed up in. Joe wouldn't donate to a cause like that, much less get involved in it."

"We're arguing generalities."

"I agree," Hong said.

"Was there anything else on the machine?"

"When I played the messages, that was it. But this morning the burglars played the tape and I heard another message—one that obviously came in after I last played the machine. It was a woman, the same voice I'd heard when the messages were played for me in New York. The accent was soft, but distinctive. I'm assuming it was Elaine Chang."

"What did she say?" Plavec asked.

"She said she couldn't or didn't want to come to the meeting—presumably the fateful meeting last night—and she suggested that Joe come see her afterward. Then—and this is very interesting—she said she needed his final decision, now or never. At that point the message was cut off."

"You figure she was talking about this deal you've been referring to?" Plavec asked.

"That would be my theory."

Dickson Hong pondered what he heard. Nick watched him.

"What do you think?" Nick asked.

"I'm not so sure it's an either-or situation. A couple of

different things could be going on. Both you and Ms. Fox could be right."

"But only one entanglement got them killed," Nick rejoined.

"Yes. And it'll be our task to figure out which."

Mike Doolan came to the booth, asking for a few minutes with Hong and Plavec.

Billie said, "Unless there's something else, Dick, I'm going to go out into the big bad world and earn some money."

"No, I don't have anything else. You've been very helpful and generous with your time. Mayor Green and the people of San Francisco are grateful."

"If you think I'm going to go easy on you the next time we face off in court, Dick, you've got another think coming."

"I would never be that naive."

Saluting them, the inspectors left the booth. Billie finished gathering her things. Nick watched her, the curiosity he felt a bit surprising.

"How's your daughter bearing up, if you don't mind me asking?"

"She's confused, doesn't really understand or know how to deal with it. She'll survive, though. I'm actually going home to be with her, but I wanted Dick to feel badly about all the time he took."

"You're a very sneaky woman."

She grinned. "You just figured that out?"

Billie slid out of the booth. Nick did, as well. They faced each other. She was tall, about Bree's height. But the resemblance ended there. In fact, Billie Fox was like no woman Nick had been friendly with, much less one he'd been attracted to.

"I'm no doctor," she said, "but you might want to have somebody look at that nose."

"Bad?"

"It brings back memories of the time I got punched out by an old boyfriend back during my cocktail-waitress days."

"You were a cocktail waitress?"

"That was before Sonny, before the law, before I went legit and got a real day job as a legal secretary."

"So your boyfriend punched you out."

"He sucker punched me, broke my nose. I still have a bump, see," she said, turning her face.

"Nice guy."

"I was so pissed, I kicked him in the balls. Damn near killed him. We ended up in the same emergency room. They had four security guards trying to keep us apart. Never saw the sonovabitch again, which was fortunate for him."

"I'm glad you're on my team," he said. "And I want to thank you again for saving my life. I wish I could think of something I could do for you."

Billie hesitated. "Buy me dinner sometime."

"By all means. In fact, whenever you're in the neighborhood drop in and have a free dinner on the house."

"Personally cooked?"

"It could be arranged."

Billie smiled, her lips sensuous-looking. She extended her hand. "Nice meeting you, Nick."

"Let's stay in touch," he said, keeping her hand in his. "Dickson's a good cop, but we bring a lot to the party, especially as a team."

"Nick, we don't agree on a damn thing."

"That makes us all the more effective, don't you think?"

She laughed. "I think you'd better go get your head examined."

With that, she picked up her briefcase and left.

THE RICHMOND

When Billie got home she found a herd of wildebeests running across the TV screen. Her father was in the front room ironing sheets as he watched an animal show on the Discovery Channel. The volume was down, which told her Emily was still asleep.

"Hi, Pop."

"Billie! How'd it go with the police?" Mel asked, putting down the iron.

"It was an exciting morning. I saved a guy from getting killed." She told him about throwing the sign through the plate-glass window as Nick was about to be shot.

"Nobody can say you've lived a boring life, Billie."

"I was in good form today. I don't know why. Sonny was murdered last night, I'm worried about Emily, but I still sucked it up and played hardball with the big boys."

"That's been your life, honey."

"I know, but sometimes I forget and surprise myself. It's not easy being a girl in a man's world. And, if I can't admit that to you, who can I admit it to?"

"That's what fathers are for." For several moments she watched the wildebeests, then glanced toward the back of the house. "Emily still asleep?"

"All morning."

"She had a rough night." Billie checked her watch. "I'm going to look in on her." She went into her daughter's room. Emily was in a deep sleep, her skinny legs tangled in the sheets. Billie did what she could to untangle the child without awakening her.

The previous evening, for some inexplicable reason, Emily had awakened shortly after Martin Fong had left. With a prescience known only to children, she'd said, "Mommy, what happened?"

Knowing she'd have to be told eventually, Billie decided to get it over with. She sat Emily down and gave her the terrible news. The girl was stunned and confused, then began to cry. Billie and her dad had done their best to console her. "I'll never ever see him again?" Emily implored, probably hoping the terrible misfortune was subject to change. Not unexpectedly she'd also inquired about Martin. "Is he dead, too?"

"No," Billie had assured her. "Martin is very sad, but he's just fine."

Billie hadn't wanted to make any promises with regard to Martin until she'd spoken with him, but her hope was that he'd remain in Emily's life. The logistics, though, could be awkward. But there would be time to consider all that.

Emily had insisted on sleeping with Billie, a request that could hardly be denied. Eventually she'd fallen asleep, and Billie let her stay in her bed until morning, when she'd carried the child to her own room. Emily might have liked the security of her mother's bed, but it meant Billie hadn't gotten more than two or three hours of sleep.

After pushing the child's light brown locks back off her forehead, she returned to the front room where Mel folded his last sheet. "Can I help you, Pop?"

"No, just have to put away the board. You sit down and rest. You look tired."

She sat on the sofa and stared at the TV. The camera was on a lion stalking his prey.

"I'm worried," Billie said to her father.

"About what?"

"Emily."

"She'll adjust, honey."

"No, I don't mean because of that. I mean because she's lost one parent and the other one could be on the way out."

"Billie, don't talk that way."

"You know as well as I do that I could have a relapse. The thought of dying and leaving Emily without a mother has haunted me, but now she has no father. Thank God for you, Pop, but if I'm not exactly feeling young at forty-three, then you... Well, you know what I mean."

"We have to make do as best we can. All of us. You gain nothing by worrying."

Billie smiled gratefully. "What would I do without you?"

"You'd manage."

She stared at the lion on TV, stealthily advancing on a hapless wildebeest. But her mind drifted to the conversation she'd had with Nick Sasso, Dickson Hong and Carl Plavec at the Yankee Clipper. She knew she was right about Sonny, and it frustrated her that she couldn't prove it. It bothered her that the evidence seemed to support Nick's contention that Sonny was mixed up with Joe Sasso in some scheme. That had to be wrong. Sonny had always been something of a Don Quixote figure, in his own mind as well as others. He had once described his practice as an exercise in tilting at windmills—a loner up against the system, a guy living in a fanciful world where justice actually meant something, though perhaps only to him.

Poor Sonny. Billie remembered how tired and dispirited he'd looked at lunch on Tuesday. He'd insisted he was fine, but obviously he wasn't—not given what had happened. She was sorry now she hadn't pressed him, though even if he had confided in her, chances were she couldn't have done anything to save him. Sonny always did everything his own way, even suffer.

On the TV the stalking lion rose from the grass and pounced on an unsuspecting wildebeest that had strayed from the herd. The poor creature couldn't have taken more than half a dozen strides before the huge predator knocked it violently to the ground. Billie shuddered.

Oddly, what came to mind was the first man she'd dated after she and Sonny split up. But then, as she thought about it, it really wasn't that odd. The guy's name was Leo—a nifty irony that her subconscious mind must have spotted. The lion and Leo were an obvious association, but even more potent may have been their common brutality.

Leo was six-three and two-hundred-and-twenty-pounds of testosterone, a steel worker with a jaw like Bluto and all the finesse in bed of a Mack truck. Basically, he was a fucking machine, which is what Billie had been looking for at the time. After her husband left her for another man, her femininity and self-confidence had been shattered. She had but one goal, and that was to prove to herself she was desirable, if not irresistible.

She'd met Leo at a Giants game. This was back when the team still played at Candlestick Park. Billie and her father sat in the same box as Leo, who'd brought his nephew, a handicapped teenager, to the game. She assumed that indicated a spark of humanity beneath the bulging biceps, the massive shoulders, the pecs. In fact, Leo turned out to be a decent guy, if somewhat single-minded. His sole interest in women was sex, which he regarded as a contact sport.

During the game she'd fantasized about inviting Leo to fuck her until she cried uncle, especially after they'd exchanged looks and a few quips about the action on the field. The deal was sealed when he'd favored her with a grin and a wink. After the last out had been made and everybody got up to go, Billie handed Leo her card without so much as a word. He looked at it and stuck it in his pocket, then sauntered off with his nephew.

Billie hadn't held out any hope that something would come of it. It was just an impulsive gesture, a meaningless bit of bravado on her part. But, to her surprise, he called her office the next day. "It's Leo, from the game," he said by way of introduction. "So did the card mean you think I need a lawyer or that you want to go out for a few beers?"

"A few beers."

"When and where?"

Billie hadn't been so bold as to suggest his place, so she picked a bar located south of Market which attracted an eclectic, mostly young crowd. Leo she judged to be a few years younger than she, but blue-collar and therefore not particularly hip.

She arrived in the briefest dress she owned, high-heel sandals and bikini panties. That was it. Leo was nicely showered and dripping with cologne. He had on designer jeans and a polo shirt that barely contained his rippling muscles. They had two beers, talked about the Giants and working on high-rise buildings. Leo did ask what kind of law she practiced, then quipped, if he ever ran afoul the law, he'd be sure to give her a call.

His proposition was soon in coming and it was direct. "So you want to go to my place and get laid?"

"Sure, why not?"

Billie followed his pickup, knowing that afterward she'd want her own transportation close at hand. Leo had a modest flat in Ocean View, a long drive out. He had enough integrity to admit that he'd been separated from his wife for two years, but that she'd only recently filed for divorce. The way Billie saw it, he could have had three wives and it wouldn't have mattered, given her intentions.

Leo got them each another beer from the refrigerator, and she went into the bathroom to undress and put on some lubricant, just in case the foreplay was unduly brief. It was a good thing.

When she came out of the bath, Leo was sitting on the bed—naked, except for a condom—sipping a beer. A flicker of second thoughts did go through her, but she reminded herself this was therapy and that it was essential to her emotional health. He handed her the other bottle. They drank the beers and Leo played with her tits as they chatted intermittently about the horrors of married life and divorce. The alcohol notwithstanding, she was tight as a piano wire, but did her damnedest to appear relaxed. Then he kissed her as a courtesy, if not out of desire.

"So, how do you like it?" he asked her as he kneaded her mound.

"Rough," Billie replied, summoning all her courage.

"That's right down my alley."

She soon discovered he wasn't kidding. Their lovemaking started with a semi body slam, followed by a lionlike pounce. Leo clearly considered himself king of the bedroom and was determined to prove it. The sex was more vigorous than actually violent, but Leo taught her what it meant to be ravished. Billie was far from innocent, despite the modesty of her married sex life. Even so, it took her a while to get into the spirit of Leo's exuberant rooting.

Throwing every ounce of strength into it that she had, Billie somehow managed to work herself into a frenzy. She was amazed and delighted when she came, though even in her delirium she realized it was an orgasm born of desperation as much as friction. "Jesus Christ," she said afterward, feeling like she'd just copulated with a horse.

"Like that?" Leo asked between gasps for air, his cologned body dripping with sweat.

"You're terrific," she told him, knowing that would please him nearly as much as a blow job.

"There's more where that came from," he said immodestly.

Billie had proceeded to avail herself of his ready supply of libido, screwing him the three subsequent weekends. She found she needed a week to recover, but was ready when her opportunity to get reamed came again.

A month was all it took. Courtesy of Leo, she'd gotten the carbon blown out of her carburetor and was a new woman. Her time with the man of steel behind her, Billie was ready to go on with life.

"Sometimes that's a little hard to watch, isn't it?" her father said as he peered over her shoulder at the TV screen. At the moment the lion was tearing the carcass of his prey limb from limb, blood running down his chin.

"Predators are a necessary part of life, I guess."

"Somehow I don't think that wildebeest would agree, honey."

"True, but they might enjoy the near misses—thrill of the chase and all that."

Mel Fox smiled. "You must identify with lions."

"They have their uses, Pop," Billie quipped.

A commercial came on. Mel sat down in his easy chair and turned to her. "Tell me," he said, "what was Nick Sasso like?"

Her father's instincts positively amazed her at times. Or was it that she developed some sort of glow in the presence of animal magnetism that stayed with her hours after the fact? Even so, her first instinct was denial. "He was okay."

"That's all?"

"Pop, the first words we exchanged were right after he regained consciousness. He looked like he'd been through a meat grinder."

Her father shrugged. "Maybe I'm wrong."

"About what?"

"You had that look."

"Well, you *are* mistaken," she said, flushing, realizing she'd been caught yet again. The fact was that Mel Fox had always been able to tell when she'd developed an interest in somebody. During her high-school years, it had been downright embarrassing. The night she'd lost her virginity, her junior year, she was positive he knew as surely as if he'd been there. He'd said nothing, but he didn't have to.

The program came back on, drawing her father's attention. Billie, though, remained lost in thought.

Ironically, the only relationship she'd had that her father totally misread was the one with Sonny. Mel hadn't seen that one coming, right up to the day she told him she was getting married. He'd never questioned her about her motives, but what it boiled down to was that her prior experiences with men had been less than exemplary and Sonny at least was honorable and had a certain nobility about him. Then, too, she had reached her thirty-fifth year with the old biological clock ticking away at double time.

Yes, she'd given Sonny Culp the prime years of her life, coming out of the marriage older and far less eligible. She'd been philosophical about it, though. There was more to life than romantic love, she reasoned. That was why it annoyed the hell out of her every time she'd meet some guy who'd set off a little bell in her head.

Much as she hated it, Nick Sasso was such a guy.

During her drive home she flushed with embarrassment for having all but asked him to take her out to dinner. True, he'd been quick to take the hint, but what else could he do? She *had* saved his life. Even so, she was ashamed, humiliated, embarrassed. It was one thing to be needy, and another to let it show. The only face-saving course of action was to avoid him, which was what she vowed to do. A prideful reaction, maybe, but necessary.

Besides, she had no idea what his domestic status was. He didn't wear a ring, but that didn't mean there wasn't somebody in his life. And to think, she'd made a pass at him without finding out. It was enough to make her want to crawl in a hole.

"You know," her father said, "I'm worried about Martin." Billie blinked. "Why?"

"He's a fragile person and last night he was terribly upset."

Her father was right, as he usually was in such matters. She, too, felt badly for him, and she wondered if maybe it wasn't incumbent on her to reach out to the poor man. Plus, she was convinced Martin probably held the key to why Sonny had been killed.

The police might have talked to him by now and culled the information they needed. She wondered if she dare phone Martin and ask? Chances were he didn't care about that much at this point and to bring it up might be crass, but there certainly wasn't any reason why she couldn't touch base with him. He'd done her the kindness of coming by last night, after all, and they did share a concern for Emily. And Billie was sincere about wanting Martin in her daughter's life. It would be good for them both.

"Maybe I'll give Martin a call," she told her father.

"Good idea."

Billie got up and went to the phone and dialed Sonny and Martin's apartment on Nob Hill. The place had actually belonged to Martin. Sonny had moved in once their relationship had become committed.

The phone rang a couple of times, then she got the answering machine. It was Sonny's voice, which gave her a momentary start. "We're not home. Please leave a message."

After the beep, she said, "Martin, it's Billie. If you're there, please pick up. I want to talk to you about Emily. Martin? Are you there?" She waited a moment. "Please give me a call then," she said.

Billie was about to hang up when there was a click and she heard Martin Fong's voice, sounding weak and lethargic. "Hello. I'm here."

"Martin, did I wake you?"

"Yeah, I didn't sleep last night, so I took some pills."

"I'm sorry."

"That's all right," he said, slurring his words, sounding dopey. "I should be up. What time is it, anyway?" He really sounded out of it.

"Martin, are you okay? How many pills did you take?"

"A lot. I wanted to sleep." He sniffled.

"Maybe I should call an ambulance."

"No, no, I didn't take that many, though I thought about it. I just wanted to sleep for a long time. I can't tell you how much it hurts, Billie."

"How long ago did you take the pills?"

"Oh, hours. They've mostly worn off. I'm really all right. But it's nice to know you care."

The irony struck her. "I can tell you're having a rough time."

"I loved him, Billie. I truly did."

She bit her lip, glancing over at her father. It was amazing how crazy life could be—she and Martin Fong, of all people, crying together. "Sonny will be missed," she said, her eyes filling.

"Oh, God..." Martin Fong broke into heart-wrenching sobs.

She let him cry for a few moments then said, "Would you rather I call back later?"

"No, actually, I feel like talking, if you can put up with me." There was a hitch in his voice. "Did you say you wanted to talk about Emily?"

"Yes, I wanted to know how you feel about seeing her from time to time. I thought, for example, you might come over for dinner occasionally. I'm no expert in these matters, but I thought continuity might be good for her."

"I'd love that. And it's damn decent of you to ask me, considering," Martin said, sniffling again.

"We've all had a loss and it's best to pull together."

Martin seemed to lose it then, clearly overwhelmed with sorrow.

Billie was reluctant to hang up without making sure he was all right. She decided it would be a good idea to keep him talking.

"Martin, is there anybody you can call to come over and be with you? I don't think this is a good time for you to be alone."

"Oh, I've got a million friends, of course. But they're all political friends. They're in the business of wanting something, not giving."

"What about your family?"

"Are you kidding? My parents have never forgiven me since I came out."

Billie knew that, but under the circumstances she thought they might be capable of showing some compassion. "How about if we get together, then, you and me?" she volunteered. "We can meet for a drink or a cup of coffee. It would do us both good to talk about Emily."

"I'd like that. Maybe when I've pulled myself together."

The criminal defense lawyer in her couldn't resist. "Martin, have the police gotten ahold of you yet?"

There was a momentary silence, then he said, "Last night I spoke with them. And there's a message on my machine from this morning when I was asleep. Why?"

She wasn't sure whether or not to press, finally deciding that she could. "I met with the homicide inspectors this morning and there seem to be conflicting indications of what was going on that got Sonny and Joe Sasso killed. I'm just curious, do you know if Sonny had any inkling he was in danger?"

"What do you mean?"

"The last few times I saw Sonny, he seemed down. I got the impression there was a case bothering him. I don't suppose you have any idea what it might have been."

"We didn't talk about his work. I was so involved in my stuff that maybe he felt he couldn't share. And maybe I failed him by...not showing...more interest." Martin's voice broke.

"Martin, it's not your fault."

"You say that, but you don't know."

"Whatever it was that got Sonny killed had nothing to do with you...unless he came up against one of your political enemies who felt he'd gotten in the way."

Billie had never had much interest in San Francisco's political power struggles, nor any patience with it. She did know that Henry Chin, the D.A., and Martin were at the vortex of the storm. They were the two most prominent Asian-American politicians in the city and at opposite ends of the political spectrum. Chin had the support of the business community and much of the Chinatown establishment. He'd earned a reputation as a ruthless prosecutor and had long had ambitions for higher office.

Martin, a liberal, was firmly in the mayor, Bobby Green's, camp and the mayor's point man in both the Asian and gay communities. He and Henry Chin were not only political enemies, but felt considerable personal animus. Billie's political sympathies lay with Martin Fong, naturally, but they had their personal issues. She found it easier to stay clear of the mess entirely.

Martin didn't react to the suggestion, so she put it to him as a question.

"Could politics have been behind these homicides, Martin?"

"Billie, I don't know. At this point I'm just confused."

"What about Joe Sasso?"

For a long moment Martin said nothing, then, "What about him?"

"What were he and Sonny doing?"

"All I know about Joe Sasso is that he always seemed to be calling and Sonny was meeting with him at all hours."

"There obviously was something big in the works," Billie said. "Something they must have gone out of their way to keep secret, since nobody seems to be able to say what it was."

"What does it matter now?" Martin said, his voice shaking.

With a natural instinct for cross-examination, Billie couldn't help but press ahead. "What about Joe's mistress, Elaine Chang? Did Sonny ever mention her?"

"Joe had a mistress?" Martin sounded genuinely shocked.

"Yes. And a wife and four kids. He was your regular all-American guy, Martin." After a very long silence, Billie said, "Martin?"

"Sonny never mentioned a mistress."

"One theory is that Sonny was advising Joe on some kind of business deal involving Elaine Chang. Whether true or not, I don't think that's what got them killed. I'm sure it's the mystery case that had Sonny so depressed. But I don't have anything to go on. Just my gut reaction."

He was again silent.

"Martin?"

"Maybe, but I'm not the one to talk to about it. Why not ask Naomi Watts? I know they have been working on something. A week ago they had a long conversation. I don't know what about because Sonny was in his office and talked right through dinner. I was pissed, I know that."

Billie had forgotten all about Naomi, though she was an obvious resource. Naomi had been a friend of Sonny's for years. They were in law school together and worked on some of the same causes then and later.

Naomi Watts was an old-line liberal. Her mother was Jewish and her father black, important figures in the labor movement back in the thirties and forties. Naomi herself started out doing civil rights work and got a reputation as a firebrand. She'd tempered some over the years and her practice evolved into public-interest law. She made some powerful enemies when she started going after the big corporations. Several years ago she got in trouble with substance abuse. It affected her work, and the legal establishment went after her, big time. They disbarred her. The last Billie had heard, Naomi's case was being appealed.

Billie knew Sonny hired Naomi to do legal research for him, whatever he could send her way to help pay the rent. She, more than anybody, would have been privy to Sonny's work. They talked about everything, and had for years.

"Maybe I *should* give Naomi a call," Billie said. "Is she still living in South San Francisco?"

"No, I think she moved to Oakland. I don't know where,

but her number might be around here. I'll look. But to be honest, Billie, I don't feel like talking anymore. I am so depressed...I could just die."

"Are you going to be all right?" she asked.

"Yes."

There was no conviction in his voice, which worried her. "You sure?"

"Positive. Don't worry about me. If you're going to worry about anybody, make it Emily. And—" his voice trembled "—tell her I love her."

"Martin, take care of yourself. Seriously. If only for Emily's sake."

Her comment had the opposite effect from what she'd intended. Martin began weeping uncontrollably. "I'm sorry," he blubbered. "I've got to go." With that, he hung up.

Billie put the receiver in the cradle. "I'm going to check Emily again," she told her father.

"Do you think we should wake her?"

"Let's let her rest as long as she wants. Sleep's probably the best thing for her."

Billie found her child much as she'd left her. The girl moaned in her sleep. Billie stroked her cheek with the back of her hand, then returned to the front room.

"Still out like a light."

"It's her way of coping. You were like that when your mother left."

Billie and Mel rarely spoke of Betty Fox. She'd dropped completely out of their lives. Billie wasn't a hundred percent sure where her mother was, though she assumed in the South where she had family. The only contact they'd had was a call Mel had gotten some years ago from Betty's cousin, saying she wanted to know how to reach Billie. This was not long after Billie had left home and moved to San Francisco. Billie never heard from the cousin or her mother, a disappointment that only made her more resentful. Nothing at all was better than an unfulfilled promise.

The telephone rang and she went over to get it.

"Billie, it's Martin again." His tone was different. She sensed resolution in his voice. "After we spoke I went through Sonny's desk here. I found one file that would interest you."

"Yes?"

"It's labeled 'Sasso.'"

"Jesus. What's in it?"

"I just took a quick look. There are some bank statements and a bunch of legal stuff. Most of it makes no sense to me, but I think it would to you. It does seem to be about a case."

"Martin, call the SFPD and make an appointment with Dickson Hong of the Homicide Section. He and Carl Plavec are handling the investigation. They were planning on interviewing you, anyway."

"I think Plavec was the one who left the message on my machine earlier."

"Call him."

"Billie, the way I feel, I really don't want to talk to the police. Can't I just give the file to you?"

"They'll have to talk to you, anyway, and this could be important. Just do it."

"Then, would you be there when I meet them?"

"I suppose I could."

"But not here," he said.

"We can meet at their office."

"No, not the police station, either. Anywhere else."

"This morning I met them at the Yankee Clipper," Billie said. "Do you know it?"

"Sure. North Beach."

"Yeah, near Washington Square. Let's meet there."

"What time?"

"Seven?"

"That's fine," Billie said. I'll confirm with the police. If the time has to be changed, I'll let you know."

No more tears. Martin, resolute now, hung up. Billie put the phone down.

"Breakthrough?" her father asked.

"Possibly." She opened the drawer and took out the phone book and flipped through it until she found the number of the Yankee Clipper. She dialed. A woman answered. Billie asked for Nick.

"I'm sorry, he's not in. This is Linda. Can I help you?"

"Maybe you could give him a message. This is Billie Fox. Would you tell Nick that I'll be meeting Martin Fong there at the Yankee Clipper at seven this evening? And tell him I may have turned up some very interesting information."

"Just a sec, let me make a note." There was a pause, then, "What's your number, Ms. Fox?"

Billie gave it to her.

"I'll tell Nick."

"Thanks." She dropped the receiver in the cradle and shot her father a smile. "It's times like this I'm glad I went into law."

"Times like this, Wilhelmina? You mean because of Martin or because of Mr. Sasso?"

Flushing, Billie went off to the bath, refusing to dignify her father's question with a response.

COW HOLLOW

Nick, riding in the back seat of a Yellow Cab, was headed for his brother's place on Vallejo Street. He was supposed to meet Dickson Hong and Carl Plavec there at two, but he was going to be early, which would give him a chance to talk to Gina, maybe catch his breath. He'd gone to the hospital to get checked out, and it had turned out to be a more unpleasant experience than usual.

The emergency room physician sewed up his lacerated cheek, gave him a tetanus shot and confirmed that he had a concussion and a broken nose. The good news was that his ribs were only bruised. It had been suggested that he spend the night under observation because of his head injury. Nick, who'd never cared much for hospitals, not so politely declined.

The doctor had given Nick a hard time, insisting it would be irresponsible of him to drive in light of his condition. Not wanting the injury or deaths of innocent bystanders on his conscience, Nick had agreed to take a taxi wherever he went the rest of the day.

The first thing he did was trek out to see his father. Tony's condition was unchanged. After a conversation with the head nurse, Nick decided against informing him of Joe's death. The old man woke for a few minutes, but soon dozed off, leaving little opportunity for conversation. Nick figured it was probably a blessing.

Before going to see his father, Nick had called Gina to make sure she knew that he and the police were coming. She'd been calm and accepting for the most part, giving him no reason to share Dickson Hong's suspicions that she'd been involved in the murders. Nick decided her principal anxiety concerned her children. Shelly, Gina had told him, had arrived early that morning from Tahoe. Tina was flying up from Santa Barbara and was due later that morning. Gina still hadn't been able to track down Anthony.

When the taxi pulled up in front of Gina's place, Nick paid the driver and got out. Just as it drove away, a light-colored van stopped across from him. He flinched, recalling the vehicle the burglars had used at the restaurant that morning. But then he saw that it was a news truck for one of the local TV stations. The passenger door opened and a young woman with the look of a reporter got out and made her way to Gina's door.

Nick didn't want to have to deal with the press—not considering how even the New York media seemed unwilling to ignore his past. So he walked across the street, waiting for the situation to work itself out. Since he hadn't talked to Bree or anybody else in New York, he decided to take the opportunity to phone her for a status report.

He got Bree at the restaurant.

"Sorry I missed your call last night," she said.

"Yeah, well, I'm naturally anxious about how things are going."

"Everything's fine, Nick. Business is booming."

He was pleased to hear that, but he also noticed Bree hadn't offered any explanation as to why she wasn't home when he called late. Not that she owed him one. If he could have casual sex with Linda Nassari and develop an interest in Billie Fox, Bree could hang out in a pickup bar or meet Aldo, or anyone else, for a drink, as well.

The thing was, though, that Billie was an adult and Bree was just a kid, which, while not exactly making him a pedophile, did bring into question what he was doing. "No problems, then?" he asked.

"No, everything's going smoothly."

It occurred to Nick that they didn't really have anything to talk about except how things were going. He toyed with the notion of saying something like, "I miss you, babe," but it struck him as forced, and he wasn't sure if Bree would know how to take it. What he did miss was wild sex and seeing her strut her stuff. She had a great laugh and could be really sweet, but... "Well," he said, "I know the place is in good hands."

"We're doing our best. So, how's it going there, Nick?" she asked.

"Messy," he said, not wanting to get into it. Bree wouldn't appreciate the subtleties of what was going on and, truth be known, she probably wouldn't care. How could he blame her?

They chatted a bit longer, then Nick ended the call. Across the street the reporter remained at the door. Her persistence was rewarded when the front door opened. Nick's niece, Shelly, a postpubescent female version of her father with traces of Gina mixed in, spoke with the woman briefly before Gina appeared. More conversation took place as a cameraman made his way up the steps to the porch. Waving him off, Gina closed the door. The newspeople retreated to their vehicle and drove away.

Nick checked his watch, then crossed the street. As he made his way to the door, he took a brief inventory of the various pains and ailments afflicting him, realizing that hypertension was probably one he could add to the list. Fatigue was becoming a factor, too. As the afternoon had worn on, his strength had waned. He decided that after this he'd head back to the restaurant and call it a day. He rang the bell.

Shelly greeted him with an enthusiastic, "Uncle Nick!"

No sooner were the words out of her mouth, though, than her face crumbled. The girl, who it seemed had been a toddler only yesterday, threw herself into his arms and began to cry. Tina, taller, slender, yet more womanly, came to the door next. She was the family beauty. Draping an arm around her, too, he kissed her on the cheek. Tina's eyes were red-rimmed. Nick had always been partial to his elder niece and she partial to him.

Gina arrived, pulling them all inside. They trouped to the front room where Blake sat sullen, slumped in a chair. The boy scarcely acknowledged him. They'd talked some the night before, maybe leaving nothing more to be said. Blake was obviously depressed.

Gina said, "It looks like you got quite a beating, Nick. I hope the pain's not too bad." He'd told her what had happened

on the phone and advised her to warn the children he wouldn't
be a pretty sight.

"Nothing serious. I'll have a puffy face for a few days,
that's all."

"Was it the men who killed Daddy?" Shelly asked.

"We don't know, angel," Nick replied. "It's possible."

"I take it there's no news," Gina said.

"Not that I'm aware of. The cops might have something,
though." Nick consulted his watch. "They should be here any
minute now."

Gina, in an understated dress and cardigan, let her shoulders slump. She told him to sit down and sent the girls off to
make coffee. Blake asked to go to his room.

Alone with his sister-in-law, Nick looked into her quiet-
suffering eyes.

"Thanks for being here," she said, sitting on the sofa next
to him.

He took her hand, feeling compassion. She seemed older to
him, having aged since last night. Gina gave a world-weary
sigh.

"Is this going to be unpleasant?" she asked.

There hadn't been an antecedent, but Nick knew she meant
the questioning by the police. "I don't see why it should be."

For the first time he saw something in his sister-in-law's
eyes that gave him pause.

"My heartache has turned to anger, Nick. Don't let me embarrass myself."

He wasn't a hundred percent sure what she meant. "What
about the children?" he asked. "There's no need for them to
be involved, and talk about their father won't be pleasant."

"I've already talked to Tina about keeping the younger
ones occupied upstairs."

"Does she know about Joe and..."

"Yes, I thought she was mature enough to know what was

going on. I've decided not to share the details with Shelly and Blake, at least for now."

"It may be irrelevant to...the murders," Nick observed, watching for her reaction.

"Maybe."

Nick's head throbbed even more. Gina's expression turned grim.

"Have the police talked to Elaine Chang?" she asked.

"I don't know. That was their intent."

"Will they share anything they've learned?"

"It's hard to tell, Gina. It kind of depends."

"Will *you* share, Nick?"

"You really want to know everything?"

"I'd like to know the man I was married to."

Nick hoped that was the real reason she was so preoccupied.

"I couldn't sleep last night," Gina went on, "so, rather than lying there staring at the dark ceiling, I spent hours going through Joe's things. It was surprising how much I found. Some of it was painful, especially evidence of his affair—I found one of her lipsticks in his coat pocket, for example—but there was other stuff that made little or no sense."

"Like what?"

The doorbell rang and Gina got up. "Excuse me, Nick. I'll be right back."

Of course she'd leave him hanging....

Nick felt like hell, but he also felt something that was rare for him—fire in the belly. Not only was it important to help his family get through the crisis, but the events of last night had added a new dimension. Now he had his brother's death to avenge...or, at the very least, understand. And if he could redeem himself in the process, so much the better.

He heard voices in the entry, then Gina reappeared, followed by Dickson Hong and Carl Plavec.

Nick got to his feet with difficulty—his energy flagging by the minute—and shook hands with the two cops. Tina came in with coffee for her mother and Nick, returning to the kitchen for a coffee for Carl Plavec. Hong had asked for water. Nick took the pain pills they'd given him at the hospital from his coat pocket, opened the container and popped a capsule into his mouth. Taking a swig of coffee, he swallowed it.

"I'm surprised you aren't in the hospital," Hong said.

"They encouraged me to stay. I declined. I don't suppose you've tracked down the boys who worked me over," Nick said.

The inspector shook his head. "Not yet. It'd help if you looked at some pictures."

Nick snapped his fingers. "That's right, I was supposed to go downtown. Between the hospital and dealing with my father, it slipped my mind. After we're finished here, I'll do it."

Shelly and Tina arrived with drinks for the others and Gina sent the girls upstairs. Nick decided to jump in and pick the conversation up where it was headed before the interruption.

"Gina told me she's been going through Joe's things and turned up something interesting," he said. "She was about to tell me about it when you arrived."

"It was more confusing than interesting," Gina said.

"What was it?"

"In the bottom drawer of his desk Joe had a bunch of information on Myanmar. There were newspaper clippings, articles from the Internet, travel brochures, all kinds of information."

"Myanmar?" Plavec said. "What's that?"

"A country," Gina said.

"Used to be called Burma," Dickson Hong added.

"Oh," Plavec said, coloring. He made a show of taking out his notepad. "Did your husband travel a lot, Mrs. Sasso?"

"No," Gina replied, "hardly at all. He used to like to go to Reno and Las Vegas, but I had a terrible time getting him anywhere else. I nagged him for years before he finally agreed to a family vacation back East. I thought the children ought to see New York City and the nation's capital."

"I take it he didn't explain his interest in Burma." ·

"No. I had no idea he was even aware it existed."

"Maybe he didn't gather the stuff for travel purposes," Plavec said. "Was Mr. Sasso a scholar?"

"Hardly."

"Maybe he saw a show on television or something and got interested," Plavec said, obviously searching.

"That's not my husband. He simply had no interest in such things."

Plavec was doing all the talking while Hong listened. Nick watched him, aware what he was thinking. Gina, oblivious, continued to answer the junior inspector's questions.

"Was there a particular theme or slant to the information?" Plavec asked.

"I suppose you could say religion, which is just as surprising as the foreign-country aspect. Joe hadn't been to Mass or talked about religion since the day we were married."

"Religion?" Plavec said. "What do you mean, exactly?"

"There was a lot of stuff on Buddhism. Historical information. Information about temples, things like that."

"That's odd."

Nick was listening to the conversation, still observing Dickson Hong as he struggled with the daze resulting from his blazing headache. But when Gina mentioned Buddhism, he sat up, recalling the statue in Joe's office at the Yankee Clipper.

"I wondered if it could have been a result of his relationship with the woman," Gina said. "But why Buddhism in Myanmar? That's not where she's from, is it?"

"Elaine Chang?" Hong said. "No, she's from the Mainland by way of Hong Kong. To my knowledge she has no connection with Myanmar. Hardly anybody on the outside does. It's one of the most closed countries in the world. Even tourism is highly restricted."

"I think Gina could be right, though," Nick said. "It very well could have to do with Elaine Chang." He told them about the green Buddha in the office at the restaurant.

"With the initial 'E' it does make sense," Hong said. "I take it, Mrs. Sasso, that the materials you're referring to are available for us to examine."

"Yes, certainly."

"Speaking of Elaine Chang, have you been able to talk to her yet?" Nick asked.

Hong said, "No, and that's a concern. The lady seems to have left town. The neighbors think she took off in the middle of the night, but nobody is sure. The building superintendent didn't have a clue. Needless to say, we're looking for her."

"Is she a suspect?" Gina asked.

"Let's just say we'd like to question her." Hong continued to peer at Gina. "Has anything else turned up, or are you aware of any reason someone might want to kill your husband?"

"Not other than me," Gina replied.

Nick was taken aback by the brazenness of her response.

"He was having an affair with that woman," Gina went on to explain. "Naturally, I wanted to kill him. I hired a detective to find out who the woman was."

"What's the detective's name?"

"Rolando Inocentes," Gina replied.

Hong and Plavec looked at one another. Hong inched forward in his seat, making eye contact with Gina. "Nick told us how you followed your husband and Ms. Chang. Would you mind going over it with us in detail. I'd like to hear everything that happened."

Gina began to recount her experience of the day before. Nick listened as closely as the cops, looking for hints of something behind her words. His sister-in-law was amazingly composed, though signs of hurt and bitterness occasionally surfaced.

Reaching the point in her account where she'd followed Joe and Elaine to Tiburon, she recounted how they'd met with the man on the deck at Sam's. "He was Chinese, I think," she said. "Asian for sure. Middle-aged. Had on a white suit and large sunglasses. He was a little pudgy, I'd say." Then she stopped, her eyes rounding.

"What's the matter, Gina?" Nick said.

"I just remembered something Joe said. I heard only snippets of conversation, but at one point he said something like, 'This Buddha's going to be the death of me.'"

"You're alluding to the religious materials in your husband's desk drawer," Hong said.

"And there's that green Buddha at the restaurant," Nick interjected.

"Where are we, then?" Hong said. "Mr. Sasso had some kind of interest in Buddhism, evidently."

"He said it was going to be the death of him," Gina noted.

"That just could have been a figure of speech."

"But he *is* dead," she rejoined.

"Right," Plavec said, "but we won't be putting Buddha on the suspect list."

Dickson Hong did not appear pleased by his partner's remark. "Can you tell us more about the Asian gentleman at the restaurant, Mrs. Sasso?"

"I got a good look at him," Gina replied. "The sunglasses masked his face pretty well, but he did have a distinctive scar above his eyebrow. It was half an inch long."

"Which eyebrow?"

"Right, I believe. Yes, right. He walked right past me."

"Pudgy, middle-aged Chinese guy with a scar over his right eyebrow," Hong said to himself as much as anyone else. "Ring any bells, Carl?"

Plavec shook his head.

"What happened then?" Hong asked Gina.

"At that point I'd seen enough. I wanted to go home, so I left."

Hong nodded, glancing at the floor. "Is there anything else in the house, Mrs. Sasso, anything you've found, anything your husband said that might be helpful in determining why he was killed and by whom?"

"Well, Joe was in a lot deeper trouble than I thought."

"What do you mean?"

"In one of the other drawers in his desk, I found a foreclosure notice from the bank. We may lose the house."

"Your house is in foreclosure?" Plavec said.

"It will be soon."

Given the extent of Joe's financial woes, Nick was not surprised by the news, but it was tragic that his brother had allowed his problems to endanger his family's well-being. He felt even worse for his sister-in-law.

"And you had no idea?" Plavec continued.

Gina shook her head. "No, I'm ashamed to say I left everything in Joe's hands. In retrospect it was stupid, but Joe had always done well by me and the children, and I had no reason to doubt him. Of course, that was before this Chang woman came into the picture. I'm sure she's behind this. And, if she is, I certainly hope you can prove it."

"Our investigation will be thorough," Hong said. "You can count on that."

"I want the people responsible arrested, of course," Gina said, her voice quivering slightly, "but nothing can make my family whole again. She's destroyed everything...with Joe's compliance, of course. He's at fault for not being stronger."

"Dickson," Nick said, "have you turned up anything yet that would indicate what brought Joe and Sonny Culp together?"

"No. We've checked with the courts. No pleadings have been filed. There's nothing in the public record. If their relationship was professional rather than personal, it must have been in the early stages."

Everyone sat quietly for a moment or two, then Dickson Hong closed his notepad, signaling that he was shifting gears. Nick had an inkling of what was coming.

"Mrs. Sasso," he said, "would you be good enough to tell us about your activities last evening?"

Gina hesitated. "You mean at the time someone was killing my husband?"

"Last evening, yes. But if you'd like to pick up your story from when you left the restaurant in Tiburon, feel free."

Nick found himself leaning forward right along with Hong and Plavec.

"I came home, very upset," Gina said. "I think you understand why."

"About what time was that?"

"Early afternoon. Approximately, two-thirty. I called my friend, Arianne, feeling the need for moral support."

"And you told her what happened?"

"Yes, generally."

"Then what?"

"For a while I stayed in my room, crying. Nick called me sometime thereafter from the Yankee Clipper, I can't say exactly when."

"Was anyone else at home?"

"My youngest son, Blake."

"Did you speak with him?"

"Briefly. He was in his room playing with his computer most of the afternoon."

"You didn't discuss any of your activities with your son?"

"No. I thought I'd let Joe tell his children...assuming he was man enough. But, as it turned out, he didn't have the opportunity, did he?"

"Then what?"

"I didn't feel like cooking and I didn't want to be home when Joe arrived, so I asked Blake if he wanted to go out for dinner. While we were having a pizza, I suggested we go to a movie, which we did."

"Where?"

"The theater on Union Street."

"What time did you enter the theater?"

"It must have been seven or seven-thirty."

"Returning home at what time?"

"Shortly before midnight."

Hong's eyebrows rose. "So late?"

"We saw two movies. I was not eager to get home."

Dickson Hong's eyes settled on her, cobra fashion. Gina had not flinched, nor had she shown great emotion, other than a touch of anger. Nick was surprised.

"Mrs. Sasso, would you mind if we spoke with your son?"

"Now?"

"If it's not inconvenient."

"Why? To see if I'm telling the truth?"

"We try to speak with everyone involved."

"My son is not involved," Gina snapped.

"You object then?"

"I have no objection to your talking to him about what we did last night, but I'd prefer you not go into his father's relationship with that woman. He's not aware of it and I see no reason to subject him to the shame...at least, not now."

"At the moment we're only interested in the family's activities last evening."

"That's a euphemism for whether I'm telling the truth or lying."

"We'd like to confirm the truth."

"All right, you may speak with him."

"Would you feel better if Nick were present?"

"Actually, I would. Shall I go get Blake?"

"Please."

Gina left the front room. Dickson Hong said nothing, nor did he look at Nick. So, Nick broke the ice.

"You don't believe her, do you, Dickson?"

"I'm trying to be thorough."

Nick saw his old partner wasn't going to be forthcoming with him. But what did he expect? This was his family, and he'd already proven to the world that he couldn't be trusted.

A minute or so later Blake Sasso shuffled into the front room, looking wary.

"Come sit next to me, Blake," Nick volunteered, wanting his nephew to be at ease. The poor kid had been through a lot.

Blake dropped his slender frame onto the sofa next to his uncle. He did not lean back, hunching forward instead, his bony shoulders rounded, his adolescent skin a field of blemishes.

"I'd like to ask you a few questions, Blake," Hong said.

"Why?"

"Your father was involved in a very tragic event and we want to learn as much about what happened as we can."

The boy looked skeptical, perhaps a little frightened. Nick put his hand on Blake's shoulder. "Just answer Inspector Hong's questions, Blake. Tell the truth. The more the police know the sooner they'll be able to find your dad's killer."

"What do you want to know?" the boy asked.

"Tell us what you did yesterday. Starting with the afternoon, if you like."

"I was home. I fooled around with my computer mostly."

"And what happened when your mom came home?"

"Nothing. She said hi and went to her room. Then later she asked if I wanted to go out for a pizza and that's what we did."

"And after that?"

"We went to a movie, actually two movies. Down on Union Street."

"Were you together the whole time?" Hong asked.

Blake shrugged. "Yeah. Except when she went to the bathroom. I didn't go with her, of course."

"She went to the bathroom during the movie?"

"Uh-huh."

"How long was she gone?"

"I don't know. She spends a lot of time in the bathroom, same as my sisters. When I want to get in, it seems forever."

"How long last night, when you were in the theater?"

"I didn't look at my watch."

"Approximately."

"A long time, I guess. I was watching the movie, but after a while I noticed she didn't come back."

"Fifteen minutes?"

"Probably longer."

"Half an hour?"

"Could have been even longer. I asked her what happened and she said she wasn't feeling well. But after that she was okay."

"And after the movie what did you do?"

"We came home. It was late so I went to bed. Then she woke me up and told me about Dad." He looked back and forth between Hong and Plavec. "Hey, you don't think my mom did it, do you? Is that why you're asking all these questions?"

"We're asking lots of people lots of questions," Hong replied. "That's our job. You and your mom both said you went out to dinner and a movie, which is what we needed to know."

"Is that it, then?"

"Yes, if we have more questions, we'll talk to you later. You can tell your mom she can come back."

Blake left. Again Dickson did not look at Nick. When Gina returned, the inspector jumped right back into questioning mode.

"Mrs. Sasso, how long were you absent from your seat while you were at the theater?"

"Pardon me?"

"Your son said you were in the bathroom for some time. How long exactly?"

Gina did not answer immediately, glancing at Nick. Finally, she said, "I guess it was a mistake not to tell you."

"Tell us what?"

"I sat there in the theater, oblivious to what was on the screen, knowing that Joe was probably at that very moment with his mistress and his lawyer. The theater was only seven or eight blocks away from the lawyer's office. So, on impulse, I left. Walked right out and went down to Chestnut..."

"Yes, go ahead."

"Well, as I approached the building, a police car arrived, lights flashing, followed by a fire truck. I had no idea what had happened, but I thought it wasn't a good idea to stick around, so I went back to the theater, bought another ticket and went back inside."

"Why didn't you tell us this earlier?"

"I guess because I was afraid it would look bad. Everybody knows I had a good reason to kill Joe, but I didn't want to complicate things. I didn't realize there'd been a shooting when I was there last night, of course, and when I found out later that was the reason for the police cars, all I could think was that me going there would add to people's suspicions."

"Not disclosing the information is worse."

"I see that now. But I figured it would never come up. I'm surprised Blake even remembered. He's oblivious to most things."

"Inspector Hong was very thorough with his questions,

Gina," Nick said. "Otherwise it probably wouldn't have come up."

"So I made a mistake of judgment in not volunteering the information. That doesn't mean I'm guilty of anything."

"You aren't making it any easier," Hong said.

"I'm sorry."

Hong sighed. "Is there anything else you neglected to tell us?"

"No."

He was silent for a while, then said, "For the moment we'll leave it at this, then."

"I really am sorry," Gina said. "But the truth is, I didn't kill my husband or anyone else. I hope you don't waste your time trying to prove otherwise. Elaine Chang's the person you need to talk to."

"The investigation will be conducted in a thorough and responsible manner," Hong replied a bit curtly. "We'd like to have a look at your husband's documents, materials and other personal effects. Do you want us to do it here, or take them away for examination?"

"I don't know that it makes any difference. Will it take long?"

"Depends on what we encounter."

"I suppose there's no reason to add to the turmoil here. There's plenty already. Why don't you come and get them."

"Fine. I'll have somebody drop by either later today or in the morning." Hong glanced at his associate. "Anything else, Carl?"

"No."

The two detectives got up to go.

Hong said to Nick, "We'll see you downtown, then?"

"Yes."

The cops left, Gina showing them to the door. Nick's head was killing him and he popped another pain pill. Gina returned, looking forlorn.

"Was it a terrible blunder?"

"It's never good to be less than fully truthful, Gina. I found that out the hard way. Dickson Hong values the truth above all else. You may have deepened his suspicions, but that won't make you guilty if you're innocent."

"I didn't kill Joe," she said emphatically.

Nick nodded. "I believe you. Listen, before I go downtown to look at mug shots, would you mind if I have a look at that Myanmar stuff? Once the cops take it I won't have another chance."

"No, not at all. Come on. I'll show you where it is. In fact, feel free to look through all Joe's things if you like. I'm certainly no expert when it comes to searches."

"There are lots of pieces to any good puzzle," he said.

"But this isn't a good one, Nick. And it seems to be getting worse by the minute."

"Yes," he said, putting his arm around her shoulders, "you're right about that."

SAN FRANCISCO INTERNATIONAL AIRPORT

Eve Adams dashed out of the terminal building and into the waiting taxi. The driver, a sleepy-looking Mexican, blinked at her.

"How far to Peninsula Hospital?" she demanded.

"It's just across the freeway, a couple of miles, maybe."

"Take me there. Fast." Eve reached over the man's shoulder and dropped a twenty-dollar bill in his lap. "Really fast."

The taxi took off with a lurch, the tires squealing. Eve's heart raced, partly from anxiety, partly because of the long run from the gate to the taxi stand. She'd hastily packed an overnight bag and had hardly bothered with her hair. During the entire flight from L.A. she'd prayed. She wasn't religious, but prayer somehow seemed necessary, especially after last night.

Even before Iggy had called to tell her he'd had a heart

attack, she'd been torn about whether to tell him about Viktor. But she knew there was no way now she could tell him she'd been violated. Iggy's rage would kill him for sure. Yet, a part of her wanted revenge so badly, she'd almost risk his health.

Viktor hadn't left the house until 2:00 a.m. Just as she'd expected, in a condition of relative sobriety, he'd been remorseful.

"I know you are angry," he said, "but I didn't hurt you. Was there even one moment of pain? No, you found pleasure once you allowed it."

Eve had been livid. "You nearly gave me gangrene binding my wrists, you sonovabitch!" she screamed into his blubbery face.

"It was the only way to keep you there so you would know the pleasure, my pet."

"Knock off that 'my pet' shit!" she'd snapped. "Just get out of my house and out of my life."

In retrospect, Eve realized it could have been far worse. She'd been raped and sodomized in prison, so she knew the horrors. Viktor hadn't hurt her in the physical sense, but he'd violated her just the same.

After binding her to the bed with Iggy's neckties, he'd left the room. She was certain his intent was to force himself on her, and she had visions of being suffocated under mounds of smelly flab. Even now she shuddered to think about it. But that wasn't what he had in mind.

Minutes after leaving the room, Viktor Chorny had returned with a quart of ice cream and a rubber spatula. To her utter amazement, the onetime scourge of Soviet Russia had proceeded to spread cherry vanilla ice cream over her body. Eve was incredulous.

Viktor had stood by the bed grinning and admiring his handiwork when he was done. "From the very first time my eyes fell upon you, this is my fantasy," he explained. "This is my heart's desire."

Then, for the next twenty minutes or so, the beast had licked her body clean. Every inch. Two or three times he'd plastered the ice cream between her legs and mounded it on her breasts. And two or three times he'd cleaned her off with his tongue, like a huge hog at the trough, nuzzling, snorting and lapping with frenzied abandon.

She was duly horrified, of course, but it certainly was preferable to what had happened to her in her dark cell at Mule Creek. Viktor wanted so badly for her to enjoy the experience. He kept blubbering, "Are you going to come? Are you going to come?"

She'd have died first. Giving him any satisfaction would have been the last thing on earth she'd have done. But after a while she realized he wouldn't give up until he had the satisfaction of her pleasure. And so she'd faked it, heaving and thrashing and crying out as though the heavens had split. Pressing his fat jowl against her belly, he'd wept. "Oh, thank you, thank you, my darling. Thank you."

After untying her, Viktor dropped to a knee and said, "Please, Eve, let this be our secret. I'll make it worth it to you. Neither you nor Igor has asked for my help with your enterprise, but I can be of much use to you in Russia. Let me do that in exchange for any displeasure I have caused. If you agree to quietly allow me this night, I will make certain you have success."

She'd wanted to clobber him, but the only safe course was to comply. "Okay, Viktor," she'd said. "Under one condition—that you never come here again while Iggy is away. Never, no matter what."

She'd finally gotten him out of the house and herself into the shower, where she stayed for half an hour until the hot water began to turn cold. Then she washed the sheets and mattress pad and scrubbed the bedroom carpet. It may not have been the worst experience a woman had had to endure, but Eve wanted to kill the bastard just the same. Having to pretend she'd enjoyed it was almost as bad as the worst horrors she'd endured at Mule Creek.

As the taxi raced down the freeway, Eve gazed out at the hills studded with houses. She told herself to forget Viktor Chorny. His fate would be determined later. She had something much more critical to worry about now—her husband's survival.

COW HOLLOW

Gina showed Nick into Joe's office and told him to make himself at home. Then she closed the door. Nick glanced around, vaguely recalling having been in the room before. It was after he and Cindy had split up and his life was languishing in its own private hell. His recollection was that his brother had been an officious, know-it-all. It was probably Joe's insecurities showing. Nick hadn't taken offense, he'd simply let his brother do his thing, imparting advice, playing the role of older, wiser sibling.

The present circumstances were radically different. He was in a dead man's den, among a dead man's things. It was as though Joe's world had suddenly become an enormous underwear drawer. Soon everybody would be peeping into places that had been for Joe's eyes alone. That was a curious thing about dying—in losing your life you also lost your privacy. The dead went from being people to objects of investigation, not to mention a bonanza of treasure for the next of kin.

Nick went over to his brother's desk, which had once belonged to their father, occupying Tony Sasso's den at home for many, many years. When Tony sold the family residence and moved to the nursing home, Joe and Gina had taken some of his things. Nick's only interest was in a few me-

mentos, which they sent to him in New York. The old man's
desk chair was at the restaurant. The one here Joe had owned
for years.

His brother would never sit in this chair again, Nick realized. He sat in the chair, feeling funny. It brought to mind
those occasions during his childhood when he'd steal into the
garage and climb up on his big brother's bike. Joe had strictly
forbidden him to touch it, but Nick hadn't been able to resist.
He didn't know how to ride such a large bike, but he loved
sitting on the seat and pretending his little toes could actually reach the pedals. He suspected his brother would probably feel much the same way about him sitting at his desk
now. But that was the price a guy paid when he went and got
himself killed under ignominious circumstances.

As he thought about it, Nick realized he was angry with
Joe—not because of the financial mess or even the suffering
he'd inflicted on his wife and children. What angered him was
that his brother hadn't lived up to his own high standards.
Sure, Joe was a risk taker, but he'd always managed to meet
his responsibilities. But with this fiasco, he'd failed miserably.

Nick had always had a grudging respect for his older brother,
but now that was in jeopardy. It just went to show that a moral
failure was the very worst kind. Nick knew that all too well.

Opening the lower drawer, he found the contents as Gina
had described them. It was half filled with brochures and articles that had been torn from publications, photocopied or
downloaded from the Internet. A real hodgepodge. Most of
the material concerned Myanmar or Buddhism—more particularly, perhaps, Buddhist temples and religious artifacts.
He hardly had the time, nor was he in any condition to read
through everything, but he wanted to get a flavor for the stuff
before it was carted away. He didn't expect to accomplish
much, other than to satisfy his curiosity.

As they'd told the cops, Joe wouldn't have collected the

material because of a genuine interest in the subject matter. His brother had to have had an angle, if only because that was what Joe was into: angles. But why Myanmar and why Buddhism? There had to be some sort of investment or business opportunity involved, but Nick just couldn't figure out what.

After shuffling through the stuff in the drawer, Nick looked through the rest of the desk. Most of what he found was pretty pedestrian—some supplies, a little junk mail, some audiotapes on marketing and investing. The other large drawer contained files, but they dealt mostly with the household accounts—telephone, utilities, insurance, taxes, mortgage. Nick browsed through the mortgage folder. There were letters from the lender demanding payment, with attendant threats of foreclosure. Gina hadn't been exaggerating.

One file seemed to be devoted to family matters. It consisted mostly of his children's school records and papers. Nick got a little choked up seeing the kids through their father's eyes. In the credenza behind the desk were more files, but they also dealt with family and household matters. There were several medical files devoted to Joe's MS, plus medical information on the rest of the family. There was a file with bank statements from the household account, as well as credit card statements. Nick flipped through them and saw nothing unusual except for the fact that Joe's credit had been maxed out on each account. There had been a number of cash advances stretching back over the previous three or four months. The more recent statements showed late-payment charges and past-due notices.

Nick felt sad. How miserable Joe must have been these last months as the pressure mounted. A simple, uncomplicated life had advantages. Guys who earned paychecks and bought and paid for things with the money they had were better off than they realized. Being rich often meant having big-time debts.

His head pounding, Nick decided he'd seen enough. As he pushed the middle drawer closed he had a flashback to his youth, when this desk had sat in his father's study. On Nick's sixteenth birthday the old man had taken him into his office, sat him down and given him the advanced lecture on the facts of life. As always, Tony was succinct.

"Sex is one of two different things, depending on if you're a man or a woman," his father had said. "If you're a man, it's for pleasure and to show who's boss. If you're a woman, it's for showing love and having babies. Love is all well and good, but babies you got to be ready for. A guy, if he's Catholic, is at a certain disadvantage," Tony went on to explain. "The women and the priests gang up on us and it's been that way for a thousand years. They don't want sex to be too pleasurable and they want lots of babies. That's why every man's got to have a secret drawer."

Tony then proceeded to pull out the middle drawer of the desk and put it on the desktop. Then he put his hand into the opening and removed a thin boxlike container that was suspended under the desktop and above the drawer. It contained a stash of condoms.

"If you're going out to get laid and you don't got a rubber, you come here and you get one. This secret drawer is for the Sasso men. Your ma don't know about it, and I sure as hell am not going to mention it to the priest in confession, not that I ever go, mind you. But the point is, you don't mention it, either. Understand? This is just for us."

Years later, when Nick and Joe were comparing notes, they discovered that each of them had gotten the lecture and the demonstration of the secret "rubber drawer" as they called it. Joe confessed to having availed himself of it the first time he'd gotten laid. Nick didn't tell the old man or Joe, but he already had his own stash of condoms.

Nick wondered if the rubber drawer was still there and if so, whether Joe had used it. Pulling out the center drawer and placing it on the desktop as his father had done twenty years before, he reached inside and, sure enough, found the box. Removing it, he discovered there weren't condoms inside, but there were several other items. One was a four-by-six photo of Joe with an attractive Asian woman who he judged to be in her early to mid thirties. It had to be Elaine Chang. The pair was seated at a table, their faces close together as they smiled into the camera. Nick figured it was one of those nightclub-style photos taken by girls with cleavage and short skirts. A little memento of a big night out.

Additionally there was a rather ancient-looking photo of what appeared to be a Buddhist monk seated before a gleaming Buddha. Written in pencil on the back was "Toungoo, 1938."

The third item was an address book and pocket calendar for the current year. Nick paged through the address section. He found no names entered, though there were half a dozen phone numbers scattered through the pages. There was one entry on the "C" page, one on the "E" page and one on the "L" page. Nick's home number was listed on the "N" page, another number on the "R" page, and the last was on the "V" page.

The "C" entry could have been either Chang or Culp, but in light of the fact there was an entry on the "E" page, he figured "C" was Culp and "E" was Elaine. That could be verified easily enough. As for "L," "R" and "V," Nick didn't have a clue.

In the calendar section there were very few entries. Most of the month of January was blank. On the last Wednesday of the month was the notation "B.V. at Y.C., 8." "Y.C." had to be the Yankee Clipper. The "8" probably meant eight o'clock. But what was B.V.? A person most likely. Nick ran "V" names through his head. He could only come up with one. Benny Vocino, their old family friend, the "honorary mayor of North Beach." The "B" certainly worked.

The next entry was in February in the second week. On a Friday, Joe had written, "V/ Elaine Chung 5." Nick assumed Joe had misspelled the last name. The "V" was surprising, however, at least in conjunction with Elaine. Benny and the Chinese woman were an odd combination. Oil and water. Nick wondered if he'd stumbled onto something pivotal. He shuddered to think what it might mean. In the ensuing months there were no more "V" entries, but there were numerous "E's." By May they seemed to be ubiquitous, several each week. In the more recent months, "C's" and "L's" began to appear, as well.

Nick realized he was looking at a rough diagram of what his brother had been doing the past six months or so, with little in the way of specifics. His thoughts kept going back to Benny Vocino, if indeed that was who "B.V." alluded to. There were other people with those initials, obviously, but...

Turning to the address section, Nick found the "V" page, picked up the phone on the desk and dialed. This was the quickest way to find out.

A woman answered. Nick wasn't sure if it was Benny's wife, Dora, or not. "Hi," he said, "this is Nick Sasso."

"Oh, Nick, we heard about Joe. I'm so terribly sorry."

It was Dora.

"Yeah," he said, "everybody's stunned."

"I guess you don't know yet when the funeral will be."

"No, not yet."

"Do you want to speak to Benny?"

"Is he there?"

"Yes, but he's lying down. Let me get him."

"No, don't disturb him. I was just calling to see if it would be convenient for me to drop by sometime to chat."

"I'll ask."

Before Nick could stop her, she had put down the phone and was gone. In a minute she was back.

"He said this afternoon's fine or tomorrow morning. Whenever you're in the neighborhood, just drop by. Benny doesn't make appointments when it's family."

"Tell him thanks, Dora. I'll be by later this afternoon. First I've got an appointment with the cops."

"I certainly hope they find who did this," she said.

"Yeah, me, too."

Nick hung up the phone. What did this mean? he asked himself. Benny was the only one who could answer that question.

The last item in the rubber drawer were several letter-size pieces of paper folded to fit an envelope and held together with a paper clip. Under the clip was a business card. The name on the card was "Ken Lu" and the business was "Chinese Antiquities, Ltd.," the address in Kowloon, Hong Kong.

Nick unfolded the sheets of paper. It was a photocopy of an article from a scientific publication of the early 1950s. The title of the article read, "The Mysterious Disappearance of Burma's Fabled Emerald Buddha," by Dr. Wan Lu. Under it was a photograph that seemed to be the same as the one he'd just removed from the secret drawer. He compared the two. Yes, they were identical.

His hands shaking, Nick began to skim the article. According to the author, an ancient and priceless Buddha encrusted with emeralds had been hidden in a monastery near the Burmese town of Toungoo for hundreds of years, its existence unknown to the outside world. In the course of the Japanese occupation of Burma during World War II, the Buddha was discovered by a small group of Japanese soldiers led by a lieutenant named Kozo Hiragara. The lieutenant, an anthropologist before the war, realized the importance of the piece, not only for scholars of antiquity, but for its immense value, in and of itself.

Hiragara was reported to have hidden the Emerald Buddha with the intention of returning after the war to claim it for himself. According to the author, Hiragara did, in 1947, organize an expedition to find the piece. However, the team disappeared in the jungles of Burma without a trace. Nor was

there any word about the disposition of the Buddha. Burmese
authorities claimed it had been stolen by the Japanese, but the
Japanese government insisted it had no knowledge of the
relic. Had the Emerald Buddha been reclaimed and secreted
away by the monks, the author of the article asked, or did it
remain where Kozo Hiragara had hidden it?

Nick folded the article and put it in his pocket along with
the two photographs. He again looked at the business card, realizing he had probably stumbled onto the key to the puzzle.
Ken Lu probably was the "L" in Joe's address book. The information on Myanmar and Buddhism fell into place. And that
green Buddha statue in Joe's office, plus the remark Gina had
overheard Joe make at the restaurant in Tiburon— "This Buddha is going to be the death of me," perhaps a more prophetic
statement than Joe could possibly have known. Nick put the
card in his wallet. It was time to go see the police.

But the surprises weren't over. Nick found Gina waiting
at the bottom of the stairs with a gun in her hand. He froze a
few steps from the bottom, wondering for the second time that
day if everything, including his life, had been for naught.

"This is Joe's gun," she said, extending the handle toward
him. "I thought I'd give it to you to do with as you see fit."

The air went out of him so fast his legs nearly buckled.

"I guess it can be tested to see if it was the gun that killed
Joe and the lawyer," she went on. "It wasn't, I can tell you
that now. I suppose I could have used another gun, but if this
at all puts your mind at ease, so much the better."

Nick gathered himself, coming the rest of the way down the
stairs. "Gina, I don't for a minute think you killed my brother."

"Inspector Hong has suspicions, though. And I know you
respect him."

"Dickson is just doing his job," he said, taking the gun.
"He's looking at lots of possibilities."

"You don't have to explain. I know what I've done and not

done." She touched his arm. "You'd better go. Try to get some rest, Nick."

"Kiss the kids for me." He gave her a hug and left, his heart still ticking away at a spirited pace.

BURLINGAME

When his wife appeared at the door to his room, tears began to pool in Igor Sakharov's eyes. His angel of mercy had arrived. For the first time since he'd been in the hospital, he felt hope.

Eve rushed to the bed, took his face in her hands and peered anxiously into his eyes. She bit her lip, but cried, anyway. "Oh, Iggy." Then she kissed him.

Igor held on to her really tight, afraid to let go.

"You don't know how scared I've been, you big lug. I let you out of my sight for a couple of days and look what happens!"

"I picked a bad time," he said remorsefully.

"But everything's okay, right? With the work, I mean."

"Alexei took care of things."

"Then there's nothing to worry about."

"Not if I get out of here alive."

"You will. I'll take you home as soon as they let me."

Igor kissed her hand. Eve looked at him adoringly. Already he felt stronger, at peace. He wondered if he could just get out of the bed and leave, go right to the airport with his angel and fly home.

"Tell me everything the doctors have said." Eve gave his hand a squeeze.

"They said I'm not dead yet."

"That's the obvious part."

"You'd have to ask them. They talk, but it means little. There is this test and that. If I'm careful I'll be okay. No stress. I must exercise, eat right. But it is also true I could have another attack tomorrow and drop dead."

"Iggy, don't talk that way."

"Since you walked in the door, I feel good for the first time."

"I'm going to take care of you," she said. "If it means cooking tofu, that's what I'll do."

"There'll be no ice cream with Viktor, that's for sure."

Eve suddenly turned red. She looked very uncomfortable. "Maybe I should speak with the doctor," she said. She got to her feet. "I'll have the nurse find him."

"Must you go now?"

"I'll be back in a few minutes, Iggy." She hurried from the room.

Igor was a little surprised. The mere mention of Viktor's name had set her off. Guilt, probably. She and Viktor had conspired to push him into doing this job, when they both knew he didn't want to do it. His health, perhaps his life, had been compromised for the sake of money. He could only imagine how she'd have felt if he'd died.

Igor was beginning to see this ordeal could turn out to be a blessing. There was no question now that his days as a professional assassin were over. He had that to be thankful for. Yes, maybe he should count himself fortunate. Alexei had done the job, they'd be paid, though there might be some discussion as to how the money was split. Everybody got what they wanted, so everybody ought to be happy.

Igor had been thinking about it. Alexei had gotten his feet wet, but he still needed seasoning. Perhaps Igor could serve as an adviser to him, a sort of consultant. It would be less stressful, yet he could make a little extra and give his brother a good start in his new career.

Just then, the cleaning lady he'd seen earlier entered the janitorial room across the hall with her mop and bucket. Igor had been thinking about her, his suspicious mind wondering. Talking openly, the way he and Alexei had, was a gaffe. The fact that they'd spoken in Russian didn't change that. The stupid cleaning woman may have understood every word. Even if she didn't comprehend the significance, it was a concern. Something to worry about. Exactly what he didn't need!

The door to the janitorial closet opened and the woman emerged without her mop and bucket. She had put on a sweater and changed head scarfs. This one was bright red. Perhaps her shift for the day was over and she was going home. As she locked the door, Igor called out to her in Russian. "Добрый день." *Good afternoon.*

The woman turned and peered across the hall.

"Добрый день," Igor said again.

She gave an uncertain nod. "Привет." *Hi.*

In one word, Igor had his answer. He beckoned her to come in. The woman stepped to the door, her expression wary.

"Как вас зовут?" *What is your name?* he asked.

"I am Olga Diachenko," she said in Russian.

"And you are Ukrainian."

"Да." *Yes.*

"You speak Russian well."

"No, I have forgotten," she said in English.

He beckoned her again. "Заходите." *Come in.*

"Нет. Простите." *No. Sorry.* "I must go," she added in English. "I am late. I will miss my bus." And with that, she was gone, scurrying off down the hall.

Igor pondered what had just happened. The woman spoke Russian, perhaps better than she'd let on. But she made no attempt to hide the fact. Was it because she hadn't heard or understood his conversation with Alexei? Or was she simply a fool? Had something like this happened in the old Soviet Russia, steps would be taken to find out exactly what the woman knew and didn't know. There was a certain comfort in that...if you were in his position, anyway. But this was America, the land of the free. Sensitive things, dangerous things, had to be dealt with privately, in an extralegal fashion.

Igor Sakharov was not the sort of man who left things to chance, but he also knew that doing too much could be just as dangerous as doing too little. He had a problem on his hands. He had to figure out if he was dealing with a chicken or a fox.

SOUTH OF MARKET

Henry Chin was in his office a few doors up Bryant Street from the Hall of Justice, when his longtime secretary, Mary Kelly, brought him the large sealed envelope. "A police officer dropped this off while you were on the phone."

Henry reached across the desk, taking the envelope from her. "Thank you."

When she was gone, he opened the envelope and removed the tape. He was expecting it, of course. George Kondakis had called twenty minutes earlier. "We picked something up on the wiretap you need to hear. I'll send it right over."

Henry turned to the credenza behind him, opened the cabinet door and placed the tape on the machine. Then he pushed the play button. He heard a man's voice.

"Billie, it's Martin again. After we spoke I went through Sonny's desk here. I found one file that would interest you."

"Yes?"

"It's labeled 'Sasso.'"

Henry Chin's stomach dropped. His heart began to pound like crazy.

"Jesus. What's in it?" the woman on the tape asked.

"I just took a quick look. There are some bank statements and a bunch of legal stuff. Most of it makes no sense to me, but I think it would to you. It does seem to be about a case."

"Martin, call the SFPD and make an appointment with Dickson Hong of the Homicide Section. He and Carl Plavec

are handling the investigation of the murders. They were planning on interviewing you, anyway."

The voice on the tape faded out as Henry Chin began to appreciate the fact that he was doomed. Only damage control remained. He had precious little wiggle room, probably not enough to save himself.

He became aware of the voices on the tape again.

The woman, Billie, said, *"We can meet at their office."*

"No, not the police station, either," Martin Fong replied. *"Anywhere else."*

"This morning I met them at the Yankee Clipper," the woman said. *"Do you know it?"*

"Sure. North Beach."

"Yeah, near Washington Square. Let's meet there."

"What time?"

"Seven?"

"That's fine. I'll confirm with the police. If the time has to be changed, I'll let you know."

Henry's gut was in a knot. He could see the headlines. He could see himself being taken away in handcuffs. His father would die of disgrace. He knew right then he couldn't let that happen.

Checking the clock, he realized there wasn't much time. He closed his eyes, reflecting. After a minute or two, he calmly picked up the phone, dialed a number and waited.

"Yes?"

"This is Henry Chin. I need to see your boss immediately."

BURLINGAME

By the time Eve returned, Igor had worked himself into a state of panic. She saw immediately.

"Iggy, what's wrong? Don't you feel well?"

"Eve, listen to me. There's a Ukrainian cleaning woman here at the hospital who speaks Russian. She was scrubbing the bathroom while Alexei was here and may have heard us discussing the job."

"Oh, my."

"I talked to her a few minutes ago. She seemed wary, but I'm not sure what she knows. The more I think about it, the more I'm convinced we have to find out exactly what she heard. And it's got to be done before she talks to somebody...like the police, for example."

"How are you going to do that, Iggy?"

"Obviously I can't. And Alexei's already home. You're going to have to do it."

"How?"

"I've been thinking about it," he said, wiping his wet forehead. "She said she had to catch a bus. There's got to be a bus stop nearby. Maybe you can find her there, if you hurry. Her name is Olga. She's wearing a gray sweater and a red head scarf."

"Iggy, I don't know what to say or do."

"Listen," he said, clenching her arm tightly, "my life, Alexei's life, may depend on this. She's a simple woman. Just act authoritative. Say you're with the FBI or something and you're trying to pursue Russian spies. Find out what she knows, and if it seems damning, tell her to keep her mouth shut until she hears from you again."

"But, Iggy..."

"Eve, for God's sake, just go before she gets on a bus."

Eve, her purse slung over her shoulder, hurried down the hall, her mind spinning. First Viktor, then Iggy's heart, now this. If she didn't have a nervous breakdown, it would be a miracle. To think, she'd once believed that running a string of girls was stressful. Iggy claimed he was getting old; Eve decided maybe she was, too.

At the entrance to the hospital she asked a security guard where the nearest bus stop was located.

"On El Camino, ma'am," he told her. "Follow the driveway down to the street."

Eve rushed outside. It was windy and there was a high fog. It was over a hundred yards down the sloping hospital grounds to the street. As she hurried along the sidewalk bordering the driveway, she could see a group of people gathered at the bus stop. There wasn't anyone in a red scarf. God, had the woman already gotten on her bus?

When she reached the bus stop, Eve confirmed that nobody fit the description Iggy gave her. Her heart sank. Then she noticed another bus stop on the other side of the boulevard, for northbound passengers. Sure enough, there was a stocky little woman in a gray sweater and red scarf, sitting on the bench along with two other women. Eve's spirits rose.

There was no crosswalk, but she decided to cross, anyway. As she looked both ways at the oncoming traffic, she noticed a bus approaching from the south. *Oh, Lord!* she thought.

The Ukrainian got to her feet. The southbound flow of traffic was too heavy for Eve to dash across the street in time to stop her from boarding the bus.

"Olga!" she cried. "Olga!"

The woman heard and peered at her questioningly.

"Wait, Olga! I must talk to you!"

The bus pulled up to the stop, blocking Eve's view. She stepped off the curb, but the traffic was unrelenting. "Shit," she muttered. Then she saw a break in the flow up the street, but would it be in time?

Across from her the bus's engine roared and it pulled away from the stop. Eve's heart stopped. But when it moved on, unblocking her view, she saw Olga still standing on the sidewalk, and one of the two women on the bench remained. Eve was elated.

There was a break in the traffic and she ran to the other side, coming up to the woman, breathless. "Thank you for waiting," she said between gasps.

"It was not my bus," Olga replied, her accent thick, her speech plodding. "How do you know my name?"

A small Asian woman with a large shopping bag peered at them from her perch on the nearby bench. Eve took Olga's arm and pulled her aside.

"I am with the FBI, Olga," she said in a confidential tone. "We believe there are Russian spies in the hospital and we're doing an investigation. Have you heard or seen anything suspicious?"

"What? This is true?"

"Yes, Olga."

"I must not be involved," the woman said, shaking her head.

"Yes, this is your country now, you must help us. Talk to me and you'll be safe."

Olga scrutinized her. "You are with the police? This is true?"

"Yes, undercover. Have you seen or heard anything we should know about?"

"There is a man in the cardiac unit, a patient, who spoke in Russian to me."

"Oh? What did he say?"

"Nothing important. He wanted to make some conversation, I think."

"Is that all?"

Deep lines formed on Olga's pudgy face.

"You must tell me," Eve said, "for the security of the hospital. For the security of us all."

Olga reflected for a moment, then said, "Earlier today, in the morning, this same man had a visitor."

"Yes?"

"He, too, spoke in Russian."

"Yes, Olga, and what did he say?"

"They spoke of something very dangerous. They spoke of deaths, I think. And—" she lowered her voice "—the KGB."

"No."

"Yes," Olga said, nodding solemnly. "It is very terrible. Here in America. I did not know what to think."

"It is good that you heard this," Eve told her. "It is important information. But it is also very important that you speak to no one about this."

"Oh, no. Never."

"You could be a great hero."

"This is not important," Olga said modestly.

"But we have more to do. I might need to talk to you again. Where do you live?"

Olga looked uncertain about whether she wished to answer the question. But then she did. "In San Francisco. The Excelsior District. In the basement of my daughter's house."

"You have a family, then."

"A daughter, a son-in-law and grandchildren. But they are on vacation until Sunday night, when they come home. School is Monday."

"I see. Will you be working tomorrow?"

"Not again until Monday."

"That's good, Olga. Stay at home, talk to no one and you'll be safe. I will contact you, but I need your telephone number and your address."

Olga gave her the information, which Eve wrote on the back of an envelope from her purse. A bus pulled up to the stop just then.

"And what is your name?" Olga asked her.

"Clarice," Eve replied.

Olga nodded and boarded the bus along with the Asian woman with the big shopping bag. Eve watched it pull away and sighed with relief. Now she understood what Iggy's life must have been like back in Soviet Russia.

Olga sat in the back of the bus as she always did. Her sister, who liked to sit in the front, near the driver, had been killed in Kiev in 1974 when the bus she was riding in ran headlong into a cement truck. Olga had learned from that.

Felina Estrella, the Filipina who worked in the cafeteria and who also lived in the Excelsior like Olga, put her shopping bag on the floor and sat down next to her friend. "So, who was that you were talking to?"

"I can't talk about it," Olga replied.

"Why?"

"Because it is secret."

"I know. She is from the union."

"No, much more important."

"Personnel?"

"No."

"Then what?"

"Felina, did I not say it is secret?"

"You are a very funny friend, Olga."

Olga pressed her lips together and looked out at the high fog covering the hills. "There is nothing to make you worry," she said.

"How can I worry, if I do not know the secret?"

"Okay, I will tell you this and this only. The Russians have spies in the hospital."

"What?"

"You heard."

"Olga," Felina tittered, "you're crazy."

"No, it is true, I heard the spies with my own ears. The KGB."

The Filipina shook her head, obviously not believing her.

"If it is not true, why should the FBI come to me?"

"Is that who that lady was?"

Olga turned red. Already she had betrayed Clarice's trust. But it was okay. Felina was an honest and trustworthy woman. "I will speak no more of this," she said. "And neither should you." She looked at her friend. "Will you promise to tell no one?"

THE HALL OF JUSTICE

Homicide was located on the fourth floor in the Hall of Justice. Nick could have gone directly to the records section downstairs, but that struck him as cowardly. Anyway, he was late, having taken the time to swing by the Yankee Clipper to drop off Joe's gun. The powers that be didn't look kindly on people carrying firearms into the Hall of Justice.

This was Nick's first time back in his old stomping grounds since his ignominious departure, and he decided to face it head-on. He walked into the Homicide Section, asked a clerk he didn't know for Hong or Plavec.

"Inspector Plavec is on the phone and Inspector Hong is out of the office."

"I'll wait for Plavec, then."

"Is he expecting you?"

"Yes."

"Your name sir?"

"Nick Sasso."

The clerk's eyes rounded slightly. "Oh."

What Nick couldn't be sure of was whether she was reacting to his brother's death or his own less than illustrious reputation. Every institution has its heroes and villains. Nick knew at which end of the spectrum he fell.

"Well, if it isn't Nick Sasso."

Nick turned at the sound of his name. It was Steve Buck, head of Homicide and his former boss.

"Hello, Lieutenant."

Buck, blond, square-jawed with a halfback's physique, didn't offer his hand, which pretty much told the story. He was about Nick's age, ambitious, political and determined to make captain by the time he was forty. They'd never particularly gotten along. Nick's fall from grace had put a little tarnish on Buck's star, which was not appreciated. "Tough luck about your brother," Buck said. "I'm sorry."

"Thanks."

"By the way, you don't have to wonder whether we'll do our job properly. Culp and Sasso are not the most popular names in this neighborhood, but we're professionals and we'll find out who's responsible. I hope that puts your mind at ease."

"I wasn't worried about it for a moment," Nick said.

"That said, it shouldn't be necessary for you to come around. I've got a happy shop now and I want to keep it that way."

"Sure, Steve. But please understand, I was asked to come in to make an ID. It wasn't my idea."

"Well, don't get any ideas of your own." With that, Buck turned and walked away, leaving no doubt about his sentiments.

Moments later, Carl Plavec came out of the bullpen where the inspectors' cubicles were located. "If you don't mind, Nick, I'll have somebody take you down to Records. Dickson or I'll be down as soon as we can."

"Fine."

Plavec started to go. Nick stopped him.

"Carl, mind if I ask you something?"

"No. What d'ya got?"

"What's the story the new people hear about me when they come into the section?"

Plavec frowned, pooching his lips. "Mainly you're used as a negative example, what not to do in handling evidence."

"That's understandable. Does Dickson carry a lot of emotion about it?"

"I don't know. Never has said much about you."

"That's amazing considering I fucked up his career."

"I'm his second partner since you left," Plavec said. "First thing he told me when I came in was that if I couldn't trust him enough to share my mistakes and problems, we shouldn't be partners. He said not having that trust cost him dearly once, and he didn't want it happening again. I assume he was talking about you."

Plavec's words, spoken directly but without animus, cut deeply into Nick's soul. Dickson Hong blamed himself. That was worse than if his partner had put it all on him.

Plavec said, "I've got some work to do on the phone. Let me get somebody to take you to Records."

A freckle-faced clerk took Nick to the basement to have a look through the computerized database of offenders, the mug shots. The technician on duty was able to narrow down the selection of target suspects with a few mouse clicks. In twenty minutes Nick had identified two probable assailants and two possibles. Hong arrived just as he was finishing up.

Seeing his onetime mentor, Nick wanted to tell him not to blame himself over what had happened in the Allard case. It hadn't been a question of trust—it had been misplaced pride. Nick hadn't been able to face the consequences of fucking up. He'd thought he could render the mistake harmless by keeping his mouth shut. Dickson hadn't failed *him*, it was the other way around.

But his onetime ex-partner seemed to be in no mood to indulge him. His tone was curt, his eyes focusing in the middle distance. Nick judged it wasn't the time to summon ghosts from the past.

"What do you have?" Hong asked, first putting on his eyeglasses, then taking the printouts from Nick's hand.

"The big guy was most distinctive," Nick told him. "But that top one is the guy who tried to put a bullet in my head."

"You sure?"

"As sure as I can be. That's not allowing for the possibility of identical twins."

Hong did not smile. "Or the fact that these people all tend to look alike?"

He was in a pissy mood. Nick knew from experience it was not the time you wanted to be around Dickson Hong.

"I wouldn't go that far."

"Never mind," Hong said, pushing his little eyeglasses up his nose, "this gives us something to go on. These gangbangers have family trees." They made their way to the elevators to return to the fourth floor. "It looks like you've picked some heavy hitters, their seeming youth notwithstanding," Hong said, studying the printouts. "I think you're wrong on one of these, though. I'm pretty certain Sung's in jail in Hong Kong. But seven-fifty is not a bad batting average, even for a former cop."

"Most of the time I was on the floor with a boot in my face, so a mistake is a definite possibility."

"I appreciate your honesty." He said the words, but there was no appreciation in Hong's voice.

When they got back to Homicide, they went to Hong's cubicle. Plavec was gone. Nick sat in Plavec's chair while his former partner took his own seat. Nick got a lump in his throat, remembering how once upon a time they'd shared this space, facing each other like this, discussing their cases and doing paperwork. He recalled one morning in particular when he'd agonized about telling Dickson about misplacing the gun in that goddamn Allard case. All these years later he still suffered for making the wrong choice.

"Since you seem to be an honorary member of the force," Hong said dryly, "I guess I can tell you that the doorman at Elaine Chang's building overheard her saying she was heading for Hong Kong as she left this morning, suitcase in hand.

"No shit? Hong Kong? So you think she skipped the country?"

"It's possible. Or, the words could have been uttered for effect. Ms. Chang could actually be in a motel in Bakersfield."

"If she does turn up in Hong Kong, will the authorities help you to question her?"

"As you may recall, they no longer salute the queen over there. Which is not to say the bunch in charge never cooperates, but Ms. Chang has lots of connections. Personally, I'd bet against it. But we aren't to that bridge yet."

"If my sister-in-law is to be believed, your case could have disappeared right along with Ms. Chang."

Hong took off his glasses and began polishing them with his handkerchief. "*If* is the key word. I'm not ready to brand anybody a suspect just yet, including Mrs. Sasso. But you have to admit, she had a clear motive and the opportunity. Ms. Chang may have fled to avoid arrest, or it could be innocent, a business trip or a last-minute vacation. But the biggest problem I have with her is motive. Your sister-in-law, who you have to admit has an ax to grind, may be engaged in wishful thinking. With all due respect, she's not the kind of pony I put my money on."

"Maybe you can put your money on me, then, Dickson," Nick said, taking the copy of the article out of his jacket pocket. "I think I figured out what my brother was after—he and Ms. Chang, most probably." Removing the business card, he passed the article across the desk to Hong.

The inspector took a minute to skim the article. "An emerald Buddha, huh?"

"I found that in a secret drawer in my brother's desk, along with a few personal items and this business card." He handed the card to Hong.

"Ken Lu," Hong said.

"Know him?"

Hong shook his head. "Can't say that I do."

"My guess is that Lu is promoting a scheme to find the

Emerald Buddha and that with Elaine Chang's help, Joe bought into it. That's got to be it, Dickson."

"Entirely possible, I grant you, but the skeptic in me says, 'So what?'"

"If the piece is as valuable as it seems, then there'll be passions and rivalry. Joe probably stepped on somebody's toes. Elaine Chang taking off as soon as Joe's killed would seem to add credence to my theory."

"That she killed him? Maybe she ran in fear of her own life."

"That's true. I'm not saying she's the killer, but she's definitely involved. My hunch is that if you find her, you'll get to whoever is responsible."

"Maybe. No question we need to talk to her." Hong put his glasses back on. "But the Buddha business is only a theory."

"The stuff was in a secret drawer, Dickson."

"Along with the rope, the candlestick and the lead pipe?"

"Could it be you're making fun of me?" Nick asked with a modicum of good cheer.

"No, I'm not in the best of moods. I've been told to stick around this afternoon in case my presence is requested for a meeting with the mukety-mucks, and you know how much I enjoy those occasions."

"Is it a meeting regarding this case?"

"No comment. Your privileges have their limits. Thanks for passing this along," Hong said, indicating the article.

Nick could see he was being asked, politely, to leave. "Mind if I keep the originals?" he asked. "Photocopies will do for your purposes, won't they?"

"Sure." Hong left the cubicle, returning a minute later. He handed the article and business card to Nick. "Why don't you go rest your banged-up body?"

"Not a bad idea."

"And, Nick...I do appreciate your help." No smile. Just a matter-of-fact statement.

Nick had a strong urge to plead with his old partner not to blame himself for what had happened in the Allard investigation. He wanted to tell him it had nothing to do with trust, but Dickson had already opened a file folder. Nick had been dismissed.

OAKLAND

Sonny's old pal, Naomi Watts, lived in an apartment in a shabby building on Vermont Street. It was on the hill above Grand Avenue with a view of the freeway and Lake Merritt. Billie found a parking place opposite the building. Peering up at it, she hoped she hadn't made the trek across the bay in vain. She'd tried calling Naomi from home and she did answer, but as soon as Billie identified herself, Naomi said, without ceremony, "Look, Billie, I can't talk to you, I won't talk to you. I'm sorry about everything that's happened, but please don't call me anymore." Then she hung up.

Billie had thought about that, deciding it was out of character for Naomi to snub her. They'd never been close, but during Billie's marriage to Sonny, she and Naomi had gotten along well enough. Occasionally the three of them would do something together, though it was clearly Sonny who was Naomi's friend.

After the divorce, Billie had seen Naomi a couple, maybe three times. They'd had lunch once, but again the primary connection was with Sonny. Even so, there'd never been unpleasantness or a cross word between them. It made no sense that now, right after Sonny's death, Naomi would suddenly get squirrelly. Maybe worse, Billie had detected fear in the woman's voice.

Shortly after their brief telephone conversation Emily had awakened and come into the kitchen where Billie and Mel were fixing lunch.

"Well," Billie said to her daughter, "if it isn't Sleeping Beauty. How are you feeling, honey?"

Emily wore a pouty expression, but made no great display of emotion. She was lethargic, but not nearly so distraught as the night before. Billie suspected she was mostly numb, trying to put the trauma of her father's death into the context of daytime reality.

Billie sat at the table, holding her daughter on her lap, while Mel finished preparing lunch. Emily didn't have a lot to say about her father, though she did ask about Martin. Billie had assured her he'd be coming to see her.

Lunch seemed to brighten Emily's mood. She started talking to her grandfather about going to Golden Gate Park because of a promise made before the tragic events. Mel asked Billie if she wanted to come with them, but she demurred, deciding it was important to find out what was going on with Naomi. As soon as her father and daughter left the house, Billie headed for Oakland.

Now that she'd found the place, the question was, how would she talk her way in? Getting out of the car, she crossed the street to an old stucco building that was in need of a face-lift. The mailboxes were in an outdoor entry area, the bell to each apartment on a badly worn brass panel next to the door. The name Watts was written on the card in the slot for apartment sixteen. There were sixteen units in the building altogether, which probably meant Naomi's place was on the top floor.

Billie didn't bother buzzing Naomi. Instead, she rang six or seven of the other bells. She got two voices on the intercom and somebody else who buzzed her directly in. As expected, Naomi's apartment was on the top floor of the building, *sans* elevator. Other than a little jogging, Billie hadn't done much of an athletic nature since her softball years in high school, though she'd gotten into yoga after her breast cancer ordeal. Yoga was good for the soul—and for flexibility—but it didn't do much for a person's cardiovascular system. The bottom line was she was out of shape and therefore winded by the time she reached the top floor. She vowed right then that if Naomi snubbed her, she'd kill her.

Billie knocked on the door. It took two times before there was a response.

"Who is it?" Naomi said from inside.

"It's me, Billie."

"I told you I wouldn't talk to you and I won't," Naomi said, clearly exasperated.

"Naomi, we've *got* to talk!"

"Why?"

"Have the police been to see you yet?"

"No."

"Then all the more important that you talk to me."

"Damn it, Billie, will you please go away! I don't want to talk to you. It won't do either of us any good."

"That makes me feel even better."

"Right now I don't care how you feel."

"Look," Billie said, letting her exasperation show, "I drove over the goddamn bridge to see you and I'll have to go back in rush-hour traffic, so open the door, will you?"

Several moments passed before the door opened a crack. Naomi Watts showed her smooth, milk-chocolate face, still pretty after more than fifty years of life.

She'd always been an enigma to Billie, one of those people who lived painfully in loneliness. Naomi's parents had been dead for years and she'd never married. Her love life had always been something of a mystery. When she was young, still hanging out in Berkeley, she had a relationship with a Black Panther who ended up in prison. They had a jailhouse romance of sorts, then he got out of prison and was promptly killed. So far as Billie knew, there'd never been anybody else in her life. Sonny used to say Naomi was an activist nun, the bride of Karl Marx and Che Guevara, but it was a joke. Once she'd grown up, Naomi had been reasonably responsible in both her politics and her personal life. Romance just didn't seem to be a part of it.

"All right," Naomi said, "so the door's open. What do you want?"

Billie took a breath. "I'll be brief and to the point. What was Sonny mixed up in that somebody would want to kill him?"

"I don't know."

"Damn it, don't pull that shit. Sonny never got involved in a single thing of importance in his professional life that you didn't know about."

"I haven't seen Sonny or talked to him for a long time."

"That's not true."

"Yes, it is."

"Bullshit."

"What makes you so sure?"

"Because Martin told me you and Sonny had a very long conversation on the phone just recently."

"That was personal."

"I don't believe you. I know because you're scared. If you didn't know what he's been up to, you'd be sad maybe, but you wouldn't be playing games. We'd be hugging and crying. You know I'm right, Naomi."

"Okay, let me put it this way. There's nothing I can do to help Sonny now. But I still got to look out for my own ass. The last thing I need is to give the goddamn Bar Association rope to hang me with."

"Naomi, this isn't you," Billie said, trying to shame her. "You're the woman who went to the South to register black voters. You counseled war protesters during Vietnam. You fought for the Equal Rights Amendment, you fought for women, farm laborers, students, welfare mothers and a thousand other causes, and you're telling me you won't talk to me about a single death?"

"I'm fifty-four years old. I've been without my law license for over two years and I'm at the point where the bar's talking settlement. This is my last chance, Billie. If I can practice law again, I can make a difference. Sonny understood that. Why can't you?"

"Because I believe in your heart more than your words, Naomi."

The woman's face crumbled and tears began running down her smooth cheeks. "Fuck you, Billie, just fuck you." With that, she slammed the door.

Billie heard a sob inside, then nothing. After two or three minutes of silence, Billie made her way back down the musty staircase and out the building. She'd spend the better part of the next hour getting to the bridge, crossing it and struggling through traffic to North Beach. In a sense this was worth it. If nothing else, she'd learned that whatever it was that had killed Sonny Culp and Joe Sasso, it was alive and well, and it still packed a hell of a punch.

CHINATOWN

Henry Chin couldn't take the chance of using his city limo, so he drove himself to Grant Street, leaving his Mercedes in a side alley in the care of a young man whose occupation was baby-sitting expensive automobiles.

The fish shop was on Grant between Jackson and Pacific. Henry moved through the crowds, unrecognized as a celebrity even in the community that should have been his birthright. Certain influential people in Chinatown did count themselves among his supporters, but truth be known, this really wasn't his turf. Montgomery Street, Pacific Heights, Sea Cliff, Presidio Heights, St. Francis Woods—those were the places

Henry identified with and, more importantly, the people in them identified with him.

But Henry Chin also knew how to get things done. The Chinese community, for all its quirks and idiosyncrasies, had a way of cutting corners and getting results. And in China-town money was used with much less pretense and hypocrisy than in most other quarters. But it was important to know the right people. Henry did.

To the average Westerner it would have been funny to see a well-dressed, dignified gentleman enter a fish shop where housewives haggled with clerks wearing white jackets smeared with blood and fish entrails. But to the residents of Chinatown the shop was simply what people who mattered passed through to get where they needed to go. In that sense, it was not un-like, say, the parking garage at the Bank of America Building.

But, unlike the B of A Building, there was no elevator. In-stead, a beefy man in a suit that fit him a bit too snugly directed Henry up the dark flight of wooden stairs leading to the second floor. There, in an outer office, another muscular retainer sat with a cup of tea in his hand, waiting in Foo dog fashion. Putting down his tea, he stood. Across the room a small woman—young, attractive, but unpretentious in a plain white blouse, dark skirt and bobbed hair—rose behind the desk where she sat.

"District Attorney Chin," she said, bowing slightly in the tradition of the old country, a custom Henry knew about, but to which he scarcely related.

"Miss Han."

"Will you please sit?" She gestured toward the worn Ming chair adjacent to her desk. "I will tell my father you are here."

The young woman stepped into the next room, quietly closing the door behind her. Henry knew that, in a very real way, he was coming to the seat of power as much as if Han Fat had come to see him on Bryant Street. In Chinese soci-ety there were interlocking fiefdoms hierarchically arranged in a manner known principally to the participants. Outward appearances were not necessarily a reliable guide. Han Fat, who was perhaps best likened to a godfather figure, was a sort of franchisee to one of the traditional Chinese triads, though he was himself well insulated from what went on under his auspices in streets up and down the West Coast. When it came to matters extralegal, though, Han Fat was the man to see.

To the world at large it would have seemed remarkable that Henry might come to see Han Fat, given his position as the chief law enforcement official in the city. But both men knew they could be of as much help to each other as a hindrance, and the simple fact was, Henry was very much in need. Both he and Han Fat appreciated the implications of that. Henry, being beholden, had to pay. Handsomely. And, if each of them did what was agreed upon, all would be right in the world. It was not the way Henry had learned to conduct himself at Yale, but it worked.

The door to the inner office opened just then and Han's daughter returned. "My father will see you now," she said in her quiet voice.

Henry went to the door and entered Han Fat's inner sanctum. The room was inauspicious, half the size of his own office. It was badly cluttered with papers and files and books. The dim light came through the yellowing blinds covering the windows. A blue haze of tobacco smoke hung in the air.

Seated behind a huge rosewood desk and nearly obscured by the ubiquitous piles of papers was a man whose appearance was in no way suggested by his name. Han Fat was small and slight. Though well into his sixties, his thick dark hair was scored by only a few streaks of white. Han showed his age in his face. He had huge bags under badly wrinkled eyes, mere slits in his sagging flesh. A smoking cigarette hung from his lower lip.

When Henry entered, Han Fat was hunched over, working on something in the small space on the desk that had been cleared for such purpose. The light to work by was provided by a vase lamp. He looked up and smiled, rising to his feet.

"Honorable District Attorney," he said with a slight bow. "Welcome."

Henry spoke only a few words of Mandarin, which meant English was essential to communication, even in Chinatown. Han spoke English well, though not idiomatically, and with a very strong accent.

"Please sit," Han said, placing his cigarette in an ashtray overflowing with butts and ashes. He came around the desk and joined Henry in a pair of Ming chairs that differed from the one outside only because they were covered with matching red cushions.

"May I offer tea?" Han asked.

"No, thank you."

"You said the matter is urgent. Maybe we talk."

"Yes," Henry said. "I'll be direct. I need yet another favor," he told the old man. "Most urgently."

"You have many problem, Henry. What you need now?"

Henry told him that they needed a home office searched and damning evidence removed. "This one may be the most difficult yet," he confessed.

"Don't tell me. The mayor?"

"No, Martin Fong."

Fat shook his head sadly. "Almost as bad."

"I know. And worse still, I don't think getting the computers, documents and files will be enough. He knows too much and has to be eliminated. For good."

Fat sat motionlessly, his eyes hidden behind the slits in his lids. "You ask very much, Henry." The old man thought for another long minute, then said, "This time a hundred thousand dollar. I know Martin father. Lucky for you we not too much friends. Otherwise, maybe two hundred thousand."

"That's a lot of money."

"You say urgent. My men do too much already. Very dangerous."

"Okay. A hundred thousand. Just get it done. The sooner, the better."

"Please don't ask more burglary, Henry. Before long, all my men in China and I all alone." Han grinned, appreciating his joke more than Henry.

"For both our sakes, I hope this will put a stop to it."

"Then, please, tell me exactly what you need."

NORTH BEACH

Nick had been sleeping for maybe an hour when he was awakened by knocking on the door. Linda Nassari, busty and voluptuous, stepped into the room, the swish of her skirts audible from where he lay.

"Sorry to bother you, Nick, but your sister-in-law is on the phone. She said it's urgent."

He blinked himself into consciousness, having been in a very deep sleep. "Gina?"

"Yes."

Nick had taken off his trousers and shirt to lie down. And, since Linda was not exactly a stranger, he didn't hesitate to throw back the covers and get up. She watched him fumble with his trousers.

"Don't get mad, Nick," the hostess said, "but you had a call earlier, before you got back. I forgot to give you the message."

"Who from?"

"Billie Fox."

"Yeah? What did she say?"

"She told me to tell you she's meeting Martin Fong here at the Clipper at seven. Something about turning up some very interesting information. She left her number."

Nick tried to clear his muddled brain. "She wants me to meet with them?"

"I guess."

He had his pants on, but didn't bother with shoes, padding across the room barefoot on his way to the office across the hall. As he passed Linda, he tweaked her chin, giving her a wink.

"I'm working the dinner shift again tonight," she said. "Have any plans for the evening? Late, I mean?"

"Not that I know of," he said, sharing a conspiratorial smile. "Maybe I'll stick around."

Linda went down the stairs and Nick into the office. The place was still a mess, thanks not only to the gangbangers, but also the police. Straightening it up wasn't a very high priority. He'd focused on the restaurant, ordering a new plate-glass window for the front, but he'd have to find time to put the office in order, as well.

Nick sat at his brother's desk and picked up the phone to speak to his brother's wife. "Hi, Gina."

"I'm sorry to bother you, but a courier just came to the door and handed me an envelope from an attorney. It's addressed to the estate of Joseph Sasso."

"Did you open it?"

"Yes, it's a bill for legal services."

"What firm, Gina?"

"It just says Todd Easley, Attorney-at-Law."

"Must be a sole practitioner. Do you know him?"

"No."

"What's the amount?"

"Twenty-four hundred dollars. The total is seven thousand four hundred, less a retainer of five thousand."

"Does it say what for?"

"Services rendered. Then it lists Joe's various companies."

"What's the date of the invoice?"

"Today's date."

"Is there an address and phone number?"

"Yes, do you want it?"

"Please."

Gina read off the information and Nick jotted it down on a scrap of paper.

"What should I do with this?" she asked.

"Give it to the police when they come to get Joe's things."

"They've already been here."

"Then just hang on to it until I see you. How are the kids doing?"

"There are a lot of red eyes here."

"How about *you?*"

"I'm hanging on."

"As soon as you're up to it, have me over for dinner, Gina. Or, better yet, I'll bring over a couple of pizzas. I don't know if I can make the kids feel any better, but at least they'll know you aren't alone. Meanwhile, if there's anything I can do, let me know."

"Did the police say anything more about me?" she asked.

"Nothing special. Just routine stuff."

"Damn it, Nick, don't give me that 'routine stuff' comment. Just tell me."

"You haven't been eliminated as a suspect. It'll depend on if they find any physical evidence linking you to the crime."

"Is that what they said?"

"No, that's my explanation of the way these things work."

"Then I don't need a lawyer just yet."

"Not unless *you* think you need one, Gina."

"What would you do in my shoes?"

He thought for a moment. "I'd wait and see if they call you in for serious questioning. And if they read you your rights, don't say a word until there's a lawyer at your elbow."

"Okay," she said. "Thank you, Nick. Thanks for everything."

They ended the call and Nick immediately dialed the number for Todd Easley. A woman answered.

"Law offices."

"Hi," Nick said. "I'm looking for a lawyer and somebody mentioned Mr. Easley's name. Is he available?"

"No, I'm afraid he's out of the office until Monday."

"I see. Well, can you tell me what kind of law he practices?"

"Mr. Easley specializes in bankruptcy."

He hadn't expected that. "Oh. Well, this is a personal-injury situation."

"Sorry, that's not his area of expertise."

"Understand. Thanks."

He hung up. Bankruptcy. That was consistent with Joe's situation. It also meant Sonny Culp was probably not involved in that part of Joe's troubles. It seemed like a good idea for him to have a chat with Mr. Easley, though. It would be interesting to know what, if anything, he knew about the Emerald Buddha.

Easley's address was South of Market a few blocks from the Hall of Justice, not exactly a hangout for top-drawer lawyers. Billie Fox's office was in the same general area. Maybe she knew him. He'd ask. Either way, he'd give Easley a call on Monday.

Nick returned to his room and lay down. He felt as if he'd been run over by a truck. Reflecting, he decided the case had a David-and-Goliath feel, and, interestingly enough, his brother may have had a foot in each camp. Nick was sure the Emerald Buddha was at the heart of the matter. Exactly what they were fighting over and who was involved remained unknown, however. If Elaine Chang had gone into hiding, then his best hope for finding out what was going on might lie with Ken Lu, the Hong Kong antiques dealer.

Reaching over to the chair where he'd put the notes he'd made while going through Joe's desk, he found the telephone numbers he'd transcribed from the address book. Under the assumption the "L" represented Lu, he decided to call the number and see what he turned up.

Trekking back to the office, he dropped into the desk chair and dialed the number. He got a downtown residential hotel, respectable, but not glitzy by any means.

"Ken Lu, please," he said.

"I'm sorry, sir, but Mr. Lu is no longer registered."

"Do you have a number for him?"

"Not a local one."

"What do you have? His number in Hong Kong?"

"Yes. Would you like it?"

"Please."

The clerk read the number, but it was the one on Lu's business card. Nick asked if the guy had any idea what time it was in Hong Kong.

"I believe they're sixteen hours ahead, sir."

"Thanks."

Nick tried to decide if he should call now. It was early Saturday morning in Hong Kong, but what the hell, maybe the phone would ring in Lu's residence or he'd get a machine. Not having the patience to figure out how to direct dial and given the condition of his skull, he asked the operator to place the call.

He quickly got a connection. A woman answered in Chinese.

"Hello," Nick said. "May I speak with Ken Lu, please?"

There was a stony silence. Nick feared he hadn't made himself understood. "Hello?" he said.

"Who calling, please?"

"It's in regard to the Myanmar deal," he said, choosing to be circumspect.

There was another silence. Then, "Mr. Lu not in Hong Kong."

"Do you know where I can reach him?"

"Perhaps he can telephone to you, sir."

"Okay. I'm in San Francisco. The name's Nick." He gave her his telephone number.

"Thank you." The line went dead.

He shrugged, thinking he'd done the best he could. His hope was that Lu would be sufficiently intrigued to contact him...unless, of course, he'd been as spooked as Elaine Chang.

Returning to his room, he lay down once again. His brain numb, he closed his eyes and debated which was more important: sleep or making a pilgrimage to Benny Vocino's place on Telegraph Hill. His body pleaded for mercy, but deep in his soul he wanted to know what Benny was doing in Joe's calendar, paired with Elaine Chang.

A taxi wouldn't be easy to come by this time of day, though. Rationalizing that it was only a short drive to Telegraph Hill, and that he wouldn't be dangerous behind the wheel since he'd had some sleep, he decided to go see the mayor of North Beach.

Nick finished dressing, took another pain pill, and bucked himself up. He started out the door, then stopped. On an impulse, he got Joe's gun from under the mattress of the bed, stuck it in his belt, under his jacket, and left.

TELEGRAPH HILL

"Nick, when the wife told me, I was devastated," Benny Vocino said, embracing him. "Dora heard it on the news and came to me in tears."

They were in the front room of Benito Vocino's house with a view of the Bay Bridge, Treasure Island and the Oakland and Berkeley Hills. The place was within spitting distance of North Beach—close enough for Benny to consider himself still in the neighborhood. "It's all fuzzy now, anyway," Benny would say. "The Chinamen are overrunning the place, so us Italians have to go somewhere, right?" Though he could easily afford it, Benny wasn't going to live in Pacific Heights with the blue bloods, the Jews and the celebrities. No, he wanted to open his window and still smell the garlic.

"What's with the face?" Benny said, guiding him to the green sofa that looked as if it was right out of the fifties, though it had to be brand-new. "They try to get you, too, Nicky?"

"Walked in on a burglary at the restaurant this morning."

"Independent of what happened to Joey, or connected?"

"We aren't sure," Nick replied, not wanting to get into the details. "Possibly connected. The police are trying to sort it out. The guys who jumped me were Chinese."

"Figures." Benny checked out Nick's bandaged nose. "Broken?"

"Yeah."

"The bastards." He shook his head. "You look like you could use a cup of coffee." He turned toward the kitchen. "Dora!" he shouted. "Bring Nick a cup of coffee, will you?"

There was no response.

"Dora?"

Still no response.

Benny shook his head again. "Dora don't hear so good anymore. And she's got that little TV in the kitchen. Soap operas and talk shows. Whatever happened to going to the vegetable and fruit market and chewing the fat with the neighbors? I'll tell you what happened. Nowadays you order your groceries on the computer and you talk to Oprah Winfrey instead of Mrs. Rossi. That's what modern living has given us." He shook his head, like a man disgusted with the world. "Excuse me a minute, I'll tell Dora we need refreshments."

"Don't bother, Benny. I don't need anything."

"Sure you do. We both need coffee." With that he got up and shuffled off stiffly in the direction of the kitchen.

Nick sighed, leaning back on the sofa. He hadn't decided just how he'd approach Benny about his possible connection with Joe's troubles. Probably, he'd just wait for the right opportunity.

Meanwhile, he stared out at the view, watching a small

freighter moving south toward the bridge. Ships always made him think of the Far East, mostly because of the stories his late uncle Sal, a merchant marine, had told him when he was a kid. Sal had had all sorts of wild tales, including some about pirates in the Gulf of Thailand. When Nick got older, the stories tended to feature women instead of pirates, and there were some damn good ones, too.

Nick's mother never thought much of her brother-in-law Sal and was always trying to keep him from her sons. "Your uncle Salvatore has the Sasso womanizing gene," his mother had told him. "Listen to him and you'll be in big trouble. Remember that, Nicky." That little sermon had come after Sal invited him out for a drink to celebrate his twenty-first birthday. Maria Sasso hadn't elaborated on the exact nature of her concern, but Nick had gotten the point. He'd just as quickly dismissed it, though.

Thinking back on his youthful escapades, Nick again saw the pattern. Trouble, pleasure and the easy way out seemed to be the dominant themes in his life. What impressed him most was how difficult it was to turn a life around. But it was clear to him there'd be no more playing at it. Solving a murder and coping with financial ruin weren't like trying to keep your New Year's resolutions. From here on out, it was balls to the wall. He'd made his old man a promise and he was going to keep it.

"Sorry about that," Benny said, returning. "Coffee'll be right out." He picked up the cigar box on the table next to his armchair, removed the lid and offered Nick one.

"No, thanks."

Benny took a cigar for himself. Nick watched him clip the tip and light the cigar, all of which was done with methodical precision. "So what's up?" he asked, hollowing his cheeks before blowing out puffs of smoke.

Nick recalled being a little kid and watching Benny Vocino smoke. It was funny how some things never changed.

Benny waited. Nick cleared his throat.

"I was going through Joe's stuff," he began. "One of the things I found was his appointment calendar, his pocket version. Most of it was in code or abbreviations, but there were a couple of entries during the past six months or so indicating he met with B.V. I figured it was you, Benny."

"Joey put down he met with me?"

"No, with B.V."

"I guess I don't have to point out I'm not the only person with those initials," Benny said. "When did his meeting with B.V. supposedly happen?"

"There were two. The first in late January, early February. Then again several weeks ago."

Benny shook his head. "No, must have been somebody else. Now, it could be I seen Joey at the Yankee Clipper about those times, 'cause, as you know, I'm in there a lot. And Joey and me talk occasionally. But as for some formal meeting that somebody's going to put in their book, no, it had to be somebody else."

"You sure, Benny?"

"You think I'm losing it like your pa, God bless his soul? No, Nick, it's somebody else, believe me. Like I told you on the phone when you called me from New York, Joey's mistake was not coming to me about his problems when I could have still helped him. Remember me telling you that?"

"Yeah, I remember."

Benny was putting on a great show of sincerity, but to Nick it just wasn't ringing true. Besides, the only telephone number in the book listed under "V" was Benny's. That had been verified. Nick saw nothing to be gained in pointing that out because he'd put Benny on the defensive and get him pissed off. Getting on the wrong side of Benito Vocino was not a wise strategy. So Nick decided to play it differently.

"Okay, I understand you didn't meet with Joe to talk about his financial problems, but I'm wondering if maybe when you talked at the Yankee Clipper, some related topics might have come up."

Benny turned his cigar in his fingers. "Like what?"

"Well, Joe seemed to have developed an interest in Myanmar and Buddhism," Nick told him. "That and the fact that he had a Chinese girlfriend, a businesswoman named Elaine Chang, makes me think Asian stuff played a role in his troubles. He ever mention any of that to you?"

Benny shook his head solemnly. "Not a word about any of that."

The "honorary mayor of North Beach" looked him dead in the eye as he said it, but Nick's cop nose, rusty though it was, told him he wasn't hearing the whole truth.

"How about a guy named Ken Lu? That name familiar?"

"Chinaman?"

"Yeah."

"Me and the Chinese don't mix too good, Nicky. Not that I'm prejudiced or anything, but I've done business with them in the past and...well, let's just say I find it easier to do my thing elsewhere. I wouldn't be putting Joey in touch with Chinamen, since I don't do business with them much myself."

Benny had answered a question Nick hadn't asked. He hadn't inquired whether Benny had put Joe in touch with Elaine Chang or Ken Lu. He'd asked if Benny had heard Joe mention them or Myanmar or any of the rest of it.

Benny, oblivious to his slip, took a slow drag on his cigar, then blew the smoke up toward the ceiling. "You know what this proves? It proves when you do business, it's best to stay close to home and deal with people and projects you know something about."

"Then there hasn't been any talk around town about some kind of business deal Joe could have been involved in that involved Myanmar and some Chinese players."

"If the subject is Chinamen, trust me, I'm not the guy to

talk to. And I certainly didn't hear anything about it from nobody else."

Dora Vocino, a sturdy woman with white hair and painted red lips, an old-school Italian housewife always in an apron, it seemed, brought out two coffees. She'd given Nick her condolences on the phone and again at the door, but still looked at him with saintly compassion, frowning to signal her deep feelings. "You take anything, Nicky?"

"No, nothing. Black's fine. Thank you, Dora."

She nodded and left. Benny put his cigar in the large stone ashtray carved in the shape of Italy, took the single cube of sugar from his saucer and dropped it into his cup. At the restaurant, Gennaro served Benny his coffee the same way.

"I'm completely at a loss," Nick said.

"Understandable, Nicky. But take my advice and don't take the burden of this on your own shoulders. You'll have your hands full with the restaurant now that Joe's passed."

Nick hadn't given that aspect of his problems much consideration. The Yankee Clipper was a problem all right, and not just because somebody had to run it. Because of Joe's wheeling and dealing, the family was in jeopardy of losing the venerable old joint. That would kill Tony Sasso, if the news of Joe's demise didn't do him in. Add to that what was going on back in New York and Nick had more on his plate than he could handle.

There might have been a time when he'd have asked Benny Vocino for help and advice, but not now. The man who'd been like an uncle to him was apparently standing at the edge of the mess, if indeed he didn't have a foot smack-dab in the middle. "Yeah," he said, taking the pitch, "you're probably right."

Nick had no desire for coffee, but he took a sip to be polite. Benny picked up his cigar and shaped the ash on the toe of Italy. "So, have the police figured out what happened yet? I mean, like who was responsible for this terrible tragedy?"

"No, not to my knowledge."

"This is big enough that they'll catch the guy. It's not like some back-alley drug deal or nothing like that."

"Yeah." Nick thought about it for a moment, then decided to probe. "Benny, I don't suppose you know anything about Sonny Culp and how he might figure into whatever it was Joe was doing."

"Not thing one," Benny said, shaking his head. "When we saw the name in the paper, I called up my lawyers and asked who the guy was. Nobody knew much about him, beyond reputation. Small-time do-gooder was the way my people described him."

"That doesn't fit with Joe's wheeling and dealing."

"No, it doesn't, does it?" Benny said, blowing a smoke ring and watching it drift toward his wife's drapes. "Could be he was an innocent victim, in the wrong place at the wrong time."

"No, we're pretty sure he was mixed up in something with Joe, something he knew to be dangerous."

"Little guys do get ambitious sometimes and get in over their heads."

"It's confusing and full of contradictions." Nick glanced at his watch, knowing he wasn't going to learn anything. Benny was stonewalling him and that made him uneasy.

"It'll all make sense in the end," Benny said.

"I hope so."

"Anybody want more coffee?" Dora called from the door.

"No, thanks," Nick said. "I've got to go. And I can tell dinner is coming soon. Smells wonderful."

"Stay and eat," Dora said. "How often am I going to have a famous chef at my table?"

"It's not home cooking I do, Dora. I cook for the masses."

"Listen to this guy," Benny said. "There's nobody better in San Francisco. Not since Carlo Cordoni. And probably nobody better in New York, either."

"Carlo was the master," Nick agreed.

He moved to the edge of his seat and got to his feet. Benny did as well. Dora walked over to where the men stood.

"Tell Gina I'll call her," she said, "will you?"

"I will, yes."

"And you, Nick," she said, "you're the Sasso family now. Come back to San Francisco. This is your home. You need a wife and children. You need heirs. This is what your mother would want for you."

"Dora," Benny said with mock sternness, "go to the kitchen."

Dora rolled her eyes, gave Nick a hug and left. Benny walked him to the door. They embraced, clasping arms in a manly way.

"I guess it's too early to know about the funeral."

"Yeah, the medical examiner hasn't released the body."

"Let us know, because we want to attend. You're aware of my feelings for your family, Nick."

"Yeah, Benny, I am."

Nick descended the long flight of stairs to the sidewalk, feeling like hell. He was ninety percent certain that the man all North Beach revered had lied to him.

He'd parked across the street and a couple of doors up from Benny's place. Normally there was little traffic on this stretch of Montgomery Street because it dead-ended half a block farther up. Distracted, his mind on this latest twist in his brother's saga, Nick damn near stepped out in front of a vehicle that came whizzing down the street. If he hadn't jumped back, he'd have been flattened. It was past him before he realized it was a light blue van.

His glimpse of the driver was very brief. Asian. Long hair. He immediately thought of the gangbangers who'd jumped him at the restaurant. Were they trying to run him down, or was this a coincidence?

If it was a deliberate attempt to kill him, they'd picked a bad place to do it. There was no way out, other than to turn around and come back down the street. Nick knew he wasn't going to be able to flag them down, but he could use his car to bar the way.

Hurrying to his rental car, Nick jumped in, got Joe's .38 out of the glove compartment and put it on the seat beside him. Then he started the engine. He waited, deciding he'd pull in front of them at the last moment, as they came around the curve, catching them by surprise. Then he'd jump out of the car and put a gun to the driver's head before the bastard had a chance to recover.

Nick continued to wait, revving the engine as he craned his neck to see as far up the street as possible. Half a minute passed before he saw the blue van approaching. It was moving smartly, just as before.

He waited as long as he could, then gunned the engine, spinning the wheel so that his car lurched into the narrow street, blocking the passage between the rows of parked cars on either side. The driver of the van slammed on his brakes, stopping only a foot or two from Nick's car.

Nick already had the door open and, with gun in hand, raced around to the driver's side of the van. He stuck his weapon into the open window of the truck and pressed it into the driver's neck.

"I don't have any money!" she cried. "Just what's in my purse."

It wasn't the long-haired gangbanger from that morning. It was a girl, a Chinese girl. Nick was confused. He leaned back and looked at the side of the van. The sign on the side read, Mai Song's Flowers. He looked inside the van, past the flinching girl. There were several flower arrangements on the floor in back. He'd waylaid a flower-delivery girl.

"Christ," he said, lowering the gun. "I got the wrong van."

The girl's eyes remained round with fright. She was shaking. "Huh?"

"Sorry," he said. "This was a mistake."

"You mean it's not a robbery?"

"No, I screwed up. Some guys in a blue van just like this jumped me this morning and I..."

The girl shook her head, her expression going from incredulity to indignation.

"Look, I'm sorry," he said. "I apologize for any inconvenience." He stuck the gun in his belt and took out his wallet and removed a twenty. "Here, take this for your trouble."

The girl snatched the bill from his hand. "Get your damn car out of my way, will you?"

Nick returned to his car and backed it into the space where he'd lain in wait. The girl glared down at him.

"Asshole," she said, and drove off.

With a sigh, he put the gun back into the glove compartment. Checking his side mirror, Nick pulled out and drove up to the end of the cul-de-sac and turned around. Then he cruised back past Benny's place. Glancing at the upper window that looked out over the bay, he saw him. Benito Vocino didn't wave. Instead, he pulled back into the shadows.

VANCOUVER, BRITISH COLUMBIA

Elaine Chang paced in front of the huge bowed window in her suite at the Waterfront Center Hotel, only half watching the floatplanes and sea buses plying the waters of Burrard Inlet. Mostly, though, she was oblivious to the city, the brilliant blue sky and majestic, snowcapped peaks framing the view. She had other things on her mind.

Elaine understood what it was like to hang by a thread. She'd been on the edge before, though it had been a while since she'd felt such desperation. It was as though the gods were mocking her, slapping her in the face at every turn. She'd been an optimist most of her life, eschewing the fatalism of her countrymen, but for the first time ever, she truly felt damned.

Joss.

Elaine had never much cared for the word, or the sentiment behind it, but having been snake bit, she had a new appreciation for luck, both good and bad. Why, right at the moment of her biggest triumph, did Joe have to go and get himself killed? If this was what fate was all about, it was cruel.

Ironically, she didn't know who to blame, unless Joe had done something to bring this on himself. But even if he had, what good did it do her? Without Joe there was no money. Without money there was no deal. Over six months of time and effort down the drain.

The news of the murders had come as a shock. She'd been uneasy that entire evening, nervous because she knew her fate was in the hands of Sonny Culp. Then, when it grew late and there was no word from Joe, she sensed she'd been screwed. Why she'd turned on the TV, she didn't know. She wasn't a TV person. Maybe she felt at some deep level there'd be an explanation in the news.

And there was.

It was the lead story. "A maverick lawyer and a prominent San Francisco restaurateur were gunned down in the Marina this evening," the news anchor had said. Elaine didn't need to hear more.

As she'd stared at the video clips taken in the street outside Sonny Culp's office, she'd realized three things—her deal had died with Joe; she'd get dragged into the ensuing mess; the negative publicity could cost her a lot more than the deal. After turning off the TV she'd sat in silence, contemplating her options, fighting the deadly feeling of hopelessness, when the telephone rang. She expected it to be the police, but it was Ken Lu.

"Have you heard?" he said, his voice shaking. Whether from fear or anger it was hard to tell.

"Yes, Ken. It's a terrible thing."

"I guess it's over."

Elaine, never one to surrender, even in the face of certain defeat, had let her instincts speak for her. "Not necessarily."

"What? You have another Joe Sasso waiting in the wings with two million in his pocket?"

"There are always possibilities," she said. It was a reflex comment without a specific intent behind it except to cling to hope.

"I don't need empty words at this point, Elaine," he said. "Please don't insult me."

"What will you do, then?"

"My partner is in Vancouver on business now. Perhaps I will visit him. I sense this is not the time to be in San Francisco."

With that, Elaine could heartily agree. "I could use some time away myself," she'd told him. "As it turns out I have friends in Vancouver, as well, wealthy friends. Perhaps you and I could go together, Ken. I can't make promises, but the optimist in me says our venture may yet be saved." When he didn't object, she pressed ahead. "Yes, Vancouver is a very good idea. The trip will be at my expense. I insist on that. I'll get on the phone and make the arrangements. First flight out okay?"

She hadn't wanted to risk getting swept up in the police investigation so, after making reservations, she'd left her apartment and got a room at the St. Francis. Yes, she knew her disappearance wouldn't look good, but she'd deal with that later. Once her name was bandied about in connection with Joe and the murders, her enemies would be coming out of the woodwork, consuming her valuable time and energy. Better she focus on her deal while she could, dim though the prospects of success might be.

At first light Elaine and Ken Lu were in a taxi headed for the airport. By early afternoon they were in Vancouver. That was the good news. The bad news was that Elaine still had no plan, only hope.

She'd been truthful about having rich friends in the city, but it was a rare friend who'd be willing to plop down two million dollars on short notice for an exotic scheme that would seem risky even after due diligence.

As she thought about it, she realized the only possibility would be if Ken and his partner could buy her some time to find a new money partner or put together an investment group, perhaps based here in Vancouver. She'd tentatively broached the idea, but Ken had not been quick to embrace the suggestion.

"The first thing I need to do is talk to my partner," he'd said in the lobby earlier as they parted company, headed for their rooms. "After I meet with him, I'll call you."

"Let's plan on dinner," she'd said. "Bring your partner, if you like."

"We'll see."

That had been a couple of hours ago. In the interim, she'd been on the phone, milking every contact she had in Vancouver. But the time pressure and the size of the deal were too much for even the most sanguine investor. "Two million's not play money, Elaine," one said. "Two hundred thousand, maybe, but not two million." The relative secrecy of the enterprise was an obstacle for many. "Maybe a money launderer, Elaine, but not me."

She was not surprised. Look how long it took her to close Joe Sasso. She realized she needed a new angle. But what?

As she sank into despair, Elaine stared at the seaplanes, swarming the inlet like giant mosquitoes. At any given time, five or six would be in the air or putting across the water, headed for the seaport or the takeoff point. The planes reminded her of a trip she'd once made from Vancouver to Victoria in the company of a very wealthy entrepreneur from Taipei who expected fun *and* profit for his money. Elaine gave him both. It was one of the first big coups of her career. She was older now and the sums were larger. Charm and guile were no longer enough. She needed *joss*.

As she continued to fret over the recent downturn in her fortunes, there was a sudden loud rap on her door. The knocking was insistent. Elaine wondered if it could be the police.

"Who is it?" she said at the door.

"It's me, Ken," he said in Cantonese.

She opened the door to a red-faced man on the precipice of rage.

"What is going on, Elaine?" he demanded. "Who have you been talking to?"

"I have no idea what you're talking about," she said, pulling him into the suite.

"Who is Nick?" Lu insisted as she closed the door.

"Nick?"

"Yes, when I got back to my room after meeting with my partner, there was an urgent message from my wife. I phoned Hong Kong and she told me there'd been a mysterious call from a man named Nick who wished to discuss the Myanmar deal."

"He didn't give a last name?"

"No, he said he was in San Francisco, but the number he gave my wife is a New York number." Lu showed her the slip of paper on which he'd jotted down the information. "Isn't this a New York area code?"

"Yes," Elaine said after glancing at the paper, her mind working. "It could be a cell number."

"Who *is* this guy? I spoke to no one about the deal, only you and Joe."

She took him by the arm and led him over to a sofa where they sat, all the while calculating, recalling a conversation she'd had early on with Joe. Then, looking Lu in the eye, she said, "Ken, I believe that's Joe's brother."

"His brother?"

"Yes, Joe had a brother who lives in New York, but they were estranged."

"Why would he be calling me? And how would he know about the Emerald Buddha?"

"I'm not sure, but I have a hunch he wants to find out what he can."

"For what purpose?"

"*That* is the question," Elaine said.

"Could he be calling at the behest of the police?"

"I suppose that's possible, but it could also be for himself." She put her hand on Ken Lu's arm. "I wonder if this might not be the opportunity we're looking for."

"What do you mean?"

"Think about it, Ken. The family has to do something with that money."

"What are you suggesting, Elaine? That we should ask *them* for a check?"

"I think we should get back to San Francisco and give Mr. Sasso the 'full court press.'" The last she said in English.

"What does that mean?"

"A sports term, I think. Baseball, football, I don't know what. It means bringing maximum pressure to bear."

Ken Lu grew silent. He stared out at the magnificent view of Vancouver harbor. "Do you really think good can come of it?" he asked.

"Do you have a better plan?"

NORTH BEACH

Finding a parking place in North Beach was no picnic but, after circling the surrounding streets for five minutes, Billie saw a car getting ready to pull out of a spot less than half a block from the Yankee Clipper. "God, Wilhelmina," she muttered under her breath as she stopped in the street behind the departing vehicle, "you must be living right and don't even know it."

It took the driver of the other car, a vintage gas-guzzler from the seventies, some time to maneuver out of the space. He was making his second attempt to get the proper angle, when a guy in a little red Miata sports car whipped over from the center lane and stopped in front of the departing vehicle. Billie was aghast, realizing the bastard intended to steal the space.

When the driver of the gas-guzzler maneuvered around the sports car, the pirate, a black guy with sunglasses and a baseball cap on backward, started backing into the space. Billie honked and stepped on the gas, nosing her eight-year-old Chevy halfway into the spot, forcing the guy to slam on his brakes. She rolled down her window.

"Hey," she cried over the traffic noise, "this is my space!"

The guy rose out of the bucket seat, half turning around and glaring at her. "What you mean, your space? I don't see no name on it," he shouted.

"No, but you saw me waiting to pull in. You're trying to steal it from me."

"I ain't stealing nothing. This is my space because I'm mostly in it. Now get that rusty bucket of bolts out of my way, mama!"

Billie wasn't about to be intimidated by some impolite jerk. She set the hand brake, got out of her car and walked up beside the Miata. "Excuse me, but you knew perfectly well I was waiting for this space."

"Look, don't y'all know possession is nine percent of the law?"

Billie repressed a smile. "The law of civility says you respect the obvious, lawful intention of others. It's the same rule that says you don't butt in line but wait your turn."

"What are you, some damn lawyer or somethin'?"

"Yes, as a matter of fact I am."

"Oh, well, that explains everything," he said, throwing his hands in the air.

"Look, I'd suggest we arm wrestle for the space, but I wouldn't want to humiliate you in public. So, why don't you be a gentleman and drive on?"

"You sure do got a lawyer's smart mouth."

"Spoken like a man who's spent some time in court. I won't speculate on the reason."

"Yeah, well, fuck you," he said.

"Listen, this is my space, I've got an appointment shortly and I'm not about to back down. We can settle this politely or not politely. I'm ready and willing to do it either way."

"Hey, what's the problem there?" It was a cop in a patrol car who'd stopped across from them.

"Oh, motherfuck," the black guy said under his breath. "Take the goddamn space, bitch. I hope you get a ticket." With that, he pulled back into the street and roared off.

Billie waved at the cop and smiled. "He changed his mind about stealing my space, Officer."

The cop nodded. "Check your tires before you drive off later."

Billie groaned. She did not *need* to buy new tires. Maybe this was a good illustration as to why justice had little relevance to the dynamics of modern living. Victory tended to go to the biggest, the strongest, the most fleet of foot. Being right did about as much good as buying a pair of shoes two sizes too small. She returned to her car and proceeded to do a piss-poor job of parallel parking. It didn't take two attempts or even three to get within the prescribed eighteen inches of the curb. It took four. The karmic implications of that were not clear to her.

Sweating from the excitement and exertion of the parking ordeal, Billie made her way along the sidewalk to the Yankee Clipper. As she neared the door, who should be sauntering down the sidewalk the other way but her erstwhile nemesis, the driver of the red Miata. He was tall, athletically built and wearing enough gold in the chains around his neck to put Sutter's Mill back in business. He wore a white T-shirt with the bold inscription Major Leaguer across the front.

"Don't tell me," he said, recognizing her. "You like the spot I got around the corner better than the one you got."

"No, I'm perfectly content where I am, thank you."

When it became obvious they both intended to enter the Yankee Clipper, the guy said, "You eatin' at the Clipper?"

"Yes."

"Well, maybe you should tell me which table got your name on it, so you don't sue my ass."

"You're free to take any table they give you."

"Well, ain't that sweet." He didn't smile. Instead, he pulled the door open and went inside.

Billie hesitated a moment, sensing a huge moment of embarrassment looming, but told herself it was no time to lose her nerve. She followed the man into the restaurant. He went right to the hostess's podium.

"Hey, I got a reservation," he said to the buxom fortyish hostess. "Jamal Wicks."

"The baseball player, right? I remember," she said. "I wrote it down when you called."

"So, you got my table or what?"

"Yes, Mr. Wicks." She looked past him at Billie. "Is it for one or two?"

Wicks glanced back at Billie. "Hell, that old broad ain't with me, man. No way."

"You should be so lucky," Billie said, just loud enough for him to hear.

He half turned. "Better they send me back down to Fresno," he said out of the corner of his mouth. "Or even Double A."

In that instant Billie understood everything. Jamal Wicks was a professional baseball player, but the name was unfamiliar because he'd just been promoted to the Giants from their Triple A affiliate in Fresno, probably within the past few days. He was a minor leaguer who'd just made it to the big show and was full of himself—a kid too young to have learned humility, too green to understand the importance of public relations.

"I think I can seat you now, Mr. Wicks," the hostess said after checking the seating chart.

The guy glanced back at Billie smugly. She was still smarting from the "old broad" remark, but kept her cool as only a courtroom veteran could. "You know, Jamal," she said, "I'll have to tell Peter how nice it was to meet one of his rising young stars."

"Huh?"

"You know Peter McGowan, don't you, Jamal? He owns your team."

Wicks's eye grew round. "You...uh...know Mr. McGowan?"

"Why certainly. Debby McGowan and I had lunch just last week. Maybe you haven't met her, but if you happen to see Peter with an old broad like me, that would be she."

Jamal Wicks looked as if he was about to faint.

"This way, Mr. Wicks," the hostess said.

As the new Major Leaguer dragged his ass off, Billie felt a modicum of satisfaction. She earned her living making adversaries look bad and stupid, so the gratification wasn't in that. If she felt good, it was because it was salubrious for the general health of society if the big, the strong and the fleet of foot got knocked down occasionally, enabling some little person to stand tall. Billie wasn't sure how justice fit into all that, but after seeing a noble soul like Naomi Watts on her knees that afternoon, she needed a lift. Yes, she needed to see the world work right. With any luck at all, the rest of the evening could go just as well, but Wilhelmina Fox had learned never to count her chickens before they hatched.

It was bad enough that his feet wouldn't reach the pedals, but he was stark naked in front of a whole stadium of Chinese girls. How could he get out of there with his dignity intact?

Nick's anxiety intensified when somebody took him by the shoulder and began shaking him. "Nick," she said. "Nick, wake up. Your appointment is here."

He sat up with a start, sending a shock wave of pain through his skull. Linda Nassari, an incipient smile on her face, peered down into his eyes as though his nakedness was as pleasing to her as it was humiliating for him. Then he realized that wasn't possible because he wasn't naked. He was on the bed, fully clothed and in pain. "Huh?" he said.

"I said, Ms. Fox is here. Remember, she was supposed to meet with you and another man here at seven."

"Christ," Nick said, only then coming to. "What time is it, anyway?" He squinted at his watch.

"About five minutes till."

Nick sat up. He rubbed his face, forgetting his schnozz was still taped until the jolt of pain reminded him. "Shit."

"Shall I tell her you'll be down or should I have her come up here?"

"Before I do anything, I've got to take a piss," Nick said.

"I don't think she needs to know that," Linda said.

"No, you're probably right. Seat her at Benny's table and give her a glass of wine, would you? I'll be down in a few minutes."

"Sure, Nick."

Linda left the room, her fully rounded but alluring behind swinging, the lush scent of her perfume lingering in her wake. Nick tried to recall if they'd made a date for sex later or if they'd only engaged in suggestive banter. He suspected she had expectations, though he hadn't been committed to the notion. If he'd been thinking about anyone, it was Billie Fox, though obviously not in the same way. Linda, both past and present, was foremost a piece of ass. Billie...well, Billie was just a neat lady.

Nick went into the bath where he relieved himself, then washed his hands, gazing into the mirror. God, he looked terrible. The color in his battered flesh was deepening and it would get worse. Whenever he found anything in the refrigerator this color, he'd chuck it in a New York minute. The image in the mirror could have been a plastic surgery experiment gone bad. Or the monster in a B-grade horror flick. He helplessly plucked at his hair, disgusted.

Knowing his appearance was only the tip of the iceberg, he sniffed his pits. His nose was working well enough to tell him corrective measures were in order. Taking off his shirt, he gave himself a quick sponge bath, dabbing himself dry with the small hand towel. When he looked in his shaving kit for his deodorant, he found that the damn thing had disappeared. Then he recalled chucking the empty container that morning, intending to stop somewhere during the day and picking up a new stick.

Nick checked the wastebasket, but somebody had emptied it. Damn. He looked in the medicine cabinet to see what supplies were available. Joe had kept the place stocked. There was a disposable razor, a toothbrush, aftershave, cellophane-wrapped toothpicks, antiseptic, a small box of Band-Aids...ah, and a stick of deodorant.

He tossed the razor and the toothbrush in the wastebasket. Then he took the cap off the deodorant. This was what he needed, but the damn thing had been used. He thought for a moment. Joe was his brother, born of the same parents. Flesh and blood. Wincing nonetheless, he took a quick swipe at each armpit, then tossed the stick in the trash. Applying the aftershave didn't bother him but, after using it, he threw the bottle in the wastebasket, anyway. The same with everything else in the medicine cabinet, including the sealed toothpicks and Band-Aids.

Nick pictured Joe as he'd been during their brief encounter the day before, his body beginning to show the ravages of MS. He also pictured Joe at the age of twelve or so when he'd gotten that bicycle. Nick regretted the times he'd sneaked into the garage to sit on his brother's cherished bike; he regretted the plays he'd made on the ball field. He regretted the attention of all the pretty girls; he regretted his father's favoritism and his mother's special love, but most of all he regretted never telling his brother he loved him. Odd as it seemed, it had never happened. Not once. And now it was too late.

Nick knew he wasn't in the best condition for an intelligent conversation or even an unintelligent one. What he needed was to go back to bed and soak his miserable head in sleep. But duty called. And so did Billie Fox.

He found her downstairs, as expected. What he didn't expect to see was a young black stud sitting next to her. They were laughing and having a gay old time. An unanticipated but readily identifiable twinge went through him. It was jealousy.

Billie wiped tears from her eyes as he approached. "Oh, Nick," she said, taking a handkerchief from her purse. She dabbed her eyes. "This is Jamal Wicks, the Giants' new star outfielder. He sent over this lovely bottle of wine."

"The man say the most expensive bottle you got," Wicks declared.

"Wasn't that sweet?" Billie effused. Then she finished the introduction. "Jamal, this is Nick Sasso, the owner of the Yankee Clipper."

"Hey, man," Jamal said, extending a fist.

Nick reached out his own fist and they tapped knuckles. "Hi, Jamal."

"He has some of the funniest stories," Billie said. "The life of a baseball player can be a lot more interesting than you think."

"And you're a bigger fan than I realized," Nick returned.

"Hey, man, her and Mr. McGowan are just like this," Jamal said, holding up two fingers.

"Is that a fact?"

"I didn't know until she say."

"Jamal and I just met outside," Billie explained.

"That be all forgotten now, though, right?" Jamal said, indicating the bottle of wine.

"Right."

Jamal Wicks looked up at Nick. "So, when you buy this place from Joe DiMaggio?"

"Actually, it was never Joe's. My father founded the Yankee Clipper years ago. He and the DiMaggio family were friends."

"Oh, I see. Well, that be just about the same thing."

"I guess you could say that."

"That's cool." Jamal shrugged. "Well, maybe I'll get on back to my table. Just wanted to come by and say, yo. Any friend of Mr. McGowan's is a friend of mine, right?" After giving Billie a toothy grin, he scooted out of the booth.

"Bye, Jamal," Billie said.

"See you later, man," he said to Nick.

As the ballplayer sauntered back to his table, Nick slid into the spot he'd vacated. "Should I ask what that was about?"

"It's more amusing than interesting," Billie replied. "The long and the short of it is that Jamal regarded me as an old broad and a bitch until he discovered I'm fast friends with Peter McGowan."

"Which is true or not true?"

"A convenient illusion."

"It got you a seventy-five-dollar wine," Nick said, picking up the bottle and double-checking the label.

"The kid's got to do something with his signing bonus."

"You're a dangerous lady, Ms. Fox."

Billie laughed. "After the day I've had, I need a little levity."

"Tell me about it."

"I'd like to say I've seen you looking better, Nick, but considering we only met this morning, I'll have to speculate that you've had better days. How are you feeling?"

"About as bad as I look." Then he shook his head. "God, was it just this morning I got jumped? Seems more like three days ago."

"Believe it or not."

Nick looked her over. She was in a silk dress, the neckline modestly scooped yet mildly suggestive, the color a spicy brown that looked good on her. "So, you've got a hot lead, huh?"

"I spoke with Martin Fong this morning and arranged to meet him here so he can give Hong and Plavec a file he found at their apartment," she said, looking at her watch.

"What was in it?"

"Legal papers. Martin wasn't in any condition to describe them to me, except that it seemed to involve a case of some sort. But that's not the interesting part. The file was labeled 'Sasso.'"

Nick's eyebrows rose. "No shit."

"Yes, indeed," she said, beaming.

It wasn't the prettiest smile in the world, but it was infectious.

"I've turned up some very interesting things myself," Nick said. "Could make the case, as a matter of fact."

"Oh? What?"

"You first. It's your party. Did Fong know what was going on between Sonny and my brother?"

Billie picked up her wineglass and took a big sip. "No, Martin was doped up. He'd been taking sleeping pills and was not in the best shape for intelligent conversation."

"God, I know the feeling."

Her expression was sympathetic. "It's been a brutal twenty-four hours."

"Has it ever."

She fingered her glass, looking into his eyes. "Would you like some of my the-Giants-are-going-to-the-World-Series wine?"

"No, thanks," he said, chuckling. "I'll wait until they get there, which probably means a life of sobriety."

"Arrogant bastard," Billie hissed. "Just like your team."

Nick laughed. "We've definitely got to go to a game."

"You have an irresistible urge to get beer spilled all over you? The ballet would be safer, Nick. But we digress."

"Right. Martin Fong. So, the contents of Sonny Culp's Sasso file are a mystery."

"Until Martin gets here. And Hong and Plavec, for that matter. I wonder where everybody is. I told Martin he had to get the file to the police as soon as possible. He wasn't eager to do that and asked me to be with him. Since he didn't want to go to the station, we settled on meeting here."

"Well, the Clipper *is* an occasion restaurant," Nick said, rolling his tongue in his cheek.

"Plus I wanted to see your face when it's revealed that Sonny's and Joe's deaths were the result of machinations of a powerful elite, not some moneymaking scheme."

"Sorry, but you're too late. I've pretty well got the case nailed."

She leveled her gaze on him. "Do you know who the killers are, pray tell?"

"Not yet, but I know what the case is about, what they were mixed up in."

"What?"

"You finish first."

"Okay." Billie took another sip of wine.

Nick watched her hands, the way she held herself. She was a lady, but she also had a gritty, real side that was uncommon.

"In addition to talking to Martin," she continued, "I spoke with a woman named Naomi Watts who, for want of another term, was Sonny's best friend. Naomi knows everything there is to know about Sonny's professional life."

"And?"

"She wouldn't talk to me."

"That's informative."

"No, Nick, that's the point. She was scared. Someone put the fear of God in her."

"What makes you think it has anything to do with the murders?"

"Because Martin confirmed Sonny was upset about a case and that he and Naomi had spoken about it at length. Now that Sonny's dead, Naomi's in a panic. In hindsight, thinking back on the comments Sonny made about the legal establishment, I'm certain some imbroglio with important, powerful people is what got him killed."

"You're forgetting about Joe, Billie. Even if what you say is true, there'd be no reason for the power elite to go after him. Besides, lawyers might be sharks, but there aren't many who are killers."

"Okay, smarty-pants," she said, checking her watch again, "if you've got it all figured out, let's hear it."

Nick checked the time as well. It was twenty past seven. Martin and, for that matter, Hong and Plavec, were late.

"Are you sure about the meeting time?" he asked. "You seem to have a habit of showing up early."

"Only when necessary to save your right-wing, Yankee-loving ass." She gave him a self-satisfied grin. "On the other hand, you could have a point. Martin was pretty dopey when we spoke. I suppose he could have forgotten or gone back to sleep."

"And never called Dickson Hong to set up the meeting."

"Or, Dick and Carl might have insisted on getting the file right away," she said. "I suppose they could all be at Martin's apartment now."

"Solving the case without us?"

Billie laughed in that shy manner of hers that seemed incongruous with her gunslinger persona. Funny how he felt such a strong rapport with her, how they seemed to click. He'd experienced something like it on the baseball field with teammates. He'd felt it when he was a cop. What could it be? Commonality of purpose? Commitment to a shared ideal? Nick couldn't explain it, but when he was with Billie Fox, things seemed to feel right.

"If they don't show up in the next few minutes," Billie said, "I'm going to start calling. Meanwhile, I believe you're under the illusion you've solved the case."

"I'm close."

"I'm listening."

"I think it's about an emerald Buddha in Myanmar."

"Nick, I think you've been mixing some seventy-five-dollar-a-bottle wine with pain pills."

"I've had my quota of pain pills all right, but no booze."

"How did you come up with this creative notion?"

He told her what he'd found at Joe's place, the brochures and articles in the desk drawer, the old photo, the business card of the antiques dealer Ken Lu. "I figure Lu could explain, so I've tried to reach him, so far without success. I'm hoping for a call back."

"What about Elaine Chang?"

"Apparently she's dropped out of sight, maybe even skipped the country. The police don't know."

Billie listened thoughtfully, then said, "I have to come back to the same nagging question. What's Sonny's role in all this? Personally, I can't see one."

"Even the most dedicated, public-minded lawyers need money. Couldn't Sonny have taken this on so he could afford to champion other causes that didn't pay as well?"

"Not Sonny. A leopard doesn't change its spots."

"We've got a dilemma on our hands, then," Nick said. "I can't believe Joe would be mixed up in a squabble with a bunch of lawyers and you don't think Sonny could be involved in Joe's scheme with the Emerald Buddha."

"I think that pretty well sums it up."

"If we're both right, that means that one of them was in the wrong place at the wrong time."

"You're saying the gunman was after one of them, but was forced to kill the other to protect his own identity."

"Something like that."

Billie said, "We don't have enough information to draw any conclusions. Maybe Martin can resolve our dilemma. Assuming he shows up."

Nick noticed Linda Nassari watching them, not exactly looking pleased. Maybe they appeared to be having too good a time, which was ironic, considering the nature of the matter under discussion.

"Is it my imagination, Nick, or is that woman giving me the evil eye?" Billie asked, having picked up the same thing.

"I guess she's the jealous type."

"Jealous? You didn't bring her with you from New York, did you?"

Nick could see his honesty had gotten him in trouble. He was reluctant to explain what was essentially inexplicable—from a woman's perspective, some things could never be justified—so he tried to circumvent the issue. "Years ago she was involved with my father. I guess Linda is protective of the Sasso men."

"Protective or possessive?"

Nick laughed, trying to make light of it. "I don't think so, Billie." Even as he said it, he felt like a heel. Considering what he'd been doing with Linda when Gennaro rushed in with the news of Joe's death, he'd been less than forthright. But that had been an anomaly, a spontaneous walk down memory lane that meant nothing. Surely, the spirit of truthfulness didn't require that he share every detail of his love life. Wasn't the moral truth as important as the literal truth?

"Maybe she has her eye on the new guy in charge," Billie quipped.

"I've got other things to worry about," he said, realizing he was on a slippery slope with no easy route of retreat.

"You aren't married, are you?"

"No," he replied. "I've got an ex, though."

"Let me guess," Billie said, "you were the perfect husband and she was a bitch."

"I wasn't perfect by any means. But Cindy definitely was a bitch. Plus she fooled around with an old boyfriend while she was married to me."

"Ouch."

"A little hard on one's pride and self-esteem," Nick said.

"Tell me about it. But at least you didn't lose her to another woman. That's the cruelest cut."

"You think?"

"Maybe it's different losing a husband to another man. Speaking of which, where in the hell is Martin? I think it's time I give him a call." Billie dug into her purse, looking for her cell phone. Finding it, she dialed and waited. A minute passed. "That's funny. I'm not getting an answer, not even his machine."

"Let's call Homicide and see what Hong and Plavec are up to."

"Know the number?"

Nick had to scour his memory, but managed to come up with it. Billie dialed. She asked for either Hong or Plavec. Her eyebrows rose at the response. "Do you know if they were on their way to a meeting?" Billie listened. "Okay, thanks." She hung up. "They've both gone home for the evening," she told Nick.

"We've been stood up."

"It's a cinch Martin didn't get ahold of them."

"Unless he saw them earlier. Then, too, he could be on his way here," Nick said. "Why don't we go ahead and order dinner?"

Billie was quiet for a moment, then said, "I'm concerned, Nick."

"You have to eat. If he's not here by the time we finish, we can go find him."

"All right."

Nick caught Gennaro Ravara's eye. "Bring the lady a menu, will you?"

Billie drank the last of her wine and Nick refilled her glass.

"Ever heard of a guy named Todd Easley?" he asked.

"The name's vaguely familiar. Who is he?"

"A lawyer. I just found out this evening that Joe had hired him to represent him in a bankruptcy proceeding. Easley sent Gina a final bill. Has an office South of Market. A sole practitioner, evidently."

"Now I remember him. Never had any dealings with the guy. Bankruptcy is a narrow specialty. I had a client once that Easley had represented, however. My impression was that he was a sleazeball."

"Could well be."

"That's the type of guy who gets involved in a client's get-rich schemes, Nick, not people like Sonny."

Nick chuckled. "We need Martin badly—if not to help solve the case, at least to instill a little humility in one of us."

"I won't rub your nose in it," she said, poking her tongue in her cheek.

"You're pretty confident."

"I'm an old warhorse, Nick."

"Want to put some friendly money on it?"

"You're proposing a wager?"

Gennaro arrived with a menu for Billie.

"Yeah," Nick said. "I say Joe and Sonny were killed because of some investment scheme gone bad. It involves Myanmar, the Emerald Buddha, Elaine Chang and maybe half the Chinese population of San Francisco, including the four thugs who decided to put a hairpin curve in my nose."

"Your brother may have been mixed up in all that, I grant you," Billie said, "but my contention is that it had nothing to do with why Sonny was killed. It was something else."

"A year's free dining at the Yankee Clipper," Nick said. "One meal a month."

"That's what you're putting up?"

"Yeah."

"What can I offer to wager?" she asked. "I don't own any restaurants. My principal asset is an eight-year-old Chevy."

"How about twelve hours of legal work?"

"You expect to need a lawyer?" she chided.

"The way things are going, it wouldn't surprise me. Could be I'll have a fight on my hands, just keeping control of the Yankee Clipper."

"Fair enough."

Nick extended his hand and Billie took it. He liked the sparkle in her eye. There was something about a woman with intelligence....

Billie had veal scallopini, which Nick had gone into the kitchen to prepare himself, over her objection. "I haven't won the bet yet."

"This way you'll owe me," he'd said, winking.

Now she was certain. He was definitely flirting, though she wasn't sure why. Reflex, maybe. There were guys who by virtue of their appeal were dangerous and Nick Sasso, she judged, was one. To see the poor dear's mangled face, some people might laugh at the suggestion, but his charm and allure came right through the bandages and bruises. This was a guy to be kept at a distance.

A woman needed a self-destructive impulse to get involved with somebody like Nick. Unfortunately she was prone to succumb. All maturity had done for her was make her aware of what she was doing—it didn't necessarily stop her from doing it. And a crush in middle age was sort of like keeping track of the calories while on an eating binge.

Billie noticed similarities between Nick's effect on her and Leo's, the man of steel. For some women testosterone worked like a pheromone. It was amazing how the danger men posed could be so alluring. And the greater the danger, the greater the allure, it seemed. It made no sense, unless it was one of Mother Nature's little tricks for assuring diversity of the gene pool. Another of life's ironies—even the modern, self-sufficient, independent-thinking woman remained a prisoner of Neolithic reproductive patterns. How else could "Take me, you brute!" and "ERA now!" resonate so passionately in the same tender breast?

Yet deep in the most libidinous female's heart was a yearning for tenderness and subtlety. Leo, a bipedal phallus, was good for only three or four weeks. Wilson Dahl had a smaller cock, but he was dangerous because of his savoir faire and his intellect. Nick, she judged, fell somewhere in between. Plus, he was conflicted about his predatory impulses. And that was his saving grace. Perhaps.

But who did he think he was kidding? There was nothing innocent about the man. He'd bagged the hostess, or led her to believe he wanted to, which was virtually the same thing. It was written all over the woman's face.

Billie couldn't quite fathom his interest in an old court-room warhorse like her. She had at least five years on him and enough baggage to sink the Sausalito ferry. But she was also quick, ballsy and she had a sharp tongue. A lot of men liked that, if only because it added interest to the seduction game. That was one of the things she liked least about being a woman—being used by men as a yardstick for measuring their own egos.

Billie couldn't help taking satisfaction in the resulting sense of power it gave her, knowing that she'd always been seen as a challenge. It was, after all, a boost to her self-esteem. And, it was what had made Leo and Wilson essential to her post-divorce, two-step recovery program. But neediness also made her vulnerable. It was sort of like being a chocoholic. You knew chocolate made you fat, but you ate it, anyway.

Nick, not surprisingly, was a fabulous cook. Good food suggested sensuality and finesse. A sexy man with subtlety made for wet panties no matter the context. And the more sensitive he was to the heart beating in a woman's breast, the easier his access to it. Maybe Nick Sasso didn't quite have the soul of an artist, but he came close.

While they ate, they talked about cooking. She cajoled him to tell his story about Julianna, the little Italian girl with whom he'd fallen madly in love as a young man. He recounted the tale with such reverence and tenderness that Billie was moved, especially when he got misty. A woman without a man was a sucker for cheap sentimentality, even when she was being manipulated and knew it. Not that she was about to let it show, however.

"You ever have an experience like that?" he asked.

"A summer romance? No, nothing like that. I went to summer camp when I was twelve and developed a terrible crush on the boys' counselor, who was all of eighteen or nineteen. Naturally, it was unrequited love. I wore braces and was just as tall as him. But that summer, I discovered the joys of masturbation and poison oak—not at the same time, fortunately. That isn't quite the equivalent of a passionate love affair in Tuscany, though, is it?"

Nick about choked laughing. "Billie," he said, shaking his head, "you're too much."

That pleased her. And it explained her outrageous behavior. It was always better to overshoot the mark than fall short.

When the waiter brought Billie her coffee, Nick took another pain pill. They checked the time and decided something was definitely amiss with Martin. He was an hour and a half late and they hadn't heard so much as a peep out of him. Billie tried calling again, with the same result as before.

"Shit," she said. "I hope he didn't take more pills, like maybe too many."

"Was he that depressed?"

"Martin's more fragile than you'd think."

"So, what do we do? Call the cops, or go investigate?"

"I'd hate to embarrass him by sending the police," she said.

"Let's go rattle his cage, then."

NOB HILL

Martin Fong's apartment was on California Street at Jones, behind Grace Cathedral. Since street parking was at a premium, particularly in places like Nob Hill, most larger buildings had passenger loading zones in front, zealously guarded by the doorman. Commercial deliveries were rare at night, so it was a bit surprising to see a van, rather than a Mercedes or Lexus, sitting in the white zone in front of Martin's building.

"Jesus Christ," Nick said when he saw it. He was driving

because Billie felt she'd had too much wine and didn't want to chance a DUI. They'd stopped at the light on Jones.

"What?"

"See that van? It's like the one the guys who jumped me were driving."

"Are you sure?"

"Not a hundred percent. I've already suffered a couple of cases of mistaken identity today. Lousy batting average. At least it's not a flower truck."

"What do you mean?"

"I'll tell you later."

"I've got my cell," Billie said. "Should I call the cops?"

"Maybe we should check it out, just to be sure."

When the light changed, Nick crossed Jones and pulled right up behind the van. The rear end of his car was in the crosswalk, making it problematic for anyone to turn off of Jones onto California. But, by nudging his bumper right up to the van, he'd effectively pinned it in.

Before he got out, he reached over and took the .38 out of the glove compartment.

"You obviously were a Boy Scout," Billie said.

"No, I got burned this morning. Maybe you should wait here."

"Bullshit."

He got her point.

Once he was out of the car, he stuck the gun in his belt. Billie got out and they met on the sidewalk. They went to the van. Nick looked inside. There was nobody in front. The side cargo door was closed but unlocked. He slid it open. Inside was a computer and a couple of cardboard boxes that appeared to contain files. He rifled through one box, spotting the name Culp on an invoice.

"Something shady is going on," he said. "Let's go in and talk to the doorman."

They walked past the carefully planted beds in front of the glass entry to the building. Nick pulled on the door handle, but it was locked. Inside they could see the security desk, but nobody was there.

"Usually the doorman is right there, keeping an eye on things," Billie said. "Every time I've visited, he's had the door open before I got close enough to ring."

Nick pushed the button for the door buzzer. "Maybe he's in back."

They waited, but there was no response. Then one of the elevators opened and a couple of kids, a lanky teenage boy in baggy pants and a girl in a short skirt and jean jacket, came out. The girl had multicolored neon hair, the boy a blond mop with shaved sides. He had on a headset. When they reached the outside door, the boy pushed the security handle and opened the door. They exited, laughing, the boy talking loudly over the sound of the music in his ear.

Nick caught the door and they went inside. The kids disappeared up the street.

"So far so good," Nick said. "What floor is Martin on?"

"The eighth. But the doorman usually calls to announce visitors. I wonder where he is."

"Maybe taking out the garbage. We may as well go on up."

They got in the elevator car and Billie pushed the button. The car rose slowly through the bowels of the building.

"I've got a bad feeling," Billie said.

"Yeah, me, too."

They reached the eighth floor and the door slid open. As they stepped out, the door of the adjoining elevator closed. Muffled voices could be heard as the car descended.

"Did that sound like Chinese to you?" Nick asked.

"I couldn't hear very well."

Billie led the way down the hall to Martin's door. She knocked.

No response.

Nick tried the door. It was unlocked.

Inside they found the lights on, but it was quiet. "Martin?" Billie called. "Are you here? Martin?"

No reply.

Stepping into the apartment, they discovered it had been ransacked.

"Time to call the cops," Nick said. "Use your cell."

Billie got out her phone and, as she made the call, Nick ventured into the apartment. The first room was an office. It was turned upside. Drawers were open and empty. Some papers were scattered about, but not many. An extension cord with a surge suppressor lay on the floor, stripped of the computer and peripherals that had likely been attached.

He didn't linger, moving on to the master suite. It was dark. Nick didn't want to turn on the light switch with his hand, so he used his elbow. The first thing he saw was a body lying in the large king-size bed, the head partially covered with a pillow. He went over, eased the pillow aside, revealing the somnolent face of an Asian man. It had been several years, but Nick recalled seeing pictures of him in the papers or on TV. It was Martin Fong.

"Billie," he called, "come back here."

The room seemed also to have been searched, though it wasn't torn up as badly as the office. He moved toward the bed.

Martin looked serene, as though sleeping peacefully, though Nick sensed he was dead. Billie came in.

Seeing Martin, she said, "Oh, my God."

Nick looked for blood and other signs of trauma, but saw none. He watched Martin's chest for movement. There wasn't any.

"Do you think he's dead?" Billie asked.

Nick reached over and pressed his thumb against Martin's

carotid artery. He shook his head as if to say, "No, he won't be waking up."

Outside, in the street below, there was the roar of an engine and the crunch of metal. Nick ran to the window. The van was trying to force its way out of the space by slamming into both his car and the vehicle in front of it.

"Mayday," he shouted as he ran for the door.

"Nick, what is it?" Billie called after him.

"Wait for the police," he shouted. "Don't touch anything."

Nick made it to the elevator and was relieved to find the car they'd taken still at their floor. The elevator descended with agonizing lethargy, like a caterpillar inching its way down a tree trunk. When it finally reached the ground floor, he pushed the defiant door open faster than it chose to go and dashed to the entry, gun in hand. As he reached the front, the van lurched backward, crashing violently into the bumper of his car.

There was a young Chinese guy in the passenger seat, the same thug who'd tried to put a bullet in his head that morning. The guy pointed a weapon at him, firing three quick shots. The rounds missed, but shattered the glass on either side of the door. Nick, who was on his belly the instant the first round was fired, shot back and hit the lurching van just behind the side window. He fired again with the same result. The rocking van did nothing for either his or his adversary's aim, but it did force enough space for the driver to make a getaway.

As the van careened down California Street, Nick ran to his battered rental car. He fumbled with the keys, dropping them once, but finally got the thing started, taking off in pursuit.

By the time Nick got rolling, the van had already gone a couple of blocks, its taillights fading. A police car came up California toward him, emergency lights flashing, siren blaring. It was obviously headed to Martin's place.

At Larkin, the van made a right. Reaching Hyde, Nick slowed, but went through the red light. When he reached Larkin, the light was against him, but he made the right turn anyway, cutting off a cab and getting a horn blast.

There was no sign of the van, which meant it probably had turned. The first cross street was Sacramento, which was one way, running west, the way they'd been going on California. Nick bet against it, barely slowing as he went through the stop sign. Next came Clay, one way, running east. Seeing nothing like the van ahead, he took a chance and made a right, headed back toward Chinatown.

His instincts were rewarded. A vehicle looking very much like the van was a couple of blocks ahead, moving smartly. Nick gunned the engine. Steam had begun billowing from the crushed front end. The vibrations didn't feel good, either. The van came to a stop at the light at Powell. A cable car rolled into the intersection and stopped. Nick was able to close the gap, pulling up behind the van.

The driver must have seen him in his rearview mirror because the van suddenly lurched forward, against the light, whipped around the cable car, over the curb and on down the hill toward Grant. Nick jumped back in his car, but as he tried to follow, the cable car moved forward, closing off the route. Nick skidded to a stop only inches from it. At almost the same instant, a car coming up Powell slammed into the left rear of his vehicle. Looking back, Nick saw it was a cop car, lights still flashing.

"Shit," he shouted, pounding the steering wheel with his fist.

The officers, a tall African-American woman with shoulders to match her hips, and an Hispanic guy, got out of their vehicle and came over, looking pissed. "What the hell you doing?" the woman said.

Nick realized it was probably a better question than it seemed.

***

Dickson Hong, out of character in a pair of chino pants, a windbreaker and athletic shoes, arrived about thirty minutes after they'd taken Nick back to Martin's building.

"So, our former cop has turned vigilante," he said dryly. "You're lucky you didn't shoot an innocent bystander. And you're lucky you hit a cop car, not some woman who was eight months pregnant."

"Actually *they* hit *me*, Dick, but I take your point."

Hong's eyes leveled on him. "There are people in the department who would like nothing better than to bludgeon you to death with this."

"You among them?"

Hong drew a long breath. "It's not as easy for me to say no as you might like," he replied, "but no."

"Then all is not lost."

Everyone was gathered in the lobby of the building, including some of the tenants. Nick sat next to Billie on one of the sofas. The medical examiner's people had been there for some time, as well as the lab people. Plavec was getting a briefing from the inspector on the scene. Billie had told Nick what had transpired while he was chasing the bad guys.

"There are two alternative theories. One is that Martin died of an overdose and the burglary was coincidental. The other is that he was suffocated by his assailants."

Nick said, "Much as I'd like to blame somebody besides Martin, the overdose works for me. If they suffocated him, there would have been signs of a struggle."

"Unless he was already unconscious or heavily sedated."

"Yes, you're right. That's a possibility. Very good, Billie."

She shrugged. "I make my living refuting cops' theories."

"Reasonable doubt is your motto, in other words."

"That's the name of the game," she said.

"Well, the autopsy will tell the story."

Her voice trembling, she said, "Until then, we won't know."

Nick could see she was trying hard to maintain the spark he'd seen in such abundance earlier in the evening, but she labored. "You okay?" he asked, putting his arm around her shoulders.

"I've been sitting here trying to figure out how I'm going to tell Emily about this," she said, her eyes beginning to glisten. "I promised her Martin was okay and that he'd be coming to see her. Now I've got to say he's dead, too."

"Kids are pretty resilient, Billie. She'll survive this, trust me."

She looked at him. "No offense, but what makes you the expert on kids?"

"I'm not."

"Then don't try to make things okay when they're not." She shook her head. "What is it about men that they've always got to do that? Sometimes things are shitty, Nick, and they're going to stay shitty for a very long time. Some suffering is unavoidable, and it can't be made better by denying it. Why not accept the fact? *Everything* can't be fixed, much as men like to think it can!"

He was taken aback but didn't say a word.

"Oh, Jesus," she said after a moment. "What am I doing, taking it out on you? I'm sorry, Nick. I didn't mean to snap. I'm just very upset...for my daughter's sake."

"Don't worry, I understand."

"Thanks for being tolerant. I don't mean to come off as just another bitch. When I'm upset, I get aggressive."

"You like to throw pots and pans, huh?"

"No, I just bellow and eat chocolate."

He chuckled, patting her hand, which she didn't seem to mind.

Actually, Nick didn't feel so good himself. He hadn't mentioned it, but he'd wrenched his neck in the collision with the patrol car, which fired up his already throbbing head. When he got out his bottle of pills and took another one, Billie asked how many he'd had that day.

"I think I've already made it to Sunday and am picking up steam."

She took the container and put it in her purse. "You're going to kill yourself."

"Actually, I know what I'm doing. I've abused this stuff before."

"I sort of had that feeling."

"So, you're going to get pushy about it, are you?"

"Yeah, Nick, that's what women do. Isn't the company of a pushy bitch the perfect touch to this otherwise wonderful day?"

"I know your game," he said, pinching her arm. "You're using reverse psychology on me, right?"

Billie laughed despite herself. "I'll leave you with your illusions."

Nick let her keep the pills.

Billie got out a handkerchief and dabbed her eyes. As she did, Nick listened to the cops' conversation.

"What happened to the doorman?" Hong asked.

"We found him tied up in the supply room in back. Shook up, but unhurt."

"How many were there?"

"Three."

"Descriptions?"

"Asian males. Twenties."

Hong and Plavec, who was in jeans and a gray sweatshirt, brought the conversation over to Nick. "You get a look at them?"

"Only one guy."

"And?"

"The same guy who tried to shoot me this morning."

"You're sure?"

"I was pretty busy ducking bullets, but I'd say ninety per-cent certain."

"We'll see if the doorman recognizes any of the guys you IDed this afternoon."

"It might be interesting, Dickson, to see if the slugs in the wall match up with the ones in my brother and Sonny Culp."

"So, from vigilante back to cop again, huh?"

"I take this case personally. So does Billie." He glanced at her. She didn't object.

"Believe it or not," Plavec said, "we've thought of the bal-listics angle."

"Nice to know our tax dollars are being productive."

"Well, don't get too self-righteous, Nick," Dickson Hong said, "you've damaged city property in pursuit of personal vengeance."

"You might want to be careful what you say, gentlemen," Nick said, "my lawyer's sitting right next to me."

Billie, who'd gotten beyond the jocular stage, said, "Why don't we talk about what happened upstairs. Everybody I know seems to be getting killed or is in fear of it. I find it a disturbing trend."

"Agreed," Hong said soberly. "You have a theory, Ms. Fox?"

"Nick and I have conflicting theories. But maybe you've got the answer already. Did you talk to Martin today?"

"Tried to, but we didn't connect."

"Oh, shit," she said.

"Martin talked to Billie and said he'd found a file marked 'Sasso' among Sonny's things," Nick explained.

"When was this?"

"Early afternoon," Billie said. "We were supposed to meet you at the Yankee Clipper at seven, and he was going to turn over the file. Martin promised he'd call you and set it up."

"Well, he didn't. I don't suppose he gave any indication what was in the file."

Billie told them what she knew, which wasn't much.

"You know," Nick said, "these burglars seem pretty damn prescient, always arriving somewhere just in time to thwart the investigation."

"Do you have a point?" Hong asked.

"Just an observation. At some stage of the game it might be good to ask why."

"Let's talk about Martin Fong," Dickson said. "What was his state of mind when you talked to him this afternoon, Ms. Fox?"

She recounted the conversation in detail.

"Sounds to me like he was pretty depressed. Could be he overdosed intentionally."

"But why would he have called me back to talk about the file? He seemed eager to share the information, set a time and place to meet. That's not the attitude of somebody who's planning on killing himself."

"Well, let's see what the autopsy report says."

They wheeled the body through the lobby then, headed for the medical examiner's vehicle in front of the building. The four of them stopped talking as though someone they'd been gossiping about had just joined them.

Once the procession was out the door, Nick said, "Do you guys mind if I go home? I feel like hell."

"No, but we'll need a formal statement," Hong said.

"Tomorrow?"

"Sure. Go. Both of you."

They went outside. The front of the building had been cordoned off, but across Jones and on the other side of California there was a congregation of media types. Three TV news trucks were on the scene, with more most likely on the way. At the moment the attention of the reporters and cameramen was on the body being loaded into the medical examiner's vehicle. Neither of them said anything as they walked, but Billie's anxiety was palpable.

Since his rental car had been towed away, they decided to walk to the Fairmont Hotel and get a taxi from there. Billie's car was still at the restaurant. As they stepped through an opening in the barricade on the other side of the street, one of the reporters asked if they were witnesses. Nick brushed the guy off.

"Just visiting a friend."

Soon they were clear of the hubbub. The air was foggy and cool and felt damn good to him, but he was fading fast. Billie saw how shaky he was and took his arm.

"You okay, Nick?" she asked.

"At the risk of belying my manly pride, no."

"You want to wait here while I get a taxi?"

"I think I'm good for another block." He said it, but he wasn't at all sure he was as good as his word.

They made their way slowly alongside Grace Cathedral. Nick looked up at the spires rising into the fog.

"When I was a little Catholic kid growing up in North Beach, Grace Cathedral was sort of like the Kremlin," he mused. "Rich, Republican Anglo businessmen came here to worship the Antichrist of Protestantism."

"Oh, so you started out as a Democrat and lost the faith."

"I never said I was a Republican. I was a Reagan Democrat, actually."

"That's worse in a way, Nick."

"Face it, Reagan was more macho than Jimmy Carter and Walter Mondale put together. Lots of guys considered that important."

"Testosterone logic."

"Scare you?"

"Do I look like somebody who'd be scared by *anything* in pants?"

He laughed. "No."

"So?"

"Let me rephrase the question," he said. "Do you hate men?" He glanced over to see her reaction.

"No," she replied calmly. "Just certain attitudes."

"And I keep stepping in it, don't I?"

"No, Nick, I'm just being unpleasant for the hell of it," she said with a laugh. "To be honest, I guess I'm tired, too. Don't take anything I say personally."

The medical examiner's vehicle rolled by. No lights. Dark as death.

"So, tell me about your daughter," Nick said. "Who takes care of her when you're playing Clarence Darrow?"

She gave him a brief description of her family situation.

"That's nice about your dad," he said.

Billie, maybe sensing his worries about his own father, squeezed his arm.

"We talked about me earlier, but not about you," he said. "You got a guy?"

"No. But in my case it really means no."

Nick chuckled to himself. Men and women felt the relationship elephant and always got different body parts. "I already admitted I date."

Her silence—pregnant with incredulity—was the equivalent of ringing condemnation.

"Okay, there's one girl in New York I see more than anybody else," he confessed, wanting to *sound* as if he was coming clean, more than actually doing it. "But it's not a committed relationship." Which was true, he reasoned.

"You don't have to explain."

"The truth feels good."

"I hate to think it's an uncommon experience for you, Nick."

He glanced at her. "You know, Billie, I've learned an important lesson tonight. Never open your heart to a trial lawyer."

She laughed for the first time in a while.

They neared the corner. The Fairmont was just across the street. They got in the taxi at the head of the queue and headed for North Beach. After they'd gone a few blocks, he turned to her.

"Maybe after this thing winds down we can go out to dinner. For pleasure."

She hesitated. "Yeah, maybe."

Her response was underwhelming, but then that was probably because she didn't know what he had in mind. Hell, even he didn't know what he had in mind. Mostly he wanted to reach out.

In five minutes they pulled up in front of the Yankee Clipper. It was closed, locked up for the night. Nick gave the driver a ten, then got out, shaky enough that he had to hold on to the door. Billie followed. As the taxi drove off, she opened her purse.

"You want your pills back?"

"Yeah, I think I'd better have them."

"Go easy, though, huh?"

"Sure, Mom, if you say so."

She put the bottle in his hand and Nick slipped it into his pocket.

"You know, I don't have your phone number," he said, struggling to maintain his balance. The goddamn street seemed to spin.

Billie got a business card from her purse and jotted something on the back. "My home number," she said, handing it to him.

He stuck the card in his wallet. Then, taking Billie's hand, he held it, savoring the connection. "Thanks for everything, Ms. Fox. Thanks for saving my life. Thanks for the moral and legal education. Thanks for getting me home in one piece."

"You going to be all right?"

"Yeah, I just need to get to bed."

He staggered toward the entrance to his building, just barely making it to the door. Billie hurried over. "Maybe I should help you upstairs."

"No, I'm okay. I just need to catch my breath."

"Nick, what if you pass out going up the stairs and take a header? Come on, at least let me walk you to your door."

He didn't resist. She took the key from him and unlocked the door. They made their way through the dark dining room to the stairs. The climb was like going up Everest. Much as his macho spirit resisted it, he was glad for her help.

When he got to his door he leaned against the frame. "Thanks again," he said. Then he leaned over and kissed her on the cheek. After taking a breath, he turned the knob, allowing the door to swing open. The light was on inside. Linda Nassari sat naked on the bed.

Nick sagged against the door frame. Linda gave a little yelp and jerked the bedspread up in front of her. Nick glanced at Billie, whose expression moved from surprise to unadulterated disgust.

Nick was so muddled, he fumbled without managing to say anything.

"He's had his quota of pain pills for the day," Billie said to Linda, sounding like a mother turning her child over to the teacher at the nursery school. "I wouldn't let him have any more until morning." She slapped the door key into Nick's hand, then turned and headed back downstairs.

Nick searched for something to say to her, but was helpless

to come up with anything. He eased himself into the room and
closed the door, but continued hanging on to it for support.

"Nick," Linda said, "I'm really sorry. I thought..."

"That's all right," he said, waving her off.

"Who was she?"

He cleared his throat. "Just somebody who saved my life."

SATURDAY SEPTEMBER 7TH

PRESIDIO HEIGHTS

Though it was 6:00 a.m. on a Saturday morning, Henry Chin was already half-awake when the phone on the bedstand rang. Even so, it startled him sufficiently that he flinched and sat up. Groaning, he took the receiver.

"Yes?"

"We need to talk."

The tone in Bart Carlisle's voice suggested disaster was imminent. What now? he wondered. "Okay," he mumbled. "When and where?"

"The playground? Say, in twenty minutes?"

"Fine."

Henry put the receiver back in the cradle and dropped his head on the pillow, though he knew it could only be for a minute. In his semiconscious state, he'd been dreaming of a woman, an alluring woman. Who? Then he recalled. It was Elaine Chang.

Since their lunch the week before, he'd been thinking of

Elaine. That was partly because he was without a mistress at the moment, and partly because her villainy was so sweet. She'd wanted no part of his offer to join his campaign, even when he'd suggested that it would ensure her direct access to the mayor's office for the duration of his term.

"I've had access to the mayor's office, Henry. I'm perfectly aware of the benefits. But I'm also very busy."

He'd hinted that he was interested in rekindling their friendship, but Elaine had put him off without rejecting him. She was the consummate tease, but that didn't keep him from lusting after her.

He heard the toilet flush in his wife's bathroom, and wondered if the phone had awakened her. Joyce had always gotten up a time or two in the night, but usually went back to sleep. Though it had been several years since they'd slept in the same bed, he assumed things were as they'd been before. Whether she was awake or asleep hardly mattered, except that he had no desire to explain his goings and comings. Just to be safe, he'd take her Lhasa Apso, Ling Ling, with him. Whenever he needed to get out of the house for a few minutes, walking the dog was a good excuse.

Henry went to the bathroom to relieve himself. Then he washed up and brushed his teeth. After dressing in a bulky fisherman's sweater and cords, he stole quietly down the stairs to the kitchen where Ling Ling snoozed in his doggie bed.

For years the diminutive Tibetan guard dog had slept with Joyce, frequently with his head on the pillow next to hers, but the incontinence that came with age had forced him into exile in the kitchen.

When Henry opened the refrigerator in search of orange juice, Ling Ling, who was half-blind, awoke, lifted his nose and gave an ineffectual bark. "It's me, you idiot!" Henry grumbled. "Don't you know the master of the house?"

Recognizing his voice, the dog dropped his chin back onto the cushion and gave a little whimper.

Henry poured himself some juice and said, "Do you want to make yourself useful and go with me for a walk?"

Ling Ling looked at him dumbly.

"Come on, you stupid hound, let's go for a walk." The dog unkinked his arthritic joints and stumbled out of his bed. Henry drank his juice, then got the dog's leash from the laundry room. Together they went to the front door where Henry deactivated the burglar alarm, put the leash on Ling Ling and took him outside, pausing on the porch to pick up the morning paper.

As expected, Martin Fong's death was the front-page, headline story. Henry glanced at the article as he and the dog made their way down to the street, one painful step at a time. The story was short on substance, the cause of death had yet to be determined. It was not clear whether the death was related to the burglary. The doorman had been overpowered by three young Chinese males who were suspects in the burglary. The question was raised as to whether Fong's death and the burglary were related to the recent double homicide in the Marina District involving Fong's partner, Sonny Culp. According to the news account, police indicated they had found no evidence of a connection, though the possibility had not been ruled out.

Then came the shocker. He read how Nick Sasso had pursued the suspects until he was involved in a collision with police officers responding to the reported burglary of Martin Fong's apartment. The question was, what was Sasso doing there? It couldn't have been a coincidence. He must have been alerted by the Fox woman, Sonny Culp's former wife.

God knows what would have happened if they hadn't had that tap on Martin's phone. Disaster had been averted, but Henry hadn't drawn an easy breath until he'd heard that Martin was dead and the evidence removed from the house. His hope was that Billie Fox would fade away. But now Sasso had gotten into the act. The police he could handle, but Billie Fox and Nick Sasso might be very dangerous if they got wind of what was going on. He and his friends did not need a reprise of Sonny Culp.

Henry could see he needed to talk to George Kondakis and find out where things stood. With timely, decisive action they could still hold this together.

Ling Ling waddled along at his habitual lethargic pace, pausing at the usual trees to leave his mark. Henry indulged him because the playground was only a few minutes away. He certainly had no desire to pick him up, which was the only proven method of making haste. In inclement weather, Henry had the Hobson's choice of carrying a wet, smelly dog or getting soaked himself.

But he had no desire at the moment to dwell on the shortcomings of his wife's animal. He was much more concerned about the Culp-Sasso business, a nightmare that was showing every indication of spiraling out of control. He'd been afraid of this from the beginning but, as Bart and the others said, what choice did they have?

The playground, while technically located in the Presidio, was literally across the street from his neighborhood. Not surprisingly, it was deserted at such an early hour. Bart Carlisle, in an overcoat and cap, paced back and forth in front of the bench located nearest the entrance. His grim expression deepened Henry's feeling of alarm.

"Sorry, Henry," Bart said. "I know it's early."

"That's all right. What's happened?"

"We've got trouble in Oakland."

"We've got trouble everywhere. You're talking about Naomi Watts?"

"Yes."

They sat on the bench. Ling Ling sat on Henry's foot. Henry kicked him away. "Stupid mutt." He turned to his friend. "What'd she do?"

Bartholomew Carlisle II wore a dyspeptic look, his habitual amused expression absent. "I'm not sure we can trust her anymore," he said.

"Why? Both her career and her freedom are in our hands."

"I know. But Billie Fox went to see her yesterday afternoon."

"Oh, Lord. Her again."

"Why do you say that?" Carlisle asked.

"She'd been talking to Fong before his untimely demise." Bart Carlisle groaned.

"You know the lady pretty well, don't you?" Henry asked.

"Yes, I subbed some criminal defense work out to her a few years ago. She struck me as kind of hot and kinky, so I introduced her to Wilson Dahl, who was in a lull at the time. They had a fling."

"Wilson Dahl and Sonny Culp's ex?"

"Ironic, isn't it?"

Henry Chin did not want to think about it; there were already too many ways the lid could get blown off this thing. "So, what do you think? How dangerous is she?"

"I don't know if she's as dangerous as her ex, but if Billie gets her teeth into something, she tends not to let go," Bart replied.

"Then we still have a problem."

"I believe so, yes."

They brooded in silence.

"Have you seen the paper this morning?" Henry asked.

"Not yet."

"It seems Sasso's brother, the former cop, has gotten into the act, as well."

"Christ Almighty."

"Yes, precisely," Henry said.

"What are we going to do?"

"Let me talk to Kondakis and find out where things stand in the department. I may have to stymie the investigation, depending on how close the inspectors are getting. But I can't use my influence to shut down Billie Fox and Sasso."

"There are other ways of dealing with them."

"As amply proven," Henry said dryly.

"We've come this far," Carlisle replied. "How can it hurt to go a step further?"

"Only if necessary."

"Of course."

THE RICHMOND

Billie, still in her nightgown, got herself some fruit juice, took her vitamins—antioxidants, she'd discovered, were a food group to cancer survivors—and made coffee for her father. Mel Fox was an early riser and would be up soon. As the coffee percolated, Billie read the newspaper at the kitchen table while she ate a banana and finished her juice.

The story about Martin's death contained no new information, which was no surprise. She knew more than the media, and she was a lot more suspicious than the police. The autopsy would be critical.

Billie had awakened, dreading one thing above all else—having to tell Emily. She again thanked God for her father. Mel Fox had been her rock and now he was her daughter's rock.

"Is that coffee I smell?" her father said right on cue. He was in his robe and slippers, looking sleepy-eyed.

"Morning, Pop."

"What time did you get in, honey? I was asleep."

"Late." Billie held up the front page of the paper for her father to see.

"I know," Mel said, getting himself a mug. "It was on the news last night."

"I wonder if we should hold off telling Emily for a while, let her recover from the loss of her father first."

"I've always felt that you're better off being straightforward with children. They know when they're being manipulated. It makes them question themselves and that's worse. Besides, you can't protect them from life."

"I'm guess you're right."

He poured himself some coffee and came to the table. Billie took her last bite of banana.

"You know what really hurts?" she said. "I told her Martin was just fine and that she'd be seeing him."

"You're not God, honey. Emily knows that."

Billie reached over and put her hand on his. "Thanks, Pop, for being here for us."

"So, how did it go with Mr. Sasso?"

"I'd like to say we've become an investigative team, but it's turning out more like the gang who couldn't shoot straight. Everything seems to go wrong."

"Life can be that way."

"I actually sort of like the guy...or, maybe I should say, *liked*. As it turns out, he's an ass."

"Why do you say that?"

"Oh, we were commiserating in a friendly way. He even suggested we go out. This was after confirming that neither of us was involved seriously with anyone." She downed the last of her juice. "So, I escort him back to his place because of his injuries and low and behold there's a naked woman waiting in his room."

"Uh-oh."

"I'd use a little stronger language, but you've got the gist of it, Pop."

"I'm sorry you were disappointed. But don't get worked up. There are lots of guys out there, most of them without naked women in their rooms."

"Worked up? I'm not worked up. Do I sound worked up?

Just because I encounter another ass doesn't mean I'm both-ered by it. Hell, I could care less."

Mel tried to repress a smile. After a moment Billie saw the humor in it, too.

"Damn, I can't even kid myself." She got up to pour her-self some coffee. She'd given coffee up years ago, but she was in both an impulsive and self-destructive mood. Basically she was pissed at being disappointed yet again.

The phone rang. Billie looked at the clock. "Who in the world..." she muttered, the sentence trailing off. She went to the telephone. "Hello?"

"Billie, have you talked to the police about me?"

It took a few seconds to figure out who it was. "Naomi?"

"Have you?"

Billie thought. With all the excitement of the previous evening, she hadn't thought to mention Naomi Watts to the police. "No, I haven't."

"You sure?"

"Yes, Naomi, why?"

"Because last night I went to the market and some white bread in a coat and tie followed me. The same sonovabitch is sitting in a car across the street right now."

"Whoever it is, it has nothing to do with me," Billie in-sisted. "Maybe somebody's stalking you. Maybe *you* should call the police."

"Yeah, sure."

Billie heard something strange in Naomi's voice. Was it just fear? "Naomi, are you all right?"

"You think I'm crazy, don't you?"

"I'm concerned."

"Well, don't be, okay? Just leave me alone."

"Naomi, you called me."

There was a long silence. Then Billie thought she heard crying before the phone went dead.

VAN NUYS

Igor Sakharov lay beside his pool, under the hazy morning sun, conscious of every beat of his heart. But his health wasn't the only thing on his mind. He knew that, because of that Ukrainian cleaning woman, they were in deep shit. Eve had done a great job scoping out the situation. He'd told her with utter sincerity that she might very well have saved his life.

"Unless you calm down, Iggy," she'd said, "you won't have a life to save. This stress is the last thing you need."

Over her protest, and the vehement objection of the doctors, he'd decided to check out of the hospital and fly home. "I've got to talk to Alexei. We need to get this problem solved," he'd explained to his wife, "and I can't risk bringing him to the hospital again."

They'd called his brother from the airport in San Francisco, but all they got was Alexei's answering machine. As soon as the plane landed at LAX they tried again. Same result. "He's off partying with some call girl," Igor had said.

Eve had taken his face in her hands and made him look at her. "Iggy, you're going to kill yourself if you get worked up like this. We're going home and you're going to rest and I'm going to find Alexei."

Late last night Eve had finally found his brother and had asked him to come over first thing in the morning. Igor had relaxed some after that, but he awoke early that morning in an anxious sweat.

Eve had been doting on him. For breakfast she'd served him fruit and high-fiber cereal with skim milk. Then she'd exacted a promise that he would go to a cardiologist, though she'd had to threaten him. "You may enjoy living on the edge, Iggy, but I don't! If you don't cooperate, I'm leaving you!" He knew she meant business.

As he idly watched the pool sweep, Eve came out to check

on him for what must have been the fifth or sixth time. "It's okay," he called over to her. "I'm still alive."

"With you, I'm never quite sure what to expect."

"No sign of Alexei?"

"No, but it's still early." Eve came over and sat next to him on the edge of the lounge chair. She stroked his forehead as she might a sick child, her eyes full of compassion. "After this is over, promise me we'll go to Mexico and lie in the sun."

"Okay, I promise."

"I've been thinking, Iggy. As soon as Lovers International is worth some bucks, let's sell out and retire."

"Retire?"

"Yeah. No more pressure. No more Viktor. No more jobs. Just sun and tropical drinks and sex...assuming they let you."

"They don't let me and I might as well be dead." Igor reached out and patted her haunch. "Speaking of Viktor, I'd better talk to him."

"Is it necessary?"

"Yes, I always report in. Would you mind giving him a call and asking him to come over? Explain I'm not feeling well."

"Couldn't Alexei do it?"

"Viktor expects to hear from me. In fact, maybe we can have him come to dinner and we'll tell him that it's over, that we're concentrating on Lovers International until we can sell out and retire."

Eve looked very uncomfortable. "How about if I get you the phone and you call?"

"Why? What's the problem? In the past you've always buttered Viktor up."

"That was when I thought we needed him. Now that we don't..."

"Now that we don't, what?"

"Oh, Iggy, the truth is, I've never liked Viktor. I've been polite because I know how important he was to your income."

"Well, hearing that would certainly disappoint the old boy. He's always been crazy about you, Eve. He envies me, truth be known."

"He *told* you that?"

"Sure. If he told me I was a lucky man once, he told me a hundred times."

She shivered. "He's actually a very disgusting, repulsive man."

"Viktor was always a little crazy. A man has to be to do the things he's done."

"But not you, Iggy," she said, stroking his cheek.

"Maybe in my way, I'm crazy, too."

She kissed his lips. "Don't say that. Don't ever say that." Inside, the doorbell rang and Eve hopped up. "That must be Alexei," she said, trotting off.

Minutes later his brother came out, but he had company. Chorny was with him. Eve was nowhere in sight.

"There's our brave hero!" the old colonel exclaimed lustily in their native tongue. "How are you feeling, Igor Andreyevich?"

"Well, I'm being treated to a visit from the entire delegation," Igor replied, trying to match his old mentor tone for tone. He lacked Viktor's zesty exuberance, though.

Igor got to his feet, accepting a bear hug from the onetime scourge of the Third Chief Directorate of the Komitet, Internal Security. Alexei kissed him.

"So, you made it home alive," his brother said.

"Miraculously, yes."

"Alexei told me of your attack," Viktor said, going to the nearby picnic table where he sat on the wooden bench. "I never thought it would be you, Igor Andreyevich. Me, perhaps, but not you."

"I was as surprised as anybody, but with Eve's help I'll return to health."

"What's with her, anyway?" Alexei asked. "When she opened the door she turned white as a sheet."

"This has been hard on her," Igor told his brother. "But never mind that, we have much to discuss. In a way, it's good you're here, Viktor, because ultimately you are as affected as the rest of us."

Igor then began to recount what had happened with the cleaning woman and Eve. Alexei listened in disbelief. Viktor, stern-faced, pondered every word. When he'd finished, Viktor Chorny was quick to speak.

"The woman must be 'terminated,'" he said, throwing in his favorite English word. "We cannot take a chance." He turned to Alexei. "You'll have to do it."

"Wait a moment, Comrade Colonel," Igor said, lapsing into old habits. "The woman is simple. I am not sure she is dangerous."

"Clearly, we can't take a chance," Chorny replied.

"I agree the matter cannot be ignored. That's why I told you about it. But why scare her to death? She thinks we're spies. She knows nothing about the lawyer Culp and the other man. And if she does talk, they'll think she's crazy. Perhaps Eve can speak with her again, say the spies have been captured but the affair must remain secret. That way we won't have to kill her."

"What's with you, Igor Andreyevich? Have you gotten soft in your old age?"

"I have never believed in killing innocent persons, Viktor Petrovich. Pointless deaths are the worst kind."

"When our survival is at stake, it's never pointless," Viktor said. "No, I've made up my mind. Alexei will kill her."

Igor knew if he'd kept his wits about him he'd have stopped Alexei from running off at the mouth with the woman close by. The price of his mistake was another death. And there was nothing he could do about it, not if Chorny was determined.

"I don't suppose there's more money in it," Alexei said.

"No," Viktor replied. "This is not the client's doing. It's ours. We must clean up our own messes. And thank God for Eve."

Igor noticed the funny little smile on Viktor Chorny's snout as he uttered the last words. How odd, Igor thought, that he'd completely missed his wife's animosity toward his old mentor. Women could be so surprising in that way. One day she's talking about buying a house in Holmby Hills with Viktor's help, and the next she wants to retire to Mexico, leaving their life behind. Could this all be because of his heart?

"How long do we have?" Viktor asked.

"The Ukrainian woman's family is returning tomorrow night. Until then she is alone," Igor said darkly.

"Then Alexei must get on a plane without delay," Viktor said, his tone commanding, as in the old days. "Give him the particulars about the woman, Igor. And while you do, perhaps I'll go inside and see if I can talk your lovely wife into making me a cup of coffee."

Igor watched the old colonel struggle to his feet, then waddle off toward the slider, leading to the family room. Oddly, he was beginning to see Viktor Chorny through Eve's eyes, and he didn't much care for what he saw.

THE HALL OF JUSTICE

Dickson Hong knew something was up when the deputy chief and honcho of the Investigations Bureau called a meeting at nine o'clock on a Saturday morning. Carl Plavec had been called in, too, along with their boss, Lieutenant Steve Buck. Captain of inspectors, head of the Personal Crimes Division, Rudy Gonzales was also in attendance. This, Dickson realized, had an unmistakable smell about it—politics.

The deputy chief, George Kondakis, who the rank and file not so affectionately called "Zeus," partly because of his Greek heritage and partly because of his autocratic management style, was clearly in a grumpy mood. Hong saw it the moment he walked in the door.

Kondakis's gray hair, gray mustache and robust demeanor had been fixtures in the department. Everybody figured he would retire never having made chief, because the mayor had passed him over and picked an outsider for the top slot when Chief Sullivan resigned.

It being the deputy chief's usual golf day, the bonhomie was kept to a minimum. Dressed in golfing attire, Zeus was in a no-nonsense mood. "Where are we in this Martin Fong thing?" he demanded.

Steve Buck spoke for them. "The lab work is being done on an expedited basis. Preliminary indications based on toxicology are drug overdose, sir. There was no note, so it could have been accidental."

"Let's hope that's the way it plays out. The last fucking thing we need is fuel for the political fires."

Dickson assumed the deputy chief was referring to the tension between Martin Fong and District Attorney Chin. Little known outside the department was that Kondakis and Chin had been cultivating one another for months. There was talk that if Chin won the mayor's race, Zeus would get the chief's job.

"All we need, then, is for the medical examiner to sign off, is that it?"

"Basically."

"Okay, as soon as that's in, I want the case deep-sixed."

Dickson and Plavec exchanged looks.

"There was a burglary, sir," Hong ventured. "And we believe it could have been connected to the Culp-Sasso homicides."

"You mean because Fong and Culp were lovers."

"That's the obvious connection, but Ms. Fox had a conversation with Fong the morning before he died and—"

"Billie Fox? She's a shit disturber. The woman's no friend

of the force. The same goes for Nick Sasso. What's with those two, anyway?"

"He's on board with her," Plavec said.

"On board or in bed?" Zeus said with a laugh.

Rudy Gonzales, on the verge of retirement and clearly wishing he were somewhere else, smiled. Steve Buck, always looking for a way to score points, guffawed. Talk was that if Zeus made it to the chief's office, Buck would get Rudy's job. Hong could see the deck had been stacked. To what end, he wasn't quite sure.

"Look, gentlemen," Kondakis said, "let's focus on the Culp-Sasso murders and let the Martin Fong thing die a quiet death—no pun intended. If we don't, sure as hell the fruits and nuts will start screaming conspiracy. Do I make myself clear, Rudy? Steve?"

"Yes, very clear," Buck said after he and the captain nodded their assent.

"That said, I want to move the Fong thing to the Property Crimes Division. Let the boys in Burglary handle it, since the burglary seems to be a concern."

"But, sir," Hong said, "we've got eyewitness testimony connecting the burglars to the assault of Nick Sasso yesterday morning."

"Who's your eyewitness? Sasso?"

"Yes, and the doorman in Fong's building."

"Sasso walked in on a burglary in progress at his restaurant, isn't that the story?"

"Yes, but the burglars were rifling through Joe Sasso's things, took his computer and any evidence that may have explained the motive behind the homicides."

"But you don't know that for a fact."

"No, but the circumstances—"

"Inspector," the deputy chief said, "I admire your tenacity, but unless and until we can make a connection, a burglary is a burglary. Rudy, let's ship the restaurant break-in to Property Crimes, too. If they turn up anything bearing on the Culp-Sasso homicides they can always send it to Steve."

Dickson Hong was livid. It was a railroad job, plain and simple. Zeus was effectively terminating the investigation. Why? he wondered. Was Henry Chin so wed to his political ambition that he couldn't even stomach sympathy for Martin Fong? Or was he afraid the mayor would somehow use it against him in the election? It seemed like an awful lot of trouble for a minor political advantage.

"So where do we stand on the homicides?" Kondakis asked, as though he'd been reading Hong's thoughts.

"The final autopsy report is pending," Hong replied. "No usable prints. We're also waiting on a ballistics report. Meanwhile, we're developing a suspect list. There's no obvious offender."

"Well, who are your possibles?"

Hong gave the deputy chief a rundown.

"So," Kondakis said, "our suspect list consists of a wife, a mistress and the members of a Chinese gang."

"We're just getting started, sir. At the moment we have two alternate theories. One is that Culp and Sasso were involved in a fast-money scheme involving Joe Sasso's mistress, an ethnic Chinese woman, and other Asian elements. Nick Sasso has brought forward physical evidence lending credence to this theory. Ms. Fox, on the other hand, maintains that Culp wouldn't have allowed himself to be drawn into that kind of scheme. She insists that Culp was mixed up in something else—probably a case he was working on—that ultimately caused his death.

"And there's some basis for her contention," Hong continued. "First, we believe Culp had been receiving threats. Second, the homicides occurred in Culp's offices. We don't yet know what the perceived source of the danger was, but it certainly warrants further investigation."

"Hold on, Inspector." Kondakis turned to Buck. "Lieutenant, have you set new policy I'm not aware of?"

"Sir?"

"From what the inspector says, SFPD homicide investigations are being directed by a hack defense attorney and a disgraced former cop. Who's in charge of your shop, anyway?"

"I am, sir."

"Are you aware how your people spend their time and who's looking over their shoulders?"

"This is the first I've heard about it, sir," Steve Buck replied, giving Dickson a dark look. "You can be assured I'll be on this the moment we walk out of this room. I haven't seen the initial report yet, but I'll be going over it promptly with a copy to you."

"Good, because I want to be updated regularly."

Dickson Hong did a slow burn. He would have objected, pointing out that he and Carl were employing proper investigative techniques in accordance with departmental policy, but he knew that wasn't what this was about. For whatever reason, Zeus was sabotaging Nick Sasso and Billie Fox. The effect, whether intentional or not, was to slow down the investigation. Plus, Steve Buck would be all over their ass. That would slow things down, as well.

Zeus looked at his watch, probably calculating how badly he'd missed his tee time. "Okay, are there any questions, gentlemen?"

"No, sir," Steve Buck said, speaking for them all.

"That's it, then," the deputy chief said, signaling for them to leave. "Oh, Rudy, could you stay a minute? We need to talk."

The others left, walking three abreast down the deserted corridor. They hadn't gone ten feet before Buck let loose. "Dick, why in the hell did you have to mention Nick Sasso and Billie Fox? You know better than anyone that both of them are *persona non grata* in this building."

"I mentioned them because they're involved in the case, they have information, and they've both been helpful, whether they're highly regarded or not. We pay known criminals good money for information, Lieutenant, there's no reason not to get it for free from Sasso and Fox."

"You heard the deputy chief. He gave me my marching orders. And I'm telling you, I don't want to see either Sasso or Fox around here unless you're bringing them in for questioning or to arrest them."

"They're due to give statements about what they saw at Fong's last night. Do you want me to tell them to forget it?"

"No, take the statements. I just don't want them deputized. Is that understood?"

"Sure," Hong said, "but let me say something, Lieutenant. I've been here for twenty-five years and this is the first time a suit in one of the big corner offices has told me how to run a homicide investigation. Something stinks and somebody, somewhere, ought to be concerned about it."

Steve Buck stopped short. Dickson and Plavec did as well.

"Listen to me, Dickson," Buck said, "you may be a top-flight investigator, but you don't know shit about politics. Just keep your mouth shut and do what you're told."

"Politics is bullshit, especially when it gets in the way of solving a crime."

"Politics can put your ass behind a desk doing inventories of evidence bags for the balance of your career, Inspector," Steve Buck said. "Now, as long as I'm in charge, we're going to do our job without stepping on toes. I'd like a preliminary report of the case on my desk in two hours. And package everything you've got last night so I can ship the file to Burglary." With that, the lieutenant turned and walked away.

Dickson Hong and Carl Plavec looked at each other.

Once the lieutenant was out of earshot, Plavec said, "What was that? Your lesson on how not to go along to get along?"

"Very funny."

"Seriously, what's the point in butting heads with the brass?"

"This isn't that kind of politics, Carl. Not *departmental* politics."

"What do you mean?"

"Somebody is trying to bury this case."

"Zeus?"

"No. He's just the hatchet man. He has no reason to give a damn."

"Then who?"

Dickson Hong wasn't ready to share his suspicions. "That's the question, isn't it?" Desperately wanting a cigarette, he headed for the elevators. "Come on, let's walk up to the corner. I'll buy you a cup of coffee."

NORTH BEACH

When Nick went downstairs to make breakfast, he discovered that Marco Falchi had already arrived. Falchi explained that he liked to come in early on Saturday to bake. "And since-a I'm-a here, let-a me make-a you some breakfast," he said in his heavy accent. "First, can I say, please, how I am-a sorry for the death of your-a brother. It is a very great-a loss. Now you're-a the boss you-a shouldn't be cooking, though. I make-a you an omelette."

While Nick sat on a stool in the kitchen, listening to Marco carrying on a dialogue with himself about family, life and cooking, his mind wandered back to the night before. He'd made a fool of himself with Billie Fox and that hurt. Still. And although he hadn't exactly invited Linda Nassari to come calling in the buff, he'd gotten involved with her once already, giving her every reason to think an overture would be welcome. Another of life's lessons—when you fucked around, you often got fucked. The worst part was that a faux pas like that wasn't easily undone. At this point his credibility with Billie had to be zero, and there was little chance of improvement.

Nick watched Falchi move his large frame around the kitchen with grace. Many of the better chefs were like ballet dancers in their kitchens, he'd noticed. In that sense, the Clipper's chef reminded him of Silvan Preno, his teacher in Tuscany, the master who'd taught him the art of Italian cuisine. There were times, like now, when the mellowness and passion he'd known in Italy seemed inviting compared to the anxiety and pressure of life in America. Or, was it just that he'd been young, carefree and didn't know the difference?

Nick remembered now that he'd dreamed that night of Italy and of Julianna. He often did when his soul was desperate for peace. Maybe it was because of all the shit he'd been through of late. Or because he'd screwed up with Billie. Not that she was in any way like Julianna—they couldn't have been more different. What was similar was that he cared in a very personal, profound way. That rarely happened.

Marco put the omelette down in front of him. "So, now that you're-a the boss, what's-a going to change, Nicolo?"

He had no idea because he hadn't begun to consider the issue. In fact, he couldn't even be sure the Clipper would remain in the family's control for long, not with Western Pacific Bank rattling its sabers. Digging into Joe's affairs and determining just how bad the situation was would be high on his list of priorities. "I don't know yet, Marco," he told the chef. "First, I have to bury my brother."

"It will-a be a sad-a day for everybody."

Nick was about halfway through his omelette, which was quite good, when his cell phone rang. The first thing that popped into his mind was that it would be Billie, though there was no basis for it other than wishful thinking.

It wasn't her. It was a man with a heavy Chinese accent. "Please," he said, "I wish to speak to Nick."

"This is Nick."

"Ken Lu here," he said. "My wife say you ask about Myanmar. What you want?"

"Mr. Lu," Nick said, gathering himself. "Thank you for calling back."

"Yes, please."

"You've been doing business with my brother, Joe Sasso, and I'm interested in...huh...maintaining the relationship. I was hoping we could talk about it."

Lu said, "Your brother, he discuss this deal with you?"

"Not in detail. I was hoping that you and I could get into it."

Lu hesitated, then said, "I wish to know better what you want."

"I want to discuss the deal and see what might be done."

"If you are the brother, does this mean you have authority?"

Nick wasn't sure what he meant at first, then it occurred to him Lu was inquiring whether he'd be standing in his brother's shoes. It struck him as an opportunity. "Yes, some authority."

Lu hesitated again. "Authority to release the money?"

"Possibly. I won't know for certain until I talk with my attorney."

"Please, you have lawyer who can say?"

Billie immediately came to mind. "Yes."

"Perhaps we can meet to talk about this problem," Lu said.

"You're in San Francisco?"

"Not far."

"Is there a place you'd like to suggest where we could meet, say, this afternoon?"

Lu took a second or two, then said, "Perhaps in the Golden Gate Park."

"That would be good."

"You know Stow Lake?" Lu asked.

"Yeah, sure."

"There is grass field south of lake, across road. If you and your lawyer will go there, bring baseball glove and wear Giants hat. I will find you playing baseball. Shall we say two o'clock, Mr. Sasso?"

"Perfect."

The man hung up.

Nick finished his omelette, glad he had an excuse to call Billie. Thanking Marco for the breakfast, he went upstairs to make his call in the privacy of his room.

A man answered. Nick assumed it was her father. He asked for Billie.

"May I tell her who's calling?"

"Nick Sasso."

"Hang on, please."

It seemed forever before she came to the phone. When she did, it was with an apology. "Sorry," she said flatly. "Emily and I are having a ladies' day. We're doing our nails and talking about her dad and her uncle Martin. What can I do for you?"

Her tone was more matter-of-fact than unfriendly. He expected her to be cold and, discovering he was wrong, he was somewhat encouraged. "I need a lawyer," he said.

"Sexual assault?" she said, not missing a beat.

He chuckled. "No, acute embarrassment."

"That's understandable, but it doesn't require the services of a lawyer. Maybe you should consult a priest. Or a shrink."

The sarcasm he took as a favorable sign. Anger in a woman was much more palatable than indifference.

"I had no idea Linda would be there," he said.

"It *is* an odd place for your father's girlfriend to hang out. Or, maybe that story about your father was a fib."

"No, that was the truth. And I knew her, too."

"In the biblical sense, obviously."

"I know it sounds really bad, but it was twenty years ago, Billie."

"Twenty years, my goodness. You must be memorable, if they come running forty-eight hours after you hit town."

He hesitated, then decided there was no point holding back now. The truth was the truth. "To be honest, we had sex the night I arrived."

"Ah. That's quite a testimonial," she said, "but more information than I'd like, to be perfectly honest. The point is, you don't owe me any explanations because we don't have a relationship and, more importantly, I couldn't care less."

"I'm being extremely candid because you think I'm a liar and a chauvinist pig, but it's not true."

"I'm sure, like most men, you're badly understood, Nick. But what does this have to do with anything? I really don't care about your love life."

"But you see, that's the problem. I want you to care. How can we be friends if you don't respect me?"

"An excellent point," she said, "but again, irrelevant. As we say in the law, you're assuming a fact not in evidence— namely, that I give a rat's ass, which I don't. The point is you're wasting your time. And mine."

"You're too pissed off to work with me on the case, is that what you're saying?"

"I don't appreciate it when someone lies to me. It doesn't matter whether it's a shoe salesman, my accountant or my congressman. Lying shows a lack of character, a lack of integrity, a lack of respect. I don't mean to rub it in, but that's what got you in trouble in the Allard case." She let that eat at him for a while, then continued. "No, I'm not pissed, Nick. I'm disappointed that you haven't learned your lesson."

That was about as deep a cut as she could have made, and he suspected she knew it. He'd come to San Francisco knowing it would be tough. Hell, he'd figured there'd be land mines everywhere...and there were. He'd tried to take the shots—the sarcasm and the insults—like a man. But it really hurt to have tried so hard with Billie, only to be called an un-reformed, unrepentant liar.

"But I know you didn't call to get a lecture," she said. "What's on your mind?"

"After that, I'm not sure I should bother telling you. Eviscerating myself might be more appropriate."

"Habits of the courtroom," she said.

"I really do need a lawyer, Billie. I spoke with Ken Lu a short while ago and he wants to meet with me and my lawyer in Golden Gate Park."

"To discuss the famous Emerald Buddha."

"Yes."

"Why don't you pester your friend, Dickson Hong?"

"Because I want this nailed down before I go to the police. Besides, Lu expects me to be playing catch with my lawyer, not a cop."

"Catch? As in baseball?"

"Yes, he wants us wearing Giants hats. It's so he can identify us."

Billie hooted. "Giants, not Yankees? My goodness but you're desperate."

"Billie, I need a lawyer, two Giants hats, two gloves and a ball." When she didn't answer, he continued. "I'll pay you double your usual fee."

"To tell you the truth, I'm tempted, just to see this charade play itself out."

"Shall I swing by a sporting goods store and pick up the equipment?"

"No, I've got everything. The fielder's glove was my father's and it's kind of crappy, but I guess it'll do."

"You've got baseball gloves?"

"I was my father's son, as well as his daughter. In other words, I was a jock—played first base on my high-school girls' softball team. We were Fresno County and South Central Valley Regional champs."

"I ask for a lawyer who can catch a ball and I get an All-Star."

"After this, we're even."

"We'd better have lunch so we can strategize. The meeting with Lu is at two."

"Lunch is a problem. I want to spend as much time as possible with Emily and I also want to go to Oakland and see Sonny's friend, Naomi Watts."

"You know we also owe Dickson Hong a statement."

"Oh, crap," she said. "I forgot about that."

"He wanted it this morning. How about I call him and schedule it for sometime this afternoon. We can work it around your trip to Oakland. Unless you object, I'll go with you. What time are you supposed to be there?"

"No particular time. I was just planning on dropping by. Somebody is harassing Naomi and I'm worried about her. Plus, she knows what Sonny was mixed up in and is too damn scared to say what it was."

"Maybe if we double team her..."

"Yeah, maybe."

"I'll talk to Dickson and let you know what he says."

"Roger."

Things had gone smoothly enough that he had a sense he was back on track. But he wanted to be sure.

"Billie, I just want to say one more thing about last night. For the record, after you left the Clipper, I apologized to Linda for starting something I shouldn't have. She said she was sorry she misread my intentions, then she got dressed, left. I went to bed alone."

"You don't have to explain."

"Like I said, I care what you think."

Billie waited a long time before saying, "Shall I meet you in the park?"

"How about if I take both you and your daughter to lunch?"

"She's not very good company, Nick. And for that matter, neither am I."

"Friends are supposed to pull together in times of crisis."

"You don't like taking no for an answer, do you?"

"No."

Billie said, "I live in the Richmond, right next door to the park."

"Got a favorite restaurant?"

"You into kiddie food?"

"I've been told I'm developmentally retarded."

Billie laughed. "Socko's is a pizza place on Clement Street that makes a killer vegetarian pizza. It's our favorite."

"Perfect. I have to get the rental car replaced, then I'll head your way. Shall we say about noon?"

Billie gave him her address, then said, "We'll be waiting with freshly painted toes."

He could hardly wait.

THE HALL OF JUSTICE

Dickson Hong and Carl Plavec had just finished their preliminary report and were putting it together when Steve Buck summoned them to his office.

"I'll get right to the point. I'm taking you guys off the Culp-Sasso case."

"Why?" Hong said.

"Command decision. You've got a heavy caseload with plenty to do without that weighing you down."

"That's why we get paid, Lieutenant. Besides, the case is fresh, perishable."

"I've made my decision."

Hong realized whatever was going on was worse than he'd thought. "Mind if I ask who you're giving it to?"

"For the time being I'll be running it myself."

"You, Steve?"

"I was an inspector before I made lieutenant."

"That's not the point. This deserves the full attention of an investigative team."

"Listen, Dickson, you already pissed off the deputy chief this morning. Don't try it with me. Bring me your report. I'll be asking various teams to help out, maybe including you two. So, let's leave it at that. End of discussion."

Hong fished a slip of paper out of his jacket pocket. After brushing away flecks of cigarette tobacco, he handed it to the lieutenant.

"What's this?"

"Nick Sasso called. He wants to know when you'd like to take his and Ms. Fox's statements about what happened last night at Martin Fong's place." His eyes narrowing as his sense of disgust grew more intense, Dickson Hong turned and walked away. Carl Plavec followed.

When they got to their cubicle, Plavec said, "At least he didn't reassign you."

"That's coming next."

"You think?"

"Whatever it takes to derail the investigation, Carl."

"You mean they're all in on it?"

"I mean they're all doing what they're told. That came from Zeus, you can bank on it."

"Why would he want you off the case?"

"The bastard knows I do my job right and that it's too late for politics to affect my career."

"So, what *are* you going to do, Dickson?"

Hong wasn't going to tell Plavec just yet, if only because he didn't want to burden him, but he'd already decided to do his damnedest to screw things up for Zeus. Not that he wanted to be a shit disturber for the hell of it, but he was determined to get to the truth. After all, he still had his pride, and that meant doing the thing right.

GOLDEN GATEWAY CENTER

They were in bed naked, lying side by side. Jessica Horton had his dumb stick in her hand, liking it more for the symbolism than any sexual connotation. No question Bartholomew Carlisle II took great pleasure in her, but the balance of power had begun to swing in her direction. It wouldn't be long before she had the leverage.

Even so, she was resentful that he continued to cling to his marriage. Every morning he set the alarm early and telephoned his wife before she could phone him. This morning it had been London.

The daily call was the first thing he did, even before breakfast. The theory was that if Bart called his wife before she called him, he could keep her from discovering he wasn't at their home. For the past two weeks he'd been staying with Jessica. Eleanor hadn't a clue, thus far. And by regularly checking the messages on his machine at home, Bart maintained the ruse. If Eleanor did call and get the machine, he'd phone her back and say he'd been in the shower or out jogging.

When Jessica first heard that Eleanor was going on a grand tour of the continent with their son, Bartholomew Carlisle III, or "Tres" as they called him because he'd been conceived in Spain, she'd been ecstatic. This would be her opportunity, she reasoned, to winnow Bart away from his wife. There was no question he'd enjoyed sleeping in her bed every night, but that damn alarm continued to go off every morning.

"How is it that you do that so well?" she asked one recent morning.

"What?"

"Deceive your wife that way."

"I'm protecting myself...and her. I don't believe in causing pain needlessly."

"It isn't necessary that you see me, is it? I mean, she couldn't be hurt if we weren't having an affair."

Bart got that little amused grin on his face. "But if I weren't seeing you, I wouldn't be maximizing life's benefits either, now, would I?"

Jessica could see that it was time to start withholding pleasure and give him the old, sure-you're-having-fun-but-what's-in-this-for-me routine. Men were shameless in their ability to use women. Of course, Jessica had her own designs, but when a woman took, it was more clearly a bargained-for exchange.

But now something else had entered the picture. It wasn't another woman, it was a problem of some sort. Bart had been distracted, especially in the last week or so. At first, Jessica thought it was his marriage, but recently she'd concluded it was something else.

There had been secretive phone calls and odd forays out of the house, either early in the morning or late at night. That day, for example, he'd been up before dawn and out the door, returning an hour and a half later. He hadn't even called London before leaving the apartment, instead making his call after he'd gotten back. Then he'd crawled into bed wanting sex. She'd accommodated him, but not until she'd questioned him about what was going on.

"It's a problem outside the office, not a case," he'd explained. "A political thing."

"Involving a client?"

"No, it's personal. It should be resolved soon. I'm sorry if I've been preoccupied."

After they'd screwed, Bart had drifted off into one of those sleeps that men with limp dicks are wont to succumb to—that "glorious lull after the storm," as one of her former beaus called it. Bart's flaccid member in her hand, Jessica asked herself whether this "problem," as he referred to it, should be a matter of concern. Her instinct was that there was danger in it. Should she be worried or simply trust him?

The thing about hitching her wagon to Bart Carlisle's star was that if he went down in flames, so, too, would she. Whatever was going on, it was shady. And what's more, it involved others. She hadn't gotten as far as she had while still on the sunny side of thirty-five without recognizing the smell of a conspiracy simmering on the barbie. But a conspiracy to do what? Forming a breakaway firm and stealing all the best clients and accounts? It was a way to double or triple a partnership share overnight. But it was also difficult to impossible to pull off. And lawsuits were almost inevitable.

She checked the time. It was getting late and, though Bart may have been up for hours, she'd gotten her beauty rest and was ready for some fun. First, she'd get cleaned up, then wake Bart and tell him to take her someplace nice for brunch. After that, she'd take him to Gump's and make him buy her the Ming vase she'd been eyeing. It was the least he could do for the best lay he'd ever have.

Jessica was in the bathroom brushing her teeth, when she heard the phone ring. She was about to rush in and get it, but then she decided to let Bart answer. That way, she wouldn't have to wake him. Given her suspicions, however, she was curious enough to listen at the door when he picked up the receiver.

"Oh, hi, Henry," he said. Then in a lower tone he added, "Hold on so I can go to another extension, will you?"

Easing the door open a crack, she saw that Bart had left the room. The receiver was lying on the nightstand. She could hear voices. *Henry,* she said to herself. Henry Chin?

Picking up the receiver, she heard the district attorney's voice all right. The tone was alarming.

"We're at the moment of truth, Bart," Chin said. "Three people stand between us and putting this to rest, once and for all."

"The woman across the bay is one. Who are the other two?"

"The brother and the ex-wife. I got an alarming report from the department this morning. The two of them are right in the middle of this thing. I think I can put a lid on the investigation, but there's only one way to shut them up."

Jessica's mouth hung open. Was she hearing what she thought she was hearing?

"What do you propose to do?" Bart asked.

"I think you'd better give your Russian contact another call. My resources are overextended. With the Fong thing I may have gone to the well once too often."

Fong? Martin Fong? Surely the district attorney wasn't saying what she thought he was saying.

"It'll be costly," Bart warned.

"I don't see that we have any choice. We either nip this in the bud or it bites us in the ass," Chin said. "And I mean but good."

"Okay," Bart said, sounding reluctant. "I'll make the call."

"The job's got to be done soon."

"How soon?"

"The next couple of days."

"I'll do what I can."

Jessica could tell the call was ending. She quietly put down the phone and hurried into the bathroom where she locked the door and turned on the shower. Then, her heart racing, she looked at her own incredulous face in the mirror. Did she misunderstand or had she been sleeping with a murderer? And more importantly, what would this do to her career? The whole damn town knew where she and Bart were headed. One thing was absolutely certain. She had no intention of being a jailhouse wife. Eleanor could have that duty. The woman was more suited for it, anyway.

SAN FRANCISCO INTERNATIONAL AIRPORT

Alexei Sakharov disembarked with the other passengers, never suspecting he'd be back in San Francisco this soon. If everything went according to plan, he'd be home in L.A. that night. The thing was, he had his own concerns. He'd been thinking about Jolie Hays, worrying that he'd left a ticking bomb in San Francisco. Would he be smart, he wondered, to take care of both problems in one trip?

Nobody would know. Hookers got shot, knifed, beaten to death every day. He would be safer with her dead, that was for sure. The bitch could have remembered more than she admitted. There'd probably be a reward for the murderer of the lawyer and the other guy and, if she put two and two together, it could be all over for him. It was ironic as hell when you stopped to think about it. And the crazy part was, he was the only one who knew.

THE RICHMOND

"Can I see those toes again?"

Emily shook her head. "Uh-uh."

"Why not?" Nick said, giving Billie a wink. "They're so pretty."

"Because."

"Because why?"

"Because you have to give me another quarter." The little girl tittered with laughter, burying her face in her mother's arm.

Billie rolled her eyes. "I hate to sound like an overly protective mother," she said, "but you realize what you're doing, don't you? You're corrupting my daughter."

"Corrupting her?" he said with mock dismay. "She's gotten a buck off me and all she's had to do is show me her bare toes."

"That's just the point. You're teaching her that a woman's ultimate destiny is to give a man pleasure in exchange for monetary remuneration."

He chuckled. "Are you using those big words to impress her or me?"

"I was hoping you'd understand and she wouldn't, but I'm beginning to see that neither of you get it."

"Let me see if they have a dictionary here."

They were seated at a table in the back of Socko's pizza parlor. He glanced around, as if he wanted to call over the waitress. Billie reached over and gave him a playful whack on the arm, which made Emily laugh. Nick pinched her cheek, getting a giggle out of her.

He was pleased that he and the child hit it off right away. There'd been some shyness at the beginning, and Emily had been a bit put off by his battered face, but she'd adjusted, as kids do. Not that she hadn't spoken her mind.

"How come your face is like that?" she'd asked earlier when Nick offered her his hand in Billie's front room.

He was down to a single bandage on his cheek, but sported lots of black-and-blue flesh. "I had a problem with some bad guys, sweetheart."

"Did they want to kill you like Daddy and Martin?"

"Yes, but your mommy saved my life. She's a very smart and very brave lady."

His comment had pleased Billie, especially when Emily had hugged her legs, saying, "My mommy is the best in the whole world!"

The visit to the pizza parlor was a success, though Nick could tell Billie was holding back. She was forthcoming when the subject was Emily, but otherwise she'd been reticent.

"Actually," Billie said, returning to the point of their conversation, "I'm not being entirely facetious about your game. That's how these things creep into the social fabric. Little girls get conditioned to think of themselves as pleasure providers, not coequal human beings."

"You think I'm turning your daughter into a hooker?"

"Mommy," Emily said, "what are you talking about?"

"We're talking in adult code."

"What does that mean?"

Nick answered for her. "It means that your mother thinks I should take off *my* shoes and show you *my* toes, but you'd have to pay me—"

"*Two* quarters," Billie interjected. "Women work for half the wages of men, don't forget."

"I think it's up to seventy or eighty cents on the dollar now," he replied.

"Oh, whoopie!"

Nick smiled. "I never should have told you I voted for Reagan."

"I could tell before you told me."

"You saw the NRA membership card in my wallet?"

"No, the swastika tattooed to your forehead was the give-away."

Nick laughed.

"All kidding aside," Billie said, "you really did vote for Reagan?"

"Bothers you, doesn't it?"

"I confess. I take politics much too seriously for my own good. I really do know that there are Republicans who are good and decent human beings, but..."

"But what?"

"I never wanted to go to a golf course or a Rotary Club to meet them."

"Well, if it helps, Billie, I was young and naive and '84 was my first election. I didn't know anything about politics."

"You mean you didn't vote for him the first time?"

"I was too young to vote."

"Oh, my God," she said, biting her nails. "This is going from bad to worse. How old are you, anyway?"

"Thirty-seven."

She put her head in her hands.

"How old are *you*?"

She looked up at him. "Even Republicans don't ask a woman that, Nick. Let's just say, *too* old."

"Thirty-nine isn't old."

She smiled. "True, that's why I've been clinging to it for so long. But thanks."

He got out his wallet. "I think we need a private consultation, Ms. Fox." He took out a five-dollar bill and gave it to Emily. "Hey, short stuff, why don't you go ask the lady for a Pepsi for you and your mom?"

Emily looked up at her mother as if to ask whether it was all right.

Billie said, "Wouldn't you rather have fruit juice, pumpkin?"

"Uh-uh."

"Okay, maybe this once, but we're not going to make a habit of it."

"Oh, goodie!"

Billie said, "I don't want one, though. I'd like mineral water instead."

Emily got off her chair, giving Nick a high five before running off toward the counter.

"Walk!" Billie called after her. Then she turned back to him. "Honestly, Nick, you're going to undo six years of diligent parenting in one afternoon. Do you get some kind of high corrupting females?"

He smiled.

She said, "Never mind, I'd rather not know."

He drained the last of his beer. "On a more serious note, you haven't forgiven me for last night, have you?"

"Forgiveness is not the issue."

"It is to me. I'd really like for there to be peace between us. For the sake of others, if not us."

Billie sighed, absently watching her daughter. "All right, you're forgiven, okay?"

Nick figured he was lucky to get that much. He sensed that more needed to be said, but this probably wasn't the time. Mainly he needed to avoid screwing up. "Thanks," he said.

"But don't push it, Nick. We've got a common interest in seeing that Sonny and Joe get justice. I'd like the focus to be on that."

"You want me to back off with Emily?"

"No, she's having fun and that's fine. Much as I hate to admit it, you're a godsend," she said, touching his arm. "I appreciate what you're doing for her."

It was a small gesture, but Nick took it as a sign that their relationship was on the road to recovery. He liked Billie a lot and he really did want things to be all right between them. "Now, if I can find a way to make Mom happy..."

There was sadness in her smile. "If I've been pissy, it's also because I'm concerned about Naomi. And I'm not real pleased that Dickson was pulled off the case."

"Yeah, that was a shocker. When he told me I almost fell over."

"Do you think it could have been at his request?"

"I don't think so," Nick replied. "Dickson really wants to nail this one. More than usual. I'd bet my very small fortune on it."

"Did you ask him?"

"Yeah, but he wouldn't talk about it."

"Something's fishy," she said.

"Yeah, I know."

Emily returned with his change, putting it on the table.

"My, what an efficient waitress," he said. "Do you think you deserve a tip?"

Emily nodded enthusiastically, but Billie gave him a look.

"Oops," he said.

"It's too late now," Billie intoned.

Nick put his hand on Emily's shoulder. "Let me tell you something, short stuff. Always remember this. Whatever you decide to do when you grow up, if you work real hard and you're honest, you'll be successful, just like your mom. There's no free lunch." He pushed a quarter over in front of her. "This is for doing a good job."

Billie seemed pleased. "You're pretty quick on your feet."

The counter girl brought their drinks. Nick glanced at the clock on the wall.

Billie said, "I think we'd better get Emily home soon."

"Are we going to have dessert, Mommy?" the child asked.

Nick had an idea. "Is there a place we can stop for an i-c-e c-r-e-a-m?"

"Yes, but aren't you going to blow all your capital on the first date?"

"I'm desperate for your approval, Billie."

The mother of the six-year-old blushed. As a diversion she took the cap off her bottle of mineral water. "Weren't we supposed to talk about Ken Lu?"

GOLDEN GATE PARK

Nick slipped on the old fielder's glove and threw the hardball into it several times. "You're right, this *is* an antique. But it'll do fine for our purposes."

Nick checked the way she pounded her first baseman's mitt with her fist. Billie wore shorts, sneakers, a Giants T-shirt and, of course, a Giants hat. She actually looked rather cute, but also savvy, like she knew what she was doing. The impression was confirmed when she spit into the pocket of the glove and worked the leather.

He recalled playing catch with Bree on Labor Day. She was cute, too, darned cute, but in a ditzy way. He realized that Bree and the girls before her were playthings, sort of a string of Marilyn Monroes with varying beauty marks, hair color and cup sizes. Billie was different. She was attractive in her way, but she had a lot more than womanly curves and a pleasing personality. She had guts and moxie and brains and heart. Tough and tender was what she was. Her uniqueness pleased him.

They were standing next to the car at the edge of the field where they were to meet Ken Lu. There were some kids playing Frisbee at the far side, some kite flyers and some picnickers under the trees at the edge of the grass. But there was a lot of vacant space in the middle of the field.

Billie began windmilling her throwing arm to loosen it up. Nick just stared at her. She noticed.

"What?"

"Nothing," he said. "I was just observing you."

"I don't want to mess up my arm," she explained. "I have a bad rotator cuff."

"Some stretching wouldn't be a bad idea."

Nick did a hamstring stretch and also worked his quads. He stretched his triceps and lats.

"You actually look good in a Giants cap," Billie told him. "Too bad I don't have a camera. A picture of you in that hat would look good on the wall at the Clipper."

"That'd give the old man a heart attack for sure."

Nick flipped her the ball. Billie told him she'd gotten it at Candlestick on a Jeff Kent home run.

Billie took a few backward steps and tossed the ball to him. They threw it back and forth, working their way into the grassy field, moving farther and farther apart as their arms loosened up. She didn't throw like a girl. Her arm motion was smooth and she followed through with her body. Before long they were thirty or forty yards apart and she was really snapping her throws, making the ball pop in his mitt.

"You're in All-star form," he called to her. "I'm impressed."

"No, I'm out of shape, actually. Throwing a baseball is like riding a bike, though. You don't forget how, you just get stiff."

Nick began lobbing high arching throws.

"You found my weakness," she called. "Never was very good at pop-ups."

He threw the ball higher and higher, but Billie managed to catch it each time until about the seventh or eighth throw, when it finally bounced off the fingers of her glove to the ground.

"I obviously haven't improved with age."

They continued playing catch at a relaxed pace, and it felt good. It was a nice sunny day and if he'd been there for any other reason than to track down a killer, it might have been perfect. As it was, he had to divide his attention between Billie and their surroundings. It being Saturday, there were lots of bikers, joggers, in-line skaters and walkers going along the path, but no one so much as hesitated who he might have identified as Ken Lu.

Nick checked his watch. They'd arrived a little before two and it was now almost fifteen after. He hoped their meeting wouldn't turn out the way it had the previous evening when they'd waited in vain for Martin to show up.

"Maybe all we're going to get out of this is exercise," Billie called after a while.

"I hope not."

"Don't get angry, but if you want to know the truth, I

think you'd save yourself a big waste of time if he doesn't show."

"You'll be eating those words before it's over, Ms. Fox."

Billie fired the ball into his glove. "Not a chance."

He'd worked up a pretty good sweat and was starting to feel it in his arm, when a man in a white suit came across the field in their direction. The guy wore sunglasses and he was Asian. Nick figured it was Lu.

Taking a final toss from Billie, he turned to face the guy who'd stopped a few yards away.

"Is it Mr. Sasso?" the man asked.

"Yes, and you must be Mr. Lu."

"Indeed."

They shook hands. Nick noted the scar above Lu's right eyebrow. Billie came sauntering over. Nick introduced Lu to her.

"Your lawyer is a woman," Lu noted.

"It does happen," Billie said.

"It is okay, as long as you know the law."

"I try."

In their strategy session, Nick had told Billie that he didn't expect any instant legal analysis. His principal objective was to buy time and learn what he could from Lu. "Try to sound positive and optimistic without being definitive," he'd said.

"If you wanted positive and optimistic, a criminal defense lawyer should have been your last choice."

"Well, I can't very well say I chose you because you have a nice ass. That would get me accused of being a male chauvinist pig."

"You're right, any reference to my ass would be politically incorrect. Why don't we say you were attracted to the modesty of my fee schedule."

"Okay, but off the record, it was your ass."

"Pig."

"Guilty."

But she had laughed. That was good.

Lu gestured toward the street. "There are benches by the lake," he said. "Shall we sit there?"

They headed for the street, Nick between them.

"I am very sorry for your brother's death," Lu said, pushing the sunglasses up off his nose.

"Thank you."

"A tragedy for your family and most inconvenient for me. As you know, I have business deal with Joe."

"Yes, but my brother and I didn't have a chance to discuss the details before he was killed."

"We will talk."

They'd come to the street. The traffic was heavy, but moving at a snail's pace. They slipped between the slow-moving cars to the other side. The lake was just ahead.

"I'm curious, Mr. Lu," Billie said. "How did you hit upon the idea of baseball and Giants hat."

"I new fan," he said, grinning. "Elaine Chang take me to game. And I know all American men like baseball. And lady, too."

"Some might debate the lady part," she said.

"Pardon?"

"Ms. Fox is being modest."

"She must be excellent lawyer, Mr. Sasso."

"The best gluteus maximus in town."

Billie gave him a wicked jab with her elbow.

Ken Lu said, "Very good."

They found an empty bench along the path at water's edge. Lu sat between them. For a short while they looked out at the swans on the lake.

"Where we begin?" Lu said.

"We're familiar with the story of the Emerald Buddha," Nick said. "We know about Kozo Hiragara's ill-fated expedition. What's a little sketchy is what you propose to do and how Joe fit into it. I assume the intent was to find the Buddha and bring it to the West."

"Yes, Mr. Sasso, you are correct. My partner is famous archeologist. He sneak into Myanmar and locate the Emerald Buddha. But it is not easy to carry something so large from jungle. This require many men and equipment. Because of Myanmar army, very dangerous."

"What do you estimate the value of the Buddha to be?" Billie asked.

"We think hundred million dollar, American. Maybe more."

Nick could see why Joe had salivated at the prospect. "And the plan was for my brother to finance the expedition?"

"Correct. I have men in Thailand waiting. Everything ready but money. Now we have short time before men leave and weather make bringing Buddha out impossible. My question, Mr. Sasso, will you be new money partner?"

"It's an intriguing prospect, Mr. Lu. But I need to know more."

"What do you need to know?"

"A bit more about your arrangement with Joe, how the deal came about and who all was involved. I assume Elaine Chang was a party to it."

"Yes. She arrange everything."

"Where is she now?"

Lu's jaw set. "I cannot say."

"Because you don't know or because you won't say?"

"Very difficult, Mr. Sasso. Please. Can we speak of the Emerald Buddha."

"Yes, certainly. But I'd like a little history. Elaine Chang introduced you to Joe, but how did she meet him?"

"I think through very important friend of Joe."

"Does the friend have a name?"

"I do not know. The friend himself invest half million, but sell his interest to Joe."

"When was this?"

"Maybe February."

February set off bells in Nick's head. "Was it Benito Vocino?"

"Perhaps."

"I see." Nick's gut began to turn. "Okay, Mr. Lu, this may be the most important question of all. Why was my brother killed?"

Lu shook his head. "This I do not know."

"An artifact worth a hundred million dollars would draw a lot of attention. You must have found this true yourself. Is there someone out there, some competitor, say, who might have wanted to kill my brother?"

"There are many who want the Emerald Buddha but have no reason to kill your brother."

"Do you feel you are in danger, Mr. Lu?"

"Perhaps some. If I knew the location of the Buddha, then most definitely, but I do not. Only my partner."

"The archeologist."

"Yes."

"Was Sonny Culp involved in the negotiations?" Billie asked.

"He was supposed to meet with us the day of the murders, but there was burglary. This is what they tell me."

Billie stiffened. "You're saying he was involved in the deal?" There was genuine surprise in her tone.

"Elaine said Joe wanted lawyer's opinion. Mr. Culp his lawyer, so..."

"Was she upset about that?" Billie persisted.

"Yes, I think she was, but she did not make complaints to me. She tell me not to worry, she take care of every-thing."

Billie, who was now on the edge of her seat, glanced at Nick before continuing her dialogue with Lu. "Could Joe and Sonny have been killed because Joe refused to go through with the deal on Sonny's advice?"

"I have no reason to believe this," Lu said. "Please. I know nothing of the murders." He turned to Nick. "I have very big opportunity I am about to lose. I need two million dollar to get the Buddha before too late. I need to know if you wish to be investor in place of your brother."

"What would my cut be?" Nick asked.

"Same as Joe. Thirty million, U.S."

"A fifteen hundred percent return on my investment."

"This correct. Thirty million to you, if you provide necessary capital. Perhaps Miss Fox say if this possible under the American law."

Nick turned to her. "Billie?"

She got a thoughtful expression on her face. "The answer is not a simple one. If Joe had a will, we'd have to examine it to determine who his heirs are. Without a will the law of intestate succession applies, which means his estate would go to those entitled under the laws of the state of California. But, as I understand it, not all of Joe's wealth was held in his name. He had corporations, partnerships and other entities, and those controlling documents would also bear on who has decision-making power."

"Please," Lu said. "I understand none of this. Can Mr. Nick Sasso become investor?"

"I'm afraid it's not a yes-or-no answer. The documents must be examined. But let me say this. If Joe's widow ends up with control, it is likely that she would give Nick the responsibility for investment decisions. A woman, being less capable and knowledgeable, would naturally turn to her husband's brother for help and advice."

"Yes, this I understand."

"I thought you would."

Nick repressed a smile. Ken Lu, oblivious, adjusted his glasses.

"How long before you know?" he asked. "I can wait, but not long."

"Give us a few days," Nick said. "We should have a better idea then."

"I will call, say, Wednesday. But if another investor come, then I will not wait."

"I understand."

Lu pulled back the sleeve of his suit coat and examined his watch. "Now I must go. Excuse, please."

They all stood. Ken Lu shook their hands, then headed off toward the street. They watched him go.

"What do you think?" Billie asked.

"I think you did that legal gobbledygook real well. I especially liked the part about the natural superiority of men in financial affairs."

"A good lawyer always plays to the jury, even if it means self-deprecation."

"But never a lie, right?"

"Oh, shut up."

He howled.

"Mr. Gluteus Maximus."

"You have to admit it was a good line."

They started walking toward the street, Billie flipping the ball up a few feet above her head and catching it.

"I think I've finally figured you out, Nick."

"Oh?"

"Yes, you're a pervert."

"But I'm a lot of fun, you have to admit."

"The jury's still out on that one. And probably will be for quite a while."

Ahead they saw Ken Lu waiting at the edge of the road. A taxi stopped in front of him and the rear passenger door opened. Nick had a glimpse of the occupant before Lu climbed in. It was the woman in the photograph Nick had found in Joe's desk. Elaine Chang.

"Elaine is in that taxi," he said.

The taxi drove off, slipping back into the slow-moving traffic.

"Here, Billie," he said, taking the car key out of his pocket, "get my car and follow them. I'll run ahead and see if I can get the number. Maybe we can find out where the taxi takes them. If we get separated, I'll meet you at the Tea Garden."

Without waiting for a reply, he took off up the pathway adjacent to Martin Luther King Drive, at a full run. The taxi was barely in sight, but he was managing to keep pace, maybe even gaining a little on it as he loped along, his lungs beginning to burn.

When the taxi made a left onto Concourse Drive, which would take it past the aquarium and the planetarium, Nick decided on a shortcut. Having run at least half a mile, he began to labor, and wouldn't be able to keep pace for long. Turning on Tea Garden Drive, he ran around the Temple of Music, where an outdoor concert was in progress, through the audience on the wide pathways, dodging children and animals, to Concourse Drive, where he caught sight of the taxi creeping along in traffic. He was only ten or fifteen yards from the vehicle, and could see Ken Lu and Elaine Chang in the back seat, when the congestion broke up and the taxi sped away headed for J. F. Kennedy Drive. Nick stopped and leaned over, exhausted, sucking wind. He hadn't caught them, but he got close enough to see the number.

THE EXCELSIOR

Olga Diachenko lay on her narrow bed, daydreaming about her teenage years in Kiev. She recalled in particular the summer she and her sister had gone to youth camp in the countryside. Practically every young person in the city had been taken in a caravan of smoke-belching buses to the dusty fields of a nearby military base where they were to sleep in army tents, develop their physical fitness and learn the fundamentals of armed combat. The last was necessary in the event the population had to take up arms to beat off an invasion by the capitalist forces. Olga recalled the jokes she and her friends had whispered about how much smarter it would be to welcome the American forces, especially if Elvis Presley was among them.

She was pondering the irony of living in America, of having American grandchildren and of helping the American police capture a Russian spy when she heard the sound of breaking glass. She froze in her bed, uncertain whether the sound had been imagined or real.

Then she heard the creak of floorboards overhead. Somebody was in the house. Olga crossed herself. She would have gone to the phone, except that it was upstairs.

Robbers? Her son-in-law, Sam, had been worried about crime and talked of putting bars on the windows. If there were thieves in the house, would they harm her? As the creaking continued, Olga's heart began to race with fear. Should she hide under the bed? she wondered. Maybe they would take what they wanted and go away.

After a couple of long, excruciating minutes, Olga heard footsteps on the stairs leading down to her basement apartment. Her heart seemed to swell to the point where she could hardly breathe.

She had only two small windows to illuminate her living space. With the shades drawn, as they were now, it was not easy to see. Then, when the man's legs appeared on the staircase, she jerked the covers up under her chin. His face came into view. Despite the faint light, she recognized him. It was the Russian spy, the visitor at the hospital.

For a moment he did not see her. Then his eyes fell upon her. He moved slowly toward her.

"Olga Diachenko?" he said, the Slavic flavor of his accent at once so familiar and ominous.

She trembled with fear, but managed somehow to speak. "Дá?" *Yes?*

"Дóбрый ýтро." *Good day.*

"Что вы хотúте?" *What do you want?*

The man raised the hand that had been hanging at his side. In it was a gun. Olga gasped, knowing the answer to her question in the split second before he fired.

HALL OF JUSTICE

"Steve Buck is an ass," Billie said as they left the Homicide Section.

"He could have been nicer to you."

"To you, too. There's no reason for impoliteness, under any circumstances."

"I'm a pimple on his career," Nick explained.

"That doesn't justify treating us like we're suspects."

"What bothers me more than that is the rush to judgment. He's going through the motions because it's more convenient if Fong's death is a simple suicide coincident with a burglary."

"Convenient for whom?"

"That's the question, isn't it?"

"Well, I don't buy it," Billie said. "Martin didn't kill himself."

"The toxicology report seems to back him up, kiddo. They'd be able to determine if he'd been asphyxiated."

"If it was an overdose, he didn't do it on purpose."

They'd come to the elevators. Billie pushed the down button.

Her voice lower, she said, "You don't think there's any chance they doctored the report, do you?"

"Billie, your paranoia is showing. That's the thing about you liberals. You see a conspiracy wherever you look."

"Maybe, but this case smells."

An elevator car arrived, the door slid open and Dickson Hong stepped out.

"Ah, just the man we want to see," Nick said.

Hong did not look as happy to see them as Nick would have liked. "You come in to give your statements?" he asked, checking out their casual attire.

"Yes, your unworthy replacement, Lieutenant Buck, did the honors."

"If you were trying to impress him with the Giants hats, I could have told you that you were wasting your time. Steve's a football fanatic and doesn't have much patience with a sissified sport like baseball."

"Well, that explains it," Billie intoned.

"I take it things didn't go too well," Hong said.

"He went through the motions and so did we."

Hong nodded without comment.

"Dickson," Nick said, "can we talk?"

The inspector took a moment before answering. "Not here. I'll walk you to your car."

The three of them got in the elevator. It was empty.

"You think the toxicology report on Martin is legitimate?" Billie asked as soon as the doors closed.

"I haven't seen it."

"Apparently an overdose was the cause of death."

"I have every confidence in the medical examiner," Hong said, "if that's your question."

"I'd have bet my eyeteeth it was asphyxiation."

"It's a good thing you didn't make the bet, then."

They'd come to the ground floor and left the building. As soon as they stepped onto the sidewalk, Hong lit a cigarette. They walked for a way in silence.

"Was there something besides the toxicology report?"

"Yeah," Nick said. "Billie and I met with Ken Lu this afternoon. He confirmed that Joe was involved in a scheme to recover the Emerald Buddha. No surprise there. What's interesting is that Elaine Chang was in the taxi that picked Lu up after the meeting."

Hong looked at Nick. "No shit?"

"Yep, had a good look at her."

"Did you tell Buck?"

"Yeah, but he wasn't overly impressed. In fact, I was so disgusted with his attitude, I didn't mention that I got the number of the taxi. I thought I'd ask if you'd find out where the driver took his fare after leaving Golden Gate Park around two thirty-five or so, and maybe share what you discover with us."

"You're not only back playing vigilante, you want me to join your gang," Hong said with only mild disapproval.

"You're off the case," Billie said. "What we're trying to do is show our superior confidence in you."

"No, what you're doing is talking to the guy in the doghouse, figuring he's pissed off enough to violate departmental policy and play your game."

"Are we wrong?"

Hong took a drag on his cigarette and returned his hand to the side of his leg, ignoring the question. "Forensic Services sent me the ballistics report, not realizing I was off the case," he said. "I took a look before passing it on to Buck. The round fired at you at the restaurant came from the same 9 mm automatic as the rounds fired at you in the lobby of Martin Fong's building."

"No surprise there, either," Nick said.

"Yeah, that's true. The weapon used in the Culp-Sasso homicides was a .38, incidentally."

On hearing that, Nick's mind did a double take. "Really?"

"Yeah, why?"

They came to the car. Nick leaned against the side of it and pondered whether to tell Hong about Joe's gun. In the end, he opted for truthfulness. "My brother had a .38."

"So?"

"Gina had access to it."

"Are you telling me you think she might have used it that night?"

"No, Dick, I'm trusting you with information that could potentially be damaging to my family...in the spirit of forthrightness. I figure that's better than holding back."

Hong's eyes met his and he took another drag on his cigarette, not breaking eye contact. "You want to confirm the gun wasn't used in the killings?"

"Gina told me it wasn't and I believe her. I think it'd be nice if you did, too."

"Where is it?"

"In the glove compartment."

"Want to give it to me?"

"Sure."

Nick got the .38 out of the car and gave it to the inspector. Hong slipped it into his pocket.

"I'll have it tested and returned to you."

"Fine."

"What's the number of the taxi?"

Nick gave it to him.

Hong hesitated. "If you call me in an hour or so, I should

be able to tell you where the taxi took Lu and Elaine Chang. Be discreet when you call, though, will you?"

"Sure."

Hong looked back and forth between them. "Anything else?" They shook their heads.

"I'll be getting back, then. Stay out of trouble, you two." With that he turned and headed back toward the Hall of Justice.

Nick and Billie looked at one another.

"You know him better than I," she said. "Where is he?"

"On board."

"So, we have a friend in high places."

"Dickson doesn't like being screwed and somebody's screwing him royally."

"How do you know?"

"That's the first time I've known him to so much as bend a rule, much less break one."

"Maybe we've started a revolution, Nick."

"Maybe."

BRENTWOOD, LOS ANGELES

Viktor Chorny lay nude on the huge heart-shaped bed in his master suite, looking at pictures of Eve Adams that he'd taken on various occasions over the years. Most were candid shots, taken in public, but included in his collection were a few more intimate photographs. His favorite was one he'd taken over the Sakharovs' garden wall with Eve standing by the pool after a topless swim. Her breasts, like big ripe melons on her slender frame, were the most gorgeous things he'd ever seen.

Now that he'd had her nipples in his mouth, felt her soft flesh with his fingers, his agony was all the greater. And, much as he'd have preferred to vanquish her from his mind, she'd been with him constantly these past days. Of all the women he'd known, she was the best. Eve Adams was perfection.

Though he'd never given it serious thought in the past, Viktor had been obsessing of late about eliminating his longtime friend, Igor, from the picture. It was the only way there would be any hope of making the woman his own.

As he fondled himself and stared at the big glossy photo of Eve Adams's breasts, the alarm on his wristwatch went off. Ah, it was time to try to reach Alexei again.

Viktor picked up the cordless phone lying next to him on the bed and pushed the redial button. He listened to the ringing, again expecting the recording that would inform him that the party he was trying to reach was unavailable. Instead, he got Alexei himself.

"Привéт *Hi,* Comrade Colonel. I was just about to call you, as a matter of fact. The job is complete."

"Ah, indeed, Alexei. Excellent. Excellent. I have good news as well. I have another job for you. Three customers this time."

"Three?"

"Yes, all urgent, all right there in northern California."

"Will it be lucrative?"

"Most lucrative."

"Tell me more."

"Not on the telephone, Alexei. We must speak in person. I will fly to San Francisco this evening." He glanced at his watch. "Can you meet me at the airport in, say, three hours?"

"Yes, of course."

"Good." Viktor gave him his flight number. "I will have complete information, including where our customers can be reached. Perhaps you can pay a visit as early as tonight."

"*Tonight?* My God, it *must* be urgent."

"The commission will be double our last sale."

Alexei began to chuckle and that pleased Viktor. Igor had been a dedicated professional but he'd never taken pleasure in the work. And it was a sad, sad day, indeed, when a man did not like his vocation.

   Viktor ended the call, kissed the photographic representa-
tions of Eve goodbye and slipped them in the drawer in the
nightstand. Then he rushed off to dress. He wondered if there
was any chance that he could convince Alexei to kill his brother.

   It was actually an excellent idea. Should it go wrong, who
would believe he'd ask a man to kill his own brother? But he
couldn't worry about Igor now. He needed to produce three
more corpses to collect his six-hundred-thousand-dollar fee.
Nick Sasso, Billie Fox and Naomi Watts. Three more step-
ping-stones on the road to riches...and perhaps a life of bliss
with his beloved Eve.

OAKLAND

   Maybe it was the rush-hour traffic, being cooped up with
his manly aroma and all that testosterone as they inched their
way across the span. Whatever the explanation, Billie Fox had
horny thoughts for the first time in a very long time and didn't
feel guilty about it.

   It shouldn't be shocking. People trapped in elevators or in
hostage situations formed bonds. Why not when stuck in an
interminable Bay Area commute? Then, too, of course, she
liked the guy. Even if he was a womanizing pig. Swordsmen
could have their sweet sides, like anyone else. And Nick
Sasso definitely had his.

   Whenever there were sexual thoughts in the air, Billie
was normally pretty good at picking up on it. The wheels
in Nick Sasso's brain were definitely turning. So, what did
she do about it?

   When finding herself in such circumstances she typically
reacted in one of two ways—she either got the hell away or
she took a good strong whiff. With this guy, she didn't want
to retreat. Animal magnetism, pure and simple. Plus, she figured she was on the brink of becoming a dirty old lady. There

wouldn't be a lot more chances to have a wild fling with a younger stud who really turned her on.

"Fling" was the key word here. As long as she thought in those terms, she was fine, just like with Leo, the Man of Steel, and Wilson Dahl. Therapeutic sex was emotionally safe. The notion of it actually turned her on. Or, was she rationalizing her weakness?

They were on the surface streets of Oakland now, headed for Lake Merritt, when Billie got a call on her cell. She dug the phone out of her purse.

"Hello, Ms. Fox, this is Dickson Hong."

"Hi, Inspector."

"I have that address for you, the destination of the taxi."

"Yes?"

He gave her a Montgomery Street address. "If I'm not mistaken, that's on Telegraph Hill. Mean anything to you?"

"Hang on." Billie related the information to Nick.

"Jesus Christ," he said.

"Inspector," Billie said, "I think we have a winner." Then to Nick. "Something you care to share?"

"That's Benny Vocino's address."

"Who's he, an old family friend?"

"Actually, that's exactly what he is."

"Can I tell Dickson?"

"Yeah, I think we're all on the same team."

Billie told the inspector what Nick had said.

"Vocino..." Hong said, ruminating. "Isn't he Nick's father's friend, Mr. North Beach or something? Yeah, I remember Nick talking about him. So, what's the significance?"

"Dick wants to know what it means and if you're going to let the rest of us in on it."

"Yeah. Tell him it's not urgent, but yeah."

Hong was satisfied. Billie ended the call.

"You going to make me wait, too?"

"No." Nick gave her a detailed account of his last meeting with Benny. "I had some suspicions he wasn't playing straight with me, now I'm damn sure."

"What are you going to do about it?"

"Talk to him. More specifically, give him the what-for."

"When?"

He came to a stoplight. "First chance I get. But I'm not even going to think about it until I've taken you out to dinner."

Billie didn't bother objecting. She was past the little-girl games and was ready for hardball. Speaking of which, it was playing catch with him that had done it, she realized. She couldn't say why, exactly. There was something about loosening up your limbs and flinging a rock at a guy and have him toss it back that really got the hormones flowing. At least for her. Ballet for the unrefined—maybe that was the way to describe it.

And maybe Nick's antennae weren't so bad, either, because he reached over and took her hand. "Hope you don't mind me saying so," he said, "but I really enjoy playing cops and robbers with you."

"I would have said cops and lawyers, but why quibble?" She gave him a smile.

Nick squeezed her hand. "And I liked playing catch with you," he added. "We'll have to do it again when we aren't on the job."

"Sure."

"Did it feel good to you?"

Billie leaned over, took his jaw in her hand and kissed him square on the mouth. "Does that give you any idea?"

Nick was taken aback, but pleasantly surprised, she could tell. And she could hear his little piggy brain cry, "Bingo!" But that was okay. She was in need of a purging. And Nick Sasso, she judged, would be the perfect man for the job.

HALL OF JUSTICE

Dickson Hong had just gotten back from the lab when Wes Welch from Vice called. "Long time no see, Wes. What's up?"

"If you have a few minutes, you might want to come by to meet somebody."

"Who?"

"We picked up a young lady named Jolie Hays for solicitation this afternoon. She's green, first arrest, not so jaded she wouldn't listen to my little lecture about the dangers of the mean streets. Anyway, she's been very talkative. In the course of our conversation she mentioned a rather unusual experience she had Thursday evening."

"Related to what?"

"Seems she had a john who got shit-faced and proceeded to tell her about a murder. I know guys say all kinds of crap in circumstances like that, but this would have been within a few hours of your double homicide in the Marina, but before the media picked it up, assuming I've got my times straight. Did a little checking. No other homicides in the Bay Area that night except one connected with a domestic dispute up in Vallejo. Looks like your case or nobody's. Thought I ought to at least bring it to your attention."

Dickson Hong felt that surge of adrenaline that came with important or interesting news. Of course, the Culp-Sasso homicides were no longer his, but his interest was still keen. "I appreciate that, Wes," he said as he considered omitting mention of the fact he'd been taken off the case. "I don't suppose the john has a name."

"We haven't gotten that far. Thought I'd call you first so you could participate...if you're interested."

"I'm *very* interested."

"You want to talk to her now?"

"Ten minutes?"

"Sure. Jolie and I are having a cup of coffee. We'll be here."

Hong put down the phone. For the first time in his life he saw how easy it was to go on a genuine crime spree. Once off the straight and narrow, it was easy to fall off again. Funny thing, though—he didn't much care.

OAKLAND

When they drove up Naomi's street and saw the array of police cars in front of her building, Billie said, "Oh, shit."

"Looks like trouble."

"If Naomi's dead, I'm going to kill myself."

"That'll do a lot of good."

Billie groaned. "Figuratively speaking, Nick. Seriously, I should have pressed her harder. Maybe she'd have let me help."

"Let's don't jump to conclusions."

They parked down the street and walked to the building. Two patrolmen were standing out front, talking. There were no ambulances. Billie took that as a good sign. The cops watched them approach.

"Hi," Billie said to them. "We're coming to see my friend, Naomi Watts. I don't suppose this has anything to do with her."

"Actually, it does," one said. "Who are you?"

"Billie Fox. Is Naomi okay?"

"Don't know," the cop replied. "We're looking for her ourselves. You know where she might be?"

"No."

Just then an attractive black woman in a business suit came out of the building.

"Sergeant Ellis," the other cop said, "these people are looking for Naomi Watts."

The woman, about Billie's age, with shiny processed hair and rimless glasses, came over, introducing herself as Angela

Ellis, a detective with the Oakland Police Department. Billie and Nick shook hands with her, giving their names.

"Sasso," Ellis said, "why is that familiar?"

"My brother was one of the victims in that double homicide in San Francisco Thursday night. The other victim was Billie's ex."

"Oh, yes, that's it. I'm sorry for your losses," the detective said. "What's your connection with Naomi Watts?"

"The long and short of it is that she was my former husband's best friend," Billie replied. "I've spoken with her since the murders and she was very upset about something but wouldn't tell me what. What's going on, anyway?"

"We've got a warrant for her arrest. Assault with a deadly weapon."

"Naomi?"

"She put a private investigator named Samuels in the hospital this afternoon. Shot him in the shoulder and fled the scene."

"Naomi complained to me she was being followed," Billie told the detective, "and was very fearful. It could be her actions were justified. Did the P.I. explain what he was doing?"

"Said he'd been retained by a San Francisco law firm to keep track of her."

"Which firm?"

"Bachman, Carlisle, somebody and somebody."

"Cummings and Glick. B.C.C.&G.," Billie said, her interest growing by the moment. "Did your guy say why he was hired?"

"They were apparently fearful she'd skip out on something, though he didn't know what. He was vague partly because he'd been sedated for surgery. We will be talking to him again. We have the weapon. Meanwhile, we're looking for Ms. Watts."

"Naomi's good people," Billie said. "She considered herself to be in danger and I personally believe it could be connected to the double homicide."

Angela Ellis's eyebrows rose. "Maybe I should have a word with the SFPD."

"Couldn't hurt," Billie said, thinking that the more pressure that came to bear, the better it would be.

"Sergeant Ellis," Nick said, "you mentioned you had the weapon Naomi used. Mind if I ask what it was?"

"Thirty-eight caliber revolver."

Billie gave Nick a sideward glance. "No way," she said under her breath.

"Am I missing something?" the detective asked.

"My brother and her ex were killed with a .38."

"I *will* be making that call," Angela Ellis said. She took a business card from her jacket pocket and handed it to Billie. "Meanwhile, if you hear from Ms. Watts or other information comes to your attention, give me a call. Nice to have met you both."

The detective left and Billie and Nick walked back down the hill to their car. He put his arm around her.

"I'd give you double odds it's not Naomi," she said.

"I'm not saying it is, but no piece of evidence can be ignored. My money's still on somebody connected to the Emerald Buddha."

"If the P.I. Naomi shot was hired by B.C.C.&G., then the legal establishment *is* behind it, like I said."

"We don't know it's connected with Sonny and Joe, though."

"We already know we disagree on that."

"Not to change the subject or anything," he said, "what say we swing by the Clipper and grab a bite to eat?"

"I thought it was a once-a-month deal."

"This isn't about the bet," he said, bumping his hip against hers. "It's comrades in arms sharing a meal."

"Nick, look at the way I'm dressed."

"Hey, I'm part owner of the joint. I'll let you dress any way you want."

"Just because I am a baseball slut doesn't mean I have to look like one."

"Billie, with those legs there isn't a place in town you couldn't walk into whenever you want."

"Tell that to the boys at the Bohemian Club."

"Well, with one exception, maybe."

"Yeah, well, I might not be a lady, but I enjoy the pretense."

"We'll eat in my private dining room, then."

"The one where you keep the naked women."

He smiled. "It's a clothing-optional establishment. But don't worry, I like you just fine fully clothed."

His voice was ripe with suggestion. It made her heart go bump, but there was also that inevitable twinge of fear. As was almost always the case when giving a man the green light, Billie worried that it could be a mistake. But then she reminded herself it was only a fling.

HALL OF JUSTICE

He didn't know if it was him, or if Vice really did smell different from other sections in the department. If so, it had to be the cheap perfume of the whores. What else?

Vice was one aspect of police work that Dickson Hong couldn't have endured. Early on in his career, he'd seen an opium den in Chinatown full of twelve-, thirteen- and fourteen-year-old girls from the Mainland who had been pressed into prostitution and that was enough. He had no desire to see more.

Not only did the vice officers' work seem fruitless and therefore pointless, nobody but the officers themselves seemed to care much about prostitution. Hong had heard serious people argue that prostitution actually served a socially useful function, as a sort of safety valve for society. Some even maintained the best way to deal with it was legalization. All Hong knew was that in one way or another prostitution was never truly consensual.

The cops who stuck with it considered policing vice to be a form of social work. Wes Welch regarded hookers as victims and struggled to save them from the mean streets and their own weakness. Protecting society was secondary. "Hookers don't create victims," Welch would say, "they *are* victims."

A clerk directed Hong back to Welch's cubicle. He was sitting on the corner of his desk, a pretty black girl in hooker clothes sat on a straight chair opposite him, her fishnet-stocking legs crossed, her arms folded under her full breasts. Seeing Hong approaching, Welch got up, extending his hand.

"Hi, Dick. Good to see you."

Welch was a fireplug of a man, short, solid, his graying hair cropped, an ex-marine who habitually wore braces. The ones he had on at the moment were red. He liked bright colors.

"You're looking fit, as always, Wes."

"The girls keep me on my toes," Welch said with a grin. "But I'm still losing them faster than I can save them." The grin faded to a solemn grimace. "Like Jolie Hays, here. She's still got a chance, but I haven't quite convinced her she's going down a dead-end alley." He looked at the girl. "Jolie, this is Inspector Hong from Homicide, one of the finest officers in San Francisco."

"Say what? I didn' kill nobody."

"That's not why I'm here, Miss Hays," Hong said, taking the chair Welch pulled over for him. He sat down near her, a bit too close, considering the potency of her perfume. But he dismissed it from his mind. "I want to talk about one of your...customers. If I understand correctly, you were with a gentleman recently who talked about a murder."

She gave a shrug as though it was no big deal. But the way she hugged herself, Hong could tell she was nervous and afraid. "Mens say all kinds of shit when they drunk," she explained.

"Maybe, but homicide is no small thing. A murderer has lots to fear, and people who protect them do, as well. What I'm telling you, Miss Hays, is that this is a good time to sharpen your memory, not begin to forget."

"Hey, man, if I know some'in', I say. But what some john bullshit about when he drunk don' mean much."

"Let me decide that, Miss Hays. Why don't we start by you telling me everything you know about this man? Did he give you a name?"

"Jerry French. That what he tell me, but I don't believe him. He didn't look like no Jerry French to me."

"Why do you say that?"

"Because he wasn't no American. He tell me he's German, but he lied. He Russian."

"How do you know?"

"He talk Russian, that's how."

"Do you speak Russian?"

"Some. I lived in Germany with my mama and stepdaddy who was a soldier."

"What exactly did Jerry say about murders?"

"Not much. Just talk. Like he say he make a hundred thousand, 'cause two mens dead. Shit like that. For all I know he talkin' trash. I didn't see no proof."

Hong contemplated her, looking for signs of sincerity. "Let's start at the beginning, Miss Hays. When did you meet Mr. French? Where were you? I want to know everything that happened. Every detail."

"Shit, man, it wasn' nothin'," she moaned. "Honest."

"Jolie," Wes Welch interjected, "solicitation's peanuts compared to this. If you don't cooperate and answer Inspector Hong's questions fully and honestly, you could be in here until you're too old to hook."

.Jolie Hays looked as if she was going to cry. "You don' tell nobody what I say?"

Dickson Hong shook his head. "What you say is between us, as long as it's the truth."

She sighed the sigh of a woman who'd suffered more than her years. "I was on Geary Street, I think, and Jerry, he pulls up next to me in a nice new rental car, lookin' for a date." Jolie squinted at him through her lashes. "You want to hear *everything?* Even what he done to me?"

"Yes, Miss Hays," Hong replied. "Everything."

CHINATOWN

Elaine Chang entered Wa-Me Chinese Antiques and Gifts on Grant Avenue not knowing what to expect. She was greeted first with the strong scent of Oriental incense, cedar and rosewood, then by a middle-aged woman in a gray shop coat who rose, bland-faced, from a stool behind the counter, beckoning her toward the back room.

Elaine followed the woman through a doorway covered by a badly worn velvet curtain. The stockroom was crowded floor-to-ceiling with boxes, stacked haphazardly, some open, a few spilling their contents over the side. A narrow walkway zigged and zagged through the mountain of boxes. Halfway along the trail they'd been following, they came to a cubbyhole where a fat man with black hair that stood out in spikes like a porcupine sat at a little desk illuminated with a bright fluorescent lamp. He had a calculator and seemed to be going over books of account. As they passed by, he gave Elaine a sideward glance without really looking at her.

The woman continued, stopping when she came to a heavy metal door at the rear of the shop. It accessed the alley in back. The woman, who was quite short, held up her hand as if to say, "One moment, please wait." She unbolted the door, pulled it open a crack, stuck her head outside, looked around, then closed the door.

"Soon," she said.

Elaine, nervous because she didn't understand what was happening, took a deep breath and rocked on her high heels. Scarcely an hour earlier she'd received a call in her room at the St. Francis.

"This is Miss Han," the speaker had said in Cantonese. "Would you be so kind as to meet with my father to discuss a business proposition?"

No more need be said for Elaine to understand that she'd been summoned by Han Fat. She'd met the father of Chinatown's dark side once before. Han had told her that he found a business deal she was pursuing at the time most inconvenient and asked her to back off. The request was accompanied by a cashier's check for five thousand dollars. Elaine, recognizing that discretion was the better part of valor, had complied without so much as asking why.

That had been several years ago. She'd had no dealings with Han Fat since. There was no indication what this was about, but she surmised that Ken Lu and the Emerald Buddha somehow figured in. She hoped it wouldn't involve another request to back off. A check for five—or even ten—thousand would be about as welcome as a token tip.

The shop woman said nothing. She didn't even look at Elaine, probably having no desire to know what was going on. The meeting place was most certainly provided as an accommodation.

A minute or two passed before there was the sound of a vehicle in the alley. The woman peered outside again, this time pushing the heavy door wide enough for Elaine to see out. A black Mercedes sedan sat only feet away, the rear passenger door was opened by a beefy man with the demeanor of a guard dog. Seated on the far side of the rear seat, looking her way through narrow eyes, was Han Fat, a slender wisp of a man who seemed scarcely to dent the plush leather upholstery. The bags under his eyes drooped halfway down his face. A thin cigarette hung from his lower lip.

No one spoke. Elaine stepped into the alley and into the back seat of the vehicle. The door slammed shut behind her. A driver was at the wheel of the sedan. The bodyguard climbed in the front passenger seat. The Mercedes moved away smartly.

"Esteemed Miss Chang," Han Fat said after a moment, "so good of you to meet me on such short notice." He spoke in Cantonese.

"I wouldn't miss the opportunity for the world," she replied. "It's been too long since I've had the pleasure of your company."

"That is certainly true."

Leaving the alley, the driver headed east toward the waterfront, crossing Grant Avenue. Elaine hadn't worried overly that some terrible fate was in store for her, having assumed that financial imposition would be unwelcome enough. But this unexplained joyride gave her pause. She refused to allow her concern to show, however, coolly crossing her legs and remaining silent.

They'd driven several blocks before Han Fat spoke again. "I have heard you had business dealings with one of the victims of the recent double homicide in the Marina District," he said.

This was headed just where she expected. "Yes, that is true," she replied. "Mr. Sasso was my client."

"Most unfortunate...his death, I mean." Han dabbed gingerly at the ashtray at his elbow with the tip of his cigarette.

"Very unfortunate."

They reached the Embarcadero and turned left, toward Fisherman's Wharf.

Han allowed several moments to pass, then said. "I believe

Mr. Sasso had placed some very large sums of money in off-shore accounts. Is that your understanding, Miss Chang?"

"Yes, it is."

"Is it also your understanding that the details of the accounts were confidential?"

"Yes, I believe his lawyer was the only other person with knowledge of the accounts."

"And he, too, is dead."

"That's correct." Elaine was very surprised by the tact of the conversation. There'd been no mention yet of Ken Lu or the Emerald Buddha. Or was that yet to come?

A few more moments passed, then Han Fat said, "Let me be direct, Miss Chang. By chance, a file has come into my possession with information on the accounts we have been discussing. The information includes account numbers, balances, everything necessary for the rightful owner to access the funds. My impression is that this file would be very valuable to certain persons. It is of no value to me, other than what I can obtain in exchange for it. I thought that you, more than anyone, would be well placed to broker a sale of the file. My price is one hundred thousand dollars. For the right person, that is a small sum, indeed."

Elaine sat very still, though her heart rattled. In her mind's eye she saw the Emerald Buddha gleaming with brilliance and promise. It was all she could do to keep from reaching over and giving Han Fat a very large, enthusiastic kiss. "Perhaps," she said.

"Of course, I must count on your utmost discretion, whether you choose to become involved or not."

"I understand."

Han Fat drew on his cigarette, holding the smoke in his lungs for several moments before letting it escape from his mouth and nose. The driver had turned on Columbus Avenue. They were headed back toward Chinatown. Elaine could hardly wait to get out of the car and get to work. As easily as Han Fat flicking away the ashes of his cigarette, the Emerald Buddha had sprung to life, the deal once again within her grasp. All that remained was to figure out how to make it happen.

THE EXCELSIOR

Normally Dickson Hong didn't drive, but Plavec had just put his take-out Mexican meal on his desk when Lieutenant Buck came in with word there'd been a homicide in the Excelsior. With his partner preoccupied with his tacos, Dickson had little choice but to take the wheel. He was not pleased.

"Some old lady getting shot by a burglar may not be the most exciting case," Carl Plavec said, munching on a taco, "but I'm not sure excitement is what you need right now. A low-stress case could be good for the mind and soul."

"What? You're a junk-food fanatic *and* a doctor all of a sudden?" Hong knew he was being pissy, but he was just in one of those moods. After interrogating Jolie Hays, he wanted to roll up his sleeves and go after the Russian. He'd heard enough to know the lead had to be pursued. But he'd also been a cop long enough to appreciate the fact that police work was shaped by events, not the preferences of the investigator.

They turned onto the street where the crime scene was located. Homicides in residential areas always drew big crowds. Hong was no expert on crowd-size estimation, but he figured a hundred and fifty souls had congregated, at least.

"Wow," Plavec said. "Maybe we'll get our pictures in the paper after all."

"Try not to get too worked up."

Hong pulled over, stopping in the first available parking place, fifty yards from the action. Plavec stuffed the last of his taco into his mouth and the two of them walked up the street. The yellow crime-scene tape had been strung up and two patrol officers were keeping the milling crowd at bay. For the younger people especially, it was a carnival atmosphere, and for others as well, though a few of the older faces wore masks of concern. *Hey, cool!* and *What if it were me?* seemed to be the two principal attitudes.

One of the cops saw them approach and lifted the yellow tape for them to pass under. "Inspectors."

The senior patrol officer on the scene was named Robinson. He met them at the door.

"What do we have?" Hong asked in his usual monotone, already looking past the officer.

"A single victim. Olga Diachenko. Female, age sixty-one. Appears she died from a single gunshot wound to the chest. The body was discovered in the basement apartment by the neighbors." Robinson consulted his notes. "Pedro and Lena Ramirez. They returned from the market and saw the broken front window. Mr. Ramirez investigated and discovered the front door ajar. When he searched the house, he found the body."

"Did the victim live alone?"

"No, sir. Her daughter, son-in-law and two grandchildren occupy the main house and the victim the basement apartment, where she was found. According to neighbors, the rest of the family has been on vacation for the past week and aren't due back until tomorrow night. The victim works at a hospital down the Peninsula."

"Interrupted burglary? Is that your theory?"

"Yes, sir, it appears so. The offender broke the window here to gain access. The victim was either in the basement at the time or fled there and was trapped and shot dead by her assailant."

"Let's have a look."

Hong glanced around the house, which was neat and orderly. Extremely clean by all appearances. They went into the basement apartment, careful not to touch the handrail on their way down. Plavec, whose rushed meal was catching up with him, belched.

Because of the window coverings, very little light filtered into the large room. Dickson asked Plavec to turn on the overhead light. He was surprised to discover the victim in bed, the covers still clutched to her chin, her eyes staring fixedly into the great beyond. There was a huge spot of blood around a hole in the covers that lay over her.

Looking closely at the body, Hong said, "I'd be willing to bet this happened in the last few hours. What time did the initial report come in?"

"Less than an hour ago. Mrs. Ramirez, the neighbor, said she's been keeping an eye on things for the daughter and was pretty sure she looked at the house on her way to the market and didn't see the broken window at that time."

"Which would confirm that it *is* recent."

"Yes, sir."

"Anything appear to have been taken?"

"No, the house seems to be intact. My theory is the burglar didn't expect to find anyone home, was surprised by the victim, killed her and fled in panic."

"You're saying she took refuge in her bed?"

"Maybe she was already in it, taking a nap, and the offender happened upon her."

"That presupposes he came to the basement first rather than ransacking the upstairs, which doesn't seem likely, does it?"

"Then maybe she did run down here."

Dickson Hong shook his head. "I don't know, Robinson. Your theory needs work." Not that he knew the answer, of course. But, based on outward appearances, he would have said the killer broke in with the intent of killing the victim, unlikely as that might otherwise seem. "I assume the family's been notified."

"Mrs. Ramirez called them right after she called us. They're on their way home."

Hong turned to Plavec. "We'll want to check if there's a large insurance policy, a sizable inheritance, that sort of thing. And, of course, we need to look into her personal life. I had a case ten, fifteen years ago where a seventy-year-old woman shot her sixty-eight-year-old friend for trying to steal her boyfriend. You never know about people."

Carl Plavec got out his pad and made a note.

"Yo, Robinson," somebody called from upstairs. "There's a woman out front who claims to have information that might be helpful."

"We'll go talk to her," Hong said.

He and Plavec made their way back up the stairs to where a patrolman waited.

"Little Filipino lady outside says she's a friend of the victim and wants to tell you something, sir."

Hong led the way out the door. A lab truck pulled up in front. The patrol officer pointed to a diminutive woman standing right at the tape.

"That's her in the blue sweater. Her name is Felina Estrella."

They descended the steps and Hong went over to the woman. "Ms. Estrella?"

"Yes, sir."

"I'm Inspector Hong and this is Inspector Plavec. You have something to tell us?"

"Yes."

Hong could see the woman seemed uncomfortable in the crowd. He lifted the crime-scene tape and invited her to step inside the cordoned-off area. They went to the porch.

"I work at Peninsula Hospital with Olga," Felina Estrella began. "We are friends. Yesterday when we come home on the bus, something very strange happen. A lady in the FBI, she comes to the bus stop and she talks to Olga."

"The FBI?"

"Yes, sir. This is what Olga tells me later. Anyway, I ask Olga what's going on and she tells me something I don't believe until now, when she is dead."

Hong glanced at Plavec. "What did she say, Ms. Estrella?"

"Olga says to me there are Russian spies in the hospital."

"*Russian* spies?"

"Yes. It sounds crazy, I know, but that's what she said. She heard the spies talking. I told her she was nuts. And she says, 'So why did the FBI come to me?' Maybe you think I'm crazy, too, sir, but I saw this FBI lady myself. She was white, very pretty."

"You're sure about the Russian part?"

"Olga should know. She is from Kiev."

Hong looked up at his partner. "Maybe the cold war isn't over, after all, Carl. Russians seem to be popping up everywhere...unless one guy really gets around."

SAN FRANCISCO INTERNATIONAL AIRPORT

Viktor Chorny, slender briefcase in hand, waddled off the plane and through the telescopic corridor to the terminal building. Alexei Sakharov, pacing nervously but with a smile on his face, waited for him. When they met, they embraced, greeting one another in Russian.

"And so, my boy," Viktor said, taking the younger man's arm, "now you are an accomplished assassin."

"It is surprisingly gratifying work, Comrade Colonel," Alexei said with a lilt.

"If you enjoyed doing the one for free, you'll adore the next three. Your cut is three hundred thousand."

"You're joking."

"No, but it must be done quickly. That is their condition. Nor will it be easy, Alexei. One, the black woman, has already dropped out of sight. But they are working feverishly to find her."

Viktor guided his charge toward an airport bar where they took a window table. After they each had ordered a vodka "straight up," a term that amused Viktor, he opened his briefcase and produced several photographs. Some were studio-type photos, but most were candid shots.

"A few of these were taken today," Viktor said, handing them to his friend.

"How did you get them so quickly?"

"Through the genius of American technology. They were e-mailed to me."

Alexei studied the photos.

"The two seated on the bench with the Asian gentleman are Fox and Sasso."

"Sportsmen, eh?"

"Yes, there's one of her throwing a baseball. Don't ask me why."

"What's happened to his face?"

"I don't know, but the injuries were recent. That's why a photo showing his current condition."

"He'll be easy enough to recognize."

"We have fewer shots of the black woman, Naomi Watts, but I'm told that she and Billie Fox have been in contact. When you kill Madame Fox, you may be able to extract from her the location of her friend, Madame Watts, assuming that hasn't already been determined. As you can see, Sasso and Fox are quite friendly. You may be fortunate enough to find them together."

"As with Culp and Sasso," Alexei said with a smile. "It's so much easier when they socialize with one another."

"This will take all your newfound skill, my boy."

"Will you please tell Igor of my success, Comrade Colonel? My brother was doubtful of my abilities and I would like for him to know he was wrong."

Viktor considered raising the issue of Igor, but decided this wasn't the time. Alexei shouldn't be distracted. He had a tremendous challenge facing him without having to fret over a clash between money and family loyalty. "Certainly," he said. "But first things first."

Viktor proceeded to go over addresses, vehicles, routines, everything about the targets that had been passed on to him. He had maps, even the floor plan of Sasso's restaurant.

"One other thing," Victor Chorny said, "normally I don't want my clients speaking to my employees, but for this operation to be a success, communication is the key. I have given the clients your cell phone number so they can contact you instantly, if need be. Keep the phone on at all times and have a backup battery ready. Only one man is authorized to call. His code name is Leland Stanford, Jr. Speak only to him and no one else."

"I must say, Viktor, you are very thorough."

"Planning and knowing how to select people has always been my strength, Alexei. That, together with my contacts and negotiating skills, justify my cut. Gunmen, after all, are easy to come by."

"But not one so skillful and loyal as me," Alexei said proudly.

"Precisely," Viktor said. "And that is why we're having this conversation. But you have much to do. Have you any questions?"

"No, but I have a gift." Alexei reached into his pocket and pulled out a wedding band, which he placed on the table in front of Viktor.

"What's this?"

"A token in remembrance of Madame Diachenko. For your collection, Comrade Colonel."

"I have no collection, Alexei," he said. Then, taking the ring and examining it briefly, he put it down in front of his friend. "My advice is to dispose of it."

Alexei picked up the ring and slipped it into his jacket pocket. He smiled, but said nothing.

WESTERN ADDITION

The taxi pulled up in front of the projects where Jolie Hays had been living most of the five months since her mother died. She hated the projects, but it was all she had. At least her apartment had a steel door that couldn't be knocked down like the one on that flat she'd had in Hunters Point, the one where the old man across the hall kicked in the door and tried to rape her. And he would have, too, if the motherfucker hadn't had an asthma attack right in the middle of ripping her clothes off.

Jolie paid the driver, earning a curse when she gave him the exact fare and no tip. "You lucky I pay you at all, motherfucker!" she screamed after him as he burned rubber, taking off up the street.

The guy gave her the finger out the window and she gave him the finger back. "Honky bastard," she grumbled, and headed for the entrance.

It was a rotten day. One arrest and no tricks. She'd tried moving to the eastern edge of the Tenderloin, closer to the expensive hotels, thinking maybe some classy businessman would pay a little extra for some nice clean soul meat. She found one all right, but he turned out to be a cop.

There was only one elevator operating and she rode up in it with a couple of twelve- or thirteen-year-old boys making rude remarks about her tits. Won't be but another couple of years and they'll be out raping and pillaging, she thought.

Jolie got out on the fifth floor and walked down the dark hallway toward the entrance to her apartment. She'd just put her key in the lock, when a voice came at her out of the shadows.

"Well, here she be, home early from work."

Jolie spun around only to see DeLon Pitts, his eyes, teeth

and gold chains gleaming in the half light. "Jesus, DeLon, you 'bout scared the piss out of me. Why the fuck you do that?"

He chuckled and came sauntering over to her door, styling his walk. "Mama, I got good news."

"Let me guess. You won the lottery and you decide to give me half."

"Almos' that good."

"What, then?"

"Ain't you goin' to invite me inside?"

"I don't see why I should."

"'Cause I come bearin' gifts, girl. Where your manners?"

"All right. For a minute, maybe."

She went inside and DeLon followed. He closed and locked the door. Jolie plopped down on the tattered flea-bitten sofa left by the previous tenant and her six cats. Jolie had since gotten immune to the fleas.

"So, let's hear your good news."

"I got you some business, babe."

"What you mean, you got me some business? You ain't my pimp, DeLon."

"No, but I be your manager after tonight. 'Fact, you beg me to be your manager."

"What the fuck you talkin' 'bout?"

"Mama, you don't got to be no street ho no more. You a call girl."

"Say what?"

"I got a call today from that honky that fucked you Thursday night. He say he want you again and tell me he pay five hundred. I say, 'No fuckin' way, motherfucker. You want my best girl, it cost you fifteen hundred.' He say that's a little steep, which it is, so we settle on a thousand. That's seven-fifty for you and two-fifty for me, Jolie. And I say to the honky motherfucker none of this all-nighter shit. Three hours and no more...unless the money go up accordingly."

"Wait a minute, DeLon. You make a deal with who? That Russian son'bitch?"

"Yeah. He pay good money. You already prove that."

"I'm not fucking that son'bitch motherfucker, DeLon. No way."

"Why not, Jolie?"

"'Cause I'm not."

"This time you get twice as much and you don't have to put up with no shit. What got you in trouble last time is you fuckin' boozed with the son'bitch. Do you whorin' right, with me lookin' over you, and you won't have no problem. That's what a good manager like me can do for you, Jolie. That and get you an extra three or four hundred."

"You say yourself he could have killed my ass. And you hear what he say about killin' those mens."

"That was all bullshit, babe. Don't mean nothin'. What I was tryin' to tell you was if these motherfuckers don't think nobody's watchin' over your ass, then maybe some'in' go wrong. But I tell the son'bitch, he's dealin' with me now, and I got rules. He understand, babe. Trust me."

"I don' trust you or him, neither one."

"Now, that ain't no way to talk to a man who's handin' you the opportunity of a lifetime. I got it all worked out. I get the room, that way I got an extra key, just in case we have a little problem. You fuck the honky and don't touch no booze. A couple of hours and you be a lot richer."

She thought for a moment, wondering if it could possibly be as good as DeLon says. "Only a couple of hours?"

"Yeah, the man say he got important business later, so can't be all night."

Jolie was tempted. "You sure, DeLon?"

"Have I ever lied to you, mama? Even once? Even one little white lie?"

She groused.

"See. You know I a straight shooter and I's the best thing that ever going to happen to you. And best of all this is only the beginning, Jolie. A thousand tonight, maybe twelve hundred tomorrow night. I got all kinds of contacts, you know."

She shook her head. As she thought about it, her ass still hurt. "I don' know, DeLon. To tell you the truth, I'm thinkin' of gettin' some work trainin' job."

"What? Where you goin' to find some work trainin' job that pay one thousand dollars for a couple hours work? You smarter than that, Jolie."

"It safer if I do work trainin'."

"You know what that sound like? Po-lice talk. They don't want to see you makin' all this money, that all. Come on, babe. A thousand for two hours, maybe an hour and a half. Shit, you can't even afford to buy clothes to go for a work trainin' interview."

Jolie thought for a minute. "You being straight with me, DeLon?"

"I swear to Jesus. What more can a man do than that?"

NORTH BEACH

As they waited at the light at the intersection of Broadway and Columbus, Nick glanced over at Billie. What was it about her that was so perfect? he wondered. The way she'd kissed him was outrageous, provocative and sweet. Billie Fox had courage. She had heart. It was a great combination, and it was sexy as hell.

She made him want to laugh and cry and play catch. He wanted to bump heads and kiss her, arm wrestle her and wrestle her in bed, if it came to that. God, it finally occurred to him—he had a crush.

"Maybe I should go in the back door," she said.

He understood her nervousness now. It wasn't him. It was

her public. "For a woman who chews them up and spits them out in court, you certainly are a wimp when it comes to appearance."

"Nick, there isn't a woman alive who doesn't worry about the way she looks...in the eyes of other women especially. Hell, men don't matter. They'd be perfectly content if everything we wore was filmy and see-through...and there's cold comfort in that, pardon the pun."

"Want me to run you home for a change of clothes, then?"

"No, but thanks for the thought," she said, putting her hand on his arm. "I'm just whining to give myself courage. I'll tough it out."

They pulled up in front of the Yankee Clipper, leaving the car with the valet. Nick went to the door and took the handle. "Just close your eyes and think of the Giants," he quipped.

Billie grabbed some skin on his stomach and gave it a good hard pinch. "Arrogant, Yankee-loving, Republican-sympathizing bastard," she muttered.

"Oh, how I love it when you talk dirty." He pulled the door open.

Billie threw back her shoulders and walked into the restaurant. Nick was relieved that Linda Nassari was not on duty. The hostess that evening was a girl named Celia. Nick had talked to her briefly once before.

"Hi, Mr. Sasso," she said, checking Billie out.

Billie stood tall, her chin slightly elevated, her Giants cap at a rakish angle. Nick was proud.

"A policeman came by a little while ago with this package for you," Celia said, taking it from the podium and handing it to him.

Judging by the size and weight, Nick figured it was Joe's .38. Dickson Hong must have had it tested.

"Also, you've had two calls," the hostess said, searching the podium for the messages. "One was from your sister-in-law and the other a long-distance from New York. Bree Davis." She found the slips, handing them to him.

"Ah," he said, as though the message from Bree was expected. He glanced at Billie. There was no special recognition, unless she was hiding it well. Mostly she seemed to be staring down the clientele. He stuffed the message slips in his pocket and peered back into the dining room.

At the moment his eye reached the DiMaggio booth, Billie said, "Looks like a special guest back there."

Nick was surprised to see who it was. "That's Benny Vocino."

"I kind of thought it might be. I suppose I'm going to have to help you interrogate the man in my shorts and T-shirt."

"Unless you want to wait upstairs."

"I'd sooner do a closing argument naked than miss an occasion like this."

Nick chuckled. "I sort of had a hunch you'd feel that way. Anyway, if I nail the case, I'd like you there to witness my triumph."

"Or pratfall," Billie said dryly.

They walked over to the booth. Benny, the collar of his shirt lying over his lapels like angel wings, an unlit cigar in his hand, stared off, not seeing them at first. Then he did.

"Nicky!" The old boy glanced at Billie, checking out her legs. "Isn't this a treat."

Nick figured he meant it both ways. "Hi, Benny. Mind some company?"

"Not if it includes the young lady."

Nick made the introductions. Billie slid onto the banquet. Nick followed, putting the package containing the gun between them. Benny had a partially eaten salad before him. As Nick recalled, the honorary mayor of North Beach liked eating at a leisurely pace.

"Have something to eat," Benny said.

"We will later," Nick replied. "We won't be disturbing you

for long. I'll be direct, which, considering we're old friends, I assume is all right."

Benny seemed to pick up on the seriousness of his tone. "Sure. What's on your mind?"

"When I came by the house yesterday, I told you about Joe's address book. What I didn't tell you was that the "V" entry had your phone number next to it. You were bullshitting about not being involved in Joe's problems, Benny, and I didn't much appreciate it."

"Hold on, son," Benito Vocino said, stabbing his unlit cigar at Nick. "We might be old friends, but you better not make accusations you can't back up."

"Then how about this? Billie and I met with Ken Lu this afternoon. After leaving us, he got in a cab with Elaine Chang. The taxi took them to *your* place, Benny. Now, how do you explain that?"

Benito Vocino looked stunned. After a moment he gave a weary sigh. "Goddamn, I guess I should have told you."

"Told me what?"

"I was less than completely honest with you, I admit," Benny said, scrunching his nose, his voice resonant with sincerity. "It was a mistake, I can see that now."

"The truth would go a long way to setting things right."

Benny flicked some bread crumbs off his lapel. "All right, here's the truth, the whole truth." He cleared his throat. "Last February I did meet with Elaine and Joey, like you suspected. Elaine had brought her Emerald Buddha deal to me. I put a little seed money into the project, but Lu needed a more committed partner and it seemed to me this was something Joey might be interested in, so I introduced him to Elaine and she took it from there."

"Why didn't you tell me this before?"

"Because I didn't want you thinking I was somehow responsible for what happened to your brother. Because I felt bad that he went overboard on the thing. Because I didn't want to be involved in the mess that's developed."

"Seems like you still are involved, Mr. Vocino," Billie said. "Elaine and Lu leave us and go directly to see you. That puts you right in the thick of things."

Benny gave her a look as if to say, "Why are you mouthing off, broad?" Seeing some explanation was required, Nick jumped in.

"Billie's my lawyer and she also happens to be Sonny Culp's former wife," he explained. "She's got the same interest in this as I do."

Benny seemed to accept that. "Well, if you're talking about the murders, Ms. Fox, I don't have nothing to do with that and I don't know nobody who does. You see, Nicky, this is why I didn't want to mention that I was responsible for Joe getting into the deal."

"Like it or not, I know now, Benny, and I want an explanation. What did Elaine and Lu come to see you about?"

"Basically, to see if I didn't want to step into Joey's shoes. They also wanted to know if you could be trusted. Of course, I said you could, but I didn't think the Buddha was your kind of thing."

"So where do things stand?"

"Up in the air. They want an investor and it's not going to be me. I'm too old for that risky shit, not at those numbers."

Benny was making a convincing argument and seemed sincere. But then, Benny always *seemed* sincere. The truth could be elusive when Benny Vocino was involved. Nick was coming to understand that.

"Well," Nick said, "if you don't know anything helpful, I guess the thing to do is to talk to Elaine Chang. Where can I find her?"

"I don't know."

"Come on, Benny, you've jerked me around enough and

I'm tired of it. I've got to talk to Elaine, no ifs, ands or buts about it. And it so happens that the police want to talk to her, too. Now I can either play the responsible citizen and tell the cops what happened this afternoon—which means they'll be on your doorstep—or I can go talk to Elaine and satisfy myself as to whether she does or doesn't hold the key to this thing. The choice is yours."

Benny rolled his cigar between his fingers, looking chastened. "Like I say, I don't know where she is, but I can probably get ahold of her and set up some kind of meeting. Will that do?"

"I suppose. As long as it's soon."

Gennaro Ravara shuffled to the table with a plate of pasta for Benny. He pushed the salad plate aside and set down the pasta. Glancing at Nick, he said, "So, you want to eat or what?"

"The lady and I will eat upstairs. Have one of the boys set up a table and chairs, will you?"

"You're the boss." He left.

Nick turned to Benny. "Anything else you've been holding back?"

The old boy scrunched his nose. "Just this. I think your brother was getting screwed by his lawyer, or somebody in his bankruptcy proceedings. We had a very brief conversation about it a while back, and I agreed with him that somebody was putting it to him. Joey was really taking it in the shorts, no doubt about it."

"What do you mean by that?" Billie said.

"I mean they was raping him, taking everything, but then I'm no lawyer, so what do I know? Maybe that's the way it has to be." He looked down at his plate of pasta. "Unless you two's got something else, I'm going to eat this."

"No, go ahead, Benny," Nick said. "We've got to go." He slid out of the booth. Billie followed.

"Nice meeting you," Benny said to her.

"Yeah," Billie said, "same here."

They went upstairs where Nick began unwrapping the gun. He hoped for a note, but there was none.

"That man is a very manipulative human being," Billie said, watching him put the bullets back in the cylinder.

"Yeah, and to think that when I was a kid I thought he was a god."

"Do you think he was telling the truth?" she asked.

"Mostly, but who knows? Benny's a lot shrewder than he seems." Nick put the .38 in the dresser drawer.

"I gathered that," Billie said. "On another subject, I'd like to wash up before dinner."

"And I should return some calls. Bathroom's right through there."

Billie gave his cheek a pinch, making him feel like a schoolboy, but in a good way, sort of like he was teacher's pet. Nick went to the office to make his calls. He started with Bree, figuring a little privacy might be nice when they talked. Though it was late, she was still at Dominick's.

"So, how's it going?" he asked, feeling distance which he could only attribute to his feelings for Billie.

"Good. We're operating to capacity. The lines weren't quite as long tonight, but they're still coming in droves. If this keeps up, you could end up a rich man," she said.

Funny how that almost seemed unimportant. It wasn't, of course—he did care, it was a dream come true—but over the past few days his life and the things that mattered seemed to have shifted to San Francisco. Dominick's California Cafe, Bree, the last five years of his life, seemed remote. His father's charge and his desire to come to terms with himself were what mattered now. "That's great, great," he muttered.

After a moment, Bree said, "There's something else I want to talk to you about, but there are too many people around.

Anyway, Eddy's ready to go over the cash receipts. Can I call you when I get home?"

"Sure, Bree. But is there some kind of problem?" he asked, his natural wariness coming to the fore.

"Yes and no. I'll talk to you about it later. Is it okay if I call on your cell phone?"

"Yeah, fine."

"Talk to you soon."

They ended the call and when he glanced up, he saw Billie standing at the door.

"Sorry, I didn't mean to intrude on something private."

"I have no secrets," he said, managing a smile.

"Sounds like you've got bicoastal women problems."

"Do I still have a problem on this coast?"

Billie shrugged. "I guess it depends on what your other problem is."

"I don't know, to tell you the truth. Bree said she'd call back later. There were too many people around."

"Uh-oh. She misses you."

"Naw, it's probably something like she suspects somebody's stealing. It's a big problem in the restaurant business. If you keep a close eye on things, you can keep it to nickels and dimes." Nick stroked his chin. "It's probably a good idea if I tell her I'm seeing somebody else."

"Do you know something I don't know?"

"I was referring to you, Billie. Haven't you figured out that I'm fond of you?"

She chewed on her lip. "I was hoping so, I guess."

"Well, I am."

"Good."

"Now that we've got that settled, why don't you come sit down? I'll give Gina a quick call, then we can eat."

"I can wait in the other room."

"No, sit down here and make yourself at home."

R.J. Kaiser

Billie dropped into the chair opposite him and crossed her legs. She looked adorable in her Giants cap, bright and perky with fresh lipstick. They hadn't kissed properly and he very much wanted to kiss her now. Especially now.

Taking the phone again, he dialed Gina's number. She answered.

"I wanted to invite you for dinner tomorrow night, Nick," she said. "I finally got hold of Anthony. He'll be arriving in the morning."

"He take it okay?"

"Yes, he's a man now."

"Good."

"I thought it would be nice for all the children if you joined us, if you're free."

"I'd like to."

"I went out to see your father this afternoon."

"How was he?"

"Much improved. Speaking a few words."

"Great."

"I talked to the nurse, Nick, and she thought he could be told about Joe. I hope you don't mind, but I went ahead and gave him the news. I figured it would be painful for you and so I did it."

"Thank you, Gina. I admit, I wasn't looking forward to it."

"Tony said he knows you're busy, but when you get a chance he'd like to see you."

"Yeah, I'll go by."

"Two more things," she said. "Inspector Hong called me and said that Joe's gun was not the murder weapon. That doesn't mean I'm off the hook, of course, but it's a step. He was kind enough to let me know."

"I should have told you I'd given him the gun, Gina."

"Don't worry about it. I know you did it with the best of intentions. Besides, if I'd used it to kill him and Mr. Culp, I'd probably have thrown it in the bay, so you didn't take much of a chance, and I suspect you know that."

"As long as you're okay with it, that's the main thing."

"I am," Gina said. "And one last thing. This just came to me this evening while I was alone in my room, thinking. Things have been so emotional dealing with the children that I haven't had a lot of time to reflect."

"Yes?"

"I thought about Thursday afternoon when I followed Joe and that woman to Sonny Culp's office."

"Hang on a second, Gina. If you don't mind, I'm going to put on the speakerphone."

"Sure."

Nick clicked on the speaker so Billie could hear. "Go ahead."

"Anyway, I recalled hearing something while I was eavesdropping on Joe's conversation with Mr. Culp that I'd completely forgotten about."

"What's that?"

"They were arguing about something, I guess Mr. Culp's commitment to Joe's business affairs, and Culp said something strange. He said, 'This is about a lot more than you, Joe.' Then he said it was very important to him, too."

"Do you have any idea what he was referring to?"

"No, but don't you think that's a strange thing for a lawyer to say to his client?"

Nick reflected. "Yes, I guess it is."

"Well, maybe it's not significant, but it was so odd, I thought I ought to bring it to your attention."

"I'm glad you did. I'll file it away in my computer and see what I can come up with."

"Is six tomorrow evening good for you?" she asked.

"Fine."

"See you then."

424   R.J. Kaiser

Nick disconnected the call. He looked at Billie and she looked at him, the incipient smile on her face building to a full-fledged grin.

"Methinks the pendulum is swinging my direction, Mr. Sasso."

"I hate to admit it, but I'm getting that same feeling. What could they both be involved in that would be more important to Sonny than Joe? Surely not the Emerald Buddha business."

Billie shook her head. "No, definitely something else. Sonny said to him, 'It's about more than you.' That's got to be key."

Nick scratched his head. "But what?"

"Sonny was so big on the integrity of the legal system, he had to be making some reference to the bigger picture. And those remarks he'd made to me recently about other lawyers being corrupt. Maybe he was railing against something that came to light in a case involving Joe."

Nick snapped his fingers. "That's it!"

"What?"

"The remark Benny made a little while ago."

"About Elaine?"

"No, about Joe getting screwed in the bankruptcy."

Billie thought. "But Sonny doesn't know shit about bankruptcy. Nobody who doesn't specialize in it does." Her eyes got round. "Wait a minute. Joe must have gone to Sonny, complaining he was getting screwed by the legal system. That would have gotten Sonny's attention. In fact, it's right down his alley!"

"And if my brother thought he was being screwed by the system, he'd go looking for a gadfly."

Billie was so excited, she jumped to her feet. Nick stood as well.

"Nick, that's it!"

She gave a whoop. They exchanged high fives over the desk.

Seeing her glow was worth the price of admission. Her glee made him happy.

Suddenly her face fell.

"What?" he said.

"This dinner tonight. Is it going to count against my twelve?"

Nick laughed. "No, it's on the house."

She gave him an endearing look. "You're such a sweet man."

Nick couldn't help himself. He went around the desk and took Billie Fox in his arms. He kissed her deeply and she kissed him back with the same energy she'd shown throwing a baseball. After a minute their mouths parted. They were both breathless. Billie ran her fingertip over his chin as though savoring the feel of the stubble.

He continued to hold her close. They were belly to belly.

"Nick?"

"Yes?"

"All this affection is going someplace, isn't it?"

"I'd like to think so."

"I'm very fond of you," she said, "but I'm also hungry. Do you mind if we eat first?"

LOMBARD STREET

Jolie Hays sat on the bed in a room in the same motel she'd been in with Jerry French Thursday night. What she couldn't decide was if it was a good sign or a bad sign. All evening long she'd gone back and forth in her head—work training or turn a quick trick for some quick money? Finally she decided. One last time. After this, no more hooking.

She'd been waiting for fifteen minutes, getting more and more nervous. That motherfucker, Jerry, was a hard man, a cruel man. She hadn't liked him—not that hookers were supposed to like their johns, but waiting like this made her think she'd made a mistake. The thousand dollars didn't seem so important anymore. As she pondered the possibility of leaving, there was a knock at the door, making her jump.

Jolie got up slowly and crept to the door. She didn't have to open it, did she? Maybe she'd let him go away. The knocking became insistent.

"Hey, sugar pie, it's me, Jerry," he called through the door. "Come on, open up. I've got a little surprise for you!"

"Hey, man, I'm not feeling so good," she moaned. "Maybe we should just forget about it."

"Jolie baby, I came all the way to San Francisco just to see you. You can't turn me away. Come on, sugar pie, let me in."

She agonized. Then she heard a sound and looked down to see a hundred-dollar bill come sliding under the door.

Jolie hesitated before bending over and picking up the bill. She couldn't very well take the money and not open the door. Sighing, she removed the security chain and turned the dead bolt. Then she pulled the door open.

Jerry stood on the outside walkway, leaning against the railing, his legs crossed at the ankles. He wore a sports jacket, but no tie. He had a paper sack in his hand and a smile on his face. "That took long enough. What's the matter?"

"If you want to know the truth, I still sore."

"I'll be gentler this time."

"I believe that when I see it."

Jerry reached into the sack and pulled out a bottle. "Stoli," he said, "the best vodka in the world."

"Oh, no, I ain't drinkin' none of that shit. No way."

His smile broadening, Jerry ambled into the room. Jolie closed the door. He sat on the bed, examining the bottle lovingly. "You don't mind if I have a nip, do you?"

"Just don't get crazy drunk, okay?"

"Fine," he said, breaking the seal on the bottle. "Take off your clothes."

Jolie undressed, and Jerry took a couple of belts of vodka as he watched her. Staring at her tits he had that same crazy look in his eye as last time.

"You are a very fine piece of ass," he said, shaking his head in a sad way.

"I worth more than any thousand."

"You know," he said, "you could be right."

"So what you want to do, Jerry?"

He reached in his jacket pocket and pulled out a small plastic packet, which he tossed to her. It was a condom. Standing, he motioned for her to approach. "Come put it on me."

Jolie remembered that he'd used a condom on their first date because she'd insisted. At least he had when they were sober. After that, God only knows. She went to the bed and he stood up.

"On your knees," he commanded.

She knelt and began unfastening his belt. By the time she got his trousers and shorts down, he had a hard-on to beat all hard-ons. Removing the condom, she put it on his cock, nervous as hell because something didn't feel right.

"Now what?" she asked.

"Get on your hands and knees on the bed."

"Ain't you goin' to take off your clothes?"

"Never mind me. Just do what you're told."

Jolie got on the bed. Opposite her was a dressing table, a mirror above it. She saw herself and she saw Jerry as he moved around behind her. "Hey," she said, looking over her shoulder, "don' you even think about my back door."

"Don't worry," he said, taking her ass in his hands. "Your cunt will do just fine."

She felt his rigid cock at her opening. The next thing she knew he rammed into her, making her gasp.

"Jesus!"

Jolie glanced up in the mirror as Jerry, the Russian, began thrusting, humping away. There was something about his face that caught her attention, that took her mind off what he was doing to her pussy. After a minute or two, he came, grunting, then muttering something in Russian. He gave her ass a slap—not a hard slap, but one that signaled finality. She wondered if that meant he was through for the night, or if this was just the opening round.

Before she could ask, the sonovabitch reached under his coat and pulled out a gun. Her blood went cold. His cock still in her, she saw him release the safety, and she knew what was coming.

Thrusting her butt back into him as hard as she could, Jolie knocked him off balance, sending him reeling. At the same moment she began screaming and clawing her way across the bed in a frantic attempt to make it to the bathroom. Still on her hands and knees, she reached the tile floor as the first bullet slammed into the wall next to her ear.

His gun must have jammed or something because she got the door shut and locked before he got off another shot. Jerry was in a rage, cursing so loud it seemed the storm of his temper would level the door. It was a small bathroom, but she managed to press her body into the corner behind the door, knowing bullets could smash through at any moment.

But they didn't come through. Instead, she heard another voice.

"Goddamn motherfuckin' cocksucker!"

There was a crash and sounds of a struggle. Jolie knew it was DeLon, coming to her rescue. She listened as the two men raged at one other, one screaming obscenities in Russian, the other in the language of the streets. She heard furniture crashing, lamps breaking as bodies hurdled about.

Jolie knew there was no way to trust who would come out

on top. The thing to do was to make her escape while DeLon had Jerry occupied. Opening the door a crack, she discovered the men rolling around on the floor, struggling for the gun. Across the room, the outside door was wide open, inviting escape. Three seconds was all she needed.

Jolie Hays muttered, "Please Jesus," and made her dash. As she ran by the men, Jerry reached out his arm, tripping her so that she fell flat on her face. She scrambled to her feet and made it out the door, running all the way to the end of the building where the stairway was located. She was halfway to the ground floor when she heard the gunshot. She didn't so much as look back, though. Instead, she ran for her life, streaking down Lombard Street, buck-ass naked, not stopping until she reached the convenience store on the corner.

The mustached clerk behind the counter stared at her with round eyes, his mouth agape.

"Call the motherfuckin' po-lice!" she cried.

As the man, shaking now, reached for the phone, dropping the receiver once, Jolie ducked behind a rack of potato chips. This was it. She'd had it. She wasn't going to be a ho no more.

NORTH BEACH

They opted for a light meal—Dungeness crab chowder and an artichoke pasta with a lemon cream sauce and a bottle of good chardonnay. For dessert they had a cheese plate and fruit. A small table had been set up in the corner of the room. White tablecloth, candle. The bed not ten feet away. What could be more blatantly, yet compellingly, seductive? Billie wondered, sipping the last of her wine.

During the meal they hadn't discussed the case a lot, though she was tempted. Nick wanted to talk about them, about relationships and feelings, which was odd for a guy. He asked her things like what she liked in a man, what she liked

doing most when she cared for someone, her favorite kinds
of intimacy, the things that turned her on and turned her off.
It was a sexy conversation. Out of the ordinary, for sure.

"It's the Boy Scout in you, Nick. Want to be prepared,
don't you?"

"Why waste a lot of time doing the wrong things?"

"I'm not afraid to give directions."

"Good. And I'm not afraid to push your limits."

"Now, that's a provocative thought," she said.

"As intended."

"What about you? You should share, too. What have you
been thinking about...besides getting laid, I mean?"

"I was thinking how much this reminds me of my summer in Italy, only better."

"Better how?"

"I idealized Julianna. She came out of my head as much
as from the person she was. You're real, Billie, and I'm mature enough to appreciate you for who and what you are. Point
is, I like what I see."

"Romantic feelings are self-delusional by definition, at
least to some degree."

"What are you saying? That there's a negative side to you
I haven't seen?"

She laughed. "I can be a bitch, of course. That goes
without saying."

"It comes with the X chromosome, no big deal."

"I could make a few choice remarks about the Y chromosome," she rejoined, "but I won't since this is a seduction and first times with a guy are supposed to be
memorable *and* pleasant. There's plenty of time later for
screaming fights."

"You see, that's what's so nice about mature love. A couple can cut right through the bullshit and get down to
what's important."

"Careful with the love word," she said. "It's much too early."

"*Lust* isn't the right word."

"Speak for yourself."

Nick's eyebrows rose. He actually looked a little hurt. "You see me as a sex object?"

"Yeah, as a matter of fact."

"That's all?"

"No, of course that's not all. Sex is mostly mental—the mind being the key erogenous zone and all that—so there has to be a lot more to it than flesh and bone. The fact that we can be having this conversation at all says a lot about us and our chemistry."

"Let me rephrase the question," Nick said. "Is getting laid your principal objective?"

"At the moment it's very high on the list, Nick. I cannot tell a lie."

"That's refreshing."

"Actually it should feel familiar. Ninety percent of men, in ninety percent of their relationships with women, think about getting laid, if they're not actually obsessed by it."

"Do you have this conversation often?" he asked.

Billie grinned. "You mean, am I a slut? Frankly, no, I'm not. I rarely meet a man I consider going to bed with. Very seldom happens, as a matter of fact."

"I'm privileged, then."

"No, your timing's good."

Again he looked disappointed.

"But don't worry, Nick, you've got a lot more going for you than just being available. Shall I list your charms?" Without giving him an opportunity to reply, she continued. "Never mind, every man wants to know why he's irresistible, so I'll tell you. You're nice. That's first and it's important. You're sexy. I just looked at you and I could tell you were good in bed. You have a boyish passion, and a sincerity that's appealing. And you have a sense of humor. Boy, man, mensch, stud. It's a combination that works for me. Any more questions, or can I go get in the shower now?"

"One more question."

"Yes?"

"Mind if I join you?"

She laughed. "It looked like a pretty small shower."

"Billie, that's its principal virtue."

She drew a long, slow breath. "I should warn you about my scar."

"No, you shouldn't. Just hang on to your hat."

With that, he took her hand and kissed it. Nice. Then he turned her hand over and licked her palm. That sent shivers through her.

"I claim undressing rights, by the way," he said, licking her palm again.

Billie had a very clear mental image of things to come. "Okay," she said in her soft, little-girl voice. She was willing. She was ready. It was time.

SAN BRUNO

Dickson Hong hung up the phone in Suze's bright yellow kitchen and returned to the family room where his dear wife was seated in her recliner watching her beloved Giants on the big-screen TV in the corner. Dickson glanced at the screen and saw a Giant swing and miss a pitch.

"Richy," Suze moaned, "you're killing me." It was one of Mike Krukow's expressions and Suze had made it her own. Krukow was an announcer for the Giants, a big, affable former pitcher with an energetic announcing style and passion for the game. He and Suze couldn't have been more different physically, but Dickson sometimes felt he was married to a Giants announcer, so deep was his wife's commitment.

The strikeout being the third out of the inning, a commercial came on. His wife turned to him. "You going out again?"

"I don't think so, though maybe I should," he said, dropping onto the sofa. He stared at the chessboard on the coffee table before him where he'd been working on variations of his favorite opening with black, the Caro-Kann Defense.

"What happened?" his wife asked.

"My Russian killer has struck again."

"Oh dear, who did he get now?"

"A pimp named DeLon Pitts. Killed him in a motel room after a struggle over a gun."

"Then it wasn't another premeditated murder."

"Pitts saved the life of a prostitute that my Russian apparently had decided to kill."

"The one you told me about?"

"Yes. She got away, but the point is, the Russian tried to kill her."

"He's got to be sick and demented."

"I'm not so sure, Suze. I think he was afraid she might identify him."

"Well, did they catch him?"

"No, he was gone by the time the first unit reached the scene. Needless to say, every cop in the Bay Area will be on the lookout for him. Unfortunately nobody saw his vehicle and we still don't have an ID. The question on everybody's mind is, is he through?"

"You think he's a serial killer, Dickson?"

Hong picked up a pawn, weighing it in his hand. "No. After hearing what he said to the prostitute, I think he may have been involved in the double homicide."

"And didn't you say the FBI is involved now, too?"

"Not in the homicides. We thought for a while they were investigating something at the hospital where the Ukrainian woman worked, but that proved not to be the case. Apparently it was a woman *posing* as an FBI agent. She spoke with the victim a few days ago, planting a Russian-spy story in her mind."

"A prostitute and a Ukrainian emigrant. Interesting combination," Suze said. "What could they possibly have to do with the lawyer and businessman who were killed?"

"The Russian told the prostitute he'd made a lot of money that night, and he made reference to the killings. I guess he didn't actually say he'd done it, but it's a reasonable assumption. How Olga fits in I don't..." Then it hit him. "Wait a minute. I just remembered something. Olga's friend, the Filipino woman, said that Olga overheard the *spies* speaking."

"Plural?"

"Yes, plural. That went right over my head at the time."

"Then there's more than one Russian killer?"

"More than one Russian, anyway. Olga must have heard a conversation in Russian and they realized they'd been compromised because one of them—or somebody associated with them—posed as an FBI agent and tried to intimidate her."

"Or, maybe they just wanted to find out what Olga knew."

"You're right, Suze. That's also possible. In any case, they didn't like what Olga had to say, because a few days later she ends up dead."

"So what do you do next?" his wife asked.

"The first order of business is probably a trip to Peninsula Hospital."

"Oh, damn," Suze said. "Look at that. A four-run lead and what does he do? Walks the leadoff batter."

Dickson Hong smiled to himself and began setting up the chessboard to run through another opening variation. When the Giants were playing, life got put on hold. He didn't even have the chance to relate the other tidbit that had been passed on to him. Olga Diachenko's daughter, when identifying the body, had noted that her mother's wedding band was missing. It wasn't valuable, so it was unlikely her assailant's motive was robbery. And it was just as unlikely anyone else who'd come in contact with the body would take a valueless ring. What could be the significance of that?

Suze might find that little development interesting, but not now, not while the game was still on the line. But that was okay. In a month the season would be over and once again they could have conversations that lasted longer than the between-inning commercial breaks. That was the good news. The bad news was that spring training was only five months away.

NORTH BEACH

Billie sat astride him, riding his cock, her lips pulled back over her gritted teeth. She breathed hard, mumbling, "Oh, God...oh, God...oh, God."

Her eyes were mostly closed, her head rolling. Every once in a while she'd lean forward and brace her hands on his chest, looking into his eyes with sex-fierce anger as she ground her pelvis into his. Hurt me nice, she seemed to be saying. Play hard, play rough, but keep it clean.

"Thank you for not coming, Nick," she hissed through her teeth. "I really need this. God, do I need this."

He would have come long before now if this were the first time, his desire to please notwithstanding. But they'd gotten carried away in the shower, screwing under the stream of hot water, teeth on tender lips, desperate gasps for air, nails clawing, him grasping her delicious ass and going off inside her like a fire hose, Billie, a little shocked, saying afterward, "God, condom or not, I felt that behind my eyeballs."

They'd scarcely dried off, repairing to his father's bed where she'd given him a few minutes to recover. "I know you're tired," she'd said, deciding he'd rested long enough, "so I'll do the work." She handed him another condom and, once he had it on, she climbed astride him.

It wasn't the first time a woman had wanted to be on top, but he took special joy in this because he was able to study her with detachment, watch her in her pleasure, getting harder as her excitement rose. It was probably all in his head, but with Billie there was a profundity to their copulation, a dance of body, mind and spirit that felt different to him. It wasn't love—Billie had correctly pointed out that it was too soon for that—but they shared a communion that was unique in his experience.

"Oh, Nick," she cried, grinding on him, "I think I'm going to come."

That was all it took. His fingers digging into her hips, he pulled her against him until she cried out, her body shuddering.

She collapsed on him, gasping for air, her small breasts, one with a silver scar, resting on his chest like a pair of fluffy pancakes on a griddle. After a minute she kissed the corner of his mouth and ran her cheek against his beard.

"Bastard," she said gently.

"Why?"

"For the same reason I get angry with chocolate."

"A compliment, in other words."

"No, something else to give up for Lent."

"You're giving me up already?"

"Yeah, remarkable, isn't it? Considering I'm still coming. Actually, it's more keeping you at an emotional distance than giving you up."

"I'd say you're gun-shy, Billie."

She kissed his chin. "I know." She looked into his eyes and smiled a bit shyly, as if to say, "We sure were bad." Then she hugged his neck, pressing her chest against his once again. "Thank you."

"The pleasure was all mine."

"Hardly."

There was a muffled ringing sound coming from somewhere in the room, drawing the attention of them both.

"Oh," Billie said, "that must be my cell phone."

He looked over at her purse, which was on the chair across the room. "Forget it," he said as she sat upright on him.

"No," she replied, rising, disengaging her body from his, "I'm a mother and mothers never disregard ringing phones."

She went to the chair, not quite staggering, not quite walking, either. Nick observed her body in the candlelight as she dug the phone out of her purse, loving her ass and her small breasts.

Billie pushed the talk button and tucked her hair back behind her ear. "Hello?" she said, resting her hand on her hip. "Oh, hi, Pop.... No, that's all right. What's up? ....She did? When?" There was genuine surprise in Billie's voice, though not alarm. Nick was concerned, nonetheless, thinking it was about her daughter, until Billie said, "Did she say where she was or leave a number?.... What time?.... Okay, I'll be home as soon as I can get there." She hung up and turned to Nick, giving him a forlorn look.

"Bad news?"

"Naomi called. She wants to see me and might come by the house. I'd better get home."

"You mean our eternal bliss is already over?"

"Sad but true," she said, giving him a sympathetic smile.

"Bummer."

"You got your rocks off, you've got no complaints, Mr. Sasso."

"I was hoping for a little postcoital affection, but obviously you're the wham-bam-thank-you-buddy kind of girl."

She came over to the bed and sat down next to him. Nick put his arm around her hips and she ran her fingers back through his hair in a soothing, maternal way. "Poor Nick. You must be used to girls who have nothing more important to do than get laid."

"That was delicately put."

She leaned over and kissed him softly on the lips. "Sorry.

That comes from only getting sex on a semiannual basis. When you're out of the swing of things you forget how fragile the male ego can be."

"I was hoping you'd be able to spend the night."

"That would be nice," she said, "but duty calls. Maybe another time."

"How is it that women are so adept at going from warm to cold in a matter of seconds?"

"I don't know, must be a natural impulse that enables us to deal with male commitment avoidance. Either that, or we're so good at faking things we forget what's real and what's not."

"So this was all an act."

"Yeah, I prostituted myself for the sake of your ego." She pinched his cheek. "All in a day of the life of a woman, big boy." She got up and began gathering her clothing. "Are you going to drive me home or make me walk?"

"Do I get a rematch?"

"I could probably find some time for you on my calendar."

"I'll drive you home, then."

Billie gave him a smile. "Nick, you are a true saint."

Now his cell phone rang. They both laughed.

"Timing could have been worse, I suppose," he said, getting up from the bed. He took the phone from the top of the dresser. "Hello?"

"Hi, it's me," came Bree's voice.

"Hi," he said, "What's up?"

She hesitated. "Nick, are you sitting down?"

"Why? What's the matter?"

"You'd better."

"Bree, just tell me."

He could hear her take a deep breath. "I think I'm pregnant."

"What?"

"Nick, I think I'm pregnant."

"Yeah, I heard," he said, feeling as if he did have to pick

himself off the floor. He glanced at Billie, who was digging through her purse for something. "What makes you think so?"

"Well, duh."

"I mean have you checked with anybody?" Because of Billie he was being circumspect.

"Like the doctor, you mean?"

"Yeah."

"I'm going in Monday."

Nick felt weak in the knees. "This isn't a joke...I mean, you seriously think..."

"I took a home test and it was positive," she said, her tone sober, no-nonsense. "They're not foolproof, but they're fairly accurate."

He swallowed hard. "I see."

"Naturally, I'll let you know after I talk to the doctor. Maybe I should have waited until after to say anything, but...well, I just wanted to be up-front."

"I appreciate that," he said vaguely.

Billie went off to the bath, giving a smile and a wave. Nick staggered over to the bed and sat down.

"Bree, I thought you were on the Pill," he said in a hushed but urgent tone.

"I am, but they're not a hundred percent. And occasionally I forget. I'm not perfect, you know. And by the way, Nick, it's not just my responsibility. There was a time or two when you got too carried away to put on a rubber, over my objection, if you'll recall."

He felt sick. How could this be happening? Now of all times. "Yeah, I know. I'm sorry. If I'm not very coherent it's because I'm in shock."

"Imagine how I feel."

"How *do* you feel?"

"Well, I don't have morning sickness, if that's what you mean."

"No, that's not what I mean. I'm asking is if you're upset."

"Nick...I...well, are *you* upset?"

It was then he knew. Maybe at some level he'd known all along that Bree Davis didn't quite take their relationship as casually as he did. But pregnancy had all kinds of implications—and unfortunately for a man in his situation, all of them were unpleasant. "I guess the honest answer is yes."

"Me, too," she said.

Nick doubted it. "Maybe we should talk after you've seen the doctor."

"Shall I call you, then?"

"Please."

"Nick, I'm sorry."

"I take my share of the responsibility," he said.

He could tell she wanted words of encouragement, compassion, maybe even love, but he just didn't have it in him, not after this evening, not after Billie.

"I'll talk to you Monday night then," she said, her voice quavering.

He felt just awful. "Hang in there, kid." It was the best he could do.

Nick was still seated on the bed, his head in his hands, when Billie returned from the bathroom, dressed.

"Hey," she said, "what's the matter?"

He looked up at her. "That was the girl I've been dating in New York."

Billie waited, then said, "Is there more?"

He drew a breath. "She thinks she might be pregnant."

She stood frozen, staring at him for a long moment. "Well, isn't that interesting. The lady certainly knows how to pick her moments."

"I'm sick," he said.

She cocked her hips, resting her hands on them. "Either

you've got lively little bullets or the two of you aren't very bright."

"Could be both."

"She's seeing the doctor, I take it."

"Monday."

"You're in for a long Sunday, then."

He looked at her beseechingly. "It was before I knew you, Billie."

"True."

"What I hate most about it is that it's coming at the end of one of the best nights of my life. I don't want anything to take away from that."

"We can't always have what we want, Nick. God can be pretty cruel. But, the way I look at it, there's usually good with the bad, though sometimes you have to look hard for it. I had a good time which, after all, was the objective."

"You aren't upset?"

"Not as much as you. But I will sleep easier if you can assure me you've changed your brand of condom."

"There's a chance it's a false alarm."

"I hope for all your sakes it is. Meanwhile, back on this coast, your date is tired and ready to go home. If you're not feeling up to it, I can take a taxi."

"No, I want to take you. The last thing I want is for the evening to end like this."

He got up to dress. Billie sat on the chair. Crossing her legs, she sat silently.

She was being rather stoic, he thought as he searched for his pants, but his news couldn't help but unnerve her. How could he blame her? If she'd just told him she was pregnant by another man, he'd be bummed as hell. Why had God dealt him a pat hand, then not let him play it out? Billie was right. There *was* cruelty in the universe. And suffering.

VAN NUYS

Igor and Eve lay in bed watching Jay Leno on TV. She snuggled up next to him, her head on his shoulder, her hand on his hairy chest. Two nights ago he'd never have dreamed he'd be here with her like this. They were blessed.

Eve, he could tell, was relieved, which he understood. Yet he sensed something was bothering her. At first he thought it was worry over his condition, but as time went on he began having doubts that was it. Their business had cash flow problems, but there was nothing new in that. He'd been concerned enough that he'd asked her about it that afternoon. "It's nothing, Iggy," she'd replied. "There've been so many things all at once. That's all."

Igor Sakharov could tell she was holding something back. He sensed no disaffection, so it wasn't her feelings for him. But she was troubled. That much he knew for sure.

Turning his head, he kissed her temple. Eve snuggled still closer. He slid his hand down over the curve of her breast, lightly brushing her nipple. She moved his hand away.

"You don't like it when I touch you anymore?"

"Of course I like it, Iggy. I adore it. But you're not well. Do you think I want my husband to die screwing me?"

"If we can't make love, what's the point of going on?"

"Is that all I'm good for?" There was pique in her voice.

"No, of course not. But you know how much I enjoy making love to you."

"We will, as soon as the doctor says it's okay."

"And if he doesn't say it's okay?"

"Then we'll live like brother and sister and be glad for what we can share."

Igor knew he should be thankful for a woman with such devotion, but his heart yearned for things as they had been before Viktor Chorny showed up with that contract. Eve gave a deep sigh. He pushed a wisp of her golden hair back off her cheek.

"Are you sure everything's all right, my darling?"

"Yes, Iggy," she insisted. "Don't worry about it, okay?" After a minute she threw the covers back and got out of bed. "I'm going to get myself a glass of wine. Can I bring you anything?"

"I'll have a glass of wine, too, please."

"Iggy, I don't think you should. Not until the doctor says it's okay."

"Goddamn it then, why don't you bring me my gun? I'll shoot myself then the doctor won't have to worry!"

She gave him a disgusted look. "All right, have it your way. I'll bring you some wine." She headed for the kitchen.

"Why do you give in on the wine, but not sex?"

"Because I'd rather you not have a heart attack while your cock's in me, thank you very much." She went out the door.

"Maybe you should bring me my gun, anyway," he called after her.

"I can't. Alexei has it."

He'd forgotten about that. In fact, he'd forgotten all about Alexei. Or maybe it was that he'd tried not to think about him. Yes, that was more accurate. Igor had been against his brother killing the cleaning woman unless it could be proven she was a danger. But Alexei—and more importantly, Viktor—were determined. Igor, disgusted and saddened by the whole business, wanted to wash his hands of it, but he couldn't. He was involved, and now he would live and die on what his brother did. It was not a comfortable thought—not knowing Alexei as he did.

Incredibly, given the hour, the phone rang, but only once. Eve must have picked it up in the kitchen. Igor, not in such a good mood as before, stared blankly at the TV, knowing he had problems which even a loving wife couldn't fix.

"Iggy!" Eve called from the other room. "It's Alexei. He wants to talk to you."

Igor, thinking there was a God, rolled over and took the receiver from the phone on the bedstand. "Приве́т." *Hi*, he said. "Что́ но́вого?" *What's up?*

"Igor, I've got to know how dangerous is it to kill witnesses. Are the police likely to catch me based only on a description? How safe is it to move about?"

A cold fear went through him but his voice was eerily calm, deliberate. "What's happened, Alexei?"

His brother began to recount the day's events. Igor stopped him.

"We can't discuss this on the telephone."

"Igor, I must know. I have very little time and three more customers."

Igor shut his eyes, knowing that this was a complete catastrophe. His brother was playing at being an assassin but he didn't have a clue as to how dangerous the work was. Viktor should have known better, of course, and the fact that he didn't told him just how desperate Viktor was, using someone so green. Igór took a deep breath and forced himself to ignore the pain in his chest. "What do you mean, '*more*'?"

"The colonel gave me three more deals to transact. All right here. The fee is incredible."

"Alexei, come back immediately. Don't go to the airport. Drive home. You are in incredible danger."

"No, Igor. If I'm going to be a wanted man, then I must have money to survive. I must do this. I am determined."

"Don't be a fool. Listen to me. I know best."

"Damn it, Igor!"

The telephone went dead in Igor Sakharov's hand. "Shit!" he cried, slamming down the receiver. A moment later, Eve was at the door.

"What happened?" she said, coming to the bed.

Igor looked into his wife's eyes, his heart pounding. How did he tell her their life here was over? He knew Alexei was doomed. His brother would be arrested or killed, which meant it was only a matter of time before the police were at their door. Dear Eve, with her big dreams for Lovers International, that house she wanted so badly in Holmby Hills—all lost now because of his stupidity and his pigheaded brother. Igor took her hands.

"Remember you spoke of going to Mexico?" he said, his voice solemn.

Terror slowly crept onto her face, then understanding. "The police are on to Alexei."

"It's just a matter of time, but he's too stupid and stubborn to realize it."

Eve threw her arms around him. "Oh, Iggy."

He kissed her head. "I'm afraid our life here is over."

She pulled back to look at him. "I don't want to go back to prison," she said, grasping his hand. "I couldn't live without you. It would kill me. Anything but that."

Igor pulled her hand to his mouth and kissed it lovingly. "I won't let that happen to you."

"How much time do we have?"

"Maybe only hours. A few days at most."

She began wringing her hands. "What will we do? How will we live?"

"There isn't time to sell the business and the house. How much cash do we have?"

"Less than ten thousand, if I clean out all the accounts. Maybe a few thousand more with cash advances on the credit cards."

"That won't get us very far. We'll have to see Viktor. He owes us a hundred thousand."

"No, let's just leave, Iggy. Tonight."

"Without money we're dead."

"I don't care, let's just go."

"Viktor owes us the money, Eve. If Alexei survives, I'll give him his share, but we must get it from Viktor. Why should he keep it? For all we know, he's already picked up and gone. We'll go to see him first thing in the morning."

Eve fell against him and began to cry. Her misery choked him up. He'd failed her so badly. Their life had had such promise. Now this. Everything lost.

"We'll make it, my darling," he said, wiping his eyes. "I promise you we will. And if we can get to Viktor in time..."

"Oh, Iggy, don't even say his name to me."

Igor looked at his wife. "You hate him that much? Eve, Viktor's our only chance."

"I don't want to see him. You go."

Something was definitely wrong. He saw it in her eyes, heard it in her voice. "Eve, what's happened? You didn't feel this way about him before, no matter what you say."

"Nothing's happened," she replied. "Just go get the money he owes us, but leave me out of it."

"No, I want you to tell me," he said, his tone sharper. "Did Viktor say or do something to you?"

"No, nothing."

"I don't believe you."

"Okay, then. Viktor propositioned me. It was while you were in San Francisco. Your old friend asked me to screw him. Are you happy now?"

Igor flushed.

"Look at you," Eve said, sitting up. "You're angry. If you don't stop and control your anger, Iggy, it will kill you. Do you see now why I didn't want to say? It wasn't the end of the world, only disgusting. Consider it a compliment that he wants me. Go to Viktor, get the money and let's leave. I don't want to go to Mexico as a widow."

Igor continued to seethe. "You're going with me to Viktor's, Eve."

"Why?"

"Because it's important to me."

"Iggy, that's insane."

"Viktor is going to apologize to us both."

Eve got to her feet. "You are a crazy Russian, Igor Sakharov. That's what you are. Your pride is more important than your life, more important than me."

"Pride is not the issue," he said, caressing her cheek. "The truth is what matters. Just the truth."

SUNDAY SEPTEMBER 8TH

NORTH BEACH

Nick woke up with mixed emotions about life. On the one hand there was Billie, and on the other there was Bree. That pretty well summed up his current state of affairs. Potential joy and looming tragedy.

There was a certain irony in that. At the beginning of the trip the situation had been reversed. He'd left behind Dominick's California Cafe and hope for the future in order to assume family burdens and confront the past. Now a pregnant woman in New York was pulling him away from newfound joy.

The helplessness he felt in the face of a larger will stayed with him through breakfast, which he prepared in the deserted restaurant kitchen before the light of day. Since it was too early to confront a sleeping world, Nick decided to go for a walk.

Leaving the Clipper in the foggy dawn, he headed down Columbus Avenue toward the wharf. At that hour on a Sunday morning there wasn't much activity in the streets and everything and everyone he encountered had a hazy surreal quality. A newspaper delivery truck, a jogger, a homeless guy pushing a grocery cart loaded with his belongings, a slow-cruising patrol car, an old Chinese woman with a shopping bag going God knows where and a flock of pigeons pecking at the grass in Washington Square.

The heavy dampness of the air was bracing but, at the same time, depressing. San Franciscans tended not to let the fog affect them emotionally, knowing that a few hundred feet above them there was sun. Yet his worries weighed on him—his father, Gina and the kids, the Clipper, Joe's elusive killer, a pregnant girlfriend three thousand miles and light-years removed and, most immediately, Billie's disillusionment with him. Though she hadn't made a big deal of his incipient paternity problem, making light of it even, he could tell she'd been disheartened. And when he'd dropped her off at her place, she'd been both stoic and a bit cool. He would have preferred anger, but he got emotional distance, instead.

Billie had said good-night the second he'd stopped the car, bussed his cheek and, patting his knee, said practically the same thing he'd said to Bree. "Hang in there, sport." The words made him feel the distance between them. After Billie had seen a nude Linda Nassari waiting for him, maybe Bree's pregnancy was just too much for her to overlook. You didn't have to wrong a woman to fall from grace. It was enough simply not to measure up. He hated that.

"Don't bother to get out," she'd said. "Give me a call in the morning so we can confabulate about our case." With that she was out of the vehicle and gone.

For several minutes after her front door closed, he'd sat in his rental car feeling sorry for himself, realizing how easy it was for yesterday's pleasures to become today's issues. Whether the cause was sins of the flesh, simple shortcomings or chance events, it hardly mattered. The bottom line was the bottom line.

As Nick had driven away, he noticed a car parked up the street from Billie's place, a guy slumped behind the wheel. He probably wouldn't have thought twice about it but for the fact that the parked car's lights came on just after he passed and the vehicle turned around and followed him. His first thought was a jealous boyfriend, a prospect which pleased him, if only because it had the feel of quid pro quo. Maybe he should have been more concerned or curious, but he was too numb to care a whole lot. Even so, he tried to convince himself the tail needed to be addressed in some way, especially when the guy showed persistence.

They were on Geary, maybe halfway from downtown, when Nick went through a traffic light on caution with a cop car plainly visible at the cross street. He was within the law, but the tail had to slam on his brakes or risk being pulled over. The upshot was that he gave the guy the slip, thereby solving his problem, though he did make a mental note to mention the incident to Billie when he called her in the morning.

It was much too early for that now, so instead Nick walked the foggy streets, occupying himself with the poignant memories of his youth. The North Beach Playground, one of his favorite childhood haunts, was ahead, just past Greenwich. After crossing with the light, he went down the block a ways and stopped to look through the cyclone fence, recalling the countless hours he'd spent at the facility, whether playing ball or swimming. It was in this very pool that, at thirteen, he'd had his first genuine sexual encounter, giving Marcia Kramer a finger job while she slipped her hand in his trunks to explore his anatomy. Neither of them had been quite sure what to do with what they found, but one thing was certain—Marcia's technique needed refining. She'd damn near killed him when she'd squeezed his balls as though they were Play-Doh.

Glancing back up Columbus, he saw a man on foot approaching the traffic light. When the light changed, the guy stayed put on the corner, not crossing, even though the light was with him. Between the fog and the distance, it was difficult to see the guy's face clearly, but Nick had a sense of his demeanor, which was definitely strange. Nervousness, maybe? Continuing toward the wharf, Nick noticed the guy crossed Greenwich against the light. Another block and it was apparent that he was trying to keep pace.

Just to be sure he wasn't imagining things, Nick crossed to the west side of Columbus. The guy followed suit. He wondered if it could be the same man who'd followed him from Billie's place. Should he confront him and give him the what-for?

North Beach was Nick's home turf and the developing game of cat and mouse got his competitive juices flowing. Maybe he'd find out just how adventurous this bozo was willing to be.

Back in their youth, Nick and his friends used to sneak into the marina where the fishing boats were tied up. On a Saturday night there'd be nobody around, so they'd slip onto a boat for drunken orgies without anybody knowing about it until Monday morning when the skipper and his crew showed up and found the mess. Naturally, they couldn't just walk out onto the docks because of the security gates, but they'd found a secret access route via the rooftops of the adjoining restaurants.

Nick couldn't be sure everything was as it had been twenty years earlier, but it was worth a try. And if the guy followed him into the maze of docks, wanting an encounter, then Nick would have the advantage of surprise. It seemed better than a confrontation on the street.

Ducking down the alley where their access route began, he hurried to the end of the building. Before going around the corner, he glanced back. The guy was still in pursuit, but now he had a gun in his hand, which changed everything. Not only did it send Nick's pulse racing, but a direct confrontation was no longer an option. Worse, there were just two ways out—

back the way he'd come or up over the roof, leaving little room for maneuver.

Seeing he'd already overplayed his hand, Nick hurried to the spot where the old rusty fire escape had afforded him and his friends access to the roof. Unfortunately the apparatus had been removed, replaced by a fancier drop-down fire escape that was well out of reach from the ground. Next to it was a Dumpster piled high with crates. Knowing he had only seconds, Nick scrambled onto the Dumpster and, from the top of the crates, dived to the lower rung of the fire escape, which he barely caught.

His sore ribs screaming to high heaven, Nick pulled himself up. His weight caused the apparatus to slowly drop toward the ground, which would give his pursuer easy access. But he didn't have time to worry about that. He could hear someone running in the alley.

Scrambling up the ladder, he reached the roof as the guy skidded around the corner, giving Nick a glimpse of his face. He was fair, fortyish and completely unfamiliar. That was all Nick could tell in the split second they faced each other. Dashing across the tar and gravel roof, he reached the far side of the broad building where he and his friends used to descend another ladder to the dock. Of course, the ladder had been removed.

Back on the other side of the building the gunman appeared, weapon in hand. Nick looked down. It was a thirty-foot drop to the dock, promising a broken leg if not a broken back. A bit farther along was a large bin filled with fishing net. It didn't pose the softest landing place, but it would be a hell of a lot better than the dock. Moving opposite the bin, he leaped, landing on his butt atop the pile of net, knocking the wind out of him. Other than a good jolt, he wasn't hurt. Struggling to get his breath, he went over the side of the bin. At the same moment, the gunman appeared above him.

The guy raised his gun to fire, but Nick ducked behind

some crates before he could get off a shot. A fishing boat was moored behind him. Nick hopped aboard and ran across the deck as a shot rang out. The bullet whistled past, barely missing him. He realized it was a hell of a lot more than a game and dived over the gunnel, onto the deck of the adjoining boat. Taking a moment to glance back, he saw the gunman leap into the bin of net, apparently determined to continue the chase.

This was his opportunity to get off the boat and run like hell. The problem was he was on a finger dock with no route of escape. Determined to put distance between himself and the gunman, he hopped off the boat and started running toward the end of the dock. As he ran, he tried to decide if he should duck onto another boat and hide, or make for the water and swim across the access channel. He'd always been a good swimmer, but he didn't have much of a lead, and for a while he'd be within easy range, a sitting duck. A close encounter with an armed man seemed worse, though, so he opted for a swim, much as he didn't relish the icy water.

Running full tilt for the end of the dock, Nick saw the shadowy profile of a fishing boat in the fog, making its way through the narrow channel off to his left, headed for the bay. It was approaching the end of the dock and would pass by about the time Nick got there. In the split second available, he thought if he timed it just right, he might be able to make a running leap onto the deck of the boat. It depended on how close the vessel passed. The bow was already gliding by, which meant he might be too late. He envisioned himself missing, landing in the water and getting sucked into the boat's wake, only to be chopped up by the propeller.

With ten yards to go, he put on a final burst of speed, leaped, sailed through the air, only to slam against the side of the boat, though he did get his arms over the gunnel. Holding on for dear life, his legs streaming in the water, he felt a hand grabbing him by the back of the collar and pulling him onto the deck.

"What in Christ's name are you doing?"

Nick, on his back, looked up into the face of a fisherman. The guy wore a stocking cap, a bushy mustache and a deep frown. Nick was too winded to speak, but he did rise to his knees with the fisherman's help. Looking back, he saw the gunman on the end of the dock, his gun hand hanging at his side, an anguished, even distressed look on his face as he faded into the mists.

BURLINGAME

"I wouldn't know what Russian sounded like if I heard it," the head nurse of the Transitional Care Unit told Dickson Hong and Carl Plavec. "Spanish, sure, maybe German and French, but Russian? Sorry."

Hong and Plavec had been roaming the hospital, talking to as many ward nurses as they could find, looking for a Russian connection. They'd already checked Admissions and, after a lengthy search through the computer with the assistance of a clerk, found that nobody with a Slavic surname had been admitted to the hospital in the past month. "Ion Pacuraru," they decided was Romanian and "Edmund Wiecowski" was most likely Polish. "Pyotr Pimenov," a probable candidate, had been admitted to the hospital in July, but died in surgery within a day.

They wanted to check out the staff, but nobody was in personnel on a Sunday at that hour. Their plan had been to work backward, learning what they could about Olga Diachenko's routine, but the cleaning-staff supervisor wouldn't be in for a couple of hours, leaving them with little to do but wander from ward to ward.

Hong asked the head nurse about the schedule of the cleaning staff.

"I believe they rotate assignments on a regular basis, but I'm not really sure," the woman said.

"Do you recall seeing a cleaning woman of Ukrainian extraction, about sixty years of age, on the floor last week?" Hong asked.

"You know, Inspector, I'm so busy I just don't notice that kind of thing."

Another nurse entered the station where Hong and Plavec stood at the counter. Plavec yawned for the fourth or fifth time since the conversation had begun. He hadn't been pleased when Hong called him that morning to say they had to get their butts down to Peninsula Hospital.

"Dickson, it's six o'clock on a Sunday morning," Plavec had said. "This is my day off."

"You can sleep later."

"I was going to watch the 49ers later."

"You can do that next week."

Plavec remained an unhappy camper.

The head nurse turned to her associate. "Polly, do you recall seeing an older woman from the cleaning staff on the floor this week, a Ukrainian woman?"

"The little heavyset one who always wears the head scarf?"

"That could be her," Hong said, brightening. "Did you see her?"

The woman shook her head. "I haven't seen her for a couple of weeks now. You might try upstairs. I think the cleaning people switch floors every week or so."

"What's upstairs?"

"Intensive Care and the Cardiac Unit."

They trooped to the elevator. Plavec, smelling of coffee after spilling some on his trousers during the drive down, said, "What makes you so sure we're looking for a patient?"

"I'm not sure, but patients come and go. The Russian gunman could work here, but I'm betting he doesn't, since nobody has said anything Russian is familiar. To me that suggests a short time presence, but I could be wrong, of course."

"What I don't understand is why this couldn't wait until tomorrow."

An elevator arrived. It was empty. They stepped inside.

"Because we've got a killer on the loose," Hong said. "God knows who else he's targeted."

"Maybe nobody," Plavec said, pushing the floor button.

"You could be right, Carl, but he knows as well as we do that he didn't get Jolie Hays. She's in protective custody, but even so I still want the bastard under lock and key. If this is connected to the double homicide, the guy could have an enemy list. There's certainly no shortage of candidates connected to Culp and Sasso."

The car reached the floor, they stepped out.

"None of it makes any sense, Dickson. I think the guy's a crazy, myself."

"That would be worse."

"Unpredictable?"

"Yeah."

They started in Intensive Care, getting the same result as before, except that a couple of nurses recalled seeing Olga on the floor, but no Russian-speaking patients. Somewhat encouraged, they went to the Cardiac Unit next.

"Yes," one of the nurses said, "she was working here this past week."

"Was there anyone in the ward speaking Russian? Someone Olga might have had a conversation with?"

All three nurses shook their heads. "All our patients this past week were Americans," one said, opening a ledger.

Hong took his glasses from his jacket pocket and slipped them on, peering over the counter as the nurse read.

"Marion Quick, Walter Brown, a black gentleman. He's still here. Thomas, Grimes, Holtzman, Cardinas—I think he was Filipino. He passed away yesterday. Grace Van Pelt is still here. Mason. Grange."

"Mason, Sue," another nurse said. "Wasn't he the one who checked out suddenly after his wife arrived?"

"Yes, Tom Mason. Dr. Crane about had a heart attack himself when Mr. Mason said he was leaving."

"He and his wife were ordinary Americans," the first nurse said. "But that first day, he had an associate with him, as I recall. He did have an accent. Was it French?" She reflected. "No, no his name was 'French.'"

Dickson Hong and Carl Plavec looked at each other. "Jerry French?" Hong said.

"You know," the nurse replied, "I believe it was. He wasn't very nice. Grumpy, actually. And, as I recall, he had an accent."

"Where can we get more information on this guy, Mason, and his wife?" Hong asked.

"Admissions is your best bet."

"Come on, Carl," Dickson Hong said. "Let's go get our court order."

"Who you going to get on Sunday?"

"Judge Cohen. It's Saturday that he doesn't want to be disturbed." He was energized. It always happened when he felt there'd been a breakthrough.

They again headed for the elevators.

Plavec said, "So we've got French visiting somebody named Mason. What's your theory? We find Mason and he gives us French?"

"Yeah, but 'Jerry French' is probably an alias."

"'Tom Mason' might be an alias, too."

"Could be, Carl. But a guy can't be in a hospital without leaving prints behind. Hell, they probably have his blood here."

"I suppose you've got Mrs. Mason pegged as the FBI agent."

"Strong possibility."

They left the elevator and headed for the parking lot.

"You know what's best about this?" Plavec said.

"What?"

"We're working the case Lieutenant Buck assigned us. I mean, it's not our fault if it leads back to the double homicide, is it?"

"Carl, you've got the heart of a thief."

NORTH BEACH

Nick was taken ashore by the harbor police. He didn't have time to futz around making a report, so he obfuscated— "Goddamn process server." Not wanting to wait until he got back to the Clipper, he called Billie from the first pay phone he could find and told her what had happened.

"I like the bit about the process server," she said with a laugh. "Nice touch. How did you explain it? Paternity suit?"

"Not funny."

"Okay, I apologize. Anyway, it's a blessing. Another little Yankee fan is just what the world needs."

"Are you through, Counselor?"

"Sorry."

"The point is you could be in danger, Billie. I can't swear it was the same guy as last night, but if it was, he knows where you live."

"How do you know he has any interest in me at all? He followed you, not me, don't forget."

"There's no point in taking a chance."

"Thanks for the concern."

"Promise me you won't go out."

"Nick, don't give me that you-poor-little-thing-let-me-protect-you shit. I was cracking heads on the playground before you were born."

He was at a loss for words.

"I'm sorry," she said, "you didn't deserve that."

"Let's change the subject," he said, craving peace. "You ever hear from your friend, Naomi?"

"Yes, she called. Said she was in fear of her life and in hiding. She'd considered turning herself in to the police, but wasn't sure she could trust them. She was obviously in need of a friend and opened up a little for the first time."

"What did she say?"

"That she was in agony because she feels she's responsible for Sonny's death."

"How so?"

"She told me she has a draft pleading of Sonny's that explained everything, but she wouldn't elaborate. I said I'd represent her, go with her to the feds, whatever was necessary. She seemed to appreciate that. Told me she'd think about it and get back in touch."

"Sounds like you made some progress."

"Yes, but what I'm not sure is how much her uncertainty about the authorities is justified and how much of it is paranoia. Her fear was definitely palpable and that bothered me."

"It bothers me, too."

"Don't worry," Billie said, "you'll be safe with me."

"That's what I've been waiting to hear."

"Okay, are we finished?" Billie said.

"No, we've got to make plans. What shall we do today? Casewise, I mean."

"I've been thinking about just that, as a matter of fact. I have an old boyfriend named Wilson Dahl who's a bankruptcy trustee. I thought I'd pay him a visit and see if he has any suggestions."

"Good idea. I'm going to be talking to Todd Easley, that bankruptcy attorney who represented Joe, on Monday. Maybe your friend will have some tips on how to deal with him, what questions to ask and so forth."

"Are you angling to go with me?"

"Would you mind?"

Billie didn't answer right away, presumably to indicate her

general disapproval with him. "Let me call and get a feel for the situation," she said. "I'll get back to you after we've spoken."

"I should be at the Clipper in fifteen or twenty minutes."

"Fine." She grunted a goodbye and hung up.

Nick called a cab. When it pulled up in front of the restaurant, Benny Vocino was pacing out front, blowing cigar smoke into the damp morning air. Nick stepped out of the taxi, taking a quick look at the street to make sure his mystery friend hadn't come back for an instant replay.

Benny checked out Nick's trousers, still wet, but no longer dripping. "What happened to you?"

"I missed the boat."

Benny didn't smile. "I won't ask."

"What brings you to the Clipper before we open?" Nick asked as he fished in his pocket for the door key.

"I wanted to talk."

"What about?" Nick opened the door and motioned for Benny to enter.

"Will I get the gas chamber for carrying this into a restaurant before hours?" he asked, indicating the cigar.

"Not if I don't report you."

Benito Vocino walked through the door, which Nick locked behind them. Benny followed him through the dark dining room.

"Hungry?" Nick asked.

"I'd take a cup of coffee."

"Let's go into the kitchen."

"Oh, if it's not made, don't bother."

"No, I'd like one myself."

They went into the kitchen. Nick made coffee in the big urn, as he'd learned to do at sixteen. Benny sat on a stool, alternately watching and shaping the ash from his cigar on the rim of a dirty cup.

They made idle conversation about Joe's impending funeral and the pennant race. When the coffee was ready, Nick put a cup in front of Benny, another on the other side of the worktable, then went and got some sugar cubes.

After the honorary mayor of North Beach prepared his coffee just so, he tapped the teaspoon on the rim and tucked it behind the cup. "Here's the deal," he said. "I talked to Elaine last night and picked up a very interesting piece of news." Benny drew on his cigar, hollowing his cheeks. Then he blew the smoke to the side with a triumphant air, as though letting the governor have it right in the face. "She says she has been offered information on the whereabouts of all Joe's money. It's a file with offshore account numbers and all that good stuff. It won't do her much good unless you and Gina want to invest it in the Emerald Buddha. But by the same token, you could have a hell of a time tracking the money down and might lose it altogether without the file."

Nick pondered what he'd just heard. If not blackmail, it was arm-twisting for sure. "And what if we're not interested in investing?"

"I think the point is that she *wants* you to be interested."

"Or else?"

"Yeah," Benny said, tapping his ash. "Or else."

"In other words, she wants me to buy a lottery ticket that may or may not pay off."

"No, actually she wants *me* to buy the ticket and give it to you."

"Why you?"

Benny studied his cigar. "Let's put it this way, I figure I owe you, and maybe I owe her, too."

"What'll it cost you, if you don't mind me asking?"

"The guy's asking a hundred G's, but I'm getting it for fifty, which I consider a bargain."

"Mighty expensive lottery ticket," Nick said, sipping his coffee.

Benny drank some of his coffee as well. "True."

"What do you get out of it?" Nick asked. "A clear conscience?"

"There's always that, yeah."

"Anything else?"

"Well," Benny said, fiddling with the handle of his coffee cup, "if you and Gina make the investment and it pays off big time, then you give me a hundred G's."

"Double your money."

"Yes, Nicky, but only if the pony comes in. I'm on the line with you. No Buddha and I'm out a Mercedes."

"I guess you didn't get rich by giving all your money to charity."

"No, it's the other way around. I got rich, which means I've got something to give to charity. There's been a time when Tony's seen a few of my nickels."

"For which we will be eternally grateful."

Benny grew serious. "Do you want to play, Nicky, or don't you? What should I tell Elaine?"

"I would like to know a little more."

"Like?"

"Where this file came from, for example."

"I don't really know. Honestly. Elaine says she can put her hands on it, and I believe her."

"Could she be the one who took it?"

"She claims she's a go-between."

"Seems to be her role in life. But you don't know who the seller is?"

"I have no idea."

"Let's talk a little more about the file. It was Sonny Culp's, wasn't it? It was the one Martin Fong had, the one he promised Billie he'd turn over to the police."

"I don't know anything about that," Benny said. "I'm assured it contains information that will enable you to put your hands on Joey's money and I'm willing to bet fifty grand it will do just that."

Nick pondered that. "Let's say, hypothetically, that Gina and I get the money out of Joe's offshore accounts. And let's say we pay off the mortgage on her house and repay what Joe borrowed from the bank against the Clipper. That much comes off the top, in other words, leaving the balance to finance the Buddha expedition."

"We're talking..."

"In round figures, a million bucks."

"But the Buddha will cost two mil."

"That's my question, Benny. Do we know anybody who'd put up the other million?"

"You saying like, for example, me?"

"That's exactly what I'm saying."

Benito Vocino thought. "And we split the cash-investor share fifty-fifty?"

"Yeah. If Ken Lu is to be believed, that's fifteen million each."

The honorary mayor of North Beach chuckled. "You got Maria's moxie and Tony's balls, you know that, Nicky."

"I take that as a compliment."

"So intended." Benny admired his cigar. "I don't know, Nicky, what do you think? Can we pull this off?"

"To be honest, I'm not eager to do business with Elaine Chang. I'm told she's been involved in shady deals and gets attention from the cops. On the other hand, now we've got nothing and she's offering to change that."

"At no particular risk to you and Gina, I might add. She gets her house paid off, there's money to clean up the Clipper's finances, plus Gina gets a lottery ticket that could pay big bucks. The guy taking the risk at this point is me."

"I've been wondering about that, Benny. How'd you get involved with Elaine Chang in the first place?"

"Let's just say the lady knows how to sniff out money." He waved his cigar at Nick. "I wasn't involved with her in any personal way, if that's what you're thinking. She knows people who know people who know me. Let's just leave it at that, okay?"

Nick considered that, seeing little downside to the deal. "When would we get the file?"

"As soon as I lay down the fifty."

Nick thought some more. "Okay, let's do it, but there's a condition. I get to talk to Elaine Chang."

"What for?"

"I have a few questions for her."

"She wants this deal to go through. I guess I could prevail upon her."

"Then we've got a deal."

Benny looked at him sternly. "Tony and I always shook hands."

Nick took Benito Vocino's hand.

BURLINGAME

Their court order in hand, Hong and Plavec returned to Peninsula Hospital where they were directed to Medical Records. The supervisor checked the order and produced Tom Mason's file. They didn't care about the medical information for the moment. The personal data was what mattered.

"It'll take a while to track this guy down," Carl Plavec said after they'd copied down Mason's address and phone number, social security number and so forth.

They'd pretty much decided Tom Mason was not only an alias, but the address in San Diego was bogus. Chances were, none of it was legitimate.

"You don't have insurance information on the guy?" Hong asked the supervisor.

She took the file and flipped through it. "It looks like the bill was paid in cash."

"Do you have a copy of the final bill?"

"Yes, I'm sure it's in here." The woman located it.

Dickson Hong studied it. "There's a phone charge, I see. Is there a record of where the call was made?"

"It wouldn't be in the file, but I should be able to get it. Could take a while."

"We have all day."

Plavec gave Hong a look.

"Carl, you'll know you're headed for the top when you're on the job and don't even notice it's Sunday."

It took a while but the woman returned with a telephone number. The area code indicated the northern portion of Los Angeles County. Hong tapped the slip of paper.

"Whoever has this number should be able to tell us something about Tom Mason," he said.

"You want to call?"

"No, let's talk to the police down there. Why give Mason any warning? I'd like them to pick him up for questioning."

"We're going to L.A.?"

"Could be."

BRENTWOOD

West L.A. was sunny and clear, the palm trees brushing the sky everywhere you looked, it seemed. As they wound their way in the hills, Igor had just one thought. The American phase of his life was about to end. That wasn't tragic, he told himself, only inconvenient. A few days ago, it had all damn near ended in a hospital up in the Bay Area. This way, at least, there was promise of another chapter in the tale of the poor Russian boy and the American stripper-madam-businesswoman he loved.

"When we get to Viktor's I'm going to stay in the car while you get the money," Eve said.

"No, you're going in with me."

"Iggy, why are you being so goddamn stubborn about this?"

"Because I want the truth and the only way I'll get it is if I can see both your faces at the same time."

"You don't trust me."

"That's not the issue."

"The hell it's not!" she said sharply. "I'm your wife and you won't accept my word. I'm insulted."

"Don't be, Eve. I know that what you're doing you're doing for me. But I still want the truth."

"Why is that so goddamn important?" she demanded.

Igor looked over at her, taking his eye off the road.

"Look out!" she screamed.

He looked up just in time to see a kid racing down the hill on a bike, headed right for them. Igor swerved, missing the kid by inches. He clutched his hand to his chest.

"You're going to be dead before we get to Orange County," she said. "I just know it."

"It's so goddamn important," he said, returning to her question, "because this way I'll never have to wonder."

"I'll tell you exactly what happened when we get to Mexico. How's that?"

"No."

"Stubborn bastard."

Within minutes they reached the driveway of Viktor Chorny's house. The place had once been owned by an Iranian millionaire, a second cousin of the shah or something. It was gaudy, even by Eve's standards, the foundations of which, she freely admitted, had been "laid in a whorehouse." Igor drove through the lion gates and stopped at the front door.

Eve looked at him, her expression bitter and fearful. "You might as well put a gun to your head."

"Did Viktor put a gun to yours, Eve?"

"Why don't you ask him?"

"I guess I'll have to," he said, opening the door.

"Iggy, please..." she groaned.

"Get out, my darling."

He went around to the passenger side, opening the door for her. She slipped out of the seat, refusing his hand. They went to the front door.

Viktor Chorny answered the door in his bathrobe, looking like a walrus enveloped in a pup tent. He had a pint of ice cream in his hand, the handle of a spoon protruding from the top.

"Well," he said with icy coolness, "if it isn't Monsieur and Madame Sakharov. To what do I owe this unexpected pleasure?"

"We've come for our money," Igor said. "The San Francisco lawyer and the other guy."

Viktor peered beyond them as though he was looking for FBI agents in the sago palms. "Come in. We can't discuss this out here."

They stepped into the marble entry embellished with a huge gold-framed mirror and Greek statuary. Viktor showed flickering signs of discomfort.

"Would you like something to eat or drink?"

"No," Igor said, "I've had my morning ice cream, thank you."

"You're in a foul mood, Igor Andreyevich. Nothing I've said, I hope."

"No, you're the hallmark of diplomacy, Viktor."

"You want your money, you say."

"Yes."

"What about Alexei?"

"Your agreement is with me," Igor said. "I'll settle with

my brother later. The work he's doing for you now is between you and him."

Chorny peered into the carton in his hand. Unable to resist, he picked up the spoon and took a large mouthful, savoring the ice cream even as he reflected. "There's a small problem. I don't have that much money on hand. Only twenty thousand or so. I can advance you that much and give you the balance in a few days."

"Give us everything you've got," Igor said.

"Why don't you go into the salon and make yourselves at home? I'll get the money."

"We'll go with you," Igor said.

"I'm just going to the bedroom."

"That's fine."

"But I would prefer you wait here."

"Viktor," Eve said, "be glad Iggy is being as polite as he is. Trust me, this could get very unpleasant. I advise you not to push your luck."

Chorny looked back and forth between them, seeming to divine the situation without having to ask. "Very well."

They followed him back through the meandering house, Viktor taking the opportunity to have a few bites of ice cream. They finally reached the master suite with its huge heart-shaped bed and paintings of naked women on the walls, some reproductions of famous pieces of art. Igor noticed his wife shiver.

Chorny gestured for them to sit in the love seat opposite the bed. Eve sat, Igor did not. Putting the carton down on a table, Viktor went to the rather artful copy of Ingres's *Odalisque* on the side wall and pulled on one end so that it swung on its hinges, revealing the huge wall safe. Turning to face them, he folded his fat hands together in a prayerful pose, looking like an albino sumo wrestler.

"Before I open the safe, perhaps you'd be good enough to

say whatever else is on your mind, Igor Andreyevich. My instincts tell me you're here to discuss more than money."

"Iggy doesn't trust me, Viktor," Eve said. "I told him that I—"

"Quiet, Eve," Igor snapped. "This is between Viktor and me." He looked hard into Chorny's eyes. "Comrade Colonel, may I ask what you did to my wife while I was in San Francisco?"

Viktor's beady little eyes narrowed in calculation, shifting back and forth between Igor and his wife. "I spoke to her inappropriately," he finally said. He waited.

"Is that all?"

Viktor Chorny shrugged.

Igor glanced at Eve, who was on the edge of the seat. Then he looked back at his longtime boss. "I don't believe you, Viktor."

Chorny threw up his hands in a helpless way. "Eve, what did *you* tell him?"

"Never mind that," Igor roared, advancing on the blimp of a man.

Viktor braced himself. Igor seized the lapels of his robe. Switching to Russian, he screamed, "Tell me what you did, you filthy scumbag!"

Eve rushed over, grabbing his arm. "Iggy, he tied me up, covered me with ice cream and licked it off!"

Igor turned. "What?" he said in disbelief.

"That's it, the whole truth. I swear."

He was in shock, disbelief.

"Please, Iggy, let it go. Your life is more important than this. It was disgusting, but it's over. He didn't hurt me." Eve's eye rounded as she looked past him. Igor spun around only to see Viktor drop to the floor like a hippo who'd been shot between the eyes. His splotchy pink thighs protruded from his robe, less repulsive than they might have been only because of the grotesqueness of the rolls on his stomach. His private parts were lost in the rubbery heap. But more importantly, Chorny clutched at his chest, making a horrible gurgling sound in his throat.

Igor could easily imagine what was going on inside the mountainous body.

"My heart," Viktor squeaked. "Call an ambulance."

Igor got the portable phone from the table beside the bed. Eve followed, snatching it from his hand. She returned to the spot where Chorny lay on the white carpet.

"What's the combination of the safe, Viktor?" she demanded.

"Oh, please, call. I'm dying."

Igor tried to take the phone from her hand, but she refused to let him have it.

"The combination, Viktor!"

Chorny gasped out the numbers, wheezing as he fought for air. Eve tossed the phone onto the bed, went to the safe and opened it. Reaching in she took out a gun, which she handed to Igor. Then she began pulling out bundles of twenty- and hundred-dollar bills.

"Get some pillowcases, Iggy," she commanded. "And leave the phone on the bed."

He got the pillowcases from the bed and brought them to Eve. She filled them with money. Igor figured there had to be several hundred thousand dollars in the sacks.

"My heart," Chorny pleaded. "Please...phone."

"Come on, Iggy," Eve said. "If he wants the phone, he can crawl over and get it." She picked up one of the sacks and headed for the door.

Igor looked down at the man whose orders he'd followed for so many years, hating him, but also feeling his pain. Chorny looked up at him like a pitiful child, a baby elephant. Igor went to the bed and got the phone. Returning to the former KGB colonel, he said in a soft voice, "What did you do to my wife that night, Viktor?"

"Licked her...ice cream...I swear."

"Nothing more?"

"Nothing more."

Keeping the phone in his hand, Igor headed for the door.

"For the love...of God," Chorny cried. "Igor. I swear it...on my soul. If there...was more. I would...say so. What do I have to...lose at this point?"

Igor, near the door, tossed the phone and Chorny caught it in the air. Trembling, he began punching the keys with his chubby fingers.

Igor Andreyevich Sakharov slung the sack of money over his shoulder and walked out of the room.

Eve waited for him in the car. She did not ask him what had happened. Igor turned to her and said, "Where to? Home to get your things?"

"No, Iggy, let's head straight for Mexico. Viktor can buy me a new wardrobe."

Igor caressed her cheek.

"I'm mad at you," she said.

"Why?"

"Because you wouldn't accept my word."

"You'd lie to keep me alive, Eve. I know you."

"What difference does it make what Viktor did? Isn't what matters what *I* did?"

He started the engine. "I just feel better knowing the truth."

"You can be a pain in the ass, Iggy, you know that?"

"Do you forgive me?"

"No."

He put the car in gear and drove into the street. They were halfway down the hill when Eve said, "Well, maybe a little."

PRESIDIO HEIGHTS

Henry Chin, pacing back and forth in the front room of his home, had been hoping for a phone call from Bart Carlisle saying that Nick Sasso, Billie Fox and Naomi Watts were dead, but it hadn't happened. Did that mean it wouldn't happen or that it simply hadn't happened yet? His life depended on the answer to that question, and until he got it, he would continue to hang in limbo, completely dependent on the capabilities of an unknown assassin.

Joyce sat in her chair by the window reading, just as she had been for the past half hour. Ling Ling was wedged next to her, his chin resting on her lap. Joyce had been silent, moving only to turn the pages of her book and stroke her dog's head. There were two sounds in the room—the clock ticking on the mantel and the whisper of Chin's slippers on the thick carpet.

From time to time he glanced at his wife, but she never looked up. Only Ling Ling's eyes followed him from one side of the room to the other. Henry hated the dog, more even than his marriage.

Joyce, for her part, was being neither impolite nor indifferent. She was respecting his wishes to be left alone. It was his wife's greatest virtue as far as he was concerned—she gave him space and she didn't intrude. Ironically, though, he yearned for interaction of some sort. With anybody. The silence was getting to him.

"I think I'd like some tea," he said.

Joyce, her hair and nails perfect, calmly placed the marker in her book and closed it. "Shall I make some, then?"

"Please," he said.

Joyce—little changed over the course of their marriage, except for the lines on her face, the slight pooch of her stomach and her self-imposed aloofness—rose from her chair and, leaving Ling Ling, went off to the kitchen. Henry continued to stride back and forth, awaiting the release of death. Not his own, of course, theirs.

The telephone rang. Henry went into the study to answer it.

"Henry," Bart Carlisle said, "we need to talk."

"The playground?"

"No, this is urgent. I'm in my car, headed your way. I'll pick you up in front of your house. Ten minutes okay?"

Henry, his heart racing in response to the urgency of Bart's tone, went upstairs for a pair of shoes. Back in the entry hall he took his car coat from the closet. He was about to go out the door when Joyce entered the front room, carrying a tray with a teapot and a pair of cups and saucers. She looked toward him questioningly.

"I don't have time now," he said. "I have an appointment." He peered out the window and saw that Bart wasn't there yet. Even so, he didn't want to stay inside. He left, descending the steps to the sidewalk where he stood waiting in the cold fog. A couple of minutes later, Bart Carlisle's Mercedes came around the corner and pulled up in front of him. Henry opened the door and slipped into the seat. Bart immediately took off.

"What's going on?" Henry demanded.

"Wilson Dahl got a phone call this morning from Billie Fox. She said she and Nick Sasso wanted to talk to him about bankruptcy."

"Oh, shit."

"Precisely. Fortunately Wilson had the presence of mind to put her off."

"Did she give any indication of what she wanted?"

"Wilson's impression was that it was a fact-finding mission, probably looking for suggestions or advice."

"Then they don't know."

"He thinks not. I'm concerned it's a trap," Bart said.

Henry reflected. "I suppose she and Sasso could be suspicious, but they can't have too good an idea what's going on, or they wouldn't blithely beard the lion in his den. And she couldn't be a front for the police. I'd know."

"What do you think's going on, then?"

"I suspect they're starting to put things together and bankruptcy came up, raising questions in their minds."

"I thought we had all of Culp's and Sasso's files and records."

"Something might have been overlooked, or a remark made that was repeated. I've worried that something like this would happen." Henry turned to him. "If she and the other two were dead, Bart, we wouldn't be having this conversation."

"I'm told my man is on the case, Henry. Naomi Watts dropped out of sight after shooting the P.I. we had watching her, so she may be hard to track down. I've got people on that, as we speak. But to the best of my knowledge, Nick Sasso and Billie Fox are wandering around oblivious."

"Let's hope they stay that way until they're eliminated."

"Yes, but we can't count on it for long," Carlisle said.

Bart Carlisle drove aimlessly toward the beach. Henry looked out the window at the fog-shrouded houses and continued to ponder the situation.

"You know, Bart, I wonder if this call Wilson got might not be the opportunity we've been looking for."

"What do you mean?"

"Perhaps we should turn the tables and set a trap for *them*," Henry Chin explained. "Wilson can call her back and invite her to meet with him at some suitable location. Your Russian can be lying in wait. He kills them and we're down to one remaining obstacle."

"They *have* handed us the opportunity, haven't they?"

"On a platter, Bart. I suggest you get hold of Wilson and your hit man. Work out a plan, get things rolling. I don't have to remind you, I assume, that time is of the essence."

"I'll arrange it," Bartholomew Carlisle II said.

The Mercedes twisted down Point Lobos Avenue, headed for the Great Highway. Henry Chin, glum, pondered life on the tightrope. This couldn't have been his father's dream for him. Somewhere, somehow, he had gone wrong. It was too late to do anything about it now, though. Bargains with the devil could not be undone.

INGLESIDE

Nick had a hard time finding a parking place anywhere near the nursing home. It was, after all, Sunday and people tended to visit on Sunday. The place somehow seemed more cheerful than his last visit, but he suspected it was due to his state of mind rather than any actual difference in conditions. The sound of children's voices emanated from some rooms, which could account for it. Though he'd had little experience with kids, people did say they were supposed to lighten the heart.

That thought was followed by one less uplifting—Bree, or more specifically, her possible pregnancy. Those four words— "I think I'm pregnant"—certainly packed a wallop. The truth was, he hadn't really come to terms with the notion. Bree's feelings about it were a mystery, though maybe deep down she'd telegraphed them more clearly than he was willing to admit. There'd been signs her feelings for him ran deeper than she'd allowed—that business with her parents, for example—but he'd turned a blind eye to the evidence. Could this be a little test she'd concocted? he wondered. Somehow he doubted she'd make it up, but he wouldn't put it past her to take advantage of the opportunity to find out where he stood.

How did he tell her he wasn't interested in pursuing a committed relationship? "Sorry, babe, but I love somebody else?" Or, "Yeah, I've only known her a few days, but the woman's fabulous, knocked me on my butt." No, that didn't seem the way to talk to someone who might be carrying your child. The simple fact was he'd gotten himself into a hell of a mess. Unless the rabbit lived.

But he couldn't worry about that now. He had to deal with his father, then get back to business, rejoin the battle. But the hell of it was, this wasn't just his fight. He and Billie were both in danger. That was the most distressing fact of all.

He'd called her again before leaving the Clipper. "I'm headed out to Ingleside to see my old man. Want to come and meet him?"

"I'd love to, Nick, but I want to spend as much time as I can with Emily and Pop."

"You're staying in, then."

"Yes, and if it'll make you feel any better, I'm keeping an eye on the street. No suspicious characters lingering about. Nobody's tried to break down the door."

"I have no doubts you can handle it even if a platoon of house invaders attack. I have every confidence in you, Billie."

"I'll hand this to you, Nick, you're a quick study."

"Maybe I should have gone to law school."

"I wouldn't go that far. A bright pasta genius is nothing to sneeze at. You're doing okay."

They weren't exactly words of hope, but he wanted to believe the shock of Bree's news had begun to wear off and that he might be allowed into Billie's good graces again. He decided to take a stab. "Okay if I swing by after I see the old man? Maybe your buddy, the bankruptcy guy, will have gotten back to you."

"Sure," she'd said, "why not?"

That had given him a lift. It was time the ball started taking a few good hops.

Nick came to his father's room. The old man was propped up in bed, watching the Giants on TV. Seeing Nick, he brightened, his mouth opening and his lip quivering before he managed to croak, "Hi...son." He got the words out, but speech was clearly a problem.

Nick went to the bed and kissed him. "What's this, you so desperate you'll watch the Giants?"

Tony waved off the comment, as if to say, "It's better than *The Price Is Right*."

Sitting beside him, Nick took his father's bony hands. "Sorry about Joey, Dad. It's a terrible, terrible thing."

Tony opened his mouth again. Nick could hear words rumbling in the old man's throat, trying to escape. "Did...they...find..."

"The guy who did it?"

The old man nodded.

"Not yet, but they're working hard on it. And so am I, by the way. Figured there was no reason to let my sleuthing genius go to waste."

Tony smiled with one side of his mouth. "Don't... quit...son."

"Don't worry, I've taken your advice to heart, Dad. Since we last spoke I've made some progress, both in getting my act together and in taking care of our problems. Benny and I are working a deal, as a matter of fact. There's a good chance I'll be able to save the Clipper and provide Gina and the kids some security. I know Joey would have wanted that."

The old man squeezed his hands, signaling his approval, but didn't try to speak. It was obviously too much of a struggle for him.

"There's no plan for the funeral yet," Nick went on, trying to anticipate everything his father would likely ask about, "but we should know something in a day or two. Gina or I will keep you posted."

More hand squeezes.

"On a happier note, I'm going to bring a lady friend around to meet you one of these days." Nick saw a sparkle in the old man's eye and he couldn't help but chuckle. "We're just friends for now, but there's sparks in the air. Don't know what it might lead to, but I like her quite a bit. Thought that might give you a lift."

Tony's lip trembled again.

"What's she like?" Nick said for him. "Well, she's smart

as hell. A lawyer, wouldn't you guess. Ballsy. Funny. And...well, if you must know, she has a great ass."

Another crooked smile. Tony's eyes filled with tears.

Nick felt his own well with emotion. There was something else he'd intended to say and he figured there may never be a better opportunity, so he launched into what was on his mind.

"On a more serious note, there's something I've been meaning to say for a long time, so if you'll bear with me." He cleared his throat. "First, I want you to know I love you. I'm sure you never doubted that. I just want to get it on the table, so that we're both clear on the point."

Nick checked and, as he feared, a tear ran down the old man's cheek. He cleared his throat again.

"The next thing is I want you to know I'm sorry for all the times I fucked up. But I'm not sorry I wasn't the second coming of Joe DiMaggio, by the way. That one you'll just have to live with. I am who I am and that's got to be good enough. But I have fallen short at times, not doing as well as I could. Those are the times I'm sorry for, especially when they hurt and disappointed you."

There was another tear on the old man's cheek. Nick wiped this one away with his thumb.

"I figured we kind of needed to clear the air about that."

Nick looked into Tony Sasso's eyes, his own filling as the painful lump in his chest grew to melon proportions. He gave a little cough, trying to get the bubble out of his throat.

"I don't want to speak for you or anything, Dad, but in case you're thinking there's a thing or two you're sorry about...well, you can figure I hear you. Everybody screws up now and again, no reason to think you're immune any more than me. Nobody's perfect. So, to the degree that's an issue, I don't want you to worry about it. Consider yourself heard."

A very firm squeeze of the hands.

Nick looked into the old man's eyes. "So, is there anything else I can do, anything you need?"

Another crooked smile, another tear, a grunt and a barely discernible, "No...son."

For a couple of minutes they watched the game together, holding hands. Nick told his father he was going over to have dinner with Gina and the kids. "Wish you could come."

A nod.

"The nurse says you're getting stronger. So, maybe next time."

A sad smile. "Maybe."

It was an exciting part of the game. The Giants were making a comeback in the late innings. Though the Sassos were inveterate Yankee fans, they were also San Franciscans and the truth was, the Giants was their second favorite team, even if they would never admit it publicly.

When Barry Bonds finally drove in the lead run with a double against the left-centerfield wall, Nick glanced at his father and found him asleep. Slipping his hand from Tony's grasp, he left the nursing home for the world—not the *real* world, he realized, because in ways *this* was the real world, what everything came down to in the end.

Walking back to his car, it cheered him to think of Billie. He hoped she'd be warmer to him. Nick Sasso was a tough customer in his way, but even the most macho stud occasionally needed a hug.

THE RICHMOND

Billie, who'd been curled up on the sofa with Emily most of the afternoon, watching the Giants, considered putting on a dress, but in the end opted to stay in her jeans. Between innings she'd added a touch of makeup—minimal and subtle because she didn't want it to look as if she was making a special effort. Men who got off the hook too easily began to take forgiveness for granted. In her experience, that was to be avoided. Then, too, there was a certain amount of confusion in her mind as to how she felt about Nick. In point of fact, he was a very confounding man.

Usually she came to pretty quick conclusions about a guy, knowing what degree of emotional and physical intimacy he'd be accorded. And, more often than not, she stuck with the judgment she made. Sonny had called her decisive, and she was. Plus, she wasn't afraid. She'd never been a fragile flower. But she did have her weaknesses. Whether by intention or accident, Nick Sasso seemed to have winnowed his way into her soft heart.

When the doorbell rang, Emily jumped up and went streaking for the door.

"Hold on, honey," Billie called after her. "Let Mommy see who's there before we open the door."

Billie shuffled to the entry in stocking feet. Looking through the peephole, she saw that it was Nick. He was nicely dressed in a jacket and tie. She immediately thought it had been a mistake not to put on a dress. Well, too late now.

"Mommy, can I open the door?"

"Okay, honey."

Emily pulled the door open. Nick stood there, his face only moderately discolored, the swelling practically gone, an ordinary Band-Aid on his cheek. Emily jumped up and down excitedly.

"Oh, goody, you're not dead!"

Billie and Nick both laughed, though it was a rather sad commentary on the state of affairs.

He said, "Yeah, sweetheart, I'm rather pleased about that myself."

Billie shook her head. "Out of the mouths of babes."

"She *does* have a point, Billie."

Emily took Nick by the hand and dragged him inside, looking up at him with such seeming pleasure. He gave Billie a wink.

"I prayed for a warm reception, but God and I apparently got our wires crossed."

"You know what they say, be careful what you wish for because you might get it."

He checked her out and Billie hated herself for not dressing up. "Everybody seems to be healthy and happy," he said as Emily tugged on his arm, leading him into the front room.

"We've had a nice quiet day," Billie said, following along behind them.

"Better safe than sorry."

They settled on the sofa, with Emily between them. The ball game had ended and the postgame wrap-up was in progress.

"I don't suppose you have any idea about the identity of your unsavory friend, do you?" she asked, referring to his game of cat and mouse, shoot and duck that morning.

"No, but I have to assume it's a result of something we've been doing."

"That covers a lot of territory."

"The one area I couldn't check out was jealous boyfriends," he said. Nick glanced down at Emily to see if he'd been sufficiently circumspect.

Billie decided to take no chances. "Hey, pumpkin," she said to her daughter, "would you go in and see what Grandpop is doing? Maybe you can keep him company for a while."

"I want to stay here," the girl protested.

"I'm sure you do, but Nick and I need to talk business and you won't find it very interesting."

Emily reluctantly got to her feet, slouching away after Billie gave her a little pat on the behind. The girl stopped at the door. "After, can we go for pizza with Nick?"

"Not today."

"Another time, Emily," he said.

"Promise?"

Nick turned to Billie. She glared at him, narrowing her eyes. "Sneaky bastard," she whispered. Then to Emily, "We'll see, honey. Now run along."

Emily left. Nick beamed. "God works in mysterious ways," he said.

"I say again, sneaky bastard."

"Back to my question. Could he have been a jealous boyfriend?"

"No, of course not."

"Why not?"

"Because I don't have any boyfriends, jealous or otherwise."

"That's surely not true."

"Well, it is, thank you very much. So, let's move on to a more fruitful line of questioning. What's your theory about the stalker?"

Nick shrugged. "I really haven't a clue, Billie. I'm out of fresh ideas. The most obvious candidate would have to be the guy who shot Joe and Sonny, I suppose, but I'm not eager to get shot just so the lab guys could do a comparison ballistics test."

"It would give new meaning to the expression 'taking one for the team.'"

"Yeah, right."

They looked at one another for a long moment before Billie folded her arms over her chest and glanced away. Being with him like this was both pleasant and uncomfortable—the tension between desire and common sense. Nick seemed to be playing it smart, which was good and bad. But there was no escaping the reality of his pregnant girlfriend. Oddly, Billie felt sorry for him, even though he'd disappointed her.

"I have some good news," Nick said, seemingly intent on keeping things positive. "It looks like we have a stab at recovering some of the money Joe squirreled away for the expedition to recover the Emerald Buddha." Nick told her about his meeting with Benny that morning, recounting Elaine Chang's offer.

Billie listened until he was finished. "So, you're going to do business with the Black Widow of Chinatown," she said, hoping her suspicions and jealousy didn't show.

"I want to find out what she knew about Joe's and Sonny's dealings, among other things."

"Could one of the other things be to find out why she's so irresistible?"

A slight smile touched his lips. "Do you really think I'm that mercenary or that stupid?"

"Nick, you're a man. But never mind, that's your problem."

The telephone rang. Billie waited to see if her father would get it and he did.

Nick looked unhappy. He'd painted himself in a corner with her and she could tell he knew it. Her own pride and self-respect prevented her from letting him off the hook. It was unfortunate in a way, but that was just the way things were.

"Wilhelmina," Mel Fox said from the kitchen door, "it's for you. Wilson Dahl."

"Oh," Billie said, getting up. "Perfect timing." She went to the phone. "Hi, Wilson."

"Billie, I'm sorry it's taken me so long to get back to you, but we've got out-of-town company, in-laws, and my wife's kept me pretty busy today."

"I understand."

"I'm looking at my calendar. Tomorrow morning is really crowded. But I had an idea. I was given a luxury box at tomorrow afternoon's game between the Giants and the Astros. I know you're a big fan. I thought we could combine business and pleasure. How about your friend? Does he like baseball?"

"Does he like baseball?" Billie said, glancing back across the room at Nick. "Wilson, he's Joe DiMaggio's illegitimate son."

"Ah, no kidding. Too bad they aren't playing the Yankees, then," Wilson Dahl quipped.

"For sure. As it happens, Nick's here now. Let me ask if tomorrow afternoon would work." She covered the mouthpiece. "He's got a luxury suite for tomorrow's game. Could you stomach the Giants for the sake of justice?"

"It'd be a sacrifice, but the real treat will be an afternoon with you."

"With me *and* a former lover."

"I'm already jealous."

Billie gave him a look, then returned to her conversation. "Tomorrow afternoon is good for both of us, Wilson."

"Fine. How about if we meet outside the stadium at the foot of the statue of Willie Mays? Shall we say twelve forty-five?"

"Perfect."

"See you tomorrow at twelve forty-five, then?"

"We'll be there in our Giants hats."

She hung up, beaming. Nick, on the other hand, looked a bit grumpy.

"What's the matter?"

"I was with you up until that last remark," he said.

"About the Giants hats?"

"Yeah."

Billie laughed. "Don't worry, Nick, wearing the enemy uniform gets you shot only in time of war."

MONDAY SEPTEMBER 9TH

SOUTH OF MARKET

Nick was waiting in the hallway outside Todd Easley's law offices when his secretary arrived. "Do you have an appointment?" she asked, unlocking the door.

"No, I thought maybe Mr. Easley could give me a few minutes of his time."

"I don't think he'll see you. It really is best to have an appointment."

"I'm sure he can find a few minutes for me," Nick replied. "When is he due in?"

"I expect him in the next fifteen or twenty minutes."

The woman, fortyish, plain, stern, humorless, was not pleased. But she allowed Nick to wait. He sat on the cracked leather sofa and watched her prepare for her day's work, storing her purse in her desk drawer, changing her shoes, turning on her computer, checking the files in her file caddy. He soon tired of her routine and stared out the window through the venetian blinds at the distant skyline of San Francisco. In the corner of his view was the top of the Hall of Justice, a few blocks away.

Nick was reminded of Dickson Hong and his former life, but with less pathos than before, probably because he'd drawn strength from his resolve to see this problem through. And his feelings for Billie had been transforming, as well—even as their relationship continued to be buffeted by events.

The evening he'd spent with Gina, his nieces and nephews, had been both sad and heartening. He'd discussed the mystery file with Gina and the older children, Anthony and Tina. They concurred in his plan. After dessert they all sat around the table talking about Joe, recalling him for his good qualities.

He'd gotten the idea to drop in on Easley when Gina gave him his bill for legal fees as he was saying his goodbyes to everyone. Now that bankruptcy appeared to be at the heart of the mess, it made sense to see if Easley could shed any light on things.

When half an hour passed without any sign of the lawyer, Nick got impatient and went to the window, where he looked down into the street. Ever since the chase down at the wharf, he'd paid special attention to what was going on around him. As best he could tell, he hadn't been followed again, but that was also a concern because it meant the guy's attention could be focused elsewhere—like on Billie, for example.

At least she hadn't been blasé about it. When they'd spoken about it before he left her place the night before, she was direct. "Emily's down to one parent. I have no desire to make her an orphan, Nick."

He was about to press the secretary for more information on Easley when the door opened and a bland-looking man in his late forties entered, a briefcase in hand. His short-cropped hair was going from blond to white, his muddy-colored eyes large behind thick glasses.

"Todd," the woman said, confirming Nick's assumption,

"this gentleman doesn't have an appointment, but he wanted a word with you."

Nick approached Easley. "The name's Nick Sasso," he said, offering his hand. "I want to talk to you about my brother."

Easley, suddenly disconcerted, shook Nick's hand with caution. "I'd like to speak with you, Mr. Sasso," he said, "but I have an appointment in a few minutes and I need to prepare."

"It'll only take a minute."

"I'm sorry, but I really can't."

"I think you will, Mr. Easley. The police are involved in this now, and you'd probably be well advised to hear from me before you hear from them."

"I have nothing to fear from the police," Easley said.

"Maybe so or maybe not."

Nick took him by the arm and led him into the private office. Easley relented, but with reluctance. Nick closed the door.

"Look, I've got nothing to say to you," the lawyer said.

"What kind of scam did my brother get caught up in? Joe was getting screwed and turned to Sonny Culp for help. What did you do to him, Mr. Easley?" Nick demanded, getting in his face.

Easley backed against the desk. "I didn't do anything except represent him in a bankruptcy proceeding. A couple of his companies were in trouble and bankruptcy was the only solution. *He* came to me. I didn't solicit the business. And I did my best by him."

"He was getting fucked and you know it, Easley."

"Look, I have no idea what you're talking about."

"You're only making it harder on yourself. I swear to God, if you fucked Joe over, you're going to pay."

Easley, clearly shaken, struggled to pull himself together. He took a deep breath. "Listen, Mr. Sasso, as his attorney I could only do so much. Most important decisions weren't in my hands. If he was screwed over, it wasn't because of me."

"Then who's responsible?"

"I have nothing more to say."

Nick grabbed him by the collar. "*Who*, Easley?"

"Take you hands off me or I'll call the police!"

"What are you afraid of?" Nick said, glaring into his face.

"Lois!" Easley called through the door.

Nick knew he'd gone as far as he could. Giving the lawyer a gentle shove, enough to make him sit abruptly on his desk, he said, "You'll talk before this is over. Trust me." Then he turned and walked out the door opened by the secretary.

HALL OF JUSTICE

Dickson Hong and Carl Plavec had been working the phones since eight-thirty that morning and it was beginning to pay off. With the assistance of Sergeant Shelby Carter of the LAPD, they'd learned that the telephone call Tom Mason had placed on Friday, September 6, from his room in Peninsula Hospital, had gone to the home of Igor Sakharov, who lived with his wife, Eve Adams, in a quiet neighborhood in Van Nuys. Adams had a criminal record, Sakharov did not. Based on descriptions provided by hospital staff and residents of Van Nuys, Hong and Plavec concluded that Mason and Sakharov were most likely the same person.

Using eyewitness accounts and descriptions, the inspectors further concluded that Mason's associate, Jerry French, who they believed also to be Jolie Hays's assailant, was in fact Igor Sakharov's brother, Alexei Sakharov. Like his sister-in-law, Alexei had a criminal record, though the convictions were mostly for misdemeanors. On one occasion, felony assault charges were brought, then dropped. A mug shot of Alexei faxed by the LAPD was shown to Jolie Hays and the staff of the Cardiac Unit at Peninsula Hospital. Everyone who'd seen Jerry French confirmed he was the individual in the mug shot.

Hong and Plavec learned that, according to neighbors,

Igor Sakharov and Eve Adams left their home on Sunday and were believed to be headed for Russia. There was no word on Alexei Sakharov, who had not been seen in the area for a few days.

At around eleven, with everything they needed in hand, Hong and Plavec took the information they'd gathered to Steve Buck and asked that an arrest warrant be issued for Alexei Sakharov for the murder of DeLon Pitts and Olga Diachenko. They also asked that Igor Sakharov and Eve Adams be picked up for questioning.

"Well, you guys certainly work fast," Buck said, looking over their report.

"Everything fell neatly in place, Lieutenant," Hong said. "We were lucky."

"So, you think this guy Alexei killed the Ukrainian woman."

"And the pimp, DeLon Pitts."

"You have a case?"

"We've certainly got enough in the Pitts shooting and the attempt on Hays for probable cause, and we think more evidence will turn up in the Diachenko case."

"Okay," Buck said, "let's pick him up, then."

"What about the brother and sister-in-law? We're afraid they're planning to leave the country, if they haven't already. Their role is murkier, but conspiracy to commit murder is a real possibility."

"Fine, let's get them, too." Buck, at his desk, looked up at them. "Anything else?"

Dickson Hong settled his gaze on the lieutenant. "What about the possible connection between Alexei Sakharov and the Culp-Sasso homicides?"

"What connection?"

"The hooker, Jolie Hays's, account of his bragging the night of the double homicide."

"That's pretty tenuous, isn't it?"

"Actually, Lieutenant, we think Sakharov's motive for killing Diachenko and his attempt on the hooker were motivated by a desire to cover up his involvement in the double homicide."

"Based on?"

"Circumstances."

Buck smiled. "I'll look into it."

"Can't we follow up on that aspect of the case?" Plavec asked.

"The best way to do that, Carl, is to arrest your Russian. If and when you turn up something concrete, then we'll talk about it."

Hong and Plavec left Buck's office.

When they got back to their cubicle, Carl Plavec said, "Why's he resisting?"

"Because he doesn't want to get his hand slapped by Zeus. If we do pick up French-Sakharov and we can make the case, all bets are off. Buck knows it. He's not going to obstruct justice, but he's not going to upset the mukety-mucks, either. That's why he put the burden on us."

"What now?

"We find Alexei Sakharov."

CIVIC CENTER

Jessica Horton entered the reception area of Superior Court Judge Jacob Cohen's chambers at precisely 11:00 a.m. and gave her name to the secretary, a trim, very proper-looking black woman with white hair.

"Judge Cohen is expecting you, Ms. Horton," the woman said, "but he's on the phone. Please have a seat and he'll be with you shortly."

Jessica sat on the soft leather sofa, which reminded her of the one in the office of her professor at Stanford Law, Kip O'Connor. Kip had been her favorite and she'd been his.

They'd screwed on that sofa two or three dozen times. "This won't help your grade," Kip had said early in the relationship. "You're already the best." Which was true. Kip was himself the best. He was brilliant and sexy. That was the reason she'd slept with him, not for grades. Of course, he'd been married and that intrigued her, as well. For some reason she was always attracted to married men, probably because the single ones were mostly young and far from the height of their powers. Jessica had a thing about power.

A well-meaning friend had once warned that her kinky predilection would eventually be her undoing. The last two days Jessica wondered if her friend hadn't been prophetic. The fact was, she was at a crisis point in her life and her career, and she was nervous, even scared.

All day Sunday she'd walked the beach at Monterey mulling over her predicament. The hell of it was, there were dangers either way. If she ignored the situation and Bart Carlisle went down, she might never dig herself out of the hole. Guilt by association wasn't fair, but it was real. On the other hand, by bringing down Bart herself—and Henry Chin, for that matter—she ran the risk of looking like a spoiler, a woman scorned, a conniving bitch. What had finally tipped the scales was the district attorney's involvement. It was one thing to turn state's evidence on a married lover, another altogether to help expose the criminality of a prominent politician, especially one responsible for enforcing the law. When this thing came down, the focus would be on Chin. That, she'd decided, would be her saving grace.

The secretary picked up her phone and said, "Judge, Ms. Horton is here." She put down the receiver. "You can go in, Ms. Horton."

Jessica got to her feet and took a fortifying breath. Dressed in her most solemn and conservative suit, a charcoal Armani, her blond hair in a businesslike chignon, she went to the frosted-glass door accessing the chambers of Judge Jacob Cohen. She'd picked Cohen because of his reputation for integrity and independence, because he was a graduate of Boalt Hall at Berkeley—about as far removed from the Stanford mafia as you could get—and because he was Jewish and unlikely to have close personal connections with a mostly gentile firm like B.C.C.&G.

Knocking, then opening the door, she found Cohen at his desk. He was in shirtsleeves and braces and a nondescript navy tie. A bit hunched as he rose to his feet, his shoulders rounded, his dark-rimmed bifocals and deeply wrinkled face testimony to his advanced years. She'd met the judge, who she thought to be approaching seventy, at a state bar function once, but doubted he'd remember.

"Ms. Horton, please come in."

Jessica closed the door and went to the leather guest armchair across from him, sitting as he indicated. She crossed her legs. Cohen dropped heavily into his high-back desk chair, the air sort of going out of him. He smiled a big wraparound smile.

"Let me say at the outset, this is an unexpected but pleasant surprise."

"I appreciate you seeing me, Judge Cohen," Jessica replied. "I'm an attorney, as I indicated on the phone. We met once, a year or so ago. I'm sure you don't remember."

"Oh, but I recall very well, Ms. Horton. If you'll allow an old man a liberty, may I say I never forget a pretty face." He shook his hand in a dismissive fashion. "But I won't say more. Courtly remarks are the stuff of lawsuits these days. I'm sure I don't have to tell you that." The lines in his forehead deepened. "But now to business. You indicated you had an urgent and delicate matter to discuss. What is your concern?"

"I'll be direct, Judge Cohen. By chance I've become aware of what I believe to be a murder conspiracy."

His expression grew quite solemn. "Indeed."

"And unfortunately it involves people I know well, a senior partner in my firm, for one."

"Isn't this a matter for the police? Why bring it to me?"

"I guess because I need somebody I can trust. You see, Judge, one of the conspirators is the district attorney, Henry Chin."

Cohen froze, hardly seeming to breathe. "You're serious?"

"Dead serious and scared to death."

"I can understand that." He reflected. "You're aware that you're making a very serious charge, of course. Is there any possibility you could be mistaken?"

"I would like nothing better than to believe that, but I can't."

Cohen folded his hands on his desk blotter. "Perhaps you could explain how you've come to your conclusion."

"Certainly, Judge Cohen."

Jessica recounted everything she knew, with special emphasis on the phone conversation she'd overheard. The judge listened attentively, his eyes narrowing, his mouth turning downward and the lines deepening as she stated the more damning facts. When she made reference to the comments about Martin Fong, the judge's eyebrows rose, and again when she recounted Henry Chin's reference to Bart's Russian contact.

"Russian, you say?"

"Yes."

"How interesting. And disturbing. There was a police officer at my home just yesterday, asking for my signature on an order to obtain evidence on a Russian suspect. A murder suspect. Well, never mind. Back to your problem. I understand your reluctance to go to the police, but as you surely know, I have no authority in matters such as this. In a sense, I'm no different than any other citizen."

"I appreciate that, Judge Cohen. I guess I was hoping for a guardian angel, if only in a psychological sense. I feel quite vulnerable, as you might imagine."

"Yes, certainly. Well, let me say this, if there is a criminal matter in which the district attorney or others in his office were accused or otherwise in a conflict of interest, the Attorney General's Office would become involved in the prosecution of the case. It occurs to me, as a matter of fact, that a conversation with one of the A.G.'s investigators might be warranted. And the FBI as well. The federal racketeering laws and even civil rights issues have been raised in instances like this, as you may know." Cohen paused. "Again, my authority is limited, but I could certainly make an introductory phone call to the A.G., if that would be helpful to you."

"I would be most grateful, Judge Cohen."

The judge picked up the phone and pushed a button. "Elizabeth, would you please get the attorney general on the phone for me? It's urgent."

CHINA BASIN

"You have to admit, he was the greatest," Billie said, glancing up at the bigger-than-life likeness of Willie Mays that rose majestically amid the palm trees of the plaza.

"Great, yeah, but the greatest?"

She pounded her fist into her first baseman's glove, rising up on the toes of her athletic shoes so she was damn near Nick's height. "If Mays had played in a bandbox like Yankee Stadium instead of Candlestick Park, he'd have broken both Ruth's and Maris's records. And probably Aaron's, too."

"You think so?"

"Yes, and it's a completely objective opinion."

Nick chuckled, looking up at the facade of the stadium. "I must say, I'm impressed with the place so far."

"I haven't been to all that many Major League parks," Billie said, "but people who have say this is the best anywhere. It wouldn't surprise me."

"My, the patriotic fervor. I must admit, I find it sexy."

"Shut up, Nick. You're still in the doghouse."

She didn't have to say so. He knew. "If that's a reference to Bree, I'm praying that no news is good news."

"Yeah, well, good luck."

As a matter of fact, he'd tried calling Bree just before he'd gone to pick up Billie, but had no luck reaching her. So much for his desire to announce with glee that he was still without child. During their drive to Pac Bell Park, the subject hadn't come up. This was the first reference to it today, though he was aware it had been simmering under the surface since Saturday night. He wanted badly to get on his cell phone right then, but it was best to keep his desperation within bounds. Besides, Bree had said she'd call with a report. Was it too early to hear from her, or was she afraid to give him the bad news?

Billie kept working her glove and glancing around. She wasn't exactly nervous, but he could tell she was a little tense.

"You okay?"

"Yeah," she said. "Why?"

"You seem uneasy."

Billie sighed. "This bankruptcy thing has me really confused."

"Isn't that why we're here? To learn what we can?"

"I keep thinking about Naomi, how scared she is."

"We already know how far these guys are willing to go," he said, touching her bare arm.

The sun had come out and it was a warm day by San Francisco standards. She'd worn a bright orange tank top and nicely tailored black slacks—Giants colors—that showed off her butt to good effect. Sunglasses and Giants hat completed her outfit. She carried a black cable-knit sweater for later when the afternoon breeze showed up, as it invariably did.

All Nick could say was that he desired her and would have given up prime seats at Yankee Stadium for a brief, well-received kiss. But Billie Fox was keeping him at arm's length. Was it pique, or was she genuinely disillusioned?

"Is there anything I should know about this old flame of yours?" he asked when nothing had been said for several minutes.

"I don't talk about past relationships," she said in a direct, though not exactly hostile, tone.

"No, I meant for purposes of our case."

"Oh. All I can tell you about Wilson's work is that he's very good at it. He's made a pile of money."

"As a bankruptcy trustee, right?"

"Right."

"What exactly does a bankruptcy trustee do?"

Billie looked off across the plaza. "He's headed this way now," she said with a nod, "so I'll let him answer the question."

Wilson Dahl was a tall, patrician-looking fellow with light brown hair streaked with wisps of gray. He wore a business suit but, given the occasion, he'd removed his tie. Dahl had a suaveness and, now that he was closer, Nick could see that his pale blue eyes and craggy face bore signs of fatigue. The bags under his eyes seemed to disappear when he smiled, though.

"Hello, hello, Billie," he said, taking both her hands before giving her a peck on the cheek. "My, but don't you look sporty and bright. Lovely as always."

"Still a flatterer, I see," she said dryly.

Nick was happy that she wasn't particularly pleased by the familiarity. She introduced him.

"This is Nick Sasso," she said. Then, gesturing. "Wilson Dahl."

"Good to meet you, Nick," Dahl said with a firm handshake that fell just short of excessive. "My sympathy regarding your brother. And Sonny, as well," he said with a glance at Billie.

"Thanks," she said, speaking for them.

"Terrible tragedy."

"Nick and I are both committed to helping find the person or persons responsible."

"Frankly, I'm surprised there hasn't been an arrest," Dahl said.

"It hasn't even been a week," Nick said.

"Yes, these things do move slowly at times. Let's keep our fingers crossed." He looked back and forth between them. "Well, shall we go inside?"

The three of them headed off, Billie between him and Dahl.

"I understand you're a New Yorker at present, Nick," Wilson Dahl said. "This your first visit to Pac Bell?"

"Yeah, as a matter of fact."

"Well, you're in for a treat. I know you've attended many games, Billie. Seen any from a luxury suite?"

"No, I'm a bleacher bum."

"You're in for a treat, as well, then. I'm so glad we have this opportunity."

"It's really nice of you, Wilson."

They reached the gate and Dahl presented the tickets, then ushered Billie and Nick through. They headed for the elevators through the teeming crowd.

The park had a nice feel, a class and sophistication that Nick associated with his hometown, though most of his life he'd been more on the outside looking in than any sort of player. Big shots like Wilson Dahl, on the other hand, tended to occupy the luxury suites at ballparks, the boxes at the opera, sailed their boats on opening day, attended the Black and White Ball, saw their names in the society columns and put them on the donor lists for charities and political campaigns. Some of them even ate at the Yankee Clipper.

Having had a few minutes to assess Billie's old beau, Nick was rather surprised they'd been an item—not because he couldn't imagine them being attracted to one another, but rather because he couldn't imagine her putting up with the phony bullshit. He wanted to take her aside and say, "Why? What was the attraction, anyway?"

"When you arrived," Billie said to Dahl, "Nick was asking what, exactly, a bankruptcy trustee does. I thought you could explain better than I."

"Nothing very exotic about it," Dahl said. "When a person or other entity files for bankruptcy, certain of their assets become sheltered against the claims of creditors, as you know, I'm sure. But what's not sheltered or exempt must go to the various creditors according to priorities established by statute. In cases where there are substantial assets, the court appoints an impartial trustee to manage those assets for the benefit of creditors and, for that matter, the bankrupt party, as well. For obvious reasons, a bankrupt obligor couldn't be expected to preserve the assets and maximize their value. A neutral, unbiased person such as myself with no interest in the proceeding or assets, other than fees, of course, is best placed to do the job." Dahl pressed the up button on the elevator and smiled. "I'm sure that's more than you cared to know."

"No," Nick said, "it's all very interesting, actually. Never having been closer to bankruptcy than a couple of weeks' pay, I'm fairly ignorant of the process."

Dahl chuckled. "You're far too modest, I'm sure."

An elevator car arrived. They stepped in and went up to the club level. Dahl led them along the concourse.

"I thought we might have some lunch before the game starts. The food here at the park is quite good. Lots of variety. They'll serve us in the suite."

Nick glanced at Billie, arching an eyebrow as if to say, "Aren't we the cat's meow." She repressed a grin.

An usher checked their tickets and showed them into the suite. It was on the first-base side with a spectacular view of a field that was absolutely gorgeous. Nick had seen it on TV, but television didn't do it justice. Wilson Dahl excused himself, saying he'd find a waitress and make a telephone call.

Nick and Billie settled into their seats. Out on the field, the ground crew was at work. A few players were stretching and doing sprints on the outfield grass.

"Pretty slick, huh?" she said.

"Yeah. Good enough to impress me."

"A shock to any Yankee fan, I'm sure."

Nick felt audacious so he reached over and caressed Billie's cheek with the back of his hand. "So tell me, when you and Dahl were friends, was it weekends in Paris and Aspen?"

"No, if you must know, it was mostly nooners at modest but discreet downtown hotels. Sometimes he bought me dinner. I did get flowers on a few occasions."

"I'm disillusioned."

"Why's that?" she said superciliously. "I've been known to screw cooks on cots in storerooms above restaurants and not complain. That doesn't mean I'm a slut. I just have modest standards."

"I believe I was just insulted."

"You were."

"Refreshing to know we're so honest with each other. You and Dahl have this kind of rapport?"

"Actually, it pretty much began and ended with sex. I was working through my breakup with Sonny when I knew Wilson."

"And Dahl was..."

"Getting laid at minimal expense. We talked, of course. You have to do something between orgasms, after all."

Nick chuckled. "You know how I know I'm not just in lust with you?"

Billie stared at him, arching an eyebrow. "How?"

"I actually hear what you say. And like it."

The door to the suite opened and Nick glanced back. The waitress, a Filipino girl, had come with menus.

"I don't even have to look at that," Nick said, handing the card back to the girl. "A big Polish and a large beer will do the trick."

"In keeping with my true nature," Billie said, "I'll have the same."

The girl left and Nick put his arm around Billie's shoulders. "You see, kid, we're made for each other."

She unwrapped his arm. "'Kid' isn't my favorite word at the moment, Mr. Sasso."

He nodded, understanding. "I still have a ways to go, in other words."

"And miles to go before you sleep...with me, anyway."

Nick's cell phone rang just then. He took it out of his pocket, gazing at it for a moment, as did Billie. He took a deep breath, the look he gave her saying, "Wish me luck."

He pushed the talk button. "Hello?"

"Nicky, it's Benny Vocino."

"Oh, hi, Benny," he said, rolling his eyes.

Billie, looking equally disappointed, turned her attention to the field.

"Listen," Benny said, "I made the deal for the file. Elaine's going to pick it up from the seller and will deliver it this evening. I suggested we meet at the Clipper at eight. That okay with you?"

"The Clipper at eight is fine. See you then."

Nick ended the call.

Billie looked at him and said, "Your Buddha?"

"My Buddha."

Wilson Dahl returned just then, the waitress in tow. "Lunch is served," he announced.

The waitress had two huge Polish sausages in buns, two beers, a chef's salad and a glass of chardonnay. As their meals were distributed among them, Billie glanced at Nick.

"You know, there are days when I'd rather be in Milwaukee than Paris," she said.

Nick took heart in her comment, figuring he was about seventy percent there.

THE RICHMOND

Mel Fox watched CNN news while he ate his sandwich and soup on a TV tray. He checked his watch. It was a late lunch. He only had half an hour before he had to pick up Emily at school. "Be real careful, Pop," Billie had warned as she went out the door with Nick, headed for Pacific Bell Park. "My friend, the former cop here, is convinced there's somebody out there on the prowl who's up to no good." "Better safe than sorry," Nick had added.

Mel had no idea what danger he and Emily could possibly be facing, but he deferred to his daughter's and Nick's superior judgment. Besides, he knew from long experience that the price of caution was hardly ever onerous.

Just then there was an insistent knock at the door, making him jump. Wary because of Billie's warning, he went to the door and peered out the peephole. A cocoa-colored woman stood on the porch, a deep frown on her face. Even through the distorted perspective of the small glass lens, she appeared anxious. There was another insistent knock.

Taking no chances, Mel asked who it was.

"Naomi Watts," the woman replied. "I'd like to talk to Billie."

He opened the door. She was a mature woman, yet quite pretty.

"Billie here?" she said.

"No, Ms. Watts, she's at the ballpark."

"Oh, shit." She peered up and down the street anxiously.

It was only then that Mel noticed the large manila envelope under her arm. She had a desperate look.

"You Billie's father?"

"Yes."

"You know who I am?"

"You're Sonny's friend."

She looked glum. "In a manner of speaking." She sighed. "I was hoping to talk to Billie, but maybe I can just leave this with you."

"That's fine, Ms. Watts, but I can probably reach her on her cell phone, if you want to talk to her. Come on in."

Again the woman checked the street. "Well, I sure as hell don't want to stand out here for long. If you don't mind..."

"Please."

Naomi stepped inside. She closed and bolted the door, slipping on the security chain for good measure. Mel was surprised. Naomi shrugged. "This is the way my life has been lately."

"I understand. Can I get you something to drink or eat?"

Naomi shook her head. "No, thanks."

"Well, sit down and make yourself at home. I'll have to go look up Billie's cell number. The old brain's not what it used to be."

"Tell me about it."

Mel smiled at her and she smiled back.

"So, what's Billie doing going to a baseball game at a time like this? Or, am I more paranoid than I think?"

"It's business. She and Nick Sasso are meeting some guy at the park. He's a bankruptcy official."

"What?" Naomi said, sounding alarmed.

"A bankruptcy trustee, I believe."

"Who?" she demanded. "What's his name?"

Mel stopped to think. "If you hadn't asked, I could have told you," he said, scratching his head.

"Not Wilson Dahl, I hope," Naomi said. "Please don't say it's Wilson Dahl."

"Why, yes, that's exactly who it is."

"Jesus Christ," Naomi said, turning gray. "Quick, call her."

Mel went to the kitchen, checked the number, which was on a slip of paper under a magnet on the refrigerator, then hurried back to the front room. He quickly dialed the number. After a few seconds they both heard a ringing in the back of the house.

"What's that?" Naomi said.

"Oh, Lord, that must be the phone back in her room. She forgot to take it."

"Shit." Naomi Watts absently chewed on her nails. "Billie could be in very serious danger, Mr. Fox," she said. "Somehow we've got to warn her. It'll take us forever to get to the park from here, and once we got there, how could we find her?"

"I know they're in a luxury suite."

"That helps, but still, something could happen before we got there."

"Let's call the police. Billie and Nick have been working with Dickson Hong."

"Yeah, I know him."

"Shall we call him?"

Naomi took a moment. "Yes, what the hell, we're talking about her life."

Mel picked up the phone again. "I guess I'll need to explain to Inspector Hong what's happening. What, exactly, is the danger?"

"Dahl was part of a conspiracy that is probably responsible for Sonny's death. They're after me and they're probably after Billie, too."

"Oh, dear Lord."

CHINA BASIN

The Astros were retired in the top of the ninth inning and the game remained tied at two to two. It was a tense game.

Both teams were in a pennant race and a lot was riding on the outcome. Even Nick, thousands of miles from his Yankees, had been drawn into the drama.

The three of them had talked about bankruptcy some, mostly between innings. Billie hadn't pressed Wilson on the various potential scams a petitioner might be subjected to, though she was beginning to sense he wasn't eager to volunteer information. Nick had asked a couple of pointed questions early on, which Wilson had sloughed over. "There's got to be opportunity for abuse," Nick had said. "I can't believe there isn't." Wilson had shrugged. "Maybe I'm just too honest to think in those terms."

Billie had asked most of the questions thereafter. Even so, the tension in their luxury suite was rising right along with the tension on the field. Wilson seemed more uncomfortable as time went on, making her wonder why. Surely he couldn't have been involved in the case.

"Forgive a stupid question, Wilson," she said, figuring she might as well get the issue on the table, "but you weren't in any way involved in Joe's bankruptcy proceedings, were you?"

"No, of course not."

"Would you have any idea who was?"

"Appointments are made by the court. There's little or no interaction between the trustees."

"How many are there?" Nick asked.

"A number. Most tend to serve a fairly broad geographical area."

"How would we find out who was working on my brother's case?"

"The easiest way would be to talk to his lawyer."

Wilson was more and more evasive. In addition to showing hints of annoyance, he'd started looking at his watch. That gave her pause. What was going on that she was missing?

Barry Bonds led off the bottom of the ninth. A walk-off

home run would end the game, so naturally the crowd moved to the edge of their seats. After a couple of balls that weren't even close to the strike zone, Bonds swung at the next pitch and hit a soaring pop-up that drifted back toward them. Billie jumped to her feet, leaning out of the box to follow the flight of the ball.

Nick peered up at the pale blue sky, as well. "There's a Major League pop-up coming your way, Billie. Off the bat of Barry Bonds. This is your chance!"

"Shut up, Nick," she said as the ball began dropping.

It was coming down right above them, the question being whether it would drift behind them, into the upper deck, or maybe toward the field, beyond her reach. Tapping her glove, she waited, craning her neck upward as the ball plummeted toward her. She reached out, stretching her glove hand out as far as she could. The ball, a missile now, slammed into the web of her mitt where it stuck, eliciting a huge roar of approval from the crowd.

Billie, laughing, held it up in triumph as the crowd continued to cheer. The voice of the TV announcer, Mike Krukow, drifted in from an adjoining box. "The lady brought her glove and got herself a souvenir. When you come to the ballpark, folks, you gotta bring your glove."

She turned to Nick, gave him a high five and got a kiss in return. Wilson, for his part, smiled stiffly, actually looking ashen.

Billie sat down in her seat and examined the ball. Again she smiled at Nick.

"You've conquered your fear of the pop-up," he said.

"Either that or I was lucky."

Her heart still pounding with excitement, Billie turned her attention back to the game. Two pitches later Bonds walked. Kent hit a deep fly ball to right center and Bonds advanced to second. Snow's infield hit off the second baseman's glove advanced Bonds to third. Dunston, who'd come into the game on a double switch in the sixth inning, came to bat.

"Squeeze play," Nick said.

Billie shook her head. "Dusty Baker's not a fan of the squeeze play."

"Bet you dinner."

"You're on."

On the second pitch, Dunston laid down a perfect bunt, which the pitcher couldn't even pick up before Bonds crossed the plate with the game-winning run. The crowd went wild. Billie and Nick hugged. Glancing back, she saw that Wilson Dahl was gone.

Amid the pandemonium, an uncertain wave of fear went through her. The noise in the stadium rose to the level of a din. The Giants players spilled onto the field, pummeling Bonds and Dunston. Nick applauded and whistled. From the corner of her eye, Billie saw the door to the suite open and a man come through it. He held a gun in his hand. He lifted it and pointed it at the back of Nick's head.

Billie reacted on instinct, hurling the baseball clutched in her fist at the intruder. The ball struck the man in the neck, jarring him as the gun went off.

Nick spun as the gunman regained his balance, still clutching the weapon. Nick lunged, grabbing the man's gun hand. They struggled. Another shot went off, silencing the crowd below. There were screams. Nick and his assailant continued to wrestle in the aisle. Both men went down, Nick ending up on the bottom.

Billie rushed over to help, grabbing the intruder around the neck from behind. Another shot went off, this one muffled, causing the man to lurch backward. The momentum of his body sent Billie reeling back, as well. She crashed against the railing at the front of the box, her body teetering on the rail. For a brief agonizing second her weight was in balance and she thought she might not go over, but it was only for a second or two. When her head began to descend toward the seats below, she knew she was lost.

The hand hit her forearm with a violent force, the weight of her body nearly wrenching her arm from its socket. She dangled, suspended over the stadium by her arm. Billie looked up in terror at Nick's bloody face, her arm slowly slipping through his fingers, not stopping until their hands locked on each other's wrists like trapeze artists.

Nick's eyes bulged from the strain. Blood dripped from his face in a stream, splattering her forehead and running into her hair. Nick struggled so hard to maintain his grip he couldn't speak. His eyes spoke volumes, though. He refused to let her go.

It was probably only seconds, but it seemed like minutes before a big ruddy cop appeared beside Nick and reached down to take her other hand. They had her back over the railing in seconds. Before they got her into a seat, she began to cry. Nick, crumpled in pain, was on his knees at her feet. Billie threw her arms around him and wept.

When Dickson Hong arrived at the club level, he found Alexei Sakharov lying on the concrete floor outside the B.C.C.&G. luxury suite. Blood ran from the corner of his mouth. A cop stood over him, telling people to back off. Hong knelt beside Sakharov, the gunman's eyes turning to him with the serenity of a dying man. Hong could see he was trying to speak.

"I...didn't kill the lawyer...and the other guy," Sakharov said, coughing, choking on his own blood. "They...were dead...when I got there. Tell my...brother I'm sorry...I lied." After a few more breaths, his eyes froze and he stopped breathing.

Getting up and dusting off the knees of his trousers, Hong

peered inside the suite. He saw Nick and Billie seated side by side. She was crying softly, her face wet. Nick clutched a bloody handkerchief to the side of his head.

"What have you two been doing?" Hong asked.

Billie looked up at him. "Nick saved my life," she said, wiping her tears away with the back of his hand.

"Good Lord, Sasso," he said, "you're a genuine hero."

Nick shrugged. "A minute before that, she saved me. I already owed her my life."

"That's not a bad incentive."

"No, actually, I couldn't let her fall because she owes me dinner. I called the squeeze play and won a bet."

Billie pressed her face against his.

"What happened to your head?" Hong asked.

"Banged it on a seat while we were struggling for the gun."

"That's how the guy got shot?"

"Yeah. Where is he, anyway?"

"Out in the hall, dead."

"He's the guy I had a run-in with down at the wharf. Who the hell is he?"

"Alexei Sakharov. A Russian living in L.A. Don't know a lot more."

"He's the one, then?" Billie said, sniffling. "He killed Sonny and Joe?"

"That's one theory, Counselor."

"How about Wilson Dahl?" Nick asked.

"He slipped away in the crowds."

"He set us up."

"Yeah, I know. We're looking for him. And several other people, as a matter of fact."

The paramedics arrived, pushing their way into the suite, hampering further conversation.

Dickson Hong went to the door. "We'll talk later, kids," he said.

He stepped out into the hall where Alexei Sakharov lay as before in a pool of blood. Hong took a deep breath, glanced at the onlookers being held back by security guards and uniformed cops, wondering what to make of Sakharov's dying words. He badly craved a cigarette, but this was California. He knew he'd have to wait.

HALL OF JUSTICE

"Thank God it wasn't my throwing arm," she said as they walked down the hall, headed for Homicide. "I already had rotator-cuff problems in that shoulder."

"Yeah," Nick said. "I figured glove hand was better, so that's the arm I went for."

She gave him a jab with her good elbow, the other arm being in a sling. "Shoulder sprain's not so bad, considering what might have been. But you know what the worst part is? I can't be mad at you anymore."

"Yeah, that is a bummer. On the other hand, you saved me from getting a bullet in the head again, so that kind of neutralizes me saving you. Technically speaking, you can still be mad at me, if you want to."

She laughed. "Nick, you're such a kind soul, the perfect gentleman."

"I'm not accused of that very often."

Billie took his hand, interlacing her fingers in his. He liked the friendliness. There'd been a few kisses in the squad car coming over from the hospital where she'd had her shoulder examined and he got a few more stitches. The kisses were nice. A friendly Billie Fox was a joy. She made him happy.

If he'd had his druthers, Nick would have taken her home or out to dinner, but Naomi had surrendered to the police, and Billie had promised to be with her when she was questioned. "They've got a warrant out for that Oakland assault," Billie told him. "Anyway, she says she can explain the whole bankruptcy scam."

They entered the Homicide Section. Steve Buck, looking a bit forlorn, sat on the corner of a desk in the reception area, his tie loose at the neck.

"They're in the interrogation room," he said, indicating with a toss of the head that they should go on back.

They found Naomi seated at a table with Dickson Hong, Carl Plavec and Angela Ellis, the detective with the Oakland P.D., and another man who was introduced as Special Agent Larry Drexel of the FBI.

"Now that Ms. Watts's attorney is here, perhaps we can proceed," Hong said.

"So, it's a federal case now, is it?" Billie said, turning to Drexel, a smallish man with a brush cut and neatly trimmed mustache.

"Quite possibly, ma'am."

Billie sat down next to Naomi. Nick took a seat against the wall, ignored, though under normal circumstances they wouldn't have allowed him in the room.

Billie took her client's hand. "How you doing?"

Naomi seemed exhausted, but at the same time relieved. "Okay."

Billie turned her attention to Hong. "So, where are we, Dick?"

"Sergeant Ellis would like to take your client to Oakland because of pending charges there, but we have other matters to discuss first. Ms. Watts has information bearing on the double homicide and a related criminal conspiracy."

"You're back on the case then, are you, Dickson?"

"Yes."

"Okay. Where do we begin?"

Naomi spoke up. "Billie, I want to get the hard part out of the way first. I've got a confession to make."

"Hold on, Naomi. Maybe we should discuss this first."

"No, I don't mean confess a crime. I'm talking about moral guilt. The reason Sonny and his client were killed is because I sold Sonny out."

"What do you mean?"

"I was approached by someone representing 'the legal establishment,'" she said, making quotation signs in the air. "I don't even know the guy's name. The bottom line was he represented people who could make it easy or impossible to get my ticket back."

"What did he want?"

"To know what Sonny was up to. I guess they knew about our relationship. Anyway, I agreed to keep them informed, hoping I could do it without any serious damage to what Sonny was involved in." Naomi's face crumbled. "Billie, I didn't know they'd kill him. I had no idea that's what the bastards had in mind." She wiped away a tear. "If I'd known, I'd never have talked to them. I'd have gone down first."

Billie put an arm around Naomi. "Don't worry about that now."

"Tell us what Sonny Culp was doing," Hong said. "What was his case?"

Naomi took a tissue from the box Carl Plavec handed her and wiped her nose and eyes. "Mr. Sasso came to him complaining that he was getting ripped off in his bankruptcy. The trustee, he said, was eating up the assets, mostly on legal fees."

"Trustee. You mean Wilson Dahl?"

"Yes. Sonny had little or no knowledge of bankruptcy, but he was intrigued with the notion of a trustee and a bunch of lawyers squeezing fees out of properties for their own personal gain. And that was exactly what Sonny found. What he hadn't expected was that it was part of an intricate scam, affecting dozens of bankruptcies. Mr. Sasso wasn't the only one getting screwed. Dahl had worked out a whole pattern of relationships among some of the heavy hitters in the biggest law firms in northern California. The lawyers would bill the trustee substantial fees for legal work in connection with foreclosures, transfers of title or whatever. Much of the work was bogus or they provided nominal services for huge fees. Dahl would sell off assets to cronies well below market value and get a kickback. He was making a fortune, and the lawyers he colluded with were able to pad their incomes, all at the expense of the bankrupt owners of the assets and their creditors."

"Culp had proof of this?" Hong asked.

"Most of it is in the draft pleading Sonny prepared," Naomi said, patting the manila envelope on the table in front of her. "He got his information from some of the bankruptcy lawyers. More often than not, they weren't even in on it. Once the trustee took over, it was out of their hands. Dahl was the one with control of the assets. The bankruptcy lawyers took the client through the bankruptcy process, but didn't always have a handle on the bigger picture. And those who were tough enough or sharp enough to cause problems, Dahl simply avoided. He chose his victims carefully."

Nick thought of the harsh words he'd uttered to Todd Easley that morning, realizing now the guy was likely as innocent as he'd claimed. That embarrassed him.

"To tell you the truth," Naomi continued, "I think there was an intimidation factor at work, too. Wilson Dahl was a powerful guy and people knew it. He had some fairly prominent lawyers eating out of the palm of his hand."

Nick caught Billie's eye and nodded as if to say, "Boy, did he ever." She flushed. He had to struggle to keep from laughing out loud. She gave him a don't-you-dare look, probably knowing she'd be getting a ribbing later.

"This scam must have been going on for some time," Drexel said.

"Years."

"How is it that it didn't come to light before now? There had to be other people who thought they were getting screwed."

"Most people in bankruptcy expect to lose everything. They're used to seeing huge bills for fees. Plus, Dahl and his buddies had a powerful friend in law enforcement."

"Who?"

"Henry Chin."

"Harry Chin was in on this?" Billie said with surprise.

"He'd been involved in the scam as a private lawyer before going into politics and the conspirators probably decided he should continue to get a cut in exchange for protection. Sonny didn't have hard evidence of that, but he had his suspicions. That's when the shit hit the fan."

"How many conspirators are we talking about?" Drexel asked.

"Sonny figured there were dozens spread among some of the top firms in town. Not all of them knew how extensive the network was, apparently. Sometimes Dahl would throw bones at people to keep them from asking questions, if nothing else. But there was an inside group. Dahl, Henry Chin and Bart Carlisle at Bachman, Carlisle, Cummings & Glick seemed to be the ringleaders. And they were the ones who profited most."

"Why didn't Mr. Culp take this to the authorities?" Drexel asked.

"Sonny said the criminal case would be tough to make and, if it started that way, all the money would be buried by the time the aggrieved parties were able to bring a civil action. He figured the way to go was to clobber them with a civil suit, then let the authorities follow up, if a criminal case could be made. What he didn't count on was how desperate these guys were and how far they'd go." Naomi looked at Billie. "And neither did I." She wiped her eyes.

"Sonny knew he was in danger," Billie said, "so it's not like he was blindsided. Nobody could have predicted they'd resort to murder."

"I guess I got what I deserve," Naomi said, lowering her head.

"You've been under duress," Billie said, directing her remarks more at Angela Ellis than Naomi. "The conspirators were apparently trying to kill you, as well as Nick and me. You were a victim, Naomi. You have to remember that."

Just then Nick's cell phone rang and everybody looked his way.

"Excuse me," he said, getting up and stepping toward the door. He caught Billie's eye. Her look said she also knew who it could very well be. Closing the door, he pushed the talk button. "Hello?"

"It's me, Nick," Bree said.

His heart seemed to stop. "Hi." He walked off in the direction of the cubicle he'd once shared with Dickson Hong.

"I know you've been anxious," she said. "I'm sorry to have taken so long, but I wanted to be with my parents, so I drove down to Philadelphia."

Nick figured that was a bad sign. A terrible ache went through him. He was dying, certain the news couldn't be good.

Bree sighed. "It was a false alarm, Nick. I'm not pregnant."

He couldn't believe it. "Really?"

"Yes."

He felt tremendous relief, palpable relief. In seconds he went from fear to elation. It was all he could do to keep from shouting, *"Yesss!"* He sat on the desk that had once been his, reminding himself that this was a person with feelings, one who, until a few days ago, had been pretty important to him. "Are you okay, Bree?"

"I'm a little embarrassed," she said.

He heard sadness in her voice. "No need for that. It could have happened."

"Nick, what if it had? What would you have done?"

He realized that was the issue as far as Bree was concerned. "Isn't the question what would *you* have done?"

She hesitated a long moment, then said, "That's your answer, isn't it?"

"Bree, I don't think people make pivotal decisions about their lives based on pregnancy anymore."

"You're right, I know that. It's just that I've never had this happen before and it made me stop and think. But now it's over and things are back to the way they were. Right?"

She said the words, but he knew she didn't mean them. "I've been too cavalier about our relationship, haven't I?" he said.

"You've been pretty up-front with me, Nick. You haven't lied."

"Lies don't just come with words, Bree. I've learned that since leaving New York."

"The point is I know how you feel," she said. "Maybe I'm the one who hasn't been as honest as I should have been. Maybe I liked you a little more than I was willing to admit, even to myself. But that's not the point. Something's happened since you got home, hasn't it?"

"A lot's happened."

"You know what I mean, Nick."

He nodded with understanding, realizing she was even more perceptive than he thought. "Yes," he said, "something has happened."

"Are you going to come back?"

"Yes," he said, "but I don't know if I'll stay."

"Hmm."

"There's a lot still unresolved."

"Well, at least you won't have to worry about this."

"I'm sorry, Bree. For everything."

She sniffled. "That's okay. As long as we understand each other. But I've got to go now. Thanks for everything, Nick. Bye." She hung up.

He sat there for a while, looking at the phone, thinking about his life, thinking of what might have been. In a sense he'd just signed off on the past without knowing where the future would take him. Funny how less than a week ago New York had been his future and San Francisco his past. Now it was just the other way around.

Looking up, he saw Billie at the entrance of the cubicle. Her clothes were bloodstained, her arm in a sling. Her hair had seen better days and, boy, did she look tired. Even her good shoulder rounded a little. But she seemed beautiful to him in the way that things familiar and dear seemed beautiful. In the short time he'd known her, she'd become special. There was no other way to put it.

She was silent but her expression asked, "So, what happened?"

"The Yankees won't be getting another young fan," he said.

She nodded soberly, a slight frown on her forehead. "Is that cause for condolences or congratulations?"

"Neither, actually. I'm relieved. I didn't want the problem, either for Bree's sake or my own."

"And how does *she* feel?"

"Sad. Not that she wanted a baby. The scare made her take an honest look at her feelings, I think. She learned something about me and I learned something about her."

"I guess that's good."

"Well, we were honest with each other."

Billie gave him a half smile. "And now you're a free man."

"*You* aren't off the hook, though," he said. "Dusty Baker called a squeeze play, just as I predicted."

"Will you let me pay off my bet tomorrow night?"

"Sure," he said, glancing at the clock. "Anyway, it's late and I've got to meet Benny and Elaine Chang before long." He inclined his head toward the interrogation room. "So, what's going on in there?"

"I'm going to try to talk Sergeant Ellis into letting me take Naomi over to Oakland in the morning to be booked so she doesn't have to spend the night in jail. Given the circumstances, I think she'll go for it. Hong and the feds need her more than Oakland does, anyway. I'm hoping to finish up and be out of here in an hour."

"Then what?"

"Home and a *very* tall glass of wine. Naomi and I both could use one."

"I wish it could be me."

"I think Elaine Chang will manage to hold your attention, Nick."

"Not the way you can."

Smiling, Billie came over to where he still sat on the desk. Caressing his cheek, she said, "That's a nice thing to say."

"And completely true."

"There'll be other opportunities."

"How about tomorrow night?" he said. "Assuming you really want to, that is. There's absolutely no obligation, you know."

"How can I say no to a man who gave me his hand when I really, really, really needed it?" Leaning over, she kissed him on the lips.

Nick watched Billie walk away. She'd only been gone a minute or so when Dickson came out of the interrogation room, joining him.

"I understand you're taking off."

"Yeah, I've got to see a man about a Buddha."

Hong grinned, shaking his head. "Walk you to your car?"

"They going to be able to get along without you in there, Inspector?"

"The fed is doing his thing now. They're going to make a federal case of it, I think."

"Bother you?"

"No, it's fine. The more the merrier. In fact, Drexel said— and this is off the record, Nick—that they've come up with a witness who could tie Chin and Carlisle to a murder conspiracy. That helps our case and maybe theirs under the federal racketeering laws."

They headed for the hall. "So, what's the theory, then? The conspirators hired the Russian to kill Joe and Sonny?"

"And you, Ms. Fox and Ms. Watts."

"That's nice and neat."

"Maybe yes and maybe no."

Nick glanced over at him. "Is that your natural caution I hear, Dickson, or something else?"

They walked in the direction of the elevators.

"I got to Pac Bell just before Sakharov died," Hong said. "He whispered a few words to me, the bottom line being he didn't kill Culp and your brother. He said they were dead when he got there."

"Really?"

"Yeah. I was surprised, to be honest."

"You believe him?"

"Deathbed confessions aren't as credible as some people think. Same with deathbed denials. Maybe he was just trying to save his brother's ass."

"So the jury's still out."

"I guess you could say that. There are contradictions for sure. They found Olga Diachenko's wedding ring in Sakharov's pocket. And we already knew he killed DeLon

Pitts. It doesn't make a lot of sense that he'd kill them if he hadn't also killed Culp and your brother."

"This *is* messy."

They came to the elevators and waited for a car.

After a while, Nick said, "Out of curiosity, why are you telling me all this?"

Hong, looking off in the middle distance, shrugged. "I don't know. Because it was your brother who died. Because you're a bright guy and you've been in the middle of things. Because we used to be partners."

They entered the empty elevator car.

"I appreciate that," Nick said. "I really do."

Hong looked up at the floor-indicator lights. "This is going to rock the city, you know. Chin going down, especially. The bankruptcy fraud is bad enough, but murder?"

"It'll be a feather in your cap, maybe a career-defining case, Dickson. Hell, they might make you a lieutenant."

Hong smiled. "You know what making lieutenant is good for? A better pension. Period." He shook his head. "No, I've been doing the work I've always wanted to do. Maybe the tragic deaths of Culp and your brother have given us both a chance to redeem ourselves, though."

"I hope so, Dickson."

The elevator door opened. In the lobby, a gaggle of reporters waited along with cameramen.

Nick said, "Oh, shit."

"You're a bona fide hero, Nick," Hong said. "I believe your public is waiting. And as for me, there's a lot of work to be done, questions to answer."

"Victory is at hand, Dickson."

Hong shrugged. "As that famous Yankee philosopher once said, 'It ain't over till it's over.'"

They made eye contact. Hong smiled. Nick felt a lump in

his throat. He was surprised, until it occurred to him what had happened. They'd made their peace.

NORTH BEACH

Nick got back to the Yankee Clipper in time to clean up, change and grab a bite before Benny and Elaine were due. He'd barely finished eating when his brother's mistress and the honorary mayor of North Beach, unlit cigar in hand, the collar of his shirt lying on his jacket lapels, entered the restaurant.

The Black Widow of Chinatown wore a red knit suit and red spike pumps. Her hair was piled up on her head in an elegant sweep. Gold glimmered at her throat and on her hands. She had a black leather document case under her arm. In it, perhaps, was the fate of his father's restaurant and his brother's family.

Nick had wondered about this Emerald Buddha, Joe's dream that seemed to be sputtering on, even after his death. He realized he was a surrogate for his brother now. This wasn't his deal. It was Joe's. The question was whether by doing this he was rectifying his brother's mistake or compounding it.

Though Billie had won their bet about the true cause of Joe's and Sonny's deaths, in a sense Nick had been right, too. The Emerald Buddha and Elaine Chang had created the conditions that led eventually to the double homicide since, without them, there would have been no bankruptcy. Of course, Joe was ultimately responsible because of the choices he'd made. Still, it had taken an intricate combination of corruption and moral lapses to get where things stood now.

Maybe, though, how they'd gotten here was no longer the point. What mattered now was the choices that were left, not just over a jewel-encrusted statue sitting in the jungles of

Myanmar, but the choices they all faced, the choices that would define the future and who they were at heart.

Benny and Elaine approached the booth. Nick slid from the banquette and stood. Benny, effusive, wielding his cigar like a conductor's baton, introduced him to Elaine Chang. Nick took the slender, cold hand of Joey's mistress. She looked into his eyes with the assurance of a woman who knew men's minds.

"Let me express my profound sadness for the death of your brother, Mr. Sasso," she said. "Joe was a dear friend to me and I am much grieved by his loss."

There was a sheen of moisture in the woman's eyes. Nick saw no point in questioning her motives. Joe had made the judgments that mattered.

"Thank you," he said. Motioning for them to sit, he took his place across from the pair.

Benny spoke first. "I hear the funeral is tomorrow at Saints Peter and Paul."

"Yes," Nick replied. "At eleven." He glanced at Elaine, whose fingers, tipped with gleaming red inch-long nails, were folded on the black case.

"I won't attend, of course," she said. "Out of respect for Joe's family."

Nick nodded.

"But my thoughts will be with him."

"I understand."

"It's a terrible shame," Benny said. "But life goes on."

"Shall we conduct business?" Elaine asked.

"Would either of you like something?" Nick asked, looking back and forth between them. "Coffee? Wine? Beer? Water?"

"I would be most grateful for a cup of tea," Elaine said.

"A glass of wine," Benny said.

Nick signaled a nearby waiter. The orders were placed, the

last of Nick's dinner dishes removed. Elaine opened the case and withdrew a file folder. It was rather ordinary in appearance, manila, worn at the edges and fairly thick. "Sasso" was written on the tab. She laid her slender, ivory hand on the folder.

"This file was taken from the residence of Sonny Culp and Martin Fong," she said. "I don't know exactly when or under what circumstances. I have no idea how it fell into the hands of the gentleman who brought it to my attention. He determined that it had value to you and Mrs. Sasso because it contains information on secret offshore accounts that Joe established to finance the expedition to recover the Emerald Buddha. He'd showed me some of the documents in this file previously. Ken Lu, who you've met, Mr. Sasso, wanted proof of the funds and that is why Joe showed me the account statements."

"Why were they in Sonny Culp's possession?"

"I can't be sure, but Joe did tell me once that because of threats, he didn't want to leave the information in his files at his office, and he was reluctant to keep it in his home because of his wife. Sonny Culp had an office in his home and I assume they decided that delicate information would be safe there. Whether records were kept elsewhere, as well, I have no idea. I assume you don't have it, otherwise this file would be of little importance to you."

"That's true," Nick said.

Benny interjected, waving his cigar. "The point is we've got it now. The information gives you and Gina access to the money. A million of it goes into the pot, along with my million. It's up to you and Gina what happens to the rest. We're agreed on that, aren't we?"

Nick nodded. "That's our agreement, yes."

The tea and glass of wine were served. Elaine Chang slid the file folder across the table.

"Your brother's documents, Mr. Sasso."

Nick stared at the cover. It seemed odd that something so pedestrian should, at the same time, have such momentous implications. "Have you looked through the file, Ms. Chang?" he asked.

"Only to verify the contents. As I said, Joe showed me the account statements. I wanted to satisfy myself that they were the same."

"And they were."

"Yes. As you can see, there is a good deal of other information in the folder, as well. It mostly has to do with their lawsuit, I believe."

"Did you know about the bankruptcy scam, Ms. Chang?"

"I knew that Joe felt he was being taken advantage of in connection with some of his investments, and that Sonny Culp was helping him with that. Joe didn't share details with me, but I'd heard rumors of bankruptcy problems."

Nick lifted the cover of the folder. The first several pages were account statements and other account information, as Elaine Chang had said. Farther into the folder he found information regarding Joe's bankruptcy petitions. Paging through it quickly, he happened upon a trustee's report signed by Wilson Dahl. It occurred to him that Dickson Hong and the FBI could have some interest in the file, as well. Nick closed the folder.

"Let's hope this does the trick," he said.

Benny, his wineglass and cigar in hand, said, "So far, I've bet a Mercedes that it will, Nicky."

"And I've bet more than half a year of time and effort that it will," Elaine said, sipping her tea.

"I've got five days, an airline ticket and several stitches invested," Nick said. "But my family's in a little deeper. I'll be getting to work on this as soon as we bury Joe."

"God rest his soul," Benny said. He downed the last of his

wine. "Well, what do you think, Elaine? Is there anything else that needs to be said, or shall we go?"

She looked into Nick's eyes. "I just want to say this to you, Mr. Sasso. Your brother was a very fine man who loved his family. I know this for a fact. He could be grumpy and impatient, but in his heart there was love. He talked to me once about his brother in New York. He said, 'Someday, Nicky will come home. He's just waiting for the right time.' I think he would want me to tell you that. He would be happy that you are here."

Benny and Elaine left then. Nick sat with tears in his eyes, his hand resting folded on the Sasso file. It said a lot about the state of affairs when a con woman moved him to tears. Elaine Chang was a wheeler-dealer, an opportunist, no doubt about it. And Benny Vocino was not much different, when you came right down to it.

Nick asked the waiter to bring him a glass of sherry. When it was served, he took it and the folder upstairs to his room.

Sitting on the bed, Nick began paging through the file more carefully. He decided to cull the information on Joe's offshore accounts, which he put in one pile. Any information on the bankruptcy scam he put in a pile to be passed on to Dickson Hong. The other tidbits he'd leave in the file.

He was perhaps two-thirds of the way through the folder, having separated out a good deal of material, when he came upon a piece of stationery with "Martin Fong" inscribed at the top. A lengthy note was written on the page in longhand, an oddity in itself. It continued to a second page. But, what caught his eye was the salutation.

Dear Billie,
Of all the people in the world, you may hate me most for what I did, but probably will understand better than anybody. I loved Sonny. I loved him too much.
    But that's not the worst. The worst is knowing I've

made a terrible, terrible mistake. How could I have been so blind? I was so sure, so sure I'd lost his love. When I went to Sonny's office I found them together, just like I suspected. Deep down I knew he'd been cheating on me, the proof was all around, but I didn't want to believe it.

They were arguing, actually yelling at each other when I walked in. I thought it was a lovers' spat. I told Sonny I hated him. Hated him for deceiving me, for breaking our trust. He was furious. He called me a silly twit and he ordered me to leave. The man I love ordered me to leave, his lover standing right there. I couldn't believe it. I lost it. I killed them both. I didn't mean to. I mean, I brought a gun with me because I wanted to scare them, punish them for the hurt they'd caused. I wanted Sonny to know the terrible thing he'd done. I wanted him to beg for my forgiveness, but instead he yelled at me, he cursed me, and so I shot them.

I was as surprised as anybody. I never thought I'd ever shoot anybody, even a burglar. Because of the crazies, I got the gun from a friend years ago when I first went into politics. The most I ever expected to do with it was scare anyone who tried to hurt me. Seeing them on the floor, dying, I couldn't believe what I had done. I ran away in tears, the horror slowly sinking in. After throwing the gun off the Golden Gate Bridge, I went home, dazed, realizing I'd killed dear Emily's daddy, the man I loved more than anything in life. But it wasn't until I talked with you and you mentioned Joe Sasso's mistress, his wife and children, that the enormity of my mistake hit me. They were innocent and I killed them! How could this have happened?

I resolved to turn this file over to the police and confess my crime. I couldn't give Emily her daddy back, or Joe Sasso to his family, but I could give them the murderer. After we talked, I sat dazed for an hour. There is no worse pain than what I feel, Billie. I wanted to be brave. I wanted to do the right thing. I still do, but I don't have the strength. They won't kill me fast enough to spare me this unbearable misery. I have no choice but to do it myself.

I have taken the rest of the pills. My final thoughts are of Emily. If ever there is a time that's right, tell her I'm sorry. I wish I had the strength and the courage to live long enough to tell her myself, but I don't. I am dying. It is over. I am sorry.

Martin

Nick, his hands trembling, fell back on the bed, incredulous. He stared at the ceiling, not believing what he'd just read.

NORTH BEACH

It was late afternoon. Nick, in a state of anxiety since the previous evening, sat in Benny's booth waiting for Dickson Hong to arrive. The inspector had called, saying he wanted to make a courtesy visit—an ironic development, considering Nick had spent much of the night and day trying to figure out whether he should hand Martin's letter over to Hong, or keep silent and let nature take its course.

He'd very nearly called Dickson the night before, reasoning that the truth was the truth, whatever the implications might be. On the other hand, Dahl, Chin, Carlisle and their cohorts had plotted murder. They'd sent a hit man to kill Joe and Sonny and they didn't know about Martin's role in this. Nobody did. Nick figured he was probably the only person alive who knew the truth. Oh, it was possible that Elaine Chang or her client had seen Martin's suicide note and chosen to keep their mouths shut. But what did they have to gain? And why would they leave it in the file for him to find? To the contrary, Elaine would have found a way to barter the information if she knew about the note. No, he was fairly certain that he alone knew the whole story.

The Russian, Sakharov, must have taken credit for the crime just to collect his fee, then killed to silence people who could identify him as the killer. How ironic and sad. Sakharov's dying denial could be explained as an attempt to save his brother, as Dickson Hong suggested. The inspector might have his suspicions, but they could be explained away.

Nick had asked himself what harm would come if the truth never came to light. The conspirators thought they were responsible for the deaths. Others had died because of their evildoings. They were far from innocent.

He'd also reflected on the benefits of Martin's suicide note never coming to light. Emily wouldn't have to face the harsh reality of one of the two most important people in her life having killed the other. The truth would be more painful than the illusion. Was some philosophical notion of justice, having little or no practical consequence, more important than that?

What was justice, after all? Nick asked himself. Was it a dry, heartless abstraction that had worth apart from its impact on the lives of real people? Was right and wrong carved on a stone labeled "truth"?

Years ago, when he'd blown that case for the prosecutors and the People of California, he'd lied in a vain attempt to see a guilty man punished. But he'd miscalculated and brought down not only himself but Dickson Hong, as well. Had his life come full circle? he wondered. Was he facing the same moral dilemma yet again?

There was an important distinction between that earlier situation and the quandary facing him now. In the Allard case, his own butt had been on the line. His pride, even his self-respect, had been at issue. He'd corrupted the system of justice and paid the price. This time the factual truth had fallen in his lap by chance. He had nothing to gain or lose because of the way this turned out. So what did he do?

As he waited for Dickson Hong to arrive, he sipped a cup of coffee and absently glanced at the *Chronicle*. The front-page headline read, Pac Bell Drama. There was a quarter-page photograph, taken by some fan in the stands, of Billie dangling from Nick's arm. He'd glanced at the picture and the first few paragraphs that morning while having his breakfast, but hadn't had a chance to read it through until now.

He'd had a busy morning. The Mass of Christian Burial for Joe had been said at Saints Peter and Paul. The interment had been in Colma. They'd buried his brother next to their mother. It was a crisp, sunny morning with lots of blue sky. Benny and Dora Vocino, along with twenty or thirty other folks from the old neighborhood, had attended the mass. Tony, Nick and Gina had decided, wasn't well enough to attend his son's funeral. The rest of the small crowd was made up of Joe and Gina's friends.

Afterward, Nick had taken Gina and the children to lunch at the Cliff House overlooking Seal Rock because that was where Joe had taken Gina on their first date "a lifetime ago," as she'd put it.

They'd watched the seals and gulls. Gina, who rarely drank, had a Tom Collins as Nick answered their questions about the events leading up to Joe's death, as well as the recent developments in the case. He didn't tell them about Martin Fong's suicide note. He recounted the official version.

"I'm astounded," Gina said, "I thought surely the Chinese woman was involved."

"Yeah," Nick said, "for a long time I did, too."

Anthony, who resembled Nick more than his father, was the only one to express anger, perhaps because it was the manly thing to do. "At least you got the sonovabitch, Uncle Nick."

His nephew's comment made him feel like a fraud, even though Sakharov was no angel, even though he'd killed others and had come after him and Billie with the same intent. "Mostly by accident," Nick said.

"Incredible to think the district attorney, among others, could be responsible for this," Gina said.

"It's a working hypothesis," he told them. "Just a working hypothesis."

After he saw his brother's family home, Nick had gone out to Ingleside to see his father. The old man's speech had improved, though genuine conversation was still not possible. On his way home, Nick had called Billie with the idea of dropping by to see how she was doing, and to see if he might find something in her eyes to help him with his dilemma. But she wasn't there. Mel told him she was still in Oakland.

Staring vacantly toward the front, Nick became aware of Dickson Hong outside on the sidewalk. The inspector was finishing a cigarette. He took a final drag, then stepped over to the curb and bent down. Nick knew the butt would be going into the side pocket of the inspector's jacket. His old partner was a creature of habit.

Hong entered the Clipper. Linda Nassari greeted him, sending him back to the booth. There was a lightness in his step that Nick hadn't seen since his return.

"How's the celebrity?" Hong said, shaking his hand. "Read all about it in the paper."

"A lot of to-do for a guy who just happened to be in the right place at the right time."

"I think Ms. Fox would consider the to-do justified."

"Can I offer you anything?"

"Not a thing," Hong replied. "Thanks."

Nick finished his coffee. "Well, what's the latest?"

"A lot's happened, actually. The FBI arrested Henry Chin this morning, walking his dog. They picked up Wilson Dahl at his mother's house in San Mateo and Carlisle was at the airport, trying to board a flight for Europe. Two dozen other attorneys are either under arrest or warrants have been issued."

"That ought to keep the rest of the lawyers in town busy for a year or so."

"Yeah, Ms. Fox could probably make a fortune if she could stomach the thought of defending the bastards."

"I'm sure she'll pass."

"Yeah, I know."

"So, you think the case is ironclad?" Nick asked.

"The pieces keep falling into place. It looks like Dahl, Chin and Carlisle are going to be fighting it out to see who gets to turn state's evidence. But we may be able to nail them all without one of them turning. Checking phone records we've made a connection between Carlisle and a guy in L.A. named Chorny, also a Russian. We think he was probably the go-between. Unfortunately, he died of a heart attack Sunday night. The Attorney General's Office has gotten involved. They'll probably handle the prosecution."

"So, are you satisfied that in Sakharov you've got your man?"

Dickson Hong stared off into the middle distance. "I'd feel better if we'd been able to track down the brother and confirm that he was in on it. That deathbed confession still bothers me a little. I have a hunch, though, that the brother and his wife have given us the slip, which means we may never know for sure."

Now it was Nick who looked away, feeling a little like Solomon. Never mind justice. What was right?

"There have been developments down at the Hall of Justice," Hong continued. "The deputy chief, George Kondakis, resigned this morning. He gave us a statement that he'd been passing on information about departmental activities directly to Chin. He had also been running illegal wiretaps for Chin, in hopes of giving him political advantage in the campaign. He vehemently denies involvement in the plot, but he's likely to face charges of some sort."

"Dickson, you might end up getting his job."

Hong laughed. "If I get to retirement without being made a crossing guard, I'll consider my career a success. Nailing Chin and the rest of them gives me all the satisfaction I need."

"Do you think the prosecutor will ask for the death penalty?"

"My gut feeling is they'll go for a life term, but Ms. Fox could tell you better than me. It'll probably turn on how strong the evidence is and whether they sell each other out."

Nick pondered that.

"What are your immediate plans?" Hong asked.

"To be honest? I'm trying to decide whether to make your day or ruin it entirely." He waited for the quizzical expression on Hong's face to gel. "And you want to know something even funnier? Of the two choices I have, I haven't got a clue which will have which result."

"You're not making sense."

Nick looked into his old partner's eyes and said, "After the Allard case, you once said to me, 'If you'd only trusted me.' In the years since, I've kicked myself, wishing I had. And you know what? I'm kind of at that place again."

"I still don't follow."

Nick realized then what he had to do. The answer had been in Dickson Hong's eyes. "What if I were to tell you I know for a fact Sakharov didn't kill Joe and Sonny?"

"I'd say you better have proof."

"And what if I said it wasn't anybody else connected with the conspirators?"

"I'd probably ask you what you'd been smoking. What is this, Nick, a parlor game?"

Nick reached down and took the manila envelope that was lying on the banquette next to him and handed it to Hong.

"What is it?"

"The proof."

Hong's eyes partially closed, cobralike. He unfastened the clasp and opened the envelope. Removing Martin Fong's suicide note, he took his glasses out of his breast pocket and read. When he'd finished, he removed his glasses and put Martin's letter down on the table. Then he gazed intently at Nick.

Nick took a long, slow breath. "I found that last night in a file containing information on my brother's finances. My assumption is that it had been stolen from Martin's place, probably during the burglary. The suicide note was stuck in the middle of a pile of papers. Martin must have left it on his desk for you to find. At least, that's my assumption. Instead, it got swept up with everything else that was carted off."

Hong was silent for a long time. Then he said, "What made you decide to give it to me?"

"It came down to playing God or not playing God. My ego could probably handle the God role, but then I asked myself if it really ought to be my choice. The world might be better off if the note never came to light, but was I entitled to make that call? And if not me, who? What if the person deciding wasn't trustworthy? What if he or she weren't so pure of heart as, say, you or me?" He smiled. "I guess the rules of justice have weight that are bigger than individual lives, but I don't really know. After all, who am I? A pasta artist and former would-be Major League shortstop."

"You called the squeeze play, Nick."

"Yeah, well, this is the real thing," he said, tapping the letter with his finger. "Bottom line is, I've decided to put the problem in your capable hands."

"You know what I'm likely to do."

Nick shrugged. "I trust you, Dickson. It's as simple as that."

An hour and a glass of wine, later Billie arrived to take him out to dinner—someplace "where there isn't a pennant race going on." She wore a pretty, taupe dress with a sassy skirt, a dress she admitted she'd purchased that day. They ended up at a funky little Greek restaurant on Clement Street, out in the avenues. Under boughs of plastic grapevines and twinkling electric lights they ate dolmas and moussaka and talked. Nick didn't mention his meeting with Dickson Hong.

After they'd finished eating, he took her hands and gazed into her eyes, intensely enough that she blushed. After a moment she chuckled, shaking her head as if to say, no, I can't take this anymore.

"You know, one of the worst things about being a woman is waiting to get propositioned," she said. "So I'm going to be my usual outrageous self and cut to the chase. Want to go to a hotel?"

"How could I say no to an offer like that?"

They both leaned forward, their lips touching midway across the small table. Billie paid the bill, getting waspish when he tried to grab the check. "A bet is a bet. Anyway, I've got a bunch of free meals at the Clipper coming. You'll get your chance."

Nick wasn't about to correct her misconception. They'd both been wrong. Joe and Sonny hadn't died because of the bankruptcy scam *or* the Emerald Buddha. They'd died because of jealousy and a foolish mistake made by an otherwise decent human being. It was a truth that would bring disappointment and hurt in several quarters. It would turn the course of justice in a direction no one had contemplated.

He hadn't decided when he would tell her. Maybe tomorrow. Maybe at breakfast. Maybe at some wistful moment as they drove home, a moment when truth seemed ineluctable. But it wouldn't be before they'd made love. Nick Sasso was neither a saint nor a fool. It hadn't begun as a wonderful day, but that's the way he was determined it would end.

TWO YEARS LATER

Henry Chin, Bartholomew Carlisle II and Wilson Dahl, along with twenty-six other lawyers around northern California, were convicted under various federal and state racketeering laws. Chin, Carlisle and Dahl were also charged with conspiracy to murder. Under the felony murder rule, charges were also brought against the three in connection with the deaths of Olga Diachenko and DeLon Pitts. State prosecutors agreed to plea-bargain, and the defendants were sentenced to terms of twenty years to life, to be served upon completion of the ten-year terms they are serving under federal charges. Chin, Carlisle and Dahl are presently incarcerated in a low-security federal correctional facility in Arizona.

Jessica Horton, whose testimony sealed the prosecutor's case, left Bachman, Carlisle, Cummings & Glick to become an associate in the San Diego law firm of Peabody, Wilsey & Morrison. She subsequently became the second wife of

Charles Morrison, the managing partner of the firm, and was herself made partner.

Assault charges against Naomi Watts were dropped by the Alameda County District Attorney's Office. After a hearing, her membership in the State Bar of California was reinstated. She is now a staff attorney with Legal Aid in Oakland.

Igor Sakharov and Eve Adams reside in Mazatlán, Mexico, as expatriate Americans, under the names George and June Emory. George is part owner of a sport-fishing boat in partnership with a wealthy retired Mexican police official still known in criminal circles as "El Gordo." Once or twice a week George takes a fishing party out into the Gulf of California, but most of the time he supervises the grounds crew of Paradise, June's oceanside fat farm, the hot new in-place for the Hollywood set.

Bree Davis left Dominick's California Cafe and returned to her show business career with zeal, winning a part in the chorus of the new Broadway musical comedy *Baby, Baby*. The show closed after only four weeks, but Bree met the show's principal financial backer, a thirty-year-old high-tech entrepreneur from Boston named Andrew Gross. After a whirlwind romance, they married. At present the Grosses are expecting twin sons.

Jolie Hays completed a work-study program sponsored by the city of San Francisco. She received her high-school equivalency and is presently training to be a dental hygienist.

Dickson Hong was promoted to lieutenant just prior to his retirement. He and Suze divide their time between Scottsdale, Arizona, where the Giants have their spring-training facility, and the Bay Area. Her feelings about Henry Chin have evolved, as has her characterization of the friendship of their youth. Hong, as before, is content with his life. He is a part-time instructor in police science at City College, works regularly on his chess game and is writing a mystery novel. Every couple of months he and Suze drop by the Yankee Clipper for a meal.

Nick Sasso was successful in recovering the funds from his

brother's offshore accounts. The mortgage on Gina's house was paid off, as well as the encumbrances on the Yankee Clipper, which was restored to financial health. Nick sold Dominick's California Cafe to the chef, Aldo, and a group of financial backers, for six hundred thousand dollars. He used five hundred thousand to purchase Gina's interest in the Clipper.

With a war chest of two million dollars, Ken Lu and his partner launched an expedition into Myanmar to recover the famed Emerald Buddha. According to reports, the Buddha was located, but before it could be removed from the country the expeditionary force was ambushed by the Myanmar army. Only Lu's partner escaped with the knowledge of the Buddha's new hiding place. Lu vowed to make another attempt to recover the treasure, but Benny, who'd died within six months of being diagnosed with lung cancer, and Gina wanted no part of it. Elaine Chang brokered a deal whereby Gina and Benny's widow sold their interest in the enterprise to a Chinese shipping magnate from Singapore, receiving fifty cents on the dollar. Gina used the half million to establish a college fund for her children.

Elaine spent several months in Hong Kong, returning to San Francisco shortly after Bobby Green was elected to his third term as mayor. Deciding that closer ties with City Hall were good for business, Elaine curried favor with the mayor and was soon appointed to the unofficial post of first mistress.

In the aftermath of San Francisco's great bankruptcy scam, Nick and Billie Fox became a couple. Once the dust settled, they took a ten-day trip to Tahiti where, on their last night under the tropical stars, Nick broached the subject of marriage. Billie demurred, saying she wasn't so sure great sex, even great love, was justification for marriage. Anyway, what Nick needed was a young wife to bear him children, a woman who didn't have the threat of cancer hanging over her head. His protest to the contrary fell on semi-deaf ears.

Within three months of Nick and Billie's return from Tahiti, her father married a fifty-six-year-old widow who taught at Emily's school. At about the same time, Tony Sasso died of a massive stroke, leaving his interest in the Clipper to Nick and a hundred thousand dollars to each of his grandchildren. Before dying, the old man asked Nick why he hadn't married Billie. Nick told him it was because Billie wouldn't have him. Not surprisingly, Tony's advice was, "Don't quit."

A couple of months after his father's death, Nick bought a house near the Marina Green with a partial view of one tower of the Golden Gate Bridge. It took some cajoling, but Billie and Emily moved in with him. Billie continues to practice criminal defense law with a vengeance, promotes breast cancer research, champions liberal causes and regularly attends Giants games.

The Marina Green is their playground. Given their odd schedules, Nick and Billie can be seen at various times of day with their gloves and a ball, playing long toss on the Green or simply strolling along the bay, hand in hand, watching the sailboats. Sometimes Emily and Nick fly kites in the ocean breezes, and the two of them spend a lot of time together in the kitchen. They are a family, and Nick remains hopeful that one day Billie will see that as clearly as he.

At the end of that first season, Jamal Wicks was traded to the New York Yankees for a left-handed journeyman relief pitcher. In his second year, Wicks became the Yankees' regular center fielder, batted .302 and stole thirty-seven bases batting in the leadoff spot. He was voted the American League's Rookie of the Year. Nick never tires of ribbing Billie about that. It doesn't help his marital aspirations, but by the same token, he finds her adorable when she's pissed.

Of course the Yankees won another pennant, and the Giants were knocked out of the play-offs in the first round. Nick finagled two tickets to the first game of the World Se-

ries. Billie went to New York with him for the game, but still
groused, "Wait till next year."

Nick no longer presses Billie on the subject of marriage.
While he hasn't given up hope, he's moved on to plan B—
he takes his happiness where he can find it, one day at a time.
Billie took a while but was finally able to admit that she
loves him. The way Nick sees it, that's enough for now. Pennants are rarely won in April.

The headquarters of Yee Industries were located in Kowloon in a cylindrical architectural marvel sixty stories above Victoria Harbor. Jimmy's suite was on the penthouse floor. They accessed it via a private elevator. As Jonas stepped out, the sight took his breath away, though he did his best not to gape.

He'd seen some nice office suites in his time, but Jimmy's digs were magnificent. The walls were constructed almost entirely of glass, a crystal doughnut encircling the building's central core. It was like being in a giant, glass-enclosed eagle's nest, a twenty-first-century version of Mount Olympus, complete with a silver-haired god of finance and industry in a handcrafted gray suit and vermilion tie.

Opposite them, standing next to a receptionist desk about the size of a motel swimming pool, was a tall slender woman of forty. Neither the words *pretty* nor *beautiful* nor *handsome* described her, though she was a touch of each. She had the obsequious grace of a courtesan. She wore a simple gray wool skirt, white silk blouse, dark stockings and a string of fine white pearls. Her ebony hair was twisted loosely, but carefully, on her head. Her manner screamed discretion, integrity, intelligence, loyalty. She moved toward them to take their coats, bowing slightly as Jimmy laid his coat in her arms.

"Jonas, this is my longtime assistant, Joy Wu. Joy, Mr. Lamb."

"Welcome, Mr. Lamb," she said, her eyes sparkling with a sincerity that made him want to throw an arm around her shoulders. Then the woman leaned close to her employer and whispered a few words in Chinese.

"Ah," Jimmy said. "An urgent matter has come up, Jonas. There's a chap in Tokyo I must ring up. It shouldn't take but five or ten minutes. Will you indulge me?"

"Of course, Jimmy. Take as much time as you need."

"Thank you. Joy will show you to my office and I'll join you shortly."

Jimmy headed off, and after Joy Wu took Jonas's coat she led the way into Jimmy's private office, which had to be the better part of three thousand square feet, occupying a large chunk of the doughnut. The office was more landscaped than furnished. There was a running stream, plans in abundance, a virtual ecosystem. To the north were the New Territories and the mountainous face of the most populous nation on earth, stretching to infinity. To the south, the sparkling skyline of Hong Kong Island and the South China Sea beyond.

The furniture was oversize. Jimmy's desk, itself a hardwood sculpture the size of a small dance floor, was the focal point. *Zeusian* was the word that kept entering Jonas's mind as he glanced around.

Joy Wu showed him to a grotto of ferns containing two overstuffed couches, located some distance from the massive desk. She gestured for him to sit.

"Please make yourself comfortable, sir. I will bring tea." She bowed and left.

Alone, Jonas glanced around, wondering if something like this could be in his future. His heart raced at the prospect. And though he remained nervous over what lay ahead, he was hopeful, feeling like a guy on a first date with a woman who seemed to be sending all the right signals.

For a man with a checkered past, Jonas was as humbled by his good fortune as he was elated. There'd been others who'd bloomed late, realizing their destiny on the eve of their first social security check, but they were few and far between. His good fortune had begun when Patrick, the son he hadn't seen in years, phoned out of the blue the previous August. Jonas had planned to take Elise to a concert in the summer series that night, but she hadn't felt up to it, so he'd given the tickets to a neighbor, just having walked in the door when the phone rang.

"It's your son, Patrick," the strange voice had said. "Have any plans for dinner?"

Jonas was shocked.

"I'm not a kid anymore," the boy said. "I've got a Ph.D. There's no reason I can't take the first step."

Jonas was flattered and pleased by the overture. They had

dinner (on Patrick) then talked until three in the morning in Elise's front room, catching up, expressing regrets and getting hurt feelings off their chests. Jonas, having lived with so much guilt about his paternal shortcomings, felt better afterward and told Patrick so. "That makes two of us," the boy replied. "I move we wipe the slate clean."

As far as Jonas was concerned, their reconciliation couldn't have come at a more propitious moment. He'd never felt the need for family, but with Elise failing and dreary times looming, Patrick was a godsend. Over the course of the previous twenty-five years, he'd seen the boy a grand total of perhaps a dozen times. Not that he'd planned it that way, but with the matrimonial landscape changing year to year, how could a boy of eight or ten or twelve be expected to understand his father's capricious approach to conjugal relations?

Which is not to say the two of them had no relationship. Jonas liked to think of their encounters as "quality time" in the purest sense. Patrick wasn't quite as sunny in his recollections of those years. During their heart-to-heart conversation that first night, he'd confessed that while had had some fond memories of time they'd spent together, there were periods when he would have had trouble picking Jonas out of a lineup.

It was during a subsequent backpacking trip in the Sierras—undertaken for bonding purposes—that Patrick first revealed his other, more pragmatic reason for the reconciliation. A microbiologist by training, he had made a scientific discovery of earthshaking import, but didn't know what to do with it. Maybe Patrick, who was an idealist, more into realizing scientific and philosophical objectives than making money (a notion that was as alien to Jonas as debt service), simply needed his old warhorse of a father to help him realize his destiny.

Jonas listened, incredulous, his eyes glistening in the light of the campfire, as his son told him about the genetically modified organism (GMO) he'd created that converted the sugar in corn into a substance that changed the character of ethanol, thus affecting the oxygenation process of petroleum fuels. Incredibly, Patrick's GMO enhanced the energy yield of a tank of gas, for example, tenfold.

Jonas didn't understand the science, but he was no fool. He saw the opportunity of a lifetime rising out of the ashes of a misspent life. A chance at redemption in the hands of his very own son!

"Do you have any idea of the import of what you're saying?" Jonas asked. "You could single-handedly turn the word economy on its head."

This was not hyperbole. Jonas knew a thing or two about economics and quite a bit about business. He'd seen the sunny side of a seven-figure net worth more than once in his financial life, though the dark side of seven figures—the *very* dark side—was more familiar territory.

"It has to be proven outside the laboratory," his son replied. "There are a few hurdles to get over, and to do that I need money."

Jonas hadn't spawned a dolt. The timing of their reconciliation did correspond with Patrick's need for a cash infusion, but what the hell, human beings had kept their love and their money in the same purse since Cro-Magnon subtlety had supplanted Neanderthal implacability. So how could a man who changed wives as frequently as he changed his long-distance company complain about the symbiosis of devotion and gold?

"Odds?" he asked, hearing the tinkle of cash register bells more clearly that the gurgling of the nearby stream.

"Seventy-five-percent probability I can pull it off," Patrick replied.

"Fifty-fifty and a man would be a fool not to put his life savings into it," Jonas said, meaning it. (Hell, maybe even borrow the money and put up his soul as collateral.)

"Then perhaps the world economy *is* going to get turned on its head."

They decided to form a company to market the technology. Jonas would own and operate it as a front man, with Patrick a silent partner. The boy wanted to be insulated from public scrutiny, with his participation a secret. "It's the best way to protect the technology," he'd argued. After giving it some thought, they settled on the name Global Energy Technologies.

There was a minor problem, however. While Jonas lived well and appeared rich, in fact his lifestyle was a product of his wife's largesse. He told Patrick he didn't have much in the way of investment capital, but he thought he could get the money from Elise, as a sort of advance on his "inheritance." Her cancer was terminal by then and she was in a settling-of-one's-affairs state of mind, though it gave her pause when he told her he wanted to form an investment firm but that the undertaking was so sensitive that even the broad outlines of the enterprise could not be revealed. He did, however, suggest that she might serve as an officer of the corporation, since the law required at least two officers. (Out of respect to his son's wishes, he didn't tell Elise about Patrick's involvement.)

Her skepticism notwithstanding, Elise was inclined to accommodate him, provided Jonas would look her in the eye and tell her it was the right thing to do. "There are never any guarantees," he'd replied, "but if the money was coming from my life's savings, I wouldn't hesitate to write the check." Bravado, he learned that day, was like toilet paper during a shortage—something best used sparingly and only when absolutely necessary.

"In a sense it *is* coming from your life savings, dear," she'd replied, the flick of her brow reminding him once again there were no free lunches. "I'll give you the money, but I'm sure my attorney will be particular about how it's done."

He'd patted his wife's hand. "I understand fully."

The attorney, not surprisingly, wanted Jonas tied up every conceivable way. He proposed that 90 percent of GET's stock would be issued in Elise's name. Jonas had the option of purchasing the stock from her at any point during her lifetime for a hundred thousand dollars plus interest. Upon her death, Jonas would inherit the stock under the terms of her will, provided the million-dollar bequest in his favor was reduced by one hundred thousand dollars. If for any reason Elise changed her will, Jonas had the option of purchasing the stock for a hundred thousand dollars plus interest.

Microeconomically speaking, Elise hadn't lost a thing by doing the deal. But in a world ruled by the twin gods of capitalism and plunder, money wasn't the issue, at least for

Jonas—the issue was the opportunity money bought. What he hadn't shared with his dear wife was that he was convinced that Patrick's project would make him king of the world. (Why distress a dying woman with appearances of selfishness?)

In the months since Elise had written him that check, he had formed Global Energy Technologies, Inc., renting a small suite on Montgomery Street in the shadow of Telegraph Hill. Elise held the title of secretary of the corporation, though her signature on the incorporation documents was the extent of her involvement. With capital available, Patrick pressed ahead with his research, reporting that experiment after experiment had come up roses. Still, it would be a while before they had the results of what Patrick had termed "the definitive test, in the only laboratory that counted—Mother Earth."

Had it not been for Elise's cancer, Jonas would have been on cloud nine. (For all his pecuniary preoccupation, he did have a sense of decency.) Sadly, though, his dear wife was moving into the final phase of her illness. The doctors were giving her a couple of months at most. Again the terrible dichotomy of sorrow and joy.

Recently Jonas had been spending half his time with Elise and the other half at the office, with occasional forays to the houseboat. Time moved with agonizing deliberateness. Everything seemed to be hanging in abeyance. So he worried, not just about his wife, but his revolutionary venture with Patrick.

For all his bravado, Jonas was smart enough to realize he was probably over his head, given the scale of their dream. At the beginning of the month he'd called for a powwow with Patrick.

Jonas had been direct. "Our capital will only last so long. I think we need a money partner, Patrick. And I don't just mean for seed capital. If we're going to knock the world on its collective ass, we'll need hundreds of millions, not hundreds of thousands."

"What are you getting at, Jonas? That we take it to an energy company?"

"No, that's only good for a nice fat annuity. We need somebody who'll put up the capital to create, then control, the world market for your little organism thingy."

Patrick had laughed at Jonas's rather unscientific description of the GMO. "I was going to make this a surprise for later," he'd told his father, "but maybe this is the time to tell you. I've given the organism a name. I'm calling it 'Black Sheep,' in honor of you."

Jonas had been touched. He'd told his son how his own mother had bestowed that epithet on him—the family "black sheep." It wasn't intended as a compliment. Barbara Lamb considered her son a clone of his old man, who, in her telling, was a reprobate and a scoundrel. Even so, Jonas wore the appellation proudly, if only because it harkened to his habit of doing things his own way.

"You've made my day, son," Jonas told him. "Maybe my life."

"You can do that yourself," Patrick replied, "if you know someplace to pick up a hundred million bucks or so."

Jonas had been ready for the comment, which had come right on cue. "As a matter of fact, I do."

"Oh? Is it a secret?"

"Hong Kong," Jonas told his son.

And now here he was in Jimmy Yee's eagle's nest on the rim of the Asian continent, the future tantalizingly within reach.

R.J. KAISER

66820	HOODWINKED	___ $6.50 U.S.	___ $7.99 CAN.
66625	FRUITCAKE	___ $5.99 U.S.	___ $6.99 CAN.
66614	GLAMOUR PUSS	___ $6.50 U.S.	___ $7.99 CAN.
66510	JANE DOE	___ $5.99 U.S.	___ $6.99 CAN.
66460	PAYBACK	___ $5.99 U.S.	___ $6.99 CAN.

(limited quantities available)

TOTAL AMOUNT	$_____
POSTAGE & HANDLING	$_____
($1.00 for one book; 50¢ for each additional)	
APPLICABLE TAXES*	$_____
TOTAL PAYABLE	$_____

(check or money order—please do not send cash)

MRJK0803BL

Critically acclaimed author

R.J. KAISER

delivers the unpredictable, action-packed novel of love and corruption,

Black Sheep

Available September 2003 wherever hardcovers are sold.

Critically acclaimed author

R.J. KAISER

delivers the unpredictable,
action-packed novel of love
and corruption,

Black Sheep

Available September 2003 wherever hardcovers are sold.